THE SECRETS OF MORGARTEN

L.S.MANGOS

Mana Publishing

Other titles by the author writing
psychological suspense as Louise Mangos

STRANGERS ON A BRIDGE
THE ART OF DECEPTION
THE BEATEN TRACK

First edition 2023

Mana Publishing, Mana AG

Paperback ISBN 978-3-9525927-1-7

For the people of the Aegerital
who welcomed me into their fold twenty-five years ago

PROLOGUE

15TH NOVEMBER 1315, MORGARTEN

Burning arrows streaked like meteors through the air, landing around the mill and the outbuildings. One of them pierced the roof of the open-sided barn between the toll tower and the chalet. Pitch burned through the thatch and trickled onto the straw underneath. The entire barn was soon on fire, as though the rain and sleet of the past weeks had never soaked the building.

Magda studied the clouds and shivered. Her glance fell to the wisps of mist drifting through the forest canopy across the valley. She prayed the wind would not cause the flames to jump to their chalet. Walter placed his hand on her arm, urging her to stay with him on the hillside. It wasn't safe to go back to the hamlet.

He lifted the alphorn to his mouth and blew a long, haunting tone. And again, a second time. When the sound reached the opposite slope, a flurry of movement rippled across the Figlenfluh Ridge. The men from the village who'd been waiting all night in the cold scrambled like ants to their posts. Using thick pine branches and brute strength, they levered the first of the boulders over the edge. The rocks moved sluggishly at first, then picked up momentum as they rolled down the steep slope. Hefty logs from the oldest trees followed in the boulders' wake. The jumble of giant objects brought down shrubs, trees, mud and rubble along its way. Even from that distance, the ground vibrated under Magda's and Walter's feet.

After a moment of silence, the noise reached them across the narrow head of the Aegeri Valley. Magda put her hands over her ears. The thunder was as loud as any of the violent alpine summer storms she'd experienced in her nineteen years. As the assault continued, she wondered whether the whole mountain would fall down and fill the valley.

The missiles crashed onto the enemy Habsburg soldiers who had turned to try and flee the onslaught. Their advance was additionally hampered by the marshland. Horses' hooves were sucked down into the swampy depths. The soldiers on foot fared no better, the weight of their armour restricting their onward movement. They were now discarding their armour to avoid being pulled under. They would be determined not to drown in the cold boggy waters before they'd even wielded the first slash of their swords.

The men of Morgarten returned the enemy's crossbow fire, bolts reaching their mark with accuracy, surprising the Habsburg troops. The enemy horses that had broken through the first defence could no longer be urged forward, despite spurs digging red rawness into their flanks. Steam rose from their rumps, their mouths sawed at their bits, and they grunted with effort. The beasts pranced and strained on the spot, attempting to lift their legs, hooves caked in the stagnant mud of the marsh. As they reared unexpectedly onto their haunches, the formation of the foot soldiers behind them descended into chaos. Men lost their boots to the bog, but pressed on regardless.

As Magda took her hands from her ears, the screams of the horses and the blood-curdling battle cries of her people echoed between the valley walls. The smell of rotting reeds, horse sweat and the iron of blood hung on the air. Hundreds of enemy troops were spread out in a disorganised chain between the lake and the hamlet. The men of Morgarten ran into their midst, using their halberds in all of the weapon's capacities – axe blades to decapitate soldiers and smite the horses' legs, the lance tips to pierce soft organs. And when all else failed, the wooden shafts were lifted to defend Habsburg swords.

Magda focused on a horse floundering in the swamp, vapour spurting in puffs from its flared nostrils. The white of its panicked eye was visible even from her vantage point on the rocky outcrop. She thought at first it was Sébastien's handsome black stallion. But then she realised the beast was a dun, and that the blood of hundreds of men had turned the marshland and its pelt dark. The blood of hundreds of men whose deaths were surely pointless. What madness drove men on, even when what lay in front of them was already helplessly slain?

After all that had passed since spring and the arrival of first Walter and then Sébastien, she wondered whether this senseless, violent loss of life could have been avoided. They all harboured secrets, even now. She wondered whether some of their twisted truths had been used wisely.

CHAPTER ONE

Eight months ago, 15th March 1315, Schornen

MAGDA

M agda hummed to herself as she hung a swatch of newly dyed linen to dry in the courtyard between the chalet and the toll tower. Her fingers were coaxing out creases, pulling the cloth on the line, when she heard the familiar bray of Mihal's mule.

She turned to see the medicine man leading his faithful beast down the path from the pass. The animal stepped cautiously along the trail, his rump packed with an assortment of bags stuffed with gadgets and tools. Glass phials and tiny clay pots clinked and jangled in the leather boxes strapped across his saddle.

The children ran up the trail to meet Mihal, turning to skip at his side as they accompanied him to the hamlet. A group of adults gathered by the stream to welcome him, clamouring for news of relatives in neighbouring villages. Magda wiped her purple-stained hands down her apron and hurried to the chalet kitchen to fetch some refreshment for the visitor.

Once the men and women had gone back to their work at the mill or to the fields, Mihal came to the courtyard and sat on the bench. He turned his face towards the warmth of the spring sun, while Magda placed a plate in front of him.

'You're a sight for sore eyes, Magda Stauffacher,' he said.

'It's good to see you, Mihal. Please, eat. *En guete.*' Magda smiled as she took the reins of the mule and led it to the water trough, leaving Mihal to chew on some dried venison and a hunk of freshly baked rye bread. After tying the mule, Magda sat next to Mihal on the bench. He swilled his food down with the remnants of last autumn's cider *Most* and pressed his gnarled, spit-dampened finger to the fallen crumbs on the table.

'Come on, Mihal, don't keep me in suspense. Which exotic southern land have you been to this time?'

'Guess,' he said, reaching for one of his saddlebags and pulling out a skein of multi-thread twine.

'Venice? Oh, I'm so envious!'

'No. Further east. A city with spires and spices, music from magical instruments, and costumes that would make you swoon,' he said as he placed the skein in her hands.

'What's this?' she asked, gently pulling apart loops of the fine threads.

'Cotton. Found growing in the hills to the west of Constantinople. The fibres around the seeds are as fluffy as new-born lambs' tails. Weavers are already using it as far north as Milano.'

Magda sniffed the threads and rolled them between her fingers. 'It's fine, like silk, but much sturdier. It must be a dream to weave.'

'Quite different from your reed flax,' Mihal said, nodding towards the swamp lying between Schornen and Morgarten. 'How's your expertise with the *baselard* coming along?'

Magda grimaced, placed her palms on the table and studied the spider-like scars on the tops of her hands. She might be proud of how softly she could spin the fibres and weave her linen from the tough mountain flax, but harvesting the reeds to extract their core was threatening to destroy the hands she needed for sewing.

'I can't avoid the wickedness of the reeds, no matter how carefully I wield the blade,' she said. 'Edgar's no help, always excusing himself to fish in the lake. Says his role takes precedence in the village's needs.' She mimicked her brother's gruff voice: 'It's a luxury to clothe yourself in more than one outfit, Maggi, but don't forget we still need to eat.'

'You and your brother are far too contrary, Magda. These roles have been allocated to men and women since the beginning of time.'

'But it's so unfair! Casting fishing lines is suited to the soft hands of a woman. It's harvesting reeds that should be left to the battling hands of a warrior.' Magda showed him her hands. 'These would be far worse if it hadn't been for the salve you made for me. Which reminds me, I've almost run out. Is it time for a new shirt, Mihal?'

She gave him a demure smile.

'I'm working on a new recipe for the healing salve. But it's not quite ready. I'll soon have some to trade for your fine needlework, though.' Mihal puffed out his chest and brushed his palm along his tunic, from under his grey beard down to his paunch. 'Your reputation is growing, my dear. I was complimented on this when I stepped off the boat in Genoa.'

Magda beamed with pride. 'The colour has held well. I couldn't think of a better person to be a walking display of my work,' she said, nudging the tunic over his rotund belly.

'Although I fear this tunic is mysteriously shrinking,' he said. 'Too many kofta stews and baklava over the past months.'

'So, you *will* be needing a new one,' Magda said, wondering what culinary delicacies he spoke of. At the thought of food, she remembered the bread and *Torten* she should be preparing for the mid-Lent village festival. 'Will you stay for the *Mittenfastenfeuer*?' she asked.

'Sadly I must leave tomorrow,' said Mihal. 'You heathens certainly know how to throw a party. Many others in the Confederation are far more pious and will be fasting until Easter.'

'It raises our spirits after the hard winter. There were losses this year. Three more elders, two sick children,' she said, her eyes pricking with unshed tears.

'It'll be good to take your minds off the troubles beyond your border,' said Mihal.

Magda bit her lip. From where they sat, they could see over the stone wall to the Aegeri Valley spread across foreign territory. Habsburg territory. 'Damn that border! Why must it divide Schornen and Morgarten? It so cruelly splits our families and farms!'

'It's because your village is at the head of the valley,' said Mihal, waving a hand behind them. 'Politicians and geography have determined the border, not your kin.'

The sound of a staff against rock drew their attention to the trail leading down from the pass. A tall man was approaching on foot. Magda's heart raced in alarm and she glanced at Mihal. He turned towards the figure, raising his hand to shield his eyes from the sun.

'A stranger. I must fetch Papa,' said Magda.

'Don't fret. I think that's young Walter,' said Mihal.

'You know him?'

'He's from Uri. He'll be carrying a message, probably for your father. He poses no danger, but it would be good to alert Josef.'

Magda made her way down the slope towards the mill, a shadow now cast over the joyful visit of Mihal. Messages these days were lacking good tidings, as they were usually about marauders, thieves and political unrest.

She crossed the stream, glancing at the new arrival. He was alone and wore no armour. When he stopped to survey the Aegeri Valley, she watched him breathe in the spring air. Pride bloomed in her chest, as though she was the one responsible for what he could see from his vantage point. She turned to share his view. The forested

cliffs to the west dropped sharply into the crescent-shaped lake –
the Aegerisee. The village of Morgarten was spread along the eastern shore. The water reflected the clear blue of the sky, drawing
the eye to the furthest point, with green meadows surrounding
the distant farmhouses and chalets.

Magda sighed and stepped through the door into the darkness of the mill house as a harsh swear word from her brother
Edgar echoed through the space. Edgar, bare-chested with flecks
of something dark on his muscular arms, was pushing a long
metal lever under a deep-toothed iron cog. Her father stood up
from where he'd been bent over on the other side of the giant
millstone and pushed his fist into the small of his back to ease
some unseen pain.

'A messenger is at the tower, Papa. You should come.'

Her father waved his hand in her direction without looking and
bent back down to the task of fixing the contraption on the mill.

'I'll be there as soon as we get... this...' His mouth clamped with
effort as he and Edgar strained to align the cog on the mill.

Magda returned to the chalet, where the stranger was deep
in conversation with the medicine man. As she approached, she
picked up their conversation.

'Are you heading north?' the young man asked Mihal, his voice
friendly. 'I must have missed you in our village. I heard no news
of your passage.'

'Delivering tinctures to the brothers at the abbey in Einsiedeln,'
said Mihal. 'But it's always worth the small detour to Schornen
to order some new clothes or to sample Magda's delicious food.'

Mihal winked at Magda as she cleared the table. She studied the
stranger surreptitiously. A row of healthy white teeth accentuated his youth; he was perhaps only a little older than herself. His
skin was clear, the smoothness of his cheek having barely seen the
coarseness of a beard. He turned to smile at her and his blue eyes
held her stare. She looked away. Although only a messenger, she

thought him brave to be walking without protection or an obvious weapon. Even Mihal carried a dagger.

'What message do you bring to Schornen, Walterli?' asked Mihal. 'No, don't answer that! Let's enjoy this moment in the spring sunshine. I'm curious to know about that cantankerous old father of yours. Is he still killing rogue Habsburg emissaries?'

'I wish you wouldn't call me that, *Michi*,' said the young man, bristling, but with what seemed to be tolerant humour. 'I've grown out of my childhood nickname. And as for my father, his aim is still true, but his draw weakens a little with age.'

Magda approached the table with an extra mug and fresh water in the jug. She poured three mugs and pushed one of them towards the stranger. He smiled his thanks. Magda was silently vexed with Mihal for not introducing them.

'Aside from messenger duties, are you still honing your tracking skills?' Mihal asked.

Magda watched the stranger as his gaze returned a moment later to the old man.

'Against my father's wishes, Mihal. I still refuse to become a soldier. And against my late mother's wishes I don't want to become a farmer either. I tracked down a thief in Altdorf last week, earning myself a few *Taler*. There's not much reward in it I'm afraid. At least when I'm delivering messages, I get to see the beauty of our land.'

Walter's gaze fixed again on Magda. She was furious with herself for feeling her cheeks blush after he uttered the word 'beauty'.

'Might I know who your father is?' she asked, to change the subject and force an introduction.

Walter raised his chin, and Magda expected contempt if he was living with a father who didn't agree with his ambitions. But instead he continued jovially.

'He's both a rebel and a compatriot, but nevertheless well loved by us all. My father is Wilhelm Tell.'

'Oh! Herr Tell!' she said. 'I met him once. He was here for a meeting with my father and Uncle Werner. He is indeed an imposing man,' she ended in a whisper.

'Then we can already be considered acquaintances, Magda Stauffacher,' he said, bowing with one hand across his chest and the other offered in official greeting.

She took his hand. His hold was stronger than she would have imagined, but his palm was not yet calloused with years of physical labour. Her breath caught for a moment in her throat, before the crunch of boots on gravel distracted them both.

'Papa!' Magda exclaimed as he approached from the mill. 'This is Wilhelm Tell's son, Walter. He's brought a message.'

'A pleasure to meet you, Walter.' Her father's frown smoothed to friendliness. 'Josef Stauffacher.'

They shook hands. A younger, darker version of her father appeared behind, wiping his fingers on a leather cloth. He looked at Walter with hooded eyes. Even after he'd heard the messenger's name, a wariness remained on Edgar's features.

'And this is my brother, Edgar,' said Magda.

Edgar stood behind her father. He took his time wiping his palms, leaving Walter's arm hanging a moment between them.

'Sorry,' Edgar said, finally shaking Walter's hand. 'Pig fat from the mill wheel. She's been sticking.'

'Come on, lad, spit it out. What do we have to fear this time?' Josef asked Walter.

'Your brother Werner is cautioning extra vigilance along this border. There've been a few raids through Arth on the Lake of Zug. It seems Heinrich von Hünenberg has been up to his terrorising tricks again.'

'I hate that man,' said Magda. 'He's despicable.'

'Ach, Maggie, didn't you know we've been saving you to offer as his concubine in exchange for peace in the valley.' Edgar roared with laughter and slapped his thigh.

'Stop teasing your sister, Eddi,' said Josef. 'Tell me, Walter, will my brother send troops to protect us?'

Magda felt sorry for Walter as he paled a little.

'He can't spare any men. They're expanding the forts at Altdorf and Schwyz. He was hoping you could muster help from the men of your village, sons of the farmers.'

Josef pounded the table. The mugs juddered along its surface. Quickly gathering his temper, he looked at Magda. 'Have you a plan for dinner, my girl, or are you expecting food to fall in our laps?'

This was a sign for Magda to retreat to the cottage.

'I'm sorry, I didn't realise how late it was.' Walter voiced her own thoughts. 'I was distracted by the company.'

Magda suppressed a smile and Edgar narrowed his eyes.

'You must stay tonight!' her father said, surprising everyone. 'Any son of Wilhelm Tell is welcome in our home. A worthy soldier to follow in his father's footsteps.'

Walter's compliment to Magda was forgotten and he flushed. A little part of her admired him for his refusal to become a soldier and she awarded him a sympathetic smile. But she wondered what shrewd words he would use to worm his way out of a military discussion with her father and brother.

'We can put fresh hay in the mill. Mihal will sleep in the tower. There would be plenty of room there for both of you, but you will undoubtedly be kept awake all night with his snoring. Mihal has the lungs of a stag in rut. The mill might be a little damp, but it will be quieter,' her father told him. 'And you must join us for a meal.'

'The soup should stretch to a couple of extra bowls,' said Magda with a hint of sarcasm.

'I imagine there'll be none for anybody if you don't go and rekindle that fire,' said her father. 'Come with me, young Walter.'

Her father took Walter to the mill house while Edgar and Magda made their way to the chalet.

'Walter seems a little forward,' said Edgar, his voice lowered. 'Do you think he's considering setting his cap at you?'

'No!' she said vehemently. 'Mihal introduced us. They know each other. He seems like a good person. In truth he feels more priest than husband material.' Magda laughed and punched Edgar playfully on his arm. It would be a new experience for him to be protecting his sister's virtue.

'I don't think we're ready to let you go just yet, Maggi,' he said with affection.

'You mean no one to darn your socks? You'd better find yourself a wife soon.'

Edgar glanced towards a square of tilled earth by the stream, where one of the village girls, Brigitta, was pushing seeds into the soil. His face softened, and Magda was sure he already had one in mind.

Her father often said the hamlet was in desperate need of more sons. More of them to fight the constant threat of the Habsburgs ravaging their land, raiding their stores, and leaving them hungry.

How could they possibly stop the enemy with so few men?

CHAPTER TWO

15th March 1315, Schornen

WALTER

A tallow lamp guttered between them in the Stauffacher's
little chalet. They were crowded round the table, their bellies
full of Magda's fine parsnip soup and rye bread. The charcoal smell
of embers from the fire mingled with the fermented sweetness of
the cattle in the stalls below. Walter was glad to spend time in
the kitchen before going to sleep in the mill, where there were no
animals to warm his bed of hay. An icy chill still stung the alpine
night at that altitude, and every one of the beasts was required to
keep the sleeping spaces warm.

'If you're my uncle's messenger, why aren't you wearing a Confederate uniform?' asked Edgar.

His curiosity held a menacing edge; one of jealousy or scorn,
Walter wasn't sure.

'These clothes are better suited for speed and agility while I'm
delivering messages. I don't work solely for your uncle, although
he's become my greatest source of income. Our village of Bürglen is
close to Altdorf's garrison, and he's a great friend of my father. But

I've also earned a small living from tracking, and my knowledge of letters serves other purposes.'

'You can read and write?' asked Magda, her admiration obvious.

He nodded. 'I was taught by a Benedictine monk in Altdorf. I helped him duplicate several copies of the *Bundesbrief*.'

'A useful skill, along with the knowledge of dialects,' said Mihal, nodding with approval.

'Is it true your father shot an apple from your head to prove himself to the Habsburgs?' asked Edgar.

Walter nodded.

'Yes, come on Walti, tell us the story,' said Mihal. 'They're all tired of my Byzantine tales.'

'I'd like to hear it too, from the horse's mouth,' said Josef. 'Such crossbow skill is to be admired.'

Walter cleared his throat. This was not the first and undoubtedly not the last time his story would be told. He was happy to enhance his father's reputation but would rather not reveal his reactions as a scared, scrawny boy. 'I must have been barely ten. It began with my father taunting Bailiff Gessler, the worst of all the emissaries ever sent from the Habsburgs,' said Walter. 'Gessler was so vain, he wanted everyone in Altdorf to bow to his hat hanging from a pole in Market Street as they passed. When my father refused, two guards grabbed us both. There was a lot of laughing and joking, but when my father realised they were about to arrest him and take him away, they soon learned the force of his anger.'

'Poor Walterli!' said Mihal.

Walter nudged the medicine man for the tease.

'Don't interrupt, Mihal!' said Josef. 'Carry on, lad.'

Walter took a deep breath. 'I was shuffled amongst the crowd. One of Gessler's men had plucked an apple from a stall and was about to take a bite, but instead placed it on my head. "Keep it there, lad," he shouted, and everyone backed away, making space. I remember experiencing a sliver of modest pride when everyone turned to look at me. That was soon quashed when I realised my own father was about to try and shoot the apple from my head. Gessler told him he'd let us both go free if he succeeded.'

Edgar didn't say anything, but kept his head tipped to one side. Walter remembered the fear, the heat of urine searing his leg.

'Go on!' Magda clapped her hands.

'Ach girl, who pulled your bell rope?' asked Josef. 'Give him a chance!'

Walter smiled uncertainly. 'After he'd uttered the words to keep me still,' he continued, 'he walked back to where Gessler's henchmen were gathered in a group. My father swung the cross-bow from his back, hauled a bolt from his quiver, and drew his arm back. His jaw relaxed, and the one eye I could see beside the bow became focused.' Walter still remembered the sharpened point of the arrowhead travelling towards him in a true line, his own eye seemingly hauling it in. The scene played out in his mind as though it was yesterday. The foreshortening of the slender projectile with the rotating feather on its shaft had been mesmerising. He would normally have had absolute faith in the unwavering accuracy of his father's aim, but doubt had flooded in with the terror that day. He thought he was going to die. 'It was all over in a split second. The apple disintegrated. We both live to tell the tale,' said Walter.

'*Gott sei Dank*,' whispered Magda, and Walter smiled.

'Your father must be disappointed to see this renewed threat to the nation he fought so hard to build,' Josef said. 'He gave more than just his brains and his brawn for the protection of our land, God rest your mother's soul.'

Walter bit his lip, trying to stifle the deep emotion any mention of his mother aroused. That was the second part of the story he preferred not to tell. With Magda being the only female presence in this house, he realised the two of them were bound in a common sadness. They had both lost their mothers too young.

Josef continued before Walter could answer. 'He'd be proud to know you're here to carry on the warrior blood through generations to come. I'm sure you'll make a fine soldier.'

Walter swallowed. The thought of lifting a crossbow turned his guts to liquid.

'You must stay an extra night with us. We have messages for you to take back to Altdorf,' said Josef. 'There's a secret meeting in Morgarten in two days' time. The *Mittenfastenfeuer*, our mid-Lent festival, is the perfect cover for a gathering of the elders.'

Edgar leaned back, narrowing his eyes. Walter, initially pleased that he would be spending another day in Schornen, had the feeling that Magda's brother trusted no one. Walter pulled his gaze back to Josef.

'You're not the first to bring a message of danger,' said Josef. 'The Habsburgs have never recognised the Confederate charter; the *Bundesbrief* is sacrosanct to us. There's a rumour Heinrich von Hünenberg will attack by the end of the year, and we're in a vulnerable position here in Schornen.'

'Von Hünenberg is the worst of Duke Leopold's lackeys,' said Edgar. 'Spies will be everywhere at the moment. Secrecy about tomorrow's meeting and its result is of utmost importance.'

He spoke with a vehemence that told Walter he should never cross Magda's brother.

✝ ✝ ✝

Walter woke only once in the night, his heart pounding in the deep darkness of pre-dawn. A regular thumping was the only sound in an otherwise silent building. As Walter stretched his stiff limbs under the rough blanket, his nightmare came back to him. Always that same damned dream. 'The apple incident' as he had come to refer to it. The retelling of the tale in the Stauffacher's chalet the night before had reawakened memories.

As his heart calmed, his eyes adjusted to the darkness. An indigo hue filtered in under the roof beams of the building. Walter looked around him at the shapes in the dark. He made out bales of wool and skeins of spun linen. The strangely comforting smell of damp wool made for a solid night's sleep until now. Outside, the water wheel was labouring with the high volume of spring melt in the stream. The extra load was causing an awkward clunking. Whatever repairs Josef and Edgar had attempted the day before, their efforts had not been completely rewarded.

It was this *thump thump thump* that had conjured the repetitive true hit from his father's crossbow to pulverise the apple in Walter's dream.

Nothing had silenced Walter as a boy more than seeing his father's bolt approach him head-on. He was, quite simply, terrified of weapons of any kind. But he had to keep that from both his enemies and his compatriots for fear of being branded a dissenter. Although he was happy to let folk think he'd been a brave young lad back then, in his heart when it came to battle, he was a coward.

The only relief from the cold perspiration now coating his body under the blanket was that each time he awoke from the nightmare, he knew he had survived.

But for how long? The quandary of how he might better help the Confederation without raising arms was growing larger. For if he were forced into battle, he knew he would surely die.

Chapter Three
16th March 1315, Troyes
SÉBASTIEN

Sébastien and Grégoire were gnawing the meat from grilled beef ribs on a large platter when the sound of scattering gravel outside the commandery announced the arrival of a horseman.

While Sébastien sucked the last of the marrow from the bone in his fist, Grégoire stood and approached the ballistraria window. He stood to one side to avoid any penetrating arrows. Pressing his shoulders flat against the thick stone wall, he turned and glanced quickly through the slit. The breeze ruffled a blond lock of hair from above his ice-blue eyes. 'It's Yves,' he said. 'And he's in great distress.' Grégoire reached for the sword he'd finished polishing before their meal, hidden in its usual place behind one of the wall tapestries.

Sébastien pushed the pewter platter aside and rose, licking his fingers. The two men went out to the courtyard to meet Yves, who slid from his saddle, pulling the hood off his habit. Of the three of them, Yves was the only one who had cropped his hair short in the fashion of a religious brother. He'd been elected to act as the eyes and ears of the group during this past year. He was their only connection to the town and the outside world. The townsmen believed that Avelleur's role was devoted only to agricultural labour and housing the occasional pilgrim.

'The king's troops are rallying,' said Yves, breathing heavily from his ride. 'We should prepare ourselves.'

Sébastien swallowed.

'Why would they come now?' asked Grégoire. 'We've done no one here any harm. We've helped the villagers with their farming, supported the pilgrims as we would protect any travellers in need.'

'He likely wants to seize Avelleur for his troops. They've always treated us with disdain as humble brothers in our caretaking role here,' said Sébastien.

'But surely the commandery is too small for his needs?' Grégoire looked up at the roof, the sharp gable a modest excuse for a church steeple. 'He would need a barracks five times the size of Avelleur for his garrison.'

'Have you heard whether there's a threat to the east?' Sébastien asked Yves as they re-entered the building.

'That's perhaps more of a concern; I heard mumblings about the Habsburgs and their alliances from several people in Troyes,' he replied. 'It won't be long before there is trouble over the entire Alps. Duke Leopold of Austria is becoming greedy.'

'Then the time has come for our most important mission,' said Sébastien.

'We must prepare to leave,' said Yves. 'Collect the things that most need protecting, and I'll saddle the other two mounts. It's time to rescue *La Ténébreuse*.'

As Yves went to the stable, Sébastien and Grégoire entered the hall.

'I'll put together as many weapons as the horses can carry,' said Grégoire. 'You sort the chests upstairs, bring the shroud, as many of the most precious treasures as possible.'

Thunder rolled from far off, in the direction of Troye. But the rumble was from no natural storm. This was the sound of soldiers, a hundred hooves pounding the road. Sébastien and Grégoire stared at each other.

'We've been betrayed!' said Sébastien. 'That is certainly no scouting party to turn the castle into a garrison. They are after blood!' Anger and disappointment made his voice tremble. 'Someone has found out who we are.'

'It was only a matter of time,' said Grégoire.

'Arrows incoming! With fire!' called Yves from outside as the sound of hooves grew louder.

Sébastien ran up the stairs, the thump of his boots on the wooden steps blending with the sound of arrows thudding on the thatched roof over his head. As he hurried through the sleeping quarters, his heart felt heavy. It had been three years since Louis succeeded King Philip of France. Sébastien and his colleagues had become complacent in their quiet Avelleur commandery. He'd even hoped he might have the chance to visit his family again before he was called to a greater duty. But now he realised it was not to be. The new king had surmised who these men living on the outskirts of Troye really were.

As Sébastien reached the secret room in the northeast corner of the building, he smelled smoke on the air. With a key hidden behind a stone in the wall, he opened the door and approached a carved cedar cupboard. Pulling a large saddlebag from a nearby shelf, he carefully folded a number of cloths and a shroud into specially sewn compartments in the bag.

'Hurry, Séb!' called the faint voice of Yves. 'They are almost upon us! And Avelleur is burning!'

CHAPTER FOUR

17th March 1315, Schornen

MAGDA

Walter was washing at the trough when Magda walked out of the chalet the next morning. As the sun crested the pass to the east, it shone on his pale, shirtless shoulders. Droplets glistened on his lean torso.

Before he could catch her watching him, she turned towards the stalls under the house to go and milk the cows and bring pails to the village. Their small herd was producing well after a long winter. She should have enough to sell to the cheesemaker and would make sure to give some to those less fortunate.

The early sunrise signalled the welcomed lengthening of the days. A gentle southerly wind softened the alpine chill of a clear morning. Once back from the hamlet with her empty pails, she joined Walter, Mihal and her family at the table outside to break their fast. After serving warmed malted milk to everyone at the table, Magda tore a hunk of bread from yesterday's loaf. 'I'd like to head up to the forest this morning to see if the wild garlic is sprouting. It's time to bring the taste of spring to our palates,' she said.

Her father, chewing on a buttered crust, shrugged.

'As Walter won't be needed until later, can he come with me?' she asked.

Josef frowned and Edgar stared at Magda. If it had been up to him, she knew Edgar would never have condoned her boldness. She could hardly believe it herself.

'Your brother is fishing today,' said her father, his objection unspoken but clear from his tone. Josef would not let her go to the forest alone with Walter.

'Then Brigitta can come with us,' she said, raising her chin to Edgar's frown. She noted the flush on his face at the mention of her friend's name, confirming her suspicions of Brigitta's place in his heart.

Walter gazed up to the forest behind tower, his lips pressed into a line.

'Oh, I'm sorry,' said Magda. 'The last thing you probably want to do, after running all over the countryside with messages, is to take a walk up the mountain.'

'I'd be delighted to join you,' said Walter. 'There may be a hole wearing through the sole of my left boot, and my feet are on the verge of blistering, but the thought of you wandering alone in a forest full of wolves, bears and brigands...'

Edgar coughed loudly. Magda ignored him.

'Do you think I need protection?' she asked. 'I've been walking these forests since I was knee-high to a marmot.'

'Then I take it back,' said Walter. 'It is probably the wolves, bears and brigands who need protection.'

Josef laughed behind his fist.

'Brigitta can come with you, but only if her father Berndt comes with you as well,' he said. 'Berndt told me he would be splitting logs in the clearing today anyway, so he can keep an eye on you all.

Walter can help carry kindling back. I trust the fauna's the only thing we need to worry about.' Josef looked pointedly at Walter.

'Of course, Herr Stauffacher,' said Walter, his hand on his chest.

Magda cleared away the mugs and plates. She carried the tray up to the kitchen, throwing the crumbs to the chickens on the way. After hastily stacking the tray away, she sat on the bench by the door. She pulled the creases from her socks, put on her boots and tied the leather laces until they were snug. Unhooking a basket from the wall, she went down to meet Walter in the yard.

As they waited for Brigitta and Berndt to join them, Magda studied Walter's face in the morning sun. He bore a fresh handsomeness she might have expected from a young soldier, for what young maiden didn't want to be wooed by a warrior? But having said he could read, she thought maybe his ambition was to be a man of God. He looked quite angelic with his fair hair and blue eyes.

'Is it your intention to become a monk?' she asked.

Walter choked on his own laughter, put his hand to his mouth and looked around to see whether anyone had heard. 'Far from it,' he said. 'The perplexing mystery of God is not one I think I can ever solve.'

Magda drew in her breath at this hint of blasphemy. How could he share such thoughts with a girl he had only just met? 'You shouldn't be uttering such words around here, Herr Tell. We might all fear the threat of the Habsburgs, but everyone fears God even more.'

'Do you fear Him too, Magda?'

'I have no reason to.'

The door to the chalet clunked heavily in its frame and Edgar walked down the stairs, pulling on his jerkin. He glanced at Walter and Magda at the table, before gathering his nets from the barn and turning reluctantly towards the lake. He would undoubtedly rather be chopping wood than fishing today.

After Brigitta arrived with her father, they all set off to climb the slope behind the toll tower.

'I'll go gently on you and your tired feet. We'll walk slowly,' Magda told Walter with a smile.

He swept his hand in front of him for her to take the lead. Brigitta followed behind Magda and they tucked the handles of their baskets into the crooks of their elbows. The two men took up the rear.

The sun filtered through the beech trees on the lower slope. The young leaf shoots of the deciduous trees around them shone brightly. Above them the forest turned darker with the evergreen needles thick on the pine trees. Tongue-shaped leaves pushed up through the undergrowth covering the forest floor. Every now and then the women stopped to pluck a handful and added them to their baskets.

'The *Bärlauch* has sprouted earlier this year. It's my favourite flavouring for meals. Here.' Magda leaned past Brigitta and crushed a leaf near Walter's face. His nose pinched as the pungent metallic smell of garlic caught in his nostrils. Berndt cleared his throat behind them. She noticed her fingers still held purple dye under the nails. Before Berndt could say anything about her inappropriate behaviour, she snatched her hand back. She skipped ahead up the path, stooping further on to pick another handful of leaves.

The crunching thud of broken twigs on the forest floor a short distance ahead made them all stop and hold their breath. Magda looked behind her as Berndt silently drew the axe from the strap across his back. Walter reached to his thigh and looked around him. Magda guessed he had lost or forgotten his weapon, if he'd even brought one at all. It was stupid not to constantly check, considering how close they were to the border.

Berndt pushed down the air in front of him with his hand. They all sank to the undergrowth on the barely visible path. Magda searched for something she could use as a projectile. Walter crouched beside her, his hand patting the ground around him until his fingers closed around a flinty stone. Brigitta remained on all fours, staring wild-eyed in the direction of the noise, which had now eerily ceased.

Could everyone hear the sound of Magda's pounding heart? She imagined the assailant above them, only four horse-lengths away, trying to work out their bearings. They had not been discreet during their ascent into the forest.

They waited. The silence drew out.

Magda stared at Brigitta's father over her shoulder. He nodded towards the rock in Walter's hand and slid his eyes in the direction they had last heard the noise. Walter pulled his arm back and threw the rock into the undergrowth. The thump of something heavy reverberated along the ground under their feet. The crashing of a great body moving through the bushes and foliage of the forest grew louder.

Walter grabbed another rock and rushed forward, putting himself in front of Magda. She sensed him bracing for the thrust of a weapon.

CHAPTER FIVE

16th March 1315, Morgartenwald

WALTER

A wild boar burst out in front of Walter on the path. He'd been expecting a Habsburg soldier with a sword or a pike, not a hairy knee-high beast with crooked tusks.

'I'd pay dearly for your father's crossbow right now!' Magda shouted over Walter's shoulder.

He hurled the rock in his hand towards the beast, the desire for pork fat on his tongue already a lost cause. His aim was surprisingly true, but the stone merely bounced off the beast's rump as it veered away from them, accelerating down through the forest. With any luck, his action would flush the animal out in the vicinity of the village and someone else would have a weapon ready.

'It's unusual to see a boar in these parts in springtime,' said Magda. 'I wonder if the beast has any young in a burrow nearby.'

'I'd as soon see a piglet than a Habsburg soldier on a roasting spit right now,' said Walter, clapping dirt and pine needles off his hands.

'Well, that gave us quite a fright. And what would you have done if it *had* been a wolf, a bear or a brigand, Herr Tell?' asked Magda. He pressed his lips together without answering.

'You'd be wise to at least make sure you're carrying a knife with you, lad,' said Berndt. 'You'll have little chance if faced with a rogue soldier.'

'An oversight on my part,' said Walter, sheepishness creeping into his voice as they continued up the path.

When they reached a clearing, Magda set the basket down and beckoned Walter towards a gap in the trees. They looked out through a forest window framed with pine branches, affording a magnificent view over the Aegeri Valley. The ground was well trodden. Log stumps, wood-chips and scatterings of old sawdust were strewn across the clearing. Magda sat on a nearby log just big enough for two. While Berndt wielded his axe, Walter joined her.

For a few moments they remained silent, gazing at the beauty of the lake and surrounding countryside. Above the forest-clad peak of the Wildspitz to the south rose the mighty anvil of the Rigi mountain, a beacon for travellers beyond the borders of the forest cantons. Walter realised he had viewed it from Luzern and was surprised to see the peak was the same shape from the opposite side.

He turned to study the swathe of reeds clogging the valley between Schornen and Morgarten. 'Has your father ever considered getting help to drain the swamp? He could cut channels, make the land good for pasture or crops.'

'And take away my livelihood? It takes a great amount of reed flax to produce my linen.' Magda answered, hiding her hands amongst the folds of her skirt. 'Besides, Papa would tell you it'll only make it easier for our enemies to walk right up to our door.'

'Fair point,' said Walter.

'It's part of our home, our lives. Eddi and I used to compete with the herons to catch frogs in the swamp when we were children.

The mud sucked the shoes from our feet. We learned new ways to free ourselves from the quagmire every year. Mutti was always furious at us for bringing home the dark stench on our clothes.'

A gentle breeze ruffled the clear waters of the Aegeri Lake, where a group of fishing boats bobbed gently off the coast of Morgarten.

'I don't think your brother likes me very much,' said Walter. He imagined the fishermen casting their lines right now, Edgar wondering what they were up to in the forest. Walter and Magda both looked at Brigitta, who was still filling her basket with *Bärlauch*.

'Oh, don't worry about Eddi. He's just being over-protective. We lost Mutti very young to a fever. Eddi took over for my father while I was too little to really know what was going on. Apparently Papa was heartbroken and quite adrift for a while.' Magda paused. 'How did your mother die? Was it recent?'

Walter cleared his throat of a sudden rush of emotion.

'You don't have to talk about it if it's too difficult,' she added.

'It's all right. It's been seven years now. Although some people still don't know.'

'What happened?' Magda asked, her voice soft.

'You'll recall the apple incident I recounted the other night?'

Magda nodded.

'Well, that's not quite the end of the story. Gessler, the emissary, had promised to let my father go free. But by the time the first bolt had met its target, my father was already reaching for the second. His intention had been, if he'd missed the apple and killed me, that the second bolt would be for Gessler. The emissary saw him draw that second bolt and soon reneged on his agreement. I managed to escape and run home but my father was arrested and Gessler instructed his men to take him to the Habsburg Castle dungeon. But he escaped on the way, then chased and killed Gessler at Küssnacht. He hid in the forest until the fuss had blown over. But Gessler's right-hand man came looking for him at home.'

Walter's mind drifted back to the memory. He bit his lip. He'd been choosing tail feathers from a dead kite to make fletchings for his father's crossbow bolts – one of his designated childhood tasks. He remembered sitting at the table in their cottage while his mother prepared soup on the fire. They heard horses approaching, hooves skidding to a stop outside their house with an air of urgency. His mother shouted at Walter to hide in the alcove at the back of the house where she and Wilhelm slept.

Walter closed his eyes and took a breath. 'I didn't know what was happening at the time. The Habsburg lackey brought three soldiers, bent on revenge. When they didn't find Father, I could hear them attacking my mother.'

Walter remembered creeping out of the alcove when he heard his mother screech. He had peered around the curtain separating the beds from the kitchen.

His voice shook as he continued. 'They forced my mother onto our kitchen table and...' Walter swallowed. He cringed as he remembered clamping his hand over his mouth to silence his spontaneous burst of laughter when he first registered his mother with her skirts tucked up around her like a pile of washing. And the pumping pale buttocks of one of the soldiers. This memory still made him hot with shame. 'I didn't understand what was happening. It wasn't until I heard my mother sobbing that I realised they were hurting her. I tried to stop them, tried to pull them off her, but I was just a scrawny lad. They threw me across the room. I only knew later that it was rape.' Walter put his palms flat over his stinging eyes and drew his hands down his face. 'She didn't die for a few days. The brutes tore her up inside. She was in pain, but no one thought to ask a midwife to look at the damage down there. And by the time she lost consciousness, it was too late.'

Walter heard an intake of breath, and lifted his head to see Magda press the back of her hand to her mouth, horror in her eyes.

'I'm sorry. I've shocked you,' he said sadly.

'Why in God's name have you never picked up the sword or the crossbow, Walter? Don't you want to take revenge on the Habsburgs?'

'I don't know, Magda. Since I was a young boy I've seen so much death and destruction. I thought I was going to die the day my father shot that bolt. I've always wondered why humans do these things to each other. It's such a waste of life. After what happened to my mother, I yearn for something else, without the blood, the anger and the retribution. I've always hoped for peace in our lifetime. I don't believe it can be achieved through violence. I'm not sure how it can be done, but I believe there is a way to work through the bigger things for the Confederation in this way too.'

'Good God, what does your father think about your... ambition?'

'You know my father's reputation. Since my mother's death, time has made him no less obstreperous. He often finds it hard to accept my current... profession.'

In the days before her violation, Walter's mother was often telling him he'd make a great spokesman one day. And yet all he could do when he'd witnessed what took place in that kitchen was sob.

To hide another wave of emotion, Walter stood up. He moved to the edge of the clearing with his back to Magda and surveyed the Aegeri Valley.

'Other than the beauty of nature, I find no evidence of God in this place. But justice must prevail before the people. If there is a God, he will surely bear witness.'

Magda gasped behind him. 'God requires us to defend our nation, to fight for our independence. He gives us the gift of food on our table and material to build our homes. He gives us the ability to build weapons to help us do this. His evidence is everywhere, Walter.'

Walter shook his head, thinking it was no good trying to convince a believer that the beauty of the land was the gift of nature itself. If He existed, God would surely not allow innocent women to be raped and murdered by men He had created in His own image.

'Schornen is strategically placed,' Walter said, to change the subject, waving his hand in the direction of the cluster of houses below them.

The toll tower dominating the village accentuated the narrowness of the pass leading into Confederate territory.

'The whole valley speaks of joining the Confederation,' said Magda quietly. 'I think that's what will be discussed tonight at the meeting of the elders. I can't imagine the other villages to the west will agree on anything though. They even argue over whose cheese melts better in a fondue. It's neither, of course. It's ours.' A mischievous glint touched Magda's eye, but Walter was unable to match her humour.

'Many communities are proud of their isolation. And they don't like change.'

Magda nodded and turned to look into the valley. 'Look! The children are helping to build the fire for the festival.' She pointed to a meadow between Schornen and the larger village of Morgarten across the stone-walled border where a pile of material for burning was being assembled. From their observation point, the figures looked like ants crawling over the field. On close inspection they could see ladders leaning against the giant conical pyre. Branches and bark were being stripped and added to it from logs which would be saved later for building homes. The woody stems of last year's reeds and rushes were also thrown on.

'Come!' said Magda.

Berndt and Walter hauled sacks of kindling over their shoulders. Breaking her promise to be gentle with him, Magda ran down the path through the forest back to the village, her basket clutched at her side to avoid spilling her harvest. The excitement of the forthcoming festival made her lift her skirt with her free hand and skip with the nimbleness of a chamois.

Putting the threat of war from his mind, Walter followed Magda, his heart swelling, glad to be staying another night. But he wondered how long the prospect of a simple festival could keep the smiles on the faces of these gentle people.

CHAPTER SIX

16th March 1315, Morgarten
Mittenfastenfeuer

MAGDA

The excitement surrounding the *Mittenfastenfeuer* was the perfect cover for the meeting of the elders in Morgarten. While the children prepared their costumes and others helped to bind and dip their sap torches for the parade, two dozen men entered the barn belonging to a family to the rear of the village.

Magda had persuaded Brigitta to exchange places with her so she could serve mead to the committee members. From across the barn Edgar frowned at Magda, mouthing, 'Where's Brigitta?' Magda made a twisting motion with her fingers, indicating she had swapped duties. Brigitta would be helping the children prepare for the torchlight parade near the church in the centre of the village. Did Edgar think Walter was the motive for the swap?

The men sat on logs or barrels or leaned against the walls. Magda poured drinks into mugs they'd brought with them. She greeted everyone in the barn. There was no animosity between the people of these two villages that had been divided by politics. It was obvious why they would want to remain within one border. Close relatives lived in both communities. The question was, which side would each of them choose?

The flame from the lantern in the centre of the barn glinted in the eyes of those closest to it. Josef and Edgar shared a barrel, perching on its edge. Walter stood behind them in the darkness, leaning against the wall.

Morgarten's spokesman was the farmer whose barn they were using. 'Men of Schornen, welcome. We're here to talk about the increasing pressure of the Habsburg emissaries to provide them with information about your hamlet for an offensive manoeuvre. Despite the binding strength of your *Bundesbrief* twenty-four years ago, the King of Austria's brother, Duke Leopold, seems to be restless and greedy. It's widely known he wishes to absorb the Confederation into his rule. But he is suspicious of our possible allegiance with Schornen and our relatives there. In short, they're asking us to spy on our own families.'

Magda's father grimaced and the farmer nodded to him.

'We're being forced to pay increasing taxes to Heinrich von Hünenberg, Josef. But he's above himself, as though he is head of the throne of Habsburg itself. We're not happy to be divided from you and want to avoid conflict. We'd like to hear your thoughts about accepting the entire village of Morgarten and surrounding farmlands into the Confederation.'

Murmurs rippled through the barn. Magda was unsure whether this indicated impatience or dissent.

'Then we must vote on it!' called a voice from the crowd. 'We are not all in accordance.'

Those in the gathering began exchanging their views both for and against an allegiance. Comments about protection, land, weapons, trading routes and taxes flew back and forth. It seemed the discussion might become heated, out of control.

'Nothing can be agreed tonight as I do not have that authority,' said Josef, his voice strong above the discussion. 'The request must first be taken to my brother, Commander Werner Stauffacher and the elders in Altdorf. We are not at liberty to decide the borders of the nation. Once we have approval, then we will have a show of your men's hands.'

Magda, who was leaning against the wall clutching a jug to her chest, cleared her throat loudly. Josef turned his blazing eyes on his daughter and pursed his mouth. It wasn't the first time she had let him know she was an advocate for the right for women to also have the vote.

'We should receive Werner Stauffacher's answer soon,' said Josef. 'We have a fleet-footed messenger who is none other than Wilhelm Tell's son.'

The crowd whispered amongst themselves, and men strained to look past those in front of them to get a look at the offspring of a legend. Magda smiled as Walter tried to make himself inconspicuous behind Josef.

'Walter will leave at first light for Altdorf,' said Josef. 'I trust him to deliver the message and bring us back an answer within a week. Then we shall meet again. In the meantime, let us forget our differences and celebrate the middle of Lent with our families at the festival!'

Magda met Walter's eyes across the room. She broke the gaze first and emptied the dregs of mead from her jug into the mug of another farmer.

The elders shook hands and clapped each other on the shoulder.

'Thank you, Josef, for your loyalty,' said the speaker. And then to the crowd: 'Come, let us head to the bonfire, but not all together. We must not draw attention from our neighbours.'

The group straggled out of the barn and walked towards the great pyre waiting like a dark ghost in the middle of the field. Its peak reached into the sky almost half the height of the toll tower in the distance.

Magda passed a large loaf of bread to one of the women preparing more refreshments for the festival before running down the track to catch up with Walter.

'Do you feel safe carrying your message to the Confederation without a sword to defend yourself, Walti?' she asked with a smile.

She hadn't meant to be cruel and hoped he could take the teasing about his negligence in the face of a wild pig in the forest earlier with good humour.

'I won't forget my weapon this time, Magda. It's likely I shall never forget it again.'

Magda boldly placed her hand on his arm. She left it there as they sat with the others in a circle around the as yet unlit bonfire.

✝ ✝ ✝

A parade of children carrying reed and pine sap torches created a snake of flickering flames from the church in Morgarten towards the pyre. As they drew near, their laughter and chatter carried to the circle of people seated on the ground in the dark.

Brigitta was at the head of the line with the oldest boy. The parade split into two and the children surrounded the pile of wood, torches lighting their ghostly faces. Several parents called to their offspring, and the children turned briefly to wave or smile. The village leader began his speech. The pungent smell of burning resin wafted on the breeze, the torches emphasising the height of the pyre.

'What's that on top?' Walter whispered to Magda, sitting cross-legged at his side.

'It's an effigy of a monster,' she whispered back. 'Do you not have such a celebration in your village? It's to ensure we have a successful spring and summer season for farming. The figure is called the *Böögg* – the Boogeyman. The children have been making it over the past few weeks. I helped too, as a child. We tried to create a more ghoulish figure each year. The more violently he burns, the more prosperous our year will be.' She paused. 'Hush, they're ready.'

'I wish we'd had something like this in Altdorf,' whispered Walter. 'I would've had great pleasure creating the Böögg in the image of Bailiff Gessler. And the greatest pleasure of all in seeing him burn.'

Their eyes met, the flicker of the torches reflecting in Walter's. Magda was pleased he would be returning with news the following week. She was warming to this young man who made her smile with his gentle humour.

'If you use your imagination, it's not too late, Walti. Let's pretend he's Heinrich von Hünenberg. Emissary Gessler has already burned in Hell.' Magda giggled and held her finger to her lips.

The Morgarten village elder finished his speech. There was a moment of quiet in the circle, except for the occasional splutter of a torch. The high-pitched yodel of Brigitta's voice rang in the night air. Magda sighed and for a brief moment regretted switching places for her role at the festival. At Brigitta's signal, the children simultaneously threw their torches into the midst of the pyre. Walter shuddered beside her.

'What is it?' Magda asked kindly.

'They look like bolts flying from a crossbow. A vision I have always had a hard time forgetting.'

'It must have been a frightening thing for someone so young, Walti. You have seen some terrible things in your youth. I'm so sorry.' Magda placed her hand on Walter's head as though touching an imaginary apple. His hair wound around her fingers.

'I cannot even imagine...' she murmured. Magda felt heat colour her cheeks as she realised she was touching Walter, and before she could withdraw it, he gently grabbed her wrist and pulled her hand towards him, placing his lips in her palm. She glanced towards Edgar sitting further around the circle. But she needn't have worried. Edgar's eyes, brimming with love and pride, were fixed on Brigitta as she completed her duties with the village children. The protection of his sister was momentarily forgotten.

'He must be proud of his future wife,' Walter said.

Their fingers remained entwined between them on the grass. Walter leaned in and kissed her full on the lips. As he drew back, Magda widened her eyes, as she felt a flutter in her stomach. She raised her other hand to touch her lips with her fingers, before their attention was diverted by the crackling of the pyre.

Thanks to the recent dry weather, the fire caught quickly and in no time became an inferno. The children turned and ran to their families. Onlookers shuffled back on the grass away from the heat. Two burly men made sure the fire didn't spread from the circle.

Through the flames on the other side of the circle, they could see Brigitta had joined Edgar. As she bent to brush his cheek with her lips before seating herself next to him, Edgar's eyes locked with Magda's. His gaze drifted to Walter at Magda's side and he frowned. Brotherly protection or disapproval? She remembered Edgar's comment about Walter tipping his hat to her. She turned back to stare at the fire, confusing emotions coursing through her. Walter had to leave early in the morning, but did she want him to? He was focusing on the top of the bonfire where the flames had now reached the zenith, with his brow furrowed. Magda looked up; the fire seemed to lean towards them.

Before either of them could exclaim, the burning head of the Böögg rolled down the side of the bonfire, cinders flying as it bounced against the pyre. In horror Magda realised it was on their side of the circle. As it hit the ground with a thud, a spray of sparks swirled upwards with the smoke. The head continued rolling towards them. As Magda stared dumbfounded, Walter shouted: 'Watch out, children!'

They all scrambled away. Walter and Magda fumbled to stand. Magda's boot caught in the hem of her skirt and they were both momentarily trapped. Her heart pounded. As the head continued towards them, Walter stuck out his boot, stopping the Böögg. He kicked the head back towards the circle of flames and it rolled around on the spot an arm's length from them, then came to a halt.

Edgar leaped to his feet and marched towards them through the smoke and sparks. He drew his sword, stabbed the head of the Böögg through the front of its face and held it aloft on the end of his blade.

'You're lucky your boot didn't catch fire,' he said to Walter. 'You continue to tempt the fates. I hear you're wandering around the countryside unarmed. You might not last long around here when trouble comes looking for you. Clever words won't save you against a Habsburg sword. It is not without reason the Böögg has sought you out. I believe this is not the first message you have been delivered to this effect.'

Edgar slung the burning head back onto the pyre, flames licking out of its slit of a mouth like a mocking tongue. He turned back to Walter. 'Just make sure our concerns are conveyed to Commander Stauffacher when you return to Altdorf. I trust you will be departing at first light.'

It was an order rather than a question. Magda was puzzled. Was Edgar jealous of Walter? She could only imagine what Edgar, with his warrior heart and fierce beliefs in the Confederation, might think of Walter's peace-mongering views. He wouldn't approve. Walter wouldn't even be able to count the supporters of his pacifism on the fingers of one hand.

Chapter Seven

17th March 1315, Troyes

SÉBASTIEN

T he oak beam above Sébastien's head creaked and popped as flames licked across the exquisitely painted ceiling of Avelleur. The King's soldiers would soon be crossing onto the commandery's land, chasing their own flaming arrows into the grounds.

'Grég, protect yourself! The burning thatch has caught. This place is going up like a tinder box.'

Sébastien watched Grégoire pull on his helmet down in the hall, the headgear crushing the blond curls that gave away his Norman Viking heritage. He retreated to the stone wall and looked up, nodding once to Sébastien on the gallery, who seized the hilt of his sword and swung at the rope securing the escape gangway to the open window on the east side of the building. The rope frayed as the blade sliced through, strands unravelling like a twirling jester. The gangway crashed onto its brace. He didn't have much time.

'Do you have the shroud and the banners?' Grégoire called up to him.

Sébastien patted the leather saddlebag slung over his shoulder in affirmation. The screech of oak against iron prevented a vocal answer as a large section of the roof came crashing down, bouncing against the balustrade. It fell onto the landing, blocking the way out through the sleeping quarters – Sébastien's escape route. The collapse sent out a spray of sparks and a cloud of smoke. As the dust settled, Sébastien searched the gaps in the beams and thatch now impeding his way. He glanced at the hole in the roof and calculated his options. Grégoire waited at the edge of the great hall, protecting himself from falling debris with one of the templar shields torn from the wall.

'Take my sword,' called Sébastien, 'It'll hinder my escape.'

He threw the heavy sword down to Grégoire, who caught the weapon in his thickly gloved hands, bending down almost to the flagstones as he absorbed the weight of it.

'I have everything we need!' Sébastien shouted, hoping Yves could hear outside. 'Ready the horses!'

Another beam collapsed to the north of the building. One of the horses squealed in the courtyard outside.

'Take your mount, Grég!' Sébastien shouted, and his colleague ran out of the hall to the courtyard where Yves waited with their beasts.

Over the sound of the crackling inferno, Sébastien heard many hooves crunching on gravel. As they drew nearer, the shouts of King Louis' troops carried to him through a fire-ringed gaping hole in the roof. Sébastien shifted the leather saddlebag across his shoulder, tightened the buckle, and shimmied up the rope now hanging loose from the gallery. When he reached the top, he put the rope in his mouth. He used his arms to swing around the gallery to the north, grabbing on to the most solid looking of the remaining cross-struts. He was glad for his thick gloves protecting him from the scorching wood.

Smoke stung his lungs and he felt his arms weakening. Saliva dripped from his mouth, wedged open with the rough rope scouring his tongue. As he reached the northeast corner, he swung up to the gallery and squeezed out through the ballistraria window hardly wide enough for a grown man. He thought for a moment he had miscalculated the size of the opening, but the saddlebag was hampering his escape. He unbuckled it and pushed it through the gap, holding onto the strap. As he forced himself through, he strapped the bag again to his body, took the rope from his mouth, held it firmly in both hands and jumped.

He dropped like a stone, praying the rope was not too long. As it drew taut, he thanked his stars he was still ten feet from the ground. But the momentum caused the rope to slide through his gloves like butter. He tumbled to the ground, rolling onto his shoulder to break his fall. The air was forced out of his lungs.

'Séb, get up! Hurry!' shouted Yves.

With his head reeling, Sébastien opened his eyes to the welcome sight of his black stallion looking down at him. The horse's nostrils flared and he nickered recognition.

'Obéron, you beauty,' said Sébastien and used the reins to pull himself up.

He scrambled onto his stallion's back, wincing as pain scythed through an old wound in his shoulder. The three knights turned their mounts and galloped down the slope into a dry moat, not visible from the main road from Troyes. They crossed diagonally through the sheep-grazed grass and passed single file through a concealed tunnel, crouching flat against their mounts' necks. By the time the King's soldiers discovered where they had exited the grounds, the three knights had vanished into the familiar embrace of the Orient Forest.

☩ ☩ ☩

When the horses began to weaken, the knights slowed them to an easy canter. They veered off the beaten path and wound their way east through the forest, a thick canopy folding over their heads.

'We should stay in the woods for the night. They'll never find us in here,' said Yves.

'The horses need water,' said Sébastien. 'But I don't think we should stop for long. We can't rest until we have crossed the Rhine.'

'We'll be at the swamp soon; we can take water and cross at Les Rives. We must press on to the Vosges,' said Grégoire.

'It would be wiser to rest the horses,' said Yves.

Sébastien noted the sweat on Yves' mount; the beast had already been ridden hard earlier that day.

'King Louis will undoubtedly send a messenger to mobilise his soldiers at Mulhouse and cut us off. We have to cross the bridge before they get there,' he said.

Sébastien thought of the shroud and banners in his bag. He must guard them with his life.

'I didn't think we would be forced to leave so quickly,' said Grégoire.

'It has been a deception,' said Sébastien. 'King Philippe turned a blind eye to Avelleur because of the financial agreement our forebears made. But his son Louis has become too greedy. This confirms he wants to see us completely wiped out.'

'We can never go back. It's surely the end of us,' said Yves.

Sébastien combed his fingers through his hair. He hadn't seen his family for several years. And now it was likely he would never see them again. He hoped they could sense he was still alive. 'Never say it's the end of us,' he said. 'They have no idea what is at stake.

But I fear the thing that must be protected most will also soon be compromised. Louis' reach will go far beyond the borders of France. Especially if he's in cohorts with the Pope, as his father was. The quiet little abbey that has housed the secret for hundreds of years may be at risk.'

'But the mountain people will not know our true calling. Most of them are probably unaware of our existence. And those who've heard of us would only think we spend our lives accompanying pilgrims through the Holy Lands.'

'Maybe the alpine folk don't know, but Pope Clément does, and he can no longer be trusted.' Sébastien crossed himself. 'It would not be impossible to imagine that the Habsburgs can sway him too.'

The three men bowed their heads, their faithful steeds carrying them onwards through the shadowed forest. Towards the most important mission of their lives. Towards the Alps.

Chapter Eight

18th March 1315, Morgarten and Schornen

MAGDA

M agda was awoken by the bell ringing frantically in the toll tower, almost but not quite drowning the voices of boys and men shouting outside the chalet. The brightness of morning shone through the gaps in the shutters. She'd slept long, exhausted from the preparations, the excitement and the lateness of the festivities finishing the night before. She pushed back the curtain of the sleeping alcove, to see her father and Edgar pulling on their boots at the door. As they clattered down the stairs to the courtyard, Magda rubbed the sleep out of her eyes and hauled herself out of bed.

'They're still in the pasture,' called the boy from the tower with urgency.

'*Gott verdammt*, I wish we had a horse,' said her father, the evidence of a hangover in the redness of his eyes and the paleness of his cheek.

'Bring your axes and pitchforks,' her brother shouted to the men in the courtyard.

With a baselard gripped in his fist and still only half-dressed, Edgar took off at a run. He leaped over the wall and disappeared from Magda's view. She hurried down the stairs, crossed the courtyard and scrambled to the top of the rough stone wall. She caught sight of him skirting the swamp on dry ground close to the forest. What or who was he chasing?

Her gaze drifted beyond the swamp to the fertile grasslands shared by the farmers of Morgarten and Schornen. At first, everything appeared normal. Several sheep were grazing in the pasture. Then she saw a figure running towards the forest above Morgarten. But Edgar wasn't giving chase. Instead he was hurrying to the centre of the field. The sheep would normally be scattering by now, but they weren't moving. Magda narrowed her eyes. The animals lay immobile on the ground and their creamy pelts, soon to be shorn after the winter, were covered in dark smatterings of blood. She counted at least five dead sheep.

Poachers! But why would they destroy the animals and not take the carcasses for their meat or wool? And why do this in the light of day? This was surely a provocation. More men were now running from Morgarten towards the pasture. The figure who'd absconded into the forest had disappeared. If he knew the lie of the land, he would easily make his escape on the forest trails running along the steep slope and be long gone. Edgar caught up to another person, though, and this one was not allowed to escape. The man was quickly overcome, and Magda feared he would soon be gored to death by Edgar and the other villagers. But instead Edgar pinned him to the ground, his knees in the man's back, and tied his arms at the wrist with a thin rope provided by one of the others. Three of them dragged the man back towards Schornen.

Magda's heart pounded. They were planning to question the man, and she didn't want to know how they would extract his answers.

As he was thrown to the ground in the courtyard between the tower and the chalet, Magda wished they hadn't brought him so close to their home. What would they do to him? He and his accomplice had killed half a dozen sheep. For what purpose? Edgar was spitting mad.

'Where have you come from?' he shouted into the man's face. He was lying prostrate on the ground. 'What kind of message is this?'

The man shook his head. Edgar tightened the twine at his wrists. 'Who are you aligned with?'

'Ow-a! That hurts!'

'So he has a voice,' whispered Magda to herself. 'But he's not from the valley.'

'Speak, man, or you'll lose your tongue before I take your life,' said Edgar.

Magda stared at her brother. This was a different man from the young boy she'd played with as a child, catching frogs in the swamp. His baselard hovered alarmingly close to the man's throat.

'Von Hünenberg sent us,' the man whimpered. 'He knows you graze your cattle on his land. It's against the law. We were told to garotte the beasts and he'll send a cart to take them to the abattoir. *His* abattoir.'

Magda swallowed. Spies were everywhere. It was the only way the Habsburgs could have known that the Schornen farmers had begun to graze their sheep on Morgarten pastures again. They'd taken a break for a few years since the time when the blood of more than a few sheep had tainted the land.

'We'll deliver this heathen to the closest garrison in Schwyz and see how they deal with this news,' said Josef. 'But it's too late to leave today. We'll lock him up and begin the journey at first light.

This man can deliver his threats to a military general, who might extract some useful information.'

'Papa, I don't want him under our roof, even down with the pigs. Is there nowhere else you can keep him?' asked Magda.

'Take him to the cellar under the mill!' Josef told Edgar. 'He'll likely enjoy the comfort of the cold and dark before being moved to more distasteful lodgings in Schwyz.'

As she watched Edgar and one of the other young men of the hamlet take the culprit away to lock him up, Magda turned to her father. 'Why don't the Habsburgs respect the charter that recognises our nation? Can't they just leave us in peace?'

'Duke Leopold of Austria would have control of the entire European continent if he could,' he answered. 'Heinrich von Hünenberg is the one who stirs up trouble on our borders for him. They hope we'll eventually give in and return to the tyrannical Austrian rule. It's why I wish we had a garrison closer to us – one of these days we'll surely suffer an attack through this valley. It's the forgotten doorway into the Confederation. Make sure you continue to keep your eyes open at all times, Maggi.'

Magda was tired of always having to watch her back. Tired of having chickens, sheep and cattle stolen by raiders and brigands, tired of having whole fields of crops torn from their roots and stolen in the night. Sometimes she wondered at the wisdom of a staunch allegiance when the villagers suffered so. But she would never mention this to her father or her brother. They were such proud patriots.

She often dreamed she might be happier if she didn't live here on this precarious border of the Confederation. Perhaps if she lived somewhere in the central mountains or lakes where she was surrounded by her fellow citizens, there might be less fear. Like Altdorf. Or Bürglen. Where the Tells lived.

If she ran away with Walter, back to his village, would he support her weaving? Perhaps he could provide safety for her to practise her skills, where her work was less likely to be ruined by usurpers or stolen by thieves.

What might it be like to be the wife of Walter Tell?

Chapter Nine

19th March 1315, Bürglen

WALTER

B efore Walter had the chance to call on the cobbler on the way back to his chalet in Bürglen, a neighbour's lad shouted to him from the door of the village tavern. He beckoned Walter urgently into the building. Walter's feet were only slightly more aching than his heart, not knowing how soon he could return to Schornen to see Magda. But his curiosity helped take his mind off the latter. The cobbler should still be earning his keep before the end of the day.

As he entered the tavern he received curt greetings from a group of men sitting at the *Stammtisch* with a piece of flattened birch bark between them. A charred stick passed from hand to hand, each drawing lines across a roughly sketched map on the pale surface. Their voices calmed only briefly when Walter entered. Looking over a shoulder at the table, he saw they were disputing a piece of land on the outskirts of the village. The parcel's proximity to the village made it valuable enough to cause a heated difference of opinion.

The tavern owner begged Walter to intervene. 'Until the dispute is solved, I am sadly lacking an income,' he said, pointing to the empty mugs on the table. 'We'd be grateful for the use of your reading skills.'

One of the potential landowners had a parchment he claimed was penned by a Confederate official in Altdorf. They hadn't been able to find anyone else who could read.

Walter gratefully received a mug of ale from the tavern owner, and set about interpreting the landownership document. It didn't take long, and it occurred to him that he could have told them anything. But they considered him trustworthy – a trait Walter automatically inherited, being the son of his father – and it was more likely this reputation secured the agreement rather than their appreciation of Walter's reading aptitude.

From this group of men he barely knew, in ten short minutes Walter made several new allies and one grumpy enemy. But he had no desire to become an arbitrator of problems on such a humdrum domestic level. He could see this way of solving disputes was infinitely better than violence, but he wasn't happy to divide his social acquaintances in this way. If this was to be his destiny, his future didn't lie in the tiny village of Bürglen.

The coins from this latest earning bypassed his purse and found their way into the palm of the cobbler with whom he left his shoes to be re-soled. The cobbler loaned him a pair of slippers to wear back to the chalet as Walter had no intention of returning barefoot under the critical eye of his father.

As it happened, his father didn't even cast an eye at Walter's feet, for he and Werner Stauffacher were in deep conversation at the table in the chalet. Commander Stauffacher was wearing a civilian tunic and they were sharing a bottle of schnapps.

'Walter, good to see you!' said Werner.

Walter feared an inquiry about his own military future.

'What news from the far reaches of the nation?' his father asked with a joviality heightened by the drink. 'How is my brother doing in that snug hamlet of Schornen?'

Walter's father straightened his back and pulled at his thick beard streaked with silver. Even seated, Wilhelm Tell's height and broad shoulders filled the space in the small kitchen.

'The hamlet may not be so snug any more,' said Walter. 'They're worried about the threat of the Habsburgs. Many of the people in Morgarten are desperate to join the Confederation. The village sees Schornen as their ally. Families have been divided over the border.'

'*Many* of the people?' asked the commander.

'There's still a difference of opinion. Some folk are torn about under which regime's rule they would feel safer.'

'Our current borders have existed less than thirty years,' said his father, his frown creasing the weathered skin around his blue eyes. 'That might seem long for a young man of your age, but the nation is only just now coming to terms with what we have. Expanding too quickly may lead to confusion and disparity.'

Werner Stauffacher said nothing.

'I don't see the point in waiting though,' said Walter, hoping he didn't sound over-bold. 'Think how we suffer after a harsh winter. Why not improve our resources while people are still enthusiastic about our progress? Especially defence resources.'

'The boy has your fighting attitude, Wilhelm,' said Commander Stauffacher, nodding slowly. 'If we can't persuade you to return full-time to Altdorf's council, perhaps we should be looking to engage young Walter here.'

His father said nothing, but pulled a slice of dried apple from the wooden bowl on the table and began chewing. Walter was perhaps the only one who knew of the aches and pains bothering his father in his old age. He had reduced his presence on the Altdorf council over the years to one or two days a month for the more important issues of the canton.

Wilhelm slid the bowl over to the commander, who helped himself to a slice, before scraping his chair back from the table as he stood.

'The people of Morgarten undoubtedly expect a swift answer,' he said. 'They'll want to know our position. Well, they shall have it soon. I'll call a meeting of my generals tomorrow and will let you know within the week. Prepare to deliver a message then, young Walter.'

The commander touched his hat as he left the chalet.

Walter tried to keep the smile from his face.

'What are you smirking about, Walterli?' asked his father. 'It's good to hear you voice your opinion about that hamlet on the edge of the Confederation. But if I didn't know better, I'd say there's another reason you've invested so much interest in it.'

Walter dropped his smile, wondering if his father could read his mind. But inside, his mood lifted, knowing he would soon be called upon to relay the next message to Magda's father.

CHAPTER TEN

25th March 1315, Schornen

MAGDA

Magda raised her head from her needlework when she heard the distant hollow clop of a hoof against flint. She'd been squinting, and it was a relief to close her eyes. She tipped her head to one side in an attempt to hear better, the absence of one sense hopefully enhancing the other. There it was again. A horse, no – horses – maybe three, walking along the trail from Morgarten.

She was sitting on the floor of the toll tower's lookout platform, leaning against the wooden wall. She often climbed up there to relieve the lads on watch and work on her embroidery, especially when rain threatened. The shuttered windows of the chalet were small, so even on the sunniest of days it was too dark inside to work efficiently. The wide, overhanging roof set on top of the tower's platform, on the other hand, kept the elements out, while offering light for Magda to practise her most intricate work. She avoided the northern corner where a group of bats occupied the roof beams for their daytime roost.

The day was hot for so early in the season, buzzing with the expectant weight of a summer yet to bloom. The metre-thick walls of stone encouraged a little coolness to waft up through the stairwell. At first, Magda thought it was Mihal on the trail, but she realised he wouldn't be approaching from the lake as he was abroad in the Confederation. And these were definitely horses' hooves, not the staccato trot-trot-trot of Mihal's sturdy mule.

She'd given the lad on watch a break and felt guilty that she'd not been paying attention. She laid the cloth she was working on to one side and stood to look westwards. Coming from the Aegeri Lake were three men on horseback. They wore typical peasant tunics made from brown cloth, and Magda wondered not for the first time why people still dyed their textiles brown when they could have vibrant greens, golds and violets. Despite their drab attire, these were no peasant horses the men rode. They appeared to be fine stock, soldiers' horses. Magda felt a frisson of alarm. Was her father expecting company? Were these men crossing the pass into Schwyz on their way south? It was late in the day for them to be travelling. She couldn't see any weapons, but they were sure to have some kind of protection under the saddlecloths of those fine beasts.

'They'd better keep their hands off my chickens,' she mumbled as she rang the bell in the tower twice to summon her father.

She returned to the balustrade to watch the horsemen approach. They were in no hurry, and judging by the reddening of the sky to the west over the Aegerital, they would probably request a place to bed that night.

Magda studied their body language, their relaxed gait on horses familiar to them. The front rider was tall. His dark hair blew across his forehead as he turned to answer something his colleague had asked. His deep voice carried to Magda. Foreign. Not Ladino or Romansch, a language she would have recognised from Mihal, who often muttered or sang in his native tongue. She thought perhaps it was French. It carried a similar softness. Walter would know. He was good with languages.

The voice matched the rider's good looks.

'Who, Magda?' her father called curtly from below.

She peered down to him in the courtyard. The axe in his hands was likely still warm from chopping wood on the other side of the barn.

'Three horsemen,' she shouted. 'They're coming from Morgarten across the marsh. They don't look like Habsburg men, but they might still be military. Be careful, Papa. Is Eddi with you?'

'He's at the mill, but he should have heard the bell. Ring twice again to be sure. And you stay up there, young lady.' He pointed at her with the axe.

She rang the bell again, and hurried back to watch the progress of the horsemen. She cupped her ear in an attempt to hear more of their conversation. A burst of laughter rang out, strong and deep, and she relaxed. They didn't seem to pose a threat. She glimpsed the sheen of brass under a blanket slung behind a saddle. A helmet. Not a design she had seen the Habsburg soldiers wear. Her curiosity was piqued. Lifting her skirts and wrapping them around her thighs, she began to climb down. After a few rungs, she gripped the outside of the ladder with her legs and slid down the middle level. She'd been doing that since she was a child and it still made her smile.

'I told you to stay in the tower,' her father barked as she crossed the courtyard. He stood watching the horsemen approach, arms folded across his chest, his axe leaning against his leg. Magda snorted softly and pulled at his arms.

'It's all right, Papa,' she said, holding his rough hand. 'Don't look so defensive. You're making your body ready for a fight before you've even discovered their purpose. I'm sure they're not a threat.'

'When did you become an expert on threat, Maggi? You can never be sure these days,' he growled. 'The Habsburgs have been sending spies all over the region. This is not the time to relax our guard.'

Magda's eyes followed the lead horseman as he guided his mount through the opening in the border wall and approached the courtyard. Her father looked from the man to her face and she cast her eyes downwards, blushing furiously.

'Put your tongue in, girl. Go feed the chickens or something. Be gone.'

'I'll be staying right here,' she hissed defiantly.

'*Gruezi Mittenand!* Greetings strangers!' her father called as the men halted their horses.

The tall one in front smiled at Magda. His dark hair shone in the sunlight, and laughter lines creased the edges of his striking green eyes. Heat rose to Magda's face. The second horseman laughed amiably, making Magda feel worse that her curiosity was so obvious.

'You'll have to excuse my daughter. Anyone would think she's never seen a horse before.'

'Papa!'

The handsome stranger removed his boots from the stirrups, and stretched his legs. He raised a gloved hand to cover a smile. Magda desperately tried to control her reactions. What was happening to her? She turned her thoughts to Walter, his fresh good looks, how he made her laugh. But it did not stop the instant feeling of attraction to this stranger, and it alarmed her that she could not control her emotions.

'It took a while to find the path around the reeds,' said the horseman, turning to point towards the marsh.

Magda was grateful he had drawn the attention away from her.

'The beasts were a little skittish in the proximity of the forest,' he continued. 'But it's hard to explain to a horse that it's better to walk on a tailored trail than wade through a swamp.'

'It's easier for us to observe the traffic,' said Magda's father. 'It requires maintenance in winter.' And in case the foreigners were unaware, he added: 'It justifies the toll we are required to charge at each passage.'

'Of course,' said Sébastien.

'What's the purpose of your journey?' her father asked with narrowed eyes.

'We understand your caution,' the second horseman said. 'We're on a transport reconnaissance mission. For textiles and the like.'

'You don't strike me as the type who'd be handy with the loom.' Magda hid a laugh behind her hand.

'Not like your lovely daughter beside you,' said the first horseman, nodding from Josef to Magda.

A renewed blush burned Magda's cheeks.

'Your reputation goes before you, *mademoiselle*,' he continued. 'They speak highly of your spinning skills at the west end of the lake.'

Magda dipped her head to one side, afraid to open her mouth and say something stupid. She would rather be recognised for her weaving and needlework than the simple task of spinning, but men seemed to think the noble job of tailoring should be left to the men.

'Are you weavers then, like me?' she asked, to press the point.

He raised his eyebrows before answering.

'No. Consider us... guardians. For the safe transport of goods.'

Magda marvelled at how well this man spoke their language. The accent softening the words he must have learned in the northern lands made her knees weak. Although she could tell all three men had to concentrate hard to understand the dialect of the forest people.

'Do you have official permission to travel through the Confederation?' her father asked, still wary.

'We've been under the employ of the French crown,' said Sébastien.

'Well, there is hardly a higher accolade,' said Josef, and Magda wondered if they could detect the hint of sarcasm in his voice.

'Perhaps this will reassure you,' said Sébastien, reaching into a pocket on his tunic.

He brought out a folded piece of birch parchment. Josef took it from his outstretched hand and hesitated before unfolding it. Martha knew he wouldn't want to reveal to these men that he could not read. She peered over his shoulder. But there were no words. The note merely contained a wax seal, and a small silver rectangle. A pilgrim's badge, decorated with four flowers and a cross. They had seen many of these carried by travellers passing through the Confederation to Einsiedeln. But none of them had ever arrived on horses. As Josef unfolded the parchment further, Magda moved closer to look at the Benedictine design on the seal, much like one that might originate from the abbey in Einsiedeln.

'If you can spare us some of your time, we would like to discuss our mission.'

This should appeal to her father's sense of pride – to be asked his advice. Josef touched his brow in acknowledgement.

'Of course,' he said, his wariness obviously easing a little.

Magda felt she could listen to the stranger speak for eternity. The deep richness of his voice and its accent was like a lullaby to her ears. As he swung his leg over the saddle and dismounted, her father stepped forward and held out his hand.

'Josef Stauffacher,' he said, and shook the handsome foreigner's hand.

'Sébastien de Molay, *à votre service*, and my colleagues Yves Querrioux and Grégoire Dupont.'

The other two riders dismounted. Grégoire's tunic flapped open, exposing a fine sword in a scabbard at his hip. Magda was standing closest to him and wondered if her father had seen. The hilt of the weapon was of a fine crafting she had never seen before. She narrowed her eyes but kept the smile on her mouth.

'Magda, take the horses, give them some hay,' said her father.

She wanted to comply, but was flustered. There were three horses, all of them towering over her, and she wasn't sure her father had worked out the coordination of this request with her lack of experience with such giant beasts. But the one called Sébastien took the reins of his own and Grégoire's mount. Magda took the reins from Yves and led his horse to the barn to tie it to the railing.

'Thank you for your help,' Magda whispered, as Sébastien followed her.

His own magnificent black mount stood patiently waiting, reins pooled on the ground, as Sébastien tied Grégoire's horse. Then he bent to pick up his own to do the same.

Magda put her hand against the neck of Sébastien's horse, and the beast nickered in a friendly manner.

'Any excuse to spend a little more time with the beautiful young weaver of Schornen,' said Sébastien.

As Magda studied his green eyes, his shiny hair, his strong jaw and his full lips now in the bow of an open smile, she put her other hand to her chest, thinking her heart might burst from her bodice.

CHAPTER ELEVEN

25th March 1315, Schornen

SÉBASTIEN

'The path from Morgarten to Schornen is precariously close to the forest,' Sébastien said as he and Magda returned to the group of men. Josef had been joined by a young man who was most certainly his son. 'But it's far enough above the high-water level to avoid getting boggy. We'd benefit from a similar lie of the land in our *marais* back home.'

Yves shot him a look and Sébastien was hit by a sudden melancholy that he would likely never again see the marshland around Troyes, let alone his real home. To take his mind off France, he studied the rough stone wall that marked the border of the Confederation. The village stream ran through a gap in the wall, and meandered to the swamp on the shores of the lake near Morgarten. The proximity of the path to the trees meant an ambush would be all too possible.

'Once the spring flood has subsided, is there still never dry ground underfoot?'

Magda shook her head. 'The marsh is deep for most of the year. Sometimes in winter we can walk on the frozen reed beds to get to the lake. But even in the driest summer, water flows from the springs along the north and south ridges. It's rare there's not enough for the wheel to turn at the mill.'

She spoke with a deep knowledge of her surroundings. She was certainly forthright. As the three knights had ridden into the hamlet earlier, Sébastien's attention had been drawn to the pretty young woman lifting her skirts to run across the courtyard from the watchtower. Until now, the knights' experience of the peasants in this land had been one of growing unease towards foreigners, especially the closer they came to the mountains.

They'd heard that the people in this tiny nation were constantly at threat from the Habsburg troops beyond their borders, that Duke Leopold wanted to take back their little nation too. The knights had seen very few young women through the western flatlands. Perhaps the mistrusting villagers were keeping their fair maidens from the eyes of strangers?

Sébastien studied Magda's face, especially her striking grey eyes, which had taken on a little blue of the sky. She was dressed becomingly, her skirts sewn with flashes of colour. She stood tall, her chestnut hair flowing wild and free as opposed to constrained and braided as was usual for peasant women. Sébastien felt something stirring in his gut, the first enjoyable emotion since the knights had fled France. But he shook his head to try and rid himself of the feeling. Their mission had no room for such distraction. He turned to Yves and Grégoire, who were already discussing their 'assignment' with Josef and his son, without revealing the true goal of their mission.

'We're doing a reconnoitre of a trade route we might be using for a consignment we are not yet at liberty to reveal,' said Yves.

Sébastien silently urged him not to say too much; they didn't want to be caught out in a deceit. Now that they could see how dangerous it would be to return westwards, the only solution would be to cross the Confederation and head south. They were going to have to bend the truth.

'Your biggest danger will be around here, on the border. What's your intended route?' asked the Stauffacher son, Edgar.

'The goods are destined for the Gotthard Pass. We'll be met by aides from Italy, who will complete the journey on the southern side of the Alps.'

'You may experience peril in the gorges. The steep granite paths through the cliffs offer yet more danger of ambush and thievery,' said Edgar.

'We have something for you to help secure the toll of our passage through the Confederation,' said Sébastien, looking up at the tower as he pulled a silver crucifix from his pocket. The piece was decorated with garnets and quartz, and down the centre were intricately carved letters in a typical Benedictine design. A faint smile touched Josef's face as he took the cross and examined it in his palm. He relaxed for the first time without his shield of caution.

'Are you monks or priests?' asked Magda. 'Why do you ride with helmets if you're not going into battle?'.

'Maggi! Mind your nosiness,' said Josef.

'It's a valid question,' said Sébastien, holding up his hand. 'Even guards of commercial goods should be prepared for the harshest attack from brigands.'

Magda must have seen the brass of their armour hidden under their horse blankets. This lass was astute.

'Guards, mercenaries. Does that mean you were once soldiers?'

Josef rolled his eyes at his daughter's continued curiosity. Sébastien thought with amusement that she must be quite a handful in the home.

'In a way,' said Yves. 'Our focus is on protection.'

Grégoire stepped forward and leaned in towards Magda. 'And we are very good at our job,' he said with a wink.

Sébastien put his hand on Grégoire's arm, to draw his gaze away from the young woman. Josef might have turned a blind eye to the attention being paid to his daughter, but they didn't need to be provoking him.

'You'll be needing lodging and food tonight for the purpose of your survey,' continued Josef. 'I had a mind to send you over the pass before nightfall, but I'd be interested to hear what you have to say about the villages to the west currently under Habsburg rule. You can sleep in the barn – there's fresh reed stalk and a little rye straw, and Magda will make sure there's enough food for all of us tonight, won't you Maggi?'

Josef threw a commanding look at his daughter. Had he expected a complaint at the short notice and extra work? Magda didn't strike Sébastien as too shy to speak up in front of strangers.

'Of course, Papa. I'll fetch another chicken for our meal.'

Judging by the raised eyebrows, she must have surprised her father with her willingness to comply.

'And I'll show you where you can sleep,' said Edgar. 'The barn is open on one side; the building is as yet unfinished. But the evening is mild and I can't smell rain, so you and your horses should stay dry.'

Sébastien stared at Magda as she made her way to the chicken coop behind the house. She turned back to steal a glance at him. The moment their eyes locked, she hurried away to her work. The stirring Sébastien had felt before was now set fully aflame.

In truth, this seemed like the perfect place to stay for a few days while they cautiously worked out the next stage of their plan, but they would be prudent to keep their real purpose a secret for as long as possible. Although the Confederation was a recognised nation, it was still under the overall rule of the Holy Roman Empire, and in collusion with the king of France, the Pope in Rome had declared the Templar Knights heretics. They didn't want their flight rendered pointless by being dragged back to France and burned at the stake.

They would first find out if they could trust Josef before they explained their true destiny. His pretty daughter might not be so admiring of them when she found out.

Chapter Twelve

25th March 1315, Schornen

MAGDA

As Magda slapped the strangled chicken on the chopping block to remove its head, she looked about her for the plucking apron and realised she'd left it in the barn. As she approached, she could hear the three men talking amongst themselves while removing the saddles from their horses. She understood not a word, but smiled at their lyrical tongue. She cleared her throat.

Sébastien slapped the rump of his beast affectionately as he came towards her. He'd removed his tunic and her heart skipped a beat as she noted the strong muscles of his shoulders and arms through his woollen undershirt. She pointed to the heavy resin-treated apron she used for plucking, lying over a stool in the corner.

'Go ahead, *mademoiselle*,' he said, sweeping his hand towards the stool.

'I'll do my work in the courtyard,' she said. 'I'll not disturb you gentlemen. Excuse me.'

As Magda reached for the apron, one of the horses stamped its foot, perhaps to rid itself of a bothersome fly. A saddlebag leaning against the partition at the back of the barn fell from where it had been propped up, and a piece of cloth spilled from within. It was white, decorated with a cloven red cross. Magda's eye was drawn to the fine weave, the bright colour and design. She raised her eyebrows. It looked like some kind of pennant or flag. As she went forward to peer at it, Sébastien stepped in her way.

'You haven't seen anything here, *mademoiselle*,' he said, assuming Magda was aware of what she'd seen.

Yves, who was shaking his blanket onto a pile of straw, said something in clipped French. Sébastien relaxed and backed away.

'We're looking forward to your fine food this evening, Mademoiselle Stauffacher,' he said, changing the subject as he guided her back to the courtyard. He set down the stool he'd carried out for her, and she donned the plucking apron. Magda was curious to know what these men were hiding. Sébastien had spoken in haste. Had he not uttered those words, her curiosity might never have been aroused. Where had these men come from? Who were they? They seemed far too sophisticated to be transport guards. As she finished plucking the second chicken, she wondered if she should tell her father. They certainly weren't Habsburg allies. And they seemed surely too open and friendly for her to consider them enemies. Magda pushed it from her mind, gutted and cleaned the fowl and went back to the chalet. Shoving the chickens whole onto a spit, one after the other, she roasted them over the fire in the chalet, turning them from time to time.

She fetched a bowl and sat at the kitchen table. She was compelled to impress these men with her culinary prowess. She beat a few eggs with some milk in the bowl, adding some sifted flour she first inspected for weevils, since it had been in the stores for several months over winter. As she rubbed the mixture into a dough, she reflected on her reaction to the handsome knight, Sébastien. She remembered Walter Tell's lips on hers at the Mittenfastenfeuer, her fondness for the person who she felt so comfortable with. She considered Walter her friend and was confused by her thoughts, only a few days earlier, that he would be good husband material. Although she hadn't known him long, Walter would be a perfect match. But it was nothing like the heat she felt every time the French knight looked her way. This was altogether something more... intense.

She shredded some of the *Bärlauch* sitting in a jar on the kitchen bench and kneaded it into the mix. Picking morsels of dough between her thumb and forefinger, she rolled them into *Spaetzli*.

The men gathered for dinner in the darkness of the chalet. Magda didn't have time to become flustered in the presence of Sébastien, so intent was she on delivering a meal they wouldn't forget. She fussed over the fire to make sure everything looked and tasted perfect. It was a tight squeeze around their table, so she decided to eat later, if there was anything left.

The Frenchmen made the right noises, complimenting Magda on the meal. When she cleared the empty plates, she produced a sweet dish for each of them of soft goats' curd from her stores in the cellar with a spoonful of a wild berry compote she'd made last autumn swirled on top. Edgar narrowed his eyes when she placed his dish in front of him. This kind of meal was only served on special occasions, Christmas or Easter. He would have thought it was a waste of their luxuries.

'A feast for kings!' Sébastien declared.

'Or brave knights,' replied Magda.

Yves and Sébastien exchanged a look, and Josef's brow sank into a frown.

'Or rather guardians of precious goods,' Magda said hurriedly.

'Speaking of which,' said Grégoire, 'We'd like to look at the area around your hamlet. It's nestled in a vulnerable spot with the valley narrowing at this point. It would be useful if you could assign someone to us who knows the woodlands and slopes surrounding the pass. It will make our task swifter if that person can show us the hidden footpaths and trails leading up to the higher points in the valley.'

'I can show them, Papa,' blurted Magda without thinking.

As her father hadn't allowed her to go unaccompanied with Walter into the forest, it was highly unlikely he would allow the same with three strangers.

'I'll take them,' said Edgar, giving Magda a stern look.

'You're certainly being thorough,' said Josef.

Magda's excitement that the foreigners might stay at least another day eclipsed the note of caution in her father's voice.

☩ ☩ ☩

'You'll allow me to come with you, Eddi, or I'll explain to Brigitta's father where you disappear off to with his daughter every other night. He thinks she's playing dice with Judith, Astrid and me.'

'Which would be frowned upon by Papa – I hear it said that the church will soon ban those games. It's not a suitable pastime for women.'

'Don't start with your "women should stay in the kitchen" speech again. You know I do more than my fair share of work around here.'

Magda thrust out her scarred hands as she spoke, reminding her brother of the battle between the reeds and her *baselard*.

'Stupid game anyway,' he said.

Magda pressed her lips to silence herself. Edgar had a hard time with his numbers. Mihal had given her the handcrafted set of six dice in exchange for a pair of soft woven socks. He taught her and Brigitta to play a game that had originated in the Arabian lands. They'd been devoted to it during many dark winter evenings, but now they were all maturing faster than heifers, there were other games playing on their minds.

'So, you'll take me?'

'Why are you so persistent, Magda? You can take a walk anytime if you're so confident you can fight off a Habsburg spy.' He paused. 'Are you warm on the Frenchman?'

Her blush spoke louder than words.

'What about the Tell lad? He seemed keen on you, though his choice of profession isn't one to be particularly proud of. Has my sister turned fickle?'

Magda put her hand to her chest and turned away. Was she being a fool? She bit her lip with self-reproach. At this point, she didn't want to risk giving away any emotions by speaking, so she remained silent.

But in the end, it was probably her mention of Brigitta that swayed Edgar.

✝ ✝ ✝

Magda assumed Sébastien would want to take the trail leading up to the lookout where they had walked with Walter the day they encountered the wild boar. Instead he asked to go to the lower rocky ridge on the other side of the marsh. It wasn't until they arrived that Magda saw why. From the sparse forest above that side of the village, they could see exposed areas on the steep slope opposite, underneath the Figlenfluh Ridge. Following the fall of the ridge down the slope, she realised it might be a place where an ambush could take place by an enemy hiding in the forest. She made out the village's wood-chopping clearing. Several dips and craggy gullies ran down to the valley from there. Edgar pointed these out to the Frenchmen, who began a lengthy discussion in their own language.

Edgar joined Grégoire and Yves on the top of a rocky knoll. He pointed out landmarks and buildings across the lake above Morgarten in Habsburg territory. The men stood on a jumble of rocks from a long-ago landslide, the lichened tops now poking through a carpet of grass cropped short by the goats. As Magda watched them chatting, she sensed Sébastien behind her, and before she could react, his warm hand fell on her shoulder close to her neck.

'That's a fine weave, Magda. They were right about your skills.'

She looked around. His eyes were on the bands of embroidered design falling from the neck of her garment to her breast. As she turned fully to face him, the back of his knuckles grazed the area below her collar bone and swept down to her breast with the movement of her body. A sharp stab of unfamiliar energy pulsed through her belly. It was so exquisite, she wanted him to touch her again, but he withdrew his hand. He narrowed his eyes in warning and Magda turned to see Edgar casting them a frown from where he stood with the others.

Sébastien pointed to the marshland in the valley. 'The swamp is much larger than it seems from below. It could both hinder and protect our position. We are only a handful of men in the event of an ambush.'

Magda nodded, not fully understanding his talk of position and attack. She was happy to mask this new, strange sensation she was feeling with conversation. 'You have the eyes and ears of our village too,' she said. 'No one wants thieves and bandits in the region, even if they are operating outside the borders of the Confederation.' She paused. 'Am I to deduce you already have experience of these things? If I'm not mistaken, you carry a battle banner with you.'

Sébastien's eyes sparked briefly.

'I saw what was folded in your saddlebags,' she said.

'Perhaps I will tell you when we know each other a little better,' he said.

She smiled at that prospect. 'Have you been professionally trained?'

Sébastien put a finger to his lips. 'Your persistence is admirable.'

'Are you spying for the Habsburgs? If you carry a religious seal, I would think not, and I don't get the feeling that you're about to destroy us all,' she said. 'But we could do with some extra men to help defend our border.'

'Rest assured, we are your allies,' said Sébastien. 'One day I will tell you a story, but you might not look upon the three of us so favourably if you know our mission.'

'How long do you think your *mission* will last?' she asked.

'Two weeks, a month, who knows? Our contract is open-ended...'

Magda sensed he was rambling, sounding purposely vague. They were definitely hiding something. But knowing they would be going back and forth in the Confederation was a pleasing prospect. 'Where will you lodge?'

He smiled, maybe guessing the question behind her question. 'Probably in Aegeri. Perhaps Morgarten. It might be more advantageous, and safer for us, to lodge somewhere inside the Confederation. We still haven't decided. We certainly thank you for the hospitality you have shown us so far.'

It wouldn't be easy to find somewhere for all three of them to stay. They might have to be billeted out to separate families. Although the Stauffacher cottage didn't have room for any more beds, she could suggest to her father that they stay in the toll tower. The open-sided barn where they were currently sleeping wouldn't be suitable in bad weather. Edgar and her father would likely see her motive, though. Every time Sébastien raised her heartbeat, she felt like everyone could see her thoughts. She was sure neither of them would approve. She wasn't sure she approved of them herself.

They returned to the village in the afternoon and Magda set about preparing another meal she hoped they, or at least Sébastien, would remember. The Frenchmen were to stay one more night before continuing to map out their routes.

After dinner, they sat outside in the courtyard. Edgar lit the brazier and threw on one of the rotten logs Magda had refused to accept for the kitchen fire. The wood smouldered and smoked until it eventually caught. Centipedes and woodlice fled from the crumbling core, the reason Magda hadn't wanted it near the house. The wood eventually burned true, and by the time the sun had set, there were enough embers to keep them warm on all sides of the brazier.

Magda was drawn to and yet repelled by these men, like tallow on water. Grégoire was a tall man with a brash voice that didn't match his golden curls. His beard was streaked with rust. She imagined he would show very little sympathy for his enemy soldiers in battle. Yves was quiet, but steady, and obviously held a deep respect for his two companions.

And yet since that afternoon, she'd been longing for another smile from the handsome Sébastien, or the touch of his hand on her body. At the same time she was terrified of her reaction to him, this new sensation that must be the driving force for why men and women couple. She tried not to think about the smouldering looks she had seen Brigitta and Edgar exchange with each other.

She tried not to think either about kind, steady Walter. Sébastien was not like him, with whom Magda could joke and play and hold hands with growing affection. Despite the soft sweetness of that one kiss, this, with Sébastien, was not like the comfort she felt in Walter's company. She was in turmoil. Sébastien had a steady, confident strength, and it had set Magda into a frenzied disarray.

Still, her father had told her to continue to keep her eyes open, and it seemed to her that these men were hiding something. She intended to find out what it was.

Chapter Thirteen

30th March, Bürglen

WALTER

W alter was sitting on the top step whittling the shaft of a fletching for one of his father's crossbow bolts when a village boy rushed up to the house.

'Walter, come with me! *Schnell*! You're needed at Frau Vogler's house.'

'*Ach*, slow down, what's the hurry? Is her house on fire?' The boy's sudden appearance caused Walter's knife to slip from the hawk feather. 'Alert the folk nearer the river. The village has stronger men than me to carry water to the flames.'

'No, Walti, I mean for your tracking and mystery-solving,' said the boy. 'A fox stole one of her chickens. But she re-counted and believes three are missing. She's as livid as a dead calf's mother. I reckon there's a reward in it for you.'

Sucking a crimson droplet from the end of his thumb, Walter followed the boy down the lane to Margrit Vogler's chalet.

The old woman was still in a state, and between her squawking – Walter sympathised with the surviving chickens – she showed him the area outside the coop where the earth had been scratched away under the willow fence. He bent to inspect the fresh marks on the ground.

'I thought they were fox-claw marks,' she said. 'But when I count the chickens, I'm sure three are missing. Could one beast carry away that many birds?'

'Those scratches were not made by an animal's claws, Frau Vogler. They are from the edge of a boot sole. Someone's intention was to make you *believe* your chickens had been taken by a fox. But their greediness has confirmed the suspicion that's been growing in your mind.'

Margrit stamped her foot like an impatient billy goat.

'I've not much, but I can pay you if you find the scoundrels.' She pulled some coins from her pocket and bounced them in her palm.

Walter tried not to smile, but was secretly pleased. His stealth and speed as a foot messenger wasn't going to last forever. At some stage, he dreamed of owning his own horse. But to purchase one, he needed extra funds. 'I'll give it a go,' he said, already examining the willow fence.

From one of the splintered posts surrounding the coop, Walter plucked a scrap of faded brown linen and tucked it into his pocket. He bent down again to examine the scuffed earth. They'd made a good job of trying to convince observers it was a fox. He spanned his hand over the size of one of the imprints and stood up.

'Here's a *Taler* now,' said Margrit. 'And you'll get the rest when you find the culprits.'

Walter touched his brow and set off down the lane. He made his way towards the forested slope leading to the river. The thieves wouldn't risk being seen through town, but Walter had an idea where they might be.

He scrambled down the bank to the riverbed where he and his friends used to build hoodoos and skin the rabbits they'd trapped.

It was a place he might find a couple of lads who would not be much younger than himself, but whose feet were not yet the fully grown size of adults.

Sure enough, there were three of them, down by the water, the remnants of a fire still smouldering within the circle of stones. He remembered choosing the best river rocks to fit snugly round the fire pit. He was sure they were still the very same stones, despite the annual spring floods threatening to roll them away.

If Walter wasn't mistaken, the lads still had the yellow grease of roast fowl on their lips. But the feathers and bones scattered in the clearing weren't enough to ascertain their guilt. They wouldn't prove the birds were Margrit's.

'Owa, ow!' The lad he picked to be the ringleader squealed as Walter lifted the front of his jerkin and then grabbed his collar. 'I ain't done nothing! Having our lunch by the stream. Where's the harm in that?'

Walter dragged the ragamuffin along the lane back past Margrit Vogler's chalet. She was still fretting, pushing earth back under the fence with a stick. Walter's fist was beginning to ache from clutching the lad's jerkin.

'Dani Baumann, you little thief,' Margrit spat. 'Wait 'til I get my hands on you.' She went to grab his arm, but Walter held up his free hand.

'We'll go before the *Schulze*, Frau Vogler. Justice must take the right path.'

'Justice, pah! It'll not bring my chickens back.'

'No, but maybe the sheriff can find a way for these lads to pay you back.'

'You can't prove nothing,' said the Baumann boy.

'We'll see about that,' said Walter as he continued into the centre of the village in search of Schulze Meyer.

He found him beside the road to Altdorf, felling a spruce whose lower branches had broken under the weight of a heavy blizzard the previous winter. The tree was in danger of falling across the road. Walter's father, who had contributed to a council discussion in town, was helping him. He stood tall, the axe an almost unfamiliar weapon in his large calloused hands, and rolled his eyes as they approached.

'He'll be wanting your job soon, that son of mine,' he mumbled to Meyer.

'Caught stealing three of Margrit Vogler's chickens,' said Walter, slinging the boy in front of them all.

The lad slipped, making Walter's presentation of him a little overdramatic as he sprawled in the road. 'I wasn't *caught*. They weren't her chickens!' the lad protested.

Walter leaned down to tear open his jerkin, the boy lying on his back.

''Ere, what're you doing?' he protested.

Walter held up the scrap of cloth from his pocket.

'I think you'll find this swatch of linen exactly matches that piece missing from his undershirt. It was attached to Frau Vogler's chicken coop at the point of forced entry,' he said.

They all looked down at the identical tear in the lad's brown linen vest.

✠ ✠ ✠

Walter accompanied the thief to the *Rathaus* and left the *Schulze* to decide on a suitable work detail for the boy to enable him to purchase three new chickens for Frau Vogler. By the time he returned to the chalet, his father was home.

He described solving the crime, although his father hadn't asked. And neither did Wilhelm Tell praise his son. He never did when it came to what he called his son's 'hobby' of tracking and mystery-solving. Before Walter could justify his achievement, there was a rap at the door and another young boy brought word that Werner Stauffacher and his generals had come to a decision about Morgarten. Walter was to call on the commander in Altdorf to collect a parchment before journeying back to Schornen the next day.

'I'll go to Altdorf and stay the night so I can start the journey at first light tomorrow,' he told his father.

Wilhelm didn't answer. Walter presumed it was because he would be obliged to prepare his own meal that evening. Since his mother's death, it had fallen upon Walter to provide for them both and to keep their house. He never complained about having to do the work of a woman. They had no relatives to provide those chores for free. Walter had developed a great respect for the role women played in the life of the village. But as Walter had been called out of the canton so often of late to deliver messages, his father was left on his own for days at a time. And although his great warrior history kept his reputation as one of the nation's saviours alive in the community, his advancing years meant he'd become lazy about performing life's more simple tasks.

As Walter announced his imminent departure, his father's mood darkened to one of his melancholies that Walter could usually cure with a couple of ales and a joke.

'Part of me wants to tell you to stay and help protect our village, son,' his father said. 'You're needed here. The work of a messenger can be left to a runner who only needs to think with his feet.'

Walter shook his head, knowing the old argument was about to raise its ugly head.

His father took a deep breath. 'After all I've fought for, I cannot believe you still refuse to join the army to help protect our nation,' he continued. 'Your mother would be so disappointed in you, considering all she went through.'

'Don't bring Mutti into this,' said Walter. 'She would've wanted to see an end to the violence. You know better than anyone military commands can be misinterpreted in the desire to conquer. I know what happened to her was undeniably wrong. But Father, I'm not refusing to protect the Confederation. Those men should've been brought to justice just like the culprits who stole Frau Vogler's chickens. The answer isn't always on the sharp end of a halberd.'

'*Gott verdammt,* Walti! We need you on the battlefield. You're a strapping lad. If only you would pick up the crossbow.'

Walter shuddered at the mention of it. No amount of cajoling would ever see him willingly use his father's weapon of choice, regardless of his expertise in repairing his bolts.

'Father, please just give me your blessing to continue delivering messages. I will still bring bread to our table. It doesn't matter if there is one man more or less in the Confederate army. I'm still helping them, indirectly. In any case, if I was conscripted, you would have to look after yourself for weeks at a time. But most of all, you know I would be useless at the hour of battle, a hopeless resource in that respect.'

Walter left his father rubbing his head, a malaise he had surely brought about himself, the worry of age and a feeling of resulting helplessness for the future of his nation clearly invading his father's thoughts. Walter closed the door quietly on his way out.

CHAPTER FOURTEEN

30th March 1315, Altdorf

WALTER

Frau Vogler's coins in Walter's leather pouch rattled and clinked gratifyingly with each footfall away from Bürglen. He shifted the purse to the far side of his belt beneath his jerkin to dampen the noise and avoid the curiosity of strangers seeking a pick-pocketing opportunity. This meagre wage was another reward for a little patience and a keen eye, but he had long understood the deception of a stealthy hand. It was, after all, helping him solve these mysteries.

He reflected on his father's disappointment in him, and was glad he had left before the chagrin turned to tears. Wilhelm Tell had been a boy himself when the three cantons of Uri, Schwyz and Unterwald signed the *Ewige Bund* – the Eternal Charter – marking the birth of the Confederation Helvetica in 1291. His widely publicised warrior's passion for his country had made him into a legend. Since he was no longer a conscripted member of the military, his father merely contributed to the more important issues on the council in Altdorf. Though his voice was still well respected in the community. But Walter sometimes found it difficult living in his shadow, especially now that he seemed to be the only one who could see his father ageing.

As he walked the trail to Altdorf, Walter reflected on the first incidents in the village that had started his interest in tracking and solving mysteries. Lost children, misplaced keys, burned haystacks, curious anomalies due to nature's own tricks. At the start, the hobby had earned him a coin or two for his labours. Frau Vogler's chicken mystery was not going to make him a rich man, but it put another notch on his belt.

✛ ✛ ✛

Walter used Frau Vogler's coins to secure himself a bed and a meal at the Bären in Altdorf. He would collect the parchment from Werner Stauffacher at the garrison the following morning. The sooner he could be on the road, the sooner he would see the commander's niece in Schornen.

The tavern was unusually busy. After replying to many greetings and satisfying curiosities about the health of his father, he settled on a corner bench near a window away from the *Kachelofen*. It was throwing out too much heat for this mild spring day. While Walter waited for a meal of beef stew to be delivered to his table, he sipped an ale and studied the other customers.

Three men sat at another table close to the bar, and Walter's attention was drawn to them speaking in a foreign tongue. French. It had been many years since the monk who taught him to write had imparted a smattering of French when his interest in Latin had waned.

Walter's intention had been initially to greet the foreigners and express his delight at being able to practise a little of their language, but his stew was delivered promptly. They were deep in conversation anyway and he thought it best to wait until their discussion dwindled. Words rolled off their tongues and he let their soft tones enhance the warm comfort of the tavern as he sipped his stew and chewed on the surprisingly tender meat.

Walter was jolted out of his reverie when he heard Schornen mentioned by one of the Frenchmen, followed by Magda Stauffacher's name. He narrowed his eyes at the three strangers and stopped chewing so he could hear what was being said.

'It is quite intriguing to see a peasant girl standing tall as she does with her untamed hair,' the dark-haired one said.

'She wears skirts with such colour, her reputation for the weave and design of her cloth is certainly justified,' said the blond one. 'She's daring, has quite the tongue on her, is not afraid to speak.'

At this, Walter pressed his mouth into a smile. On that he wholeheartedly agreed.

'The church would not condone a lowly person without royal blood to wear such colour,' the blond one continued.

'No matter, when she raised those skirts to cross the courtyard, it was a sight for sore eyes the day we rode to the village,' the tall, thin one said.

A frown wrinkled the brow of the man called Séb, who had first mentioned Magda's name. His colleague punched him playfully on the arm as though to appease him. Séb had dark hair, falling in thick waves to his broad shoulders and a beard he kept stylishly trimmed. Walter looked down at his own yellowing linen shirt and smoothed the cloth over his chest.

'You know we will have to leave as soon as our goal has been achieved. It would be unwise to get soft on her,' the blond one said. 'Don't let her beauty distract you from your cause.'

Walter imagined Séb's green eyes looking at Magda and he clenched his jaw. After they had taken swigs of their ales, their three heads leaned towards each other again over the table. Walter could only catch parts of the conversation, but tuned out all other noise around him to concentrate harder.

'*La Ténébreuse* is no longer safe. It's too dangerous for her now that the Habsburgs threaten the Confederation,' said the other man.

Walter didn't know what they were referring to. *Her?* He must have misheard. Who was *La Ténébreuse*?

'Our mission has provided us with this one chance. The villagers believe we're delivering consignments through the Confederation. It's a good cover,' said the one called Séb.

Were these men spies? Walter felt suddenly naïve, not about their association with the Confederation, but that they had a connection to Magda he was unaware of. It sounded like he might have some competition for her affections. Would he be able to match Séb's strength of character and handsome looks? Or was he allowing his emotions to cloud his judgement?

'If only the King and the Pope knew they had advanced the cause. It's as though they've fallen on their own swords,' the blond one said.

They were now talking about something other than Magda Staffaucher. Riddles. Walter should be paying attention to everything he heard to find out exactly what their 'cause' might be. But it was proving challenging as the tavern was filling up with customers.

'Don't forget that we will never be allowed to return to our homeland, Yves,' the third man said with sadness. 'We will be killed for our sins if we go back. It still makes me seethe to think they can twist God's testaments for their own advantage.'

'They've made a grave mistake,' said Yves. 'God will punish them eventually. No man should be allowed to manipulate religion like this. Even Pope Clément. Timing for this is essential.'

'One thing is fairly certain,' Séb said. 'King Louis' henchmen will not find us here. We'll be safe until our task is completed. Then we must travel east to protect *La Ténébreuse*. Returning to France will never be an option.'

The conversation made little sense to Walter. But he was alarmed for Magda and her family. They seemed to be talking about something greater than the dangers of a little village on the borders of the Confederation. They spoke of the head of the church and the King of France with something bordering on fear in their voices. And who needed protecting? Didn't the Confederation have enough to deal with from the Habsburgs?

Walter was glad to be returning to Schornen the following day. He wanted to find out who these strangers were and how they would affect Magda's village. Something did not ring true.

✝ ✝ ✝

'So you're the mystery-solver,' said the sailor as he hauled the heavy rope from the bollard at the jetty.

'That has a better ring to it than "The Son of Wilhelm Tell" or "messenger boy",' said Walter.

The sailor laughed. 'There's much talk of the young man who refuses to join the Confederate military in the footsteps of his notorious father. I'd say you've already earned a reputation. You should be careful about shunning the title of soldier. Some would call it heresy around here.'

'It's no secret that if I joined the army, I wouldn't be long for this earth. I inherited none of my father's ability with the crossbow.'

'Where are you heading today, lad?' the sailor asked, shaking his head.

'To the north-western border – Schornen in the Aegerital. Reduced to the work of messenger again, alas.' Walter patted the parchment tucked inside his jerkin. He had collected it at dawn as promised from the fort in Altdorf.

'One of the strategic gateways to the Confederation – are you bringing notice of a potential mobilisation?' asked the sailor.

'I'd rather not say. It's not news for sharing.'

'Don't worry *Junge*. I won't be spreading any rumours. I'm stuck on this old barge for at least another week and we'll not be taking many passengers. Look around you, the thing is about to fall apart.' Walter bristled at him calling him *lad*. Was his youth still so apparent despite his height? 'But that won't stop the captain insisting on relieving you of a *Taler* for your journey.'

The sailor held out his hand, a toothless grin on his face.

Walter put a coin in his palm, stepped onto the old splintered deck and helped pull the gangplank on board. He watched as the sail was raised. It filled with the stiff southerly *Föhn*, and the cumbersome vessel strained at the jetty before loping on its journey.

Instead of travelling along the precarious trail hewn into the cliffs beside the lake, Walter had used another of his hard-earned coins to purchase this passage on the cargo barge heading north across the water. He now wondered how wise this decision was, as it appeared to be the lake's oldest vessel.

The wind whipped up a froth of waves Walter thought might have them surfing on white caps towards their destination in Brunnen. Instead, the ancient flat barge bucked and rocked on the water, and several of the sailors became unwell. The vessel's hull was not designed for speed, but rather to maximise holding capacity. Walter suspected the cargo – he was told it was quartz sand dredged from the delta where the Reuss ran into the lake after the voluminous spring melt – had been poorly distributed below deck. It caused the vessel to sit unevenly in the water.

It was then Walter discovered that although he'd inherited none of his father's weaponry skills, he had at least inherited his sailing legs. He examined how loose or tight the sheet ropes should be to take optimal advantage of the wind in the sail, and how the boat fared better if it rode in exactly the direction the waves were rolling, despite being slightly off compass for their destination. He took the helm for a couple of hours while even the captain himself expelled his breakfast over the gunwales. Walter suspected his helplessness was due to an excess of local schnapps the night before.

'You can have your coin back,' said the first sailor as he tied the barge to the dock in Brunnen. 'I'm sure he was grateful for your help.' He nodded towards the captain, who was slowly coiling a rope at the stern.

The barge would soon continue along another branch of the lake towards Luzern to deliver the sand to a glassmaker. Walter bid farewell to the sailor, impatient to get to Schornen. Not to deliver his message, but to see Magda Stauffacher again.

CHAPTER FIFTEEN

31st March 1315, Schornen

SÉBASTIEN

The roof of the watch tower was a welcome sight as the knights crested the pass. Their horses picked their way down to the trail to Schornen. They greeted Edgar on the way past the mill and tied the horses up beside the barn. Taking the packs and tack, they transferred everything to the main floor of the tower where they would stay until they had established a routine.

'It takes longer than I imagined to travel in these parts. Is nowhere flat? I'm not sure whether Obéron finds the ascent or the descent more odious. He'll not get the chance of a good gallop anywhere on this terrain.' Sébastien hid his bags under his saddle blanket and fixed the strap on one of his stirrups.

'I hear there is a moor between here and Einsiedeln. You'll get your chance, Séb,' said Grégoire.

'When do you think we should visit the abbey?' asked Yves.

'It has its own garrison,' said Grégoire. 'Perhaps it's best for us not to snoop around as a group. With so many soldiers, it will take a while to work out a secure plan for the extraction.'

'Did you hear the barman in Altdorf? The entire civilian population is worried there will be a Habsburg invasion imminently. And after our impromptu meeting with Werner Stauffacher, we know there are not enough qualified senior soldiers to train new troops. We don't know which side the garrison at the abbey favours, but if their soldiers are mobilised, for whichever allegiance, it will leave the door wide open for us to go in. That will be our best opportunity.'

'And how do you propose to make that happen?' asked Yves.

'I'm forming a plan,' said Sébastien.

A wooden board in the ceiling above them creaked.

'Shh. Did you hear that?' Grégoire said. 'Hallo?' he called, and when there was no answer: 'Séb, go and see.'

'Is it the boy on watch?' Yves whispered.

Sébastien shrugged and took his sword from the corner by his bedroll. The blade preceded him up the wooden ladder.

Cloth rustled and he heard a deep yawn as though someone had just woken. Sébastien's grip on the hilt of his sword relaxed and he poked his head up through the ladder-well. It wasn't the boy on watch.

'*Bonjour, ma belle,*' Sébastien said softly.

Magda's eyes opened. Her beauty had not diminished in their absence.

'Where have you come from today?' she asked, stretching her limbs and pushing herself up to a sitting position.

'We've returned from Altdorf, through Schwyz. Were you supposed to be on watch?'

Magda's lips pressed together. An admission of her lapse in duty. 'Did you find a good route for your goods?' she asked, rubbing her eyes.

'I think so. We eliminated the notion of using boats to travel upstream on the Reuss. The flow is too strong, even though it hasn't rained.'

'The river will still be carrying the spring melt from the glaciers,' she said. 'You've yet to learn the signs of the seasons in the Alps.'

Sébastien tipped his head. Magda moved towards the ladder.

'We're not accustomed to life in the mountains,' he said. 'Where I come from, water is often scarce in the summer. You're lucky to have abundant sources here.'

Sébastien backed down the ladder and jumped the last few feet to the floor.

'And where is it you come from, Séb?' asked Magda as she stepped carefully onto the first rung of the ladder.

He smiled at the use of his nickname, but then it occurred to him she must have been listening to their conversation. Did she understand French? As she stepped down the ladder, he had a clear view of her ankles and her underskirt. He stayed close, his presence blocking both Yves and Grégoire's line of vision.

'I grew up on an orchard in the Pays d'Auge in Normandy before moving east to Troyes. Life was not so different from your fruit-farming communities here. But our fields were somewhat flatter. And the result is a calvados that I have to say is far finer than the apple schnapps we've sampled here.'

Magda wrinkled her nose as she stepped off the bottom rung of the ladder.

'I have no taste for distilled liquor. I prefer a good cider myself. So what was your work after "growing up" on your orchard?' she asked, straightening her skirts.

The three men looked at each other.

'We were a special kind of soldier,' Sébastien began. Yves frowned.

'Séb...' Grégoire began.

'It's all right,' said Sébastien with a placating hand.

She was waiting for a story and Sébastien was calculating how much they could trust her. It would be useful to have an ally in the village, especially as they were within the Confederate border.

'She's summing you up,' said Grégoire in French. 'She's not stupid. She knows how a man's tongue can loosen significantly in the presence of a beautiful woman, even without drink.'

Yves and Grégoire laughed, but Sébastien refrained, if only to reassure Magda that they weren't making any jokes at her expense.

'Have you heard of the Knights Templar?' he asked her.

Magda nodded. Behind him Yves hissed.

'She's already seen the cloth,' Sébastien said in French. 'Besides, we shall soon be needing the service of an expert with the sewing needle.'

'To safeguard the Christian pilgrims,' said Magda. 'I suspected when I saw your banner and then the Benedictine seal.' Magda pointed towards their saddles in the corner. 'But isn't that a lifelong profession? Why are you transporting goods when you have this other... obligation? And why do you hide something so sacred?'

'We are no longer employed by the French monarchy or the church,' Grégoire said.

'But you carry helmets, although you don't wear them. Surely that means you are expecting to defend? You should be proud. You're guarding a holy belief.'

'As Grég says, those services are no longer required. King Louis, like his father Philippe before him, is in cahoots with the Pope and has decided the treasury we've been controlling for hundreds of years would be better managed without us.'

'We suspect there is corruption in the Vatican,' said Yves.

Magda drew in her breath. 'You must be careful what you say. Corruption in the church?'

'Most of the Templar assets were seized by King Philippe of France last year,' said Sébastien. 'Now his son seeks to take even more power. He and Pope Clément are seeking to... disband our group.' If he were to tell her that they had been declared heretics by the two most powerful men in France, she might not look upon the knights so favourably. Most of the other knights of the order had already been killed.

'So you are fugitives? Does my father know?'

'He knows we are soldiers. But for his own safety and that of your people, it is better he doesn't find out who we really are. The church is still the ultimate ruler here, and that knowledge might upset the people. It would... complicate matters.'

Sébastien prayed Magda wouldn't alarm her father, but an idea was beginning to form in his mind.

'You have no idea about my secret-keeping prowess,' she said. 'But why are you sharing this information with me?'

'You're already curious about the cloth you saw. It would be best not to mention it to anyone else. It's important our true identity is kept from those who might seek an advantage. The King of France believes the Templars no longer exist. It is best that remains so.'

'Oh... but your profession! That's terrible. Am I in danger too, now that you've shared your secret?'

'Ah, *mademoiselle*, you do not know the whole of it, but we would value your discretion. And we may engage you for your sewing skills at some stage.'

Magda looked at each of the men's shirts as though judging what might need mending.

'And you ask too many questions,' said Yves with a twinkle in his eye.

Magda held her hand to her chest with a smile. She must have recognised the tease.

Before she could say anything, Josef shouted from the court-yard. 'Maggi! Where are you?'

She hurried out into the brightness of the day and ran down the wooden steps to the courtyard. Sébastien pressed his back against the wall near the door inside the tower to listen.

'I was making sure the men had enough fresh straw,' she said. 'I didn't know they would be back so soon, or that you had agreed they could stay here another night.'

'I'd have thought you would be glad of this,' said Josef.

In the shadows, Sébastien smiled.

'Papa, there's something I need to talk to you about,' said Magda.

Yves drew in his breath. 'Do you think she will say something about us?' he said in a hushed voice.

'Not now, girl,' said Josef. 'We have to organise another meeting. Walter Tell should arrive in the next day or two with an answer from your uncle. There's a suggestion that the men up there should be consulted.'

The three Frenchmen looked at each other.

'Papa! You don't understand, it is to do with them,' hissed Magda.

'Damn, we are doomed,' said Grégoire. 'Sébastien, you fool. Look what you have done.'

'I don't think so. I think she still wants to protect us, and I have an idea how we can help these people,' he whispered.

'Later, Magda,' said Josef, his voice fading across the courtyard. 'You must prepare extra loaves tomorrow for more visitors. Prove the dough tonight. There will be no time for it in the morning...'

'It is time to talk to Josef,' said Sébastien, turning to his colleagues.

✠ ✠ ✠

'You've changed your mind about us,' said Sébastien, watching Magda's hands knead a large quantity of bread dough at the table outside the chalet.

She stopped only for a second before continuing to roll, fold and pound the soft dough with her knuckles against the wood. The smell of yeast rose like a heady perfume between them. Her eyes didn't meet his.

'How do you know the direction of my mind in the first place?' she asked.

'I didn't intend to frighten you with our talk of things God would not approve of.'

'He knows everything. And Pope Clément was chosen by the Lord himself. He would surely not turn against His wishes. He would be punished, or excommunicated.'

'And who is there to determine this excommunication? The Pope is sovereign. There is no one higher. He is supposedly in direct communication with divinity. He does these things in the name of God, Magda. But we know God has no need for money. The kingdom of heaven has no need for material things. It's only man's greed that has led to the necessity or desire for affluence.'

'I cannot believe the Pope would defy the Lord,' she whispered. 'Tell me again why you are here. Why have you chosen our valley to hide in?'

'It will be to the advantage of you and your family too,' he said, once again failing to answer Magda's question. 'We've been given a kind of unspoken freedom. As the Habsburg emissaries pass along the routes our trades will take, we're awarded amnesty as foreigners. We can observe, listen to the rumours, alert the elders to any signs of unrest. I think the Habsburgs suspect we are men of the cross, but news of our flight from France has not yet reached the mountains.'

Magda didn't ask him to embellish on the reasons for their fugitive status.

'I don't understand why you've chosen to guard commercial goods rather than pilgrims,' she said. 'It's hardly a noble employ.'

Sébastien didn't correct what she had surmised.

'Our crusading days are over,' said Grégoire, 'Perhaps we are not as nimble as we once were. And perhaps we grow tired of being chased like game.'

Grégoire's grasp of the language was less refined than Sébastien's.

'You should meet Walti,' said Magda. 'He would like to voice his uncertainty of the existence of God with someone. You would all enjoy a good blasphemous discussion.'

'We are not disputing the existence of God. We are disputing what men choose to do with His power,' said Sébastien. 'So who, may I ask, is Walti?'

'Walter is a good friend. He's the son of Wilhelm Tell.'

'Then he must be a great warrior.'

'Not exactly...'

'We were in Altdorf yesterday. If we'd had more time, we would have called in at Bürglen to pay our respects to the indomitable *Guillaume* Tell. His reputation precedes him,' said Yves.

'So what of Walter?' asked Sébastien wondering if there was a romantic connection.

'Next to Mihal, he's one of the wisest people I know. Aside from his duties as a Confederate messenger, he is a great tracker.'

Sébastien raised his eyebrows.

'He's also a great solver of mysteries. There's not much you can hide from him,' said Magda with a touch of smugness.

Sébastien reminded himself to be cautious, should he ever meet this Walter Tell.

CHAPTER SIXTEEN

2nd April 1315, Schornen

WALTER

Walter made his way on foot the next morning along the trail towards the Aegerital. It was the first real chance he'd had to test the new soles on his boots.

The grass had begun to grow lush again in the full burst of spring. Keening red kites rose and dipped above him on the thermals. As the trail levelled out at the pass, Walter turned around and took in the view back down to the Urner Lake. He picked out the road he had travelled on, now familiar to him, snaking beside the Muota River. He could still see a ribbon of the lake, tiny white specks of waves visible even from a distance. The *Föhn* made everything crystal clear. If Walter could be one of those birds above him, the journey would be so much easier. But he didn't complain; he'd heard of lands to the west that were so flat, the boredom would lull a man to sleep on his horse before he'd travelled half a day.

He hoped he'd never have to live without that view. He hoped he'd never have to live without his freedom. If the Habsburgs were to take back the Confederation, they would all be bound to Duke

Leopold. The mournful sound of the kites reminded him of the fragility of that hope. As Walter made his way to the saddle of the pass, he had a smile on his face for another reason. He would once again be able to set eyes on the beautiful Magda Stauffacher.

Cherry and plum blossoms flurried across the path as he crested the pass to descend into the Aegerital. If it weren't for the heat of the sun and the green of the meadows, he would have sworn it was snowing. He was impatient to complete his journey, but forced himself to keep a slow pace. Arriving grubby from the dusty road and sweating like a sow on a spit would not impress Magda.

As he picked his way down the trail to Schornen, he noted a wisp of smoke curling from the Stauffacher's chalet. Magda must be home. Judging by the position of the sun overhead, she would likely be preparing a meal for her father and brother.

He forced his eyes back to the path to avoid stumbling on the steepest switchbacks. Approaching the village, he saw two people sitting at the bench in the courtyard between the tower and the chalet. As he came closer, he recognised the men, but it took a moment to place them. A third man came out of the door of the tower, and when a lock of his dark hair blew back from his face as he descended the steps, Walter recalled him from the tavern in Altdorf. Coincidences like this didn't happen very often. He remembered their discussion at the bar and wasn't sure whether they were friend or foe. In what capacity did these men know the Stauffachers?

'*Gruezi wohl!*' he called in a disarming tone as he approached.

All three men turned.

'I saw him in the tavern in Altdorf,' said one of them in French to the man Walter remembered was called Séb. 'Caution, my friends.'

These men would likely not know the extent of his knowledge of French, but Walter wondered why they would need to exercise such prudence. Were these men Habsburg spies? Walter decided against practising his French and continued in his dialect.

'I recognise you from the Bären Tavern. Yesterday. Altdorf.'

'Indeed,' said one of the other men. 'Are we to surmise this is a chance meeting, or is there a reason we've been followed?'

He moved his hand under a cloth lying on the table. Walter glimpsed the hilt of the type of sword a high-ranking soldier might carry. Walter held his open hands up between them.

'I assure you our crossing is entirely a coincidence,' he said.

He glanced towards the horses that had allowed them the luxury of completing the same journey at twice the speed. They were fine steeds, of high breeding. Definitely soldiers' horses. The three men glared at Walter, their demeanour defensive, although they were clearly not on home territory. He stepped back, suddenly feeling like the outsider. Humour might not go down well in this situation.

In the ensuing silence, Magda appeared from the little chalet, carrying a tray upon which sat a crusty loaf and a slab of butter. 'Walter, you're back.'

Walter studied her face and raised his hand to his forehead by way of a greeting. A smile flickered, but then a frown creased her brow and she glanced towards the one called Séb. She set the tray down on the table and shook a fold out of the apron as though she didn't know what to do with her suddenly free hands. Walter took a seat at the bench on the other end of the table from her. With the three burly men sitting between them, this was hardly the welcome he had been expecting.

'Sébastien, Yves, Grégoire, this is the young man I mentioned to you. Walter Tell.'

Walter was flattered she had introduced him, but that they had already discussed him made him uneasy. And he wasn't so keen on being called 'young' again. He couldn't be much younger than these Frenchmen. What exactly had she revealed to these three foreigners? He had to try and get Magda on her own to warn her of any suspicious intent.

'Ah yes, the offspring of the mighty Guillaume Tell. I'm surprised you don't carry a crossbow, young man. Where is your weapon? It's dangerous travelling these parts without some form of protection.'

'That's something I've already learned the hard way,' said Walter, remembering the wild boar thundering past him in the forest. He cast a smile in Magda's direction. 'My weapon of choice is a *baselard*. It's easier to carry as I am mostly on foot.' Walter subtly lifted his tunic to expose the leather sheath containing the long dagger. Two could play at the weaponry show-off, although his blade was distinctly smaller than the Frenchman's. 'What has brought you along the trail that preceded mine? Altdorf, and now Schornen? I should reassure you I have not been following you. But as you say, this is some coincidence.'

'What business is it of yours?' asked Sébastien.

'Sébastien,' chided Magda. 'Walti is a friend.'

Resentment at her easy manner with these men fought with the pleasure of hearing his nickname on her lips.

'We've been on a scouting mission,' said the one with the scraggy beard, who had been introduced by Magda as Grégoire. 'Studying the flow of the Reuss to see whether it's possible to take a barge as far south as possible up the valley to the Gotthard.'

'That'd be impossible,' Walter scoffed, then calmed his tone. He didn't need to be making enemies. 'Between the snowmelt and the autumn rains, the Reuss is ever powerful. Even the strongest of horses couldn't pull a vessel upstream.'

'A conclusion we also came to.'

'Trade vessels go no further than Flüelen,' Walter told him. 'Why is it so important to use the river? There are perfectly good trails from the head of the lake.'

'It's a matter of defence. We'll be transporting precious goods. Once on land, our task becomes a little more challenging.'

These men didn't look like they were ready to accept a paltry wage. Although their clothes were well worn, their saddlery, equipment and the horses currently standing at the north end of the courtyard were of a quality that spoke of wealth.

Sébastien caught Walter surreptitiously studying their horses. He turned from the beasts to look at Magda and she smiled, though not before Walter caught the preceding frown on her face. She seemed nervous. But whether she was nervous of Walter or the men, he couldn't tell.

'Come, Walti.' Magda placed her hand gently on his elbow. 'Papa will want to hear your news before meeting with the Morgarten elders again.'

She spoke quietly, but not so quietly that the other men couldn't hear. When Sébastien and Grégoire looked hard at Walter, he guessed they must be aware of the meeting.

He shook his head as though to clear it and turned towards the mill, where he was sure he would find Edgar and possibly Josef. Who were these Frenchmen? And why were they so interested in this little hamlet on the edge of the Confederation? He didn't like the tone with which they'd spoken about Magda in the tavern in Altdorf.

There were other things he'd like to ask Magda directly. But it would have to wait until after the gathering of the Morgarten folk. The parchment from the commander outlined extensive solutions for iron sources, weapons needs, and where to conceal their caches. Walter was hardly the person who could enlighten the people about the army's strategy, but he was sure Josef would ask him to accompany them to the meeting to help answer questions from the written parchment. Not because of his military knowledge, but for his reading eyes.

CHAPTER SEVENTEEN

2nd April 1315, Schornen

SÉBASTIEN

Yves and Grégoire had it in their minds to head to the forest to do some hunting, even though it was not the season. The men had not been gone an hour and Mihal's eyes began drooping where he sat at the table in the courtyard. Josef had entrusted their family friend to watch over Magda for a few hours. But he hadn't counted on Mihal's exhaustion.

'Mihal, come and rest on the cot beside the embers in the kitchen,' said Magda. 'You can keep an eye on the rack of trout smoking there.'

'I'm supposed to be keeping an eye on you, young lady. Heaven knows how much trouble you might get yourself into.' He winked at her.

'She'll be safe with me, Mihal,' said Sébastien. 'I'll be retiring shortly.'

Mihal frowned and shot Sébastien a narrow-eyed glance. 'You're probably the one I should be keeping an eye on most,' he grumbled, but heaved himself up the stairs to the chalet anyway, the prospect of resting beside the warmth of the fire likely too tempting for his old bones to worry about his chaperoning duties.

'I'll be right there, Mihal. Their lodgings will need fresh straw.'

Mihal waved above his head as he entered the chalet and Magda shook her head fondly as he disappeared into her kitchen.

'Fresh bedding would be kind. Let me help you,' Sébastien said, rising from the bench.

They gathered an armful of straw each from the back of the barn and climbed the stairs to what had now become the knights' lodgings.

'The stalk is bone dry,' said Magda. 'You must keep the lamp out of its way. We don't want our ladders to burn and the roof to be left open to the sky. God's protection is surely not divine enough to prevent the rain from falling on your head if you set fire to this place.'

'Ha, my lady begins to jest about the Lord without fear. Have you been taking lessons from your young friend, *Walti*?'

Magda drew in her breath.

'Are you a believer, Magda?' he asked after a pause.

'Of course!' Magda made the sign of the cross, should God indeed be looking into her head and her heart.

Sébastien's linen undershirt had come untied. He turned and caught her glance quickly away from his bare chest appearing through a gap. She cleared her throat. 'Where are Yves and Grégoire?'

'They fancy themselves a *petit goret* on a spit tomorrow.'

'But it's almost dark!'

'That's the best hunting time. They're in the forest above the lake. I understand the wild boar are quite numerous on that side of the valley. They may be gone for some time. They left on foot as our horses need resting. It is good they aren't here though. I have something to ask you.' He paused. 'Is the old man sleeping?'

'He's taken the cot beside the kitchen in the chalet,' she said with a smile. 'I'm supposed to go back to him right now, but I believe the warmth there will make him slumber until his grumbling stomach wakes him for breakfast.'

'Magda, it's not by chance that Mihal is with us today.'

Magda frowned.

'He's brought something from the south, something that has been delivered to us, and for which I'd like to ask you to create a very special thing for us.'

Before she could ask how this had come about, he took both her hands in his and turned them palms upwards, as though to place something in them. He was overcome with a sudden compulsion and lowered his lips to her left hand, then kissed it, his beard sweeping the fleshy base of her thumb.

'This is called the Mount of Venus,' he told her and saw her shiver.

Before he could stop himself, he took her right hand and placed it flat against his bare chest through the gap in his shirt. The sensation of her hand on his skin made his heart beat faster. His throat grew hot as her eyes glazed. He knew the same deep ache pulsed in the depths of her body. He should step away, but instead raised her chin, stroked her cheek and cupped his hand to her neck. He saw what his touch was doing to her. She could not keep the desire from her eyes.

'But you must be a believer. To create this object.'

'I believe in you, I believe in God, but you speak in riddles,' she whispered and he imagined she would follow him through fire as though he was the son of God Himself.

'Oh, Magda. You are so beautiful. How is it Josef has not yet had men knocking at his door to claim you for a wife?'

'Since Mama... I have vowed to look after him until Eddi finds a wife. Then he in turn will have someone to take care of Papa. Then I shall be free to...'

Sébastien leaned in to kiss her, his tongue seeking her mouth. She gasped, and he moved his hands to hold her around the waist. One hand rose to her bodice. He should not be doing this, but as God was his witness, he was finding it hard to stop himself. Regardless of the teachings of the Bible, God would not be sending such wonderful sensations through their bodies if He had not meant this to be. She pressed herself to him in urgency. She must want this as much as him. But he must draw the line, must stop; he did not want to sully her. And yet...

Sébastien circled his fingers around Magda's breast through her tunic, and her breath shortened. She seemed to swoon, and he held her on her feet, kissing her deeply. He looked briefly to the door of the tower, wondering whether the old man was still sleeping. He moved towards the ladder leading up to the tower, and she broke away from him.

'I... I can't,' she breathed. 'But I want to.'

He kissed her, and pushed her towards the ladder, his body leaning into her, wanting to lift her skirts, but knowing he shouldn't. She must be feeling the same thing, that same power, that same need he felt in his groin. His hand sank to her lower belly and lower, and he grasped her gently through the material of her skirt.

She gasped, and pushed herself against his fingers. 'Lightning smite me. This cannot be a sin!' Her breath quickened, until she was whimpering, pressing against his hand through the layers of soft linen.

Sébastien pushed his body towards her, moving against her hip, his hot breath heavy in her hair. He dared not undo his buttons, but as Magda swooned with ecstasy, he groaned as he felt the release, felt their hearts pounding together between them. This thing they had consummated but not consummated. A flood had been let loose. A flood of trouble.

As his breath calmed, Magda laughed at her new discovery and Sébastien felt a spike of guilt. Even though the seeds had not been sown in the true furrow, her journey to becoming a woman was a step closer.

'Now I know the rewards a woman reaps for her cooking and weaving,' she said.

Sébastien smiled, and swept a lock of her hair away from her face before taking her hand and placing it against his chest again as his heart calmed. After a moment he took her chin in his palm, swept his thumb over her lips. 'Much as I've been able to enjoy your efforts at the first, it is the second skill we require. I have a great and noble task for you to perform, Magda.'

'You mean that wasn't it?' She laughed. 'It was both great, and noble, and I personally thought it was a little holy.'

Sébastien's brow creased. He didn't want her to feel like he had used her. She should not regret what he had done to her. 'Let us just say that perhaps God has put temptation in my way to show me that you are the one chosen to use your craft for us.'

'So you have something for me to sew? Then why all the serious-ness? I thought you were going to ask me to concoct some kind of poison to slay the Habsburg troops. But tailoring? I could prob-ably sew something for you with my eyes closed.' Magda blushed. She'd implied she knew the measurements of his body intimately. Something had undoubtedly changed in her perception of men over the past hour. And Sébastien was well aware he had been the thief of her innocence.

He moved away from the ladder. Magda shook her skirts to hang straight and pushed her hair away from her face.

'Come, sit,' said Sébastien. He fetched one of his saddlebags from the wall by the door and sat down in the middle of the room. He placed the saddlebag on his lap and reached into one of the pouches. He pulled out a roll of fine linen cloth and unrolled it to reveal a skein of thread.

It might have been the setting sun appearing from behind a cloud, reflecting off the rocks on the far cliff through the door, but he swore he could see the loops of thread glow with light. She reached out to touch it. Sébastien did the same, his fingers on the other end of the skein. It was soft, but sturdy, with the strength of linen.

'It glints as though it contains the light of the stars,' said Magda.

'It has gold woven through it. This thread can be found nowhere else in the northern lands,' said Sébastien.

'Metal? Like the sovereign coins they forge to the east? How can anyone spin metal? It's so full of light.'

'The gold they use is soft, pliable. I don't know how it was spun. Here.' Sébastien placed the skein in her hands, and her arms dropped.

'It's so heavy!'

Sébastien looked around, then reached for the water jug by the door. 'Do you think you can weave a bag from this that would contain something a little smaller than this?' He poured water into two mugs and offered her a drink.

She looked at him as though she'd do anything for him right now, and he felt another twinge of guilt.

'Of course! A pouch like that is far less trouble than a jerkin or a shirt.'

'It would need to have a special design. I have another thread, one that will take a dye. But it has to be the colour red.'

Magda shook her head. 'You may have seen my work. Mihal's clothes, my skirts. Red dye is impossible to make here. The blues and purples come from forest fruits, their skins and juices. The greens from the sap of young spring herbs and the ochre from the earth in the seams that run along the trails cut into the Morgartenberg. Our soil contains no iron ore here, so it is difficult to obtain, and even if I had some, the colour red is horribly difficult to make from the ore with the resources I have here.'

'Do you think you could ask your friend Walter? He seems like a travelled and knowledgeable lad. He must know these things. We must have the colour red.'

'Why? If it is a design you are after, a symbol, a shape, I can surely find something close, a deep purple, maybe, if I find the right plums, those that come from the west, or cherries. The season is soon upon us ...'

'No, it must be crimson. Please.' How could he make her realise the importance, without giving away its secret?

'If I do this thing for you, do you agree to help our people? Help us fight the wrath of the Habsburgs?'

Sébastien raised his eyebrows and then dipped his head without answering. It would be wise to keep the extent of their missions, both the true one and the cover, a secret for as long as possible.

Magda sighed. 'What is the symbol you wish me to weave?'

He was unsure whether it was his touch on her body or the half-promise to help her people that would seal the agreement to the divine task she was being asked to perform. But their passionate fooling around might make her wonder in the morning whether he had already taken more than was proper. He rose and walked to the far wall where he removed a cloth object from the behind his saddle; as his hands spread apart, they exposed the banner she had seen spilling from his bag the day they arrived in Schornen.

'This is what we would like you to design, Magda. This symbol must appear on the bag, to mark its importance in the eyes of God.'

She gazed down at the banner, a creamy white linen that had often flown behind Sébastien and his colleagues as they had ridden their horses across the southern lands in the past. She stared at the symbol on the banner: the blood-red cross of the Knights Templar.

CHAPTER EIGHTEEN

2nd April 1315, Schornen

WALTER

Walter accompanied Josef back from the latest meeting in Morgarten, which, eventually, had had a successful outcome. The villagers listened as Josef told them Commander Stauffacher welcomed their initiative to join the Confederation and that their defence of the Habsburgs would be highly coveted.

Walter answered several questions directly from the commander's parchment, information about where the iron for blades would be sourced, the stockpile of existing weapons, and possible solutions for the forging of new ones. A number of alphorns would be stored in shepherds' huts below the ridges to use as an early warning system should the enemy be seen amassing in neighbouring valleys. The distances were too far to rely on even the strongest of yodlers.

But then came the concerns of the sceptics.

'Where will the weapons be forged?'

'How can we work if our tools are requisitioned?'

'How will we till the earth, scythe the hay, harvest the crops?'

And the question that had been forefront in his own mind.

'Who will train us to use these weapons?'

Josef assured the gathered men that the commander had a solution for this last concern, which would be revealed in good time. Walter had looked down at his parchment and back at Josef's face. This was information he did not have. In the end, it was Josef's word that swayed the men present, and they had voted overwhelmingly in favour of joining the Confederation.

As they returned cautiously to Schornen together along the trail, Josef confided in Walter. 'I've a mind to ask the brothers at the abbey in Einsiedeln if we can use a location within their walls to forge new weapons.'

'You're beginning to speak like your brother,' said Walter with a smile. 'Aren't the priests and brothers at the abbey Habsburg sympathisers?'

'No... well, it's complicated,' Josef said. 'But there is a subtle understanding between the abbey and our hamlet.'

'They're not theoretically part of the Confederation,' said Walter. 'Like the Pope's seat in the Vatican is not part of the Rome. I understood that they ally themselves with neither.'

'Officially, that's true. The abbey has its own garrison. Einsiedeln is a holy enclave, neutral to both the ambitions of the Austrian monarchy and to the Confederation. We know that the Bundesbrief was written with its first allegiance to God, and the abbey cannot be seen to be taking sides. But thanks to Magda, we've been supplying their habits and sewing needs over the years. This gives us a special connection.'

It's not the first time Walter imagined that Magda was an important figure in the survival of this little hamlet. They might have a hard time letting her go, should someone outside the village wish to propose a union. He swallowed.

'It's all very well for a large number of weapons to be forged for a battle, but who will wield them? Unless your brother can send troops, there aren't enough trained men in Schornen and Morgarten to defend against the Habsburgs.'

'God and luck may have sent us an answer to that problem,' said Josef.

Walter felt a sudden chill. As he recalled the question about who would train the men, it became clear to him who might be the most qualified for this task, in addition to whatever secret guard duties they were supposed to be performing.

The Frenchmen.

'Our watch tower is developing an extensive visitors list,' said Josef as they entered Schornen and looked up at the building dominating the hamlet. 'I have a feeling if Magda set up a tavern in its midst we could make a fine guest house out of the number of travellers. We must be taking business away from the establishments in Morgarten and Schwyz. I hope you don't mind sharing the basic accommodation with our French friends.'

At that moment Walter could think of nothing worse, but nodded to Josef with a forced smile. He could hardly take his leave and begin the journey home in the middle of the night. That would be asking for trouble on the unsafe roads.

When they entered the courtyard, the three Frenchmen were gathered around the brazier. Walter chewed on his lip. If what he surmised was true, how would the Confederation pay these men for training the men of Schornen and Morgarten? Three highly experienced soldiers would not be giving their services away for free.

Through the open door, Walter saw Magda moving about inside the chalet. She caught Walter's eye, and moved to the entrance with her finger to her lips. She pulled the door closed behind her as she came outside and stepped quietly down the stairs to the courtyard.

'Mihal is sleeping,' she said. 'I don't have the heart to wake him.'

'And where will you sleep tonight?' asked Walter, jealousy ringing a harshness in his voice that he wished he could take back.

Instead of the expected retort *What business is that of yours?* her face flushed in the light from the fire. Walter again experienced a sense of unease.

'I'll be fine in the corner with a few blankets and a shawl. How was the meeting?' she asked, almost absently.

'Finally, there is solidarity between the villages. They voted to join the fight with the Confederation. I'm sure there are still a few doubters, but in the end they raised their hands.'

She didn't react, or perhaps was unimpressed with the news. Her attention was focused on the group of men at the fire. Walter touched her elbow by way of reminding her of the significance of the decision. She looked into Walter's face with an uncertain smile. 'Walti, I need to ask you something,' she said with her voice lowered.

Walter's heart lifted. He looked at her expectantly, already preparing a speech in his head.

'I have to obtain some dye to colour thread,' she continued. 'But it has to be red. Over the years I've practised fixing the colour of the red that flows from the slaughtered bodies of chickens or cattle, even from my own finger on the spindle, but although it is surprisingly easy to fix onto linen, the colour only ever turns brown, and stinks like a bloated badger forever afterwards.'

'What about minerals?' he said, disappointed in the nature of her query. 'I see you've managed a handsome yellow.' He pointed to the stripes on her skirt sewn between a dark violet and embroidered with green. 'If you have yellow ochre, can you not find the same reds in the rock deposits around the valley?'

'That's the problem. Red is the hardest colour to source from minerals. There's a plant called the madder, and its root produces the brightest red and is easiest to extract, but it doesn't grow here. I've seen it used on Mihal's scrolls. I know you're a man of letters, so I was wondering...'

'I fear my usefulness is being exploited by the fair maiden of Schornen,' he joked, his heart now calming as he drew from a knowledge he hoped would impress Magda.

'Oh, come, Walti, don't tease. That tells me you have a solution.'

'At what price, though?'

'Perhaps I can design you a new jerkin. Mihal can vouch for my quality.'

Walter smiled. 'The Monk who copied the Bundesbrief stayed in our village for some years. One of his tasks was to illuminate several manuscripts for the church, and I remember seeing vermillion lettering. He died a few years ago and the space is now used to store those manuscripts and banners used by the church. I'm sure I can source some dye, although I'm not sure about the root. Powders, maybe.'

'Oh Walti, I'd be so grateful!'

'Why, if it is so difficult to obtain, would you insist on its use? Isn't it a bit of a luxury in these austere times?'

'It's for a special creation. Something I've been commissioned to weave,' she whispered, looking towards the Frenchmen.

Walter raised an eyebrow and followed her gaze across the courtyard to the men sitting on the other side of the fire. Sébastien was looking at Walter with an expression he could not read. The reflection of a single lick of flame from the fire glinted in his eye, matching the streak of jealous heat in Walter's throat.

✝ ✝ ✝

When it was clear Magda had retired to the chalet, Walter carried the blanket Josef had given him up the steps to the tower. As he ducked through the low door, he knew he couldn't possibly sleep in the same space as the Frenchmen. Their saddlebags and chattels were strewn across the straw. Instead, he continued up the second ladder to the platform at the top of the tower. He surveyed the dark shadow of the marshland below and stared at the shimmering lake in the distance, touched occasionally by shards of moonlight from the shrinking clouds. The following day would likely be fine for his return to Bürglen.

'I can relieve you for a couple of hours in the night if you feel sleepy,' he told the boy on watch.

Walter lay on the floor, wrapping himself entirely in the blanket. The balustraded walls of the platform provided little protection from the breeze blowing up the valley, but he breathed warm air around his body with his head tucked beneath the blanket.

As he sought sleep, he imagined Magda moving about her little house, the swish of her colourful skirts about her hips, her body bending to spread the embers on the hearth to reduce the smoke in the kitchen, using the last of the hot water to prepare herb tea for her brother and her father who had followed her inside, trying not to wake the snoring bulk of Mihal beside the fire. He imagined her settling down on a pile of blankets to sleep and how he longed to be there with her.

And then he wondered why she was so desperate to seek the red dye. This wasn't simply an artisan's whim to produce the colours of the rainbow. There was something more to her objective. What had she been commissioned to make? Why did it have to be that colour?

Some time later Walter was awoken by the three Frenchmen entering the tower to prepare for sleep. He heard them take off their boots, kick them to the stone walls and throw their leather jerkins onto their piles of possessions. As they shook out their blankets, Walter picked up the conspiratorial tone of their conversation. At first he couldn't tell who was speaking, but he strained to listen to every word. Perhaps they hadn't seen him climb up. They appeared to have forgotten his existence up on the platform. They would assume he couldn't understand their language anyway.

'These people are desperate for their farmers to be properly trained in warfare. We cannot simply leave them exposed with so many threats on their border.' The voice was Sébastien's.

'But we should have discussed a strategy before you made promises to Josef,' said one of the others. 'Are you sure that girl hasn't put a magic spell on you?'

'These are good people, Grég. If we can help them, we should.'

'We should not to draw any more attention to ourselves,' Grég replied.

'We *must not* forget our mission!' The third Frenchman was blatantly angry. 'Don't allow some pretty wench to divert you from your holy cause. Once our route out of here has been established, I say it would be better for us to quietly go ahead with the extraction and disappear south.'

Yes, thought Walter, *leave here immediately and leave Magda alone.*

'But the timing must be right to avoid all suspicion,' said Sébastien. 'I was thinking it could be after the celebrations marking the anniversary of the signing of the treaty in the summer. The brothers at the abbey won't be present at the celebrations. They don't care to mix politics with religion. But the soldiers at the garrison will likely be drawn away from the abbey for duties along the border.'

'That's leaving it a bit late, Séb. We must take *La Ténébreuse* before the beginning of winter, to allow a swift journey to the east or to the south.'

'We can discuss it after our route has been decided,' the angrier of the three conceded.

Conversation turned to banter about the discomfort of their lodgings, until the turning and settling of bodies quietened and gentle snores rose through the ladder-well. Walter lay awake, thinking about what he thought he had understood. *Suspicion? La Ténébreuse?* What or who was this thing? Why would these men need to escape, if they were friends of the community and therefore the Confederation? A warning bell rang in Walter's mind. There was something the Frenchmen had not told the Stauffachers. They spoke of an abbey. Were they referring to Einsiedeln?

These Frenchmen had an ulterior motive for finding themselves on the border of the Confederation. It sounded as though their presence was no coincidence. Walter regretted having to leave so early the following morning, but he had to report the result of the vote to Commander Stauffacher and then head home.

But he'd heard enough to be sure the Frenchmen's guard service and any agreement to help train the men of Morgarten was a cover for something more sinister.

CHAPTER NINETEEN
23rd April 1315, Schornen
MAGDA

M
agda lost count of the number of weeks it had been raining and was longing for the next full moon to bring a change in the weather. A layer of muck caked the floor of the chalet kitchen. On cold nights, the heat of the cattle in the stall below hardly penetrated the floorboards as the spaces between them were plugged with mud.

The sound of rushing water was a companion day and night as white ribbons of rainwater filled the folds and gullies along the hills behind the village, creating waterfalls that Magda didn't think had ever existed in her lifetime. It was as though the guts of some poisoned mountain monster were spewing into the valley, the frothy detritus swirling into the lake. The stream through the village had burst its banks and covered the trails, making the journey from Morgarten impossible from the valley. But although the lake came almost to their doorsteps, no boats could make their way across the swamp. The reeds impeded their passage and the water wasn't deep enough to accommodate their draft.

The path higher in the forest had collapsed in several places, and the villagers were advised not to pass alone between Schornen and Morgarten, and only when necessary. For the first few days Edgar was glad of the velocity of the water, as he'd been grinding the remainder of last season's barley. But the wheel's axle began to strain under the water load. He feared the whole thing would break with the effort, so the water was redirected and the milling had come to a halt.

The women of the village sat in their doorways or on their verandas weaving baskets or mending sacks and aprons, looking up and cursing the slanting rain preventing them from planting in the fields. They worried about foot-rot for the sheep and cattle in the boggy pastures. They hoped the pasture still had enough daylight through the shrouds of constant rain and fog to produce grass.

It had been almost two months since Magda had seen Sébastien and his colleagues. The heavy rain must have hampered whatever scouting they were still hoping to undertake. They might be reluctant to return to Morgarten or Schornen, but it didn't stop her hoping Sébastien wanted to see *her* again.

And then Walter arrived to cheer up the villagers. But his news was hardly anything to smile about. The Devil's Bridge in the narrowest part of the Schollenen Gorge leading to the Gotthard Pass had been washed out by the swelling Reuss River and would take many weeks to rebuild. All transport across the mountain pass south had been halted until the waters subsided. Although the physical presence of the Habsburgs at the borders of Zug and Luzern had decreased, they were all beginning to feel like they were under siege, not by the Habsburgs, but by the weather.

Walter spent some time at the Schornen mill where Edgar and her father were mending the wheel of one of the carts. Later he came to the chalet where she greeted him warmly. Although she yearned for Sébastien's hands on her, it was Walter she wanted to entertain her with his talk and to make her laugh. And she wondered whether he had brought anything with him.

'Mother of God, you are soaked to the skin, Walti, come dry yourself by the fire.'

'I'd be grateful for a change of shirt,' he said. 'It was a long journey. It's not the first time I wish I could afford a horse, if only for the luxury of choosing upon which part of my anatomy I develop blisters.'

Magda chuckled. Walter removed his jacket on the veranda and wrung it out, adding to the puddles in front of the chalet.

'I'll hang this by the fire,' said Magda. 'You can use the nook to the rear, but I'd appreciate you leaving your boots by the door. I can't bear to see any more mud in this house. We'll be able to grow a whole harvest of beans if the floor gets any thicker. And I have a gift for you, which seems rather appropriate right now.'

Magda went to the shelf behind her cot and pulled out a soft linen undershirt and a pair of underpants she had woven, tailored and sewn for Walter. She held up the shirt for him and his face showed open delight. Magda smiled. These were not the most difficult articles of clothing she had ever had to sew, but they were evidently appreciated.

'I have a gift for you too, Magda. But mine to you is far less refined. Thank you for this. I feel I should wash before I put on these beautifully woven items. I'm flattered you've done this thing for me. Perhaps tomorrow I can help you clear the muck from the kitchen floor, even if the rain hasn't ceased.'

Walter hadn't yet removed his boots, and strode back outside. He set his hat down on the bench beside the door and took off his jerkin and tattered undershirt. Magda stood watching him from the doorway. She couldn't help but notice the physical differences between Walter and Sébastien. She'd never seen the latter's bare chest in full, but this was the second time she had seen Walter's.

Magda looked away as she felt a flood of shame, remembering Sébastien's touch.

Curiosity pulled her gaze back to Walter, who raised his face to the rain, to this thing that had become a bane to them over the weeks. Magda saw a pleasure on his face that made her reassess the magic and the worth of the liquid now falling out of the sky. It washed the grime of travel from his head and the sweat from his skin. He drew his fingers through his fair hair, darkened with the rain. As he took a deep breath and let the deluge wash down over his chin and throat, Magda found herself smiling with the vicarious pleasure of this simple act. She marvelled at Walter's relationship with nature.

He shook his head, drops of water flying from his hair, colliding with the arrows of rain falling from the sky. He drew his fingers over his eyes and down over his face, and looked at Magda watching him from the doorway. She smiled wistfully, wishing it was this young man who made her feel the way Sébastien did. She had the feeling things would be a lot simpler if he did. They certainly had a lot more in common. There were no nagging secrets between them and she was fascinated by that clever head of his.

'I have something for you, in my bag there,' said Walti, pointing to the bench next to her on the balcony, sheltered from the rain. A large wrapped package was tucked and strapped under the flap of his leather pack.

Magda waited for him to approach the mud-splattered wooden steps. He scraped his boots on a rock at the foot of the stairs before climbing to the shelter of the balcony. He unstrapped the package from the bag and unrolled a silver-grey pelt with blue-black patches, the like of which Magda had never seen.

'It's beautiful. Thank you!'

'Wolf,' he said. 'Last week's culprit in Bürglen. A ravaging so brutal there was no doubt that the farmer's sheep was not given the same tame treatment as Mrs Vogler's chickens.'

Magda remembered the chicken story, one of Walter's mysteries he had recounted during his last visit.

The pelt had become wet round the edges with the rain, but the centre was still dry. Magda wiped her hands on her apron before stroking the soft fur, as though petting one of the village dogs.

She became aware of a pleasant peaty smell, an aroma not unlike a mixture of herbs from the forest and realised it was coming from Walter's body. It was not the sour sweat smell she often caught from her brother or her father. Walter still hadn't put on his shirt. As Magda looked at his bare chest, a muscle ticked below his shoulder. She backed off, confused by her reaction.

Had her coming of age turned her slatternly? Several years had passed since she'd become a woman, yet she had not felt desire for any man until these two marched into her life – Walter, and then Sébastien. And she could not forget what Sébastien had unleashed in her in the tower that day. She knew where her body belonged, but what about her head, and ultimately, her heart?

Walter was smiling at Magda with his clever green eyes. All she could think about was the line of his lithe body, his slim belly and his lean arms that had gained a little muscle since the first time they'd met. His pale skin was hairless and blemish-free, so different from Sébastien's. She felt a spark of something, but blushed to think that these two men were affecting her in similar ways. Was it guilt or prudishness she felt? Surely it could not be the second; she would more likely be labelled a harlot if anyone knew what Sébastien had already done to her.

'We must clothe you, Walti.'

He reached for her arm, suddenly bold.

'Are you ashamed of what you feel, Magda?' he asked.

'No... I. You will catch your death in this rain. But worse, if Papa sees you standing there like that when he comes from the mill, he will send you packing back to Bürglen. And I don't want you to go just yet.'

Walter looked towards the little mill in the hamlet and put his hand to her cheek, his fingers still damp from his shower in the rain. His touch added to Magda's turmoil. She turned into the dark of the chalet. He followed her inside.

'Dry yourself beside the fire before you put these on,' she said, picking up the garments she had sewn from the cot and holding them up between them. 'Can it be possible you have grown since I last saw you, Walti?'

In the confines of the chalet, his height was accentuated. *He must be almost as tall as Sébastien.* At the invasion of that thought, Magda cleared her throat and turned to place the garments on the edge of a chair before clearing away a tray of bowls and mugs from the morning's breakfast. She was glad to do this before her father admonished her for avoiding her household work to follow her 'frivolous creative endeavours', as he put it.

The swatch of cloth Magda had begun to cut and sew for Sébastien was spread across another chair. While Walter had his back to her, she folded it quickly and hid it behind the curtain in the alcove. Away from not only Walter's eyes, but also from those of her father and brother who would soon be home for something to eat.

Instead she spread out the wolf pelt.

'You should dress now, Walti. I will absent myself while you change your pants.'

For this, at least, Walter seemed relieved despite his earlier boldness. She retreated through the curtain to the sleeping alcove, not wanting him to bring the weather or the mud into that area of the chalet. She heard him remove the remainder of his wet clothes. A buckle clinked and his trousers rustled, and curiosity got the better of her. She allowed herself a peek through the curtain.

His long legs were surprisingly muscular, but lithe, like a runner. This man travelled everywhere on foot in the Confederation and recently he'd been delivering more than an average number of messages. Now that the blisters on his feet had hardened, he must be as fit as a fighting knight, though he would never raise a weapon. Her eyes glanced at the wolf pelt on the chair.

'You know, it's the first thing larger than a rabbit I have ever killed,' Walter called out with his back to her. Was he aware she was watching? 'I took courage in the fact that the farmer had promised me more than my fair share of *Taler* if I could rid him of the beast. It was hardly a mystery. The way his sheep's carcass had been torn apart, limb from limb, and the spine of the creature chewed bare by the crows once the beast had had his fill, I knew...' Walter looked up at Magda where she now stood in the doorway, her hand on her chest and her mouth turned down at the corners. 'Oh, I'm sorry, Magda. I'm not painting a very pleasant picture.'

At that moment they both realised he was completely naked in front of the stove. Walter looked down and laughed, but did nothing to cover himself. Magda put her hand to her mouth and retreated behind the curtain, blushing furiously, but with a smile.

'You'd think we were brother and sister the way we have forgotten our modesty,' she called from behind the curtain, though Edgar would never dare stand so boldly in front of her with no clothes on. 'You'd better dress yourself before Papa returns from the mill. He'll skin you with more vigour than your wolf if he sees you standing there like that,' she said.

It was good to hear Walter laugh.

'You can come out now,' he said after a few moments. 'I'm not completely dressed, but I want to show you how accurate your sewing skills have been.'

Magda drew back the curtain and looked at his undershirt and pants. She circled him, pulling the waist a little here, stretching the fabric across the shoulders there. She hadn't measured him properly, but had guessed at his size each time they'd been close to each other. The garments were a little snug, but would not impede his movement. And they would keep him warm.

'It's so soft. How do you give the linen its gentleness? Not even two years of wearing has given my old shirt such softness,' he said.

'I pound the fibres thoroughly before feeding them to the spindle. You'd think by the look of these hands that I've been spinning halberd blades for my entire life. Did you tan this pelt yourself?' asked Magda, holding up the wolf fur. 'I think I shall make us each a pair of *Finken* to keep our feet warm in the winter.'

Colour rose to Walter's face, and Magda pressed her lips together as she realised he thought they could share the comfort of the slippers together. There could be a promise in the words she hadn't said. He seemed to remember something and turned back to his bag still sitting on the bench on the balcony. 'You cannot continue to promise me gifts, Magda, without something in return. Here is the root you asked for. *Rubia tinctorum.*'

Magda clapped her hands with delight.

'It gives a brighter vermillion hue than the oxide minerals the old monk has on his shelves,' said Walter. 'The madder root apparently only grows in the south near the Mediterranean Sea. I'm sure when you run out, Mihal will be able to source you some more. I've heard there is a beetle whose shells are crushed to make a crimson colour.'

Magda turned one of the roots over in her hands. 'I've tried to grow this before,' she said. 'Mihal brought me a sapling when I was designing his first jerkin, but it wouldn't grow here. I think we are too high up the mountain and our summers are not long enough. Thank you, Walti. I am most grateful and I'm glad the trade against your new clothing was anticipated.'

'Better than payment in blood, I suppose,' he said, stroking the wolf's pelt.

Instead of a vision of the animal who had provided the fur, the bright red cross of the Knights Templar came to Magda's mind.

✝ ✝ ✝

The next morning Edgar and her father were called away to the stream that had swelled to the size of a river running through the hamlet. Magda could hear the rain hissing on the sodden earth from inside the chalet. Those living close would need their homes protecting from flooding.

As she opened the door to take the slops outside, Walter was digging a narrow channel across the trail for water to escape down the slope towards the river. When he finished, Magda watched him check the water was draining satisfyingly away from the courtyard.

'Morning!' she called. 'You'll be wanting some warm bread and milk after that hard work.'

Walter slapped his hands on his thighs and approached the chalet. 'I offered to stay and help,' he said. 'My next chore is to whittle some arrows and bolts and fix some fletchings for the growing collection of weapons in your arsenal. The weather should let up tomorrow and I'll be on my way.'

Was that regret she heard in his voice? Surely anyone would want to be gone from this Godforsaken place where the rain-clouds seemed to be glued to this end of the valley.

Walter sat on the bench outside the kitchen door under the roof, and when he'd finished his food and drink reached into the basket beside him. 'You have geese here?' He held up a feather. 'We don't often see them on the pastures around our villages. I have to use heron or hawk feathers.'

'These came from the western plains. I can't remember who Edgar bought them from, but I know they came from a valley on the other side of the Jura Mountains. Papa says geese feathers are the best for fletchings, though I don't know why.'

'He's right,' said Walter. 'Have you ever fletched an arrow? I often wonder why the softer hands of a woman aren't used more often for such delicate work.'

Magda tipped her head with curiosity. Walter held out a birch stick in his left hand and a whittling knife in his right. He ran his finger down the outside of the stick, and began shaving fine curls of wood.

'You start with the shaft. This is good wood, a little harder than pine. It's more difficult to whittle, but flies better.'

'Why the feathers, then?' Magda asked.

'Same reason birds need them. Feathers keep them stable in flight. It's the same with an arrow. A bare shaft doesn't travel as well, and certainly not as far. These help the arrow spin, controlling its stability through the air. You need a minimum of three feathers to create the spin. At home I use hawk feathers, but these will make even finer fletchings.'

'Why do you use one of one colour and two of another?'

'It's mostly tradition. But there is a tiny difference in the weight of these three feathers. It helps the spin. This one, on his own...' Walter splayed the dark feather he'd chosen, '...is called the cock. I'll use these for the other two fletchings. They're called the hens.'

A man and two women.

Magda thought of Walter and Sébastien, competing for her attention, likening their triangle to the flight aid of the arrow. But in this case it was a woman and two men. And she wasn't sure she could live without either of them.

'It's all about the subtleties,' continued Walter. 'Father says I'm the best fletcher in the village.'

'That's a great compliment, coming from the great Wilhelm Tell. I find it ironic you're an expert in the construction of an arrow, but you choose not to put your fingers on the bow.'

'If you must know, I quite surprised myself with the throw of my knife at the wolf in the hills above Bürglen. My aim found its way through the beast's left eye; he didn't suffer. So perhaps all is not lost with my weaponry skills.'

✝ ✝ ✝

'It's not a mineral, so I bind it with chalk from the hills above Morgarten. But first we must preserve the colour from the root in liquid form.'

She pulled a pot from above the fire, aware of her use of the word 'we', as though the work of fletching arrows and making red dye were the labours of a team. She was keen to fix the dye Walter had brought to the special yarn Mihal had delivered on behalf of the knights.

'Could you?' she asked, handing Walter the pot. The ingredients to fix dye would require urea, but she wasn't sure whether he knew that.

He raised his eyebrows.

Magda laughed. 'I'm sure yours is pure, but I need spring water first,' she said, the test of his knowledge ever a wonder to her.

Walter pulled on his still damp jacket, hat and boots and went down to the trough in the courtyard to fill it with water from the spout.

In the kitchen, Magda cut the pieces of root into chunks and scraped away their skins. After the water had heated on the stove, she added the root. Walter looked into the pot, which soon began to swirl crimson from the root. It resembled a pot of blood.

'Red is a royal colour. It engenders pride – a mortal sin according to some. Who has asked you for this commission? Surely we lowly peasants shouldn't be seen to be flaunting such brightness?' he asked.

'Perhaps God will notice us better if we flaunt the colours of his making,' she taunted.

'Now you speak in blasphemous riddles, Magda. *He* is allowed to flaunt anything.'

'After a long winter and wet spring, I'm tired of all the grey. Anyway, this is not for clothes; it's for something different. But I can't tell you right now. I've been sworn to secrecy.'

She knew Walter wanted to know. But she didn't want to sour the mood between them by talking about the knights. Walter was still treating them with a great deal of reserve. He moved his stool to the doorway and continued with the arrows. Beyond him, the rain dripped in curtains from the roof into grooves formed in the courtyard below.

'When was the last time you saw the Frenchmen?' asked Walter.

So his curiosity had got the better of him, then.

'You speak about them as though they're emissaries of the Habsburgs themselves. They're here to help us, Walti. But it's been almost two months since they were here.' Inside she felt a well of sadness, but kept her voice neutral.

'I imagine this flooding will impede whatever transport it is they have been planning.'

'I wish this rain would stop,' she said, happy to change the subject. 'It feels like the whole Morgartenberg could come down on top of us at any moment with the amount of water the ground is carrying. Papa and Eddi are using sacks of gravel and sand to keep the waters at bay, but I think we may have to move some families, including Brigitta's. The tower may yet see more temporary residents.'

'I think the Frenchmen are hiding something. I'm not sure their intentions are for the good of the Confederation. You and your people here need to be careful.'

'They... do have a secret, but it's not what you think.' Magda paused, realising it wasn't simply jealousy that was occupying Walter's thoughts. 'There's something I'll tell you, but you must share it with no one. For their safety, not ours. Sébastien and his men are fugitives from the King of France. They are not our enemy, but they are in danger. Your continuing curiosity might get them into trouble, could even get them killed. If they hadn't found refuge here, they would have been hunted down and burned at the stake.'

'Burned at the stake? Are they Templar Knights or something? I'd heard they were no longer in the Pope's favour.'

Magda's face must have confirmed his question.

He pressed his lips together and nodded. 'I think they're hiding something else,' he said. 'They speak in riddles of something they refer to as *La Ténébreuse*. I don't know if this thing is already in their possession, but the last time I heard them speak without their knowledge, I heard the words *extraction* and *escape*. It didn't sound like they were being altogether honest, in my opinion. They could be planning a theft. It sounded more sinister than words uttered by warriors of God.'

'I...' Magda looked down at the pot she held between her hands, the lines on her fingers now deeply etched with the vermillion dye. 'Yes, they have a divine secret. It is truly something religious. Perhaps something we don't understand. I should not begin to talk of this with you. I have made a promise.'

Walter raised his eyebrows, and she realised that probably didn't sound good.

'But what, then? Why is it something you cannot speak of with me? If God knows all our thoughts, then he will already forgive me for what I have swirling in my head, otherwise I would have been smitten down years ago.'

'I think you are purer than you believe, Walti. You're a good person. But so are they. You have to get over your ominous feeling. We have enough to deal with from the Habsburgs. The knights are going to help train our farmers and sons. They're going to help us defend ourselves from Duke Leopold.'

'And how do they expect to be paid for such a task?'

'They expect only the charity we can give them in the way of food and lodging, and maybe the occasional new article of clothing. They're working for the goodness of God.'

Walter sighed. 'I'm not convinced that their God is the same one as yours, Magda.'

CHAPTER TWENTY

21st June 1315, Schornen

MAGDA

Preparations for Edgar and Brigitta's wedding began as soon as the rains stopped. After a week, the lake began to recede, although the swamp remained inundated. The sun came out at the beginning of June and shone for as many days as the rain had fallen. By the solstice, it was as though they'd never had the deluge at all.

Brigitta's close family lived in Schornen, but her extended relatives living in Morgarten outnumbered those in the hamlet tenfold. Magda panicked at the thought of providing food for everyone coming for the celebrations. Contrary to most of the arranged marriages between families in the two villages, this one was born entirely out of love. Magda planned to make their alliance one they would never forget. As they would be making their home in Schornen, it was decided to organise the celebrations there too. Brigitta had become almost like a sister to Magda, and she would be moving into the chalet with Edgar. Magda was glad to be gaining a member of the family she both liked and respected.

This had been inevitable, with Edgar being the older sibling, but the months leading up to their marriage meant she must get used to the idea of losing her status as the matriarch of the family. Her father would soon be looking for a suitable husband for Magda. She hoped to guide his search in the right direction. She had two choices and knew which one her father would favour. The one who had a grounded history in the Confederation with a roof over his head and a growing reputation earning himself a regular income. Walter Tell. A match not only her father, but also everyone else, would assume was the perfect one.

Her father didn't have much to offer in the way of a dowry. The mill would go to Edgar and with a poor start to spring, they had not made much profit on grain. Magda had made more money from spinning and weaving, but her father wouldn't want to admit that to his peers.

'You know I could look after myself if I had my own roof over my head,' she said to him one evening while they were eating around the table. Edgar was absent, visiting his future relatives in Morgarten. 'You could stay here with Eddi and Bridgi and I could live on my own. Then you wouldn't need to gather a dowry for me.'

'What devil's drivel do you speak, girl! No daughter of mine will end up a spinster, although you are heading to that status now with your duties to me over the years since your mother's passing. I will find you a husband. I'll not hear of your wish to end up a shrivelled old woman without having provided sons to protect the future of our nation.'

If he was going to look for a suitor imminently, Magda wanted to tell him about *her* choices. She wanted him to ask Sébastien. But Walti had put a seed of doubt in her mind.

And while Magda pondered the possibilities, she smiled with the thought that maybe this was a practice run for the ceremony she might herself be having this time next year.

✝ ✝ ✝

Magda spent more time fussing around the bride than Brigitta's own mother on the morning of the wedding. Brigitta came to the chalet early and together they prepared posies for the ceremony. She sat on a stool in the courtyard as Magda skilfully wove flowers into her blonde hair.

'How easy it is to tease your hair into a braid, Bridgi. I fear for anyone who is tasked with combing mine for a ceremony. It's wilder than a boar's bristles.'

Brigitta laughed. 'Your chestnut tresses would be best left free anyway, Maggi, to show off their beauty. Look how the reflection of the sun on your curls turns them to fire. I would rather not tame your hair when it comes time for *me* to prepare *you* for your big day. Which I'm sure will be soon with suitors buzzing like bees around a honey pot.'

Magda sighed. 'Which honey bees though? The clover or the heather?'

'You know there is no hurry,' said Brigitta. 'I won't allow Edgar to force you to leave the home before you are ready. There is room enough for all of us.'

Magda bit her lip. 'I'm getting old. At nineteen years I should already be married.'

'It will come in its good time. I hope, like me, you choose well, that it comes to you with love and not necessity. With your skills, I am surprised you've not already been snapped up.'

Magda had long feared this might well be the reason for her spinster status; that nobody in the valley had come forward because they thought she wouldn't bear them children while she was too occupied designing jerkins. No man wanted to think his wife was somehow above him, more resourceful. Except...

'Let us enjoy this time of life, laughter and love,' said Brigitta. 'I am so happy we shall become sisters today.' She stood and pulled Magda into a hug.

'This is *your* day, Bridgi. It will be perfect. Today you shall have a sky to match your eyes. Now, let me fetch your dress.'

Magda turned away before the hot sting of tears in her throat rose in her eyes.

✛ ✛ ✛

The wedding took place in the tiny chapel halfway up to the pass. The trail was decorated with posies of primroses and pine branches full of new green cones. The wild cherries had ripened earlier in the month and the women of the hamlet made cherry bread, venison *Würst* flavoured with cherry pickles and cherry cheese. During all the food preparation, Magda still had time to fit Brigitta's dress, using rose-coloured sashes dyed with the tint from cherry skins. With marguerites woven into a marital crown, there would never be a more beautiful bride.

In the afternoon, the children of both villages gathered for a cherry stone spitting contest and the older generations celebrated their achievements with dangerous quantities of kirsch schnapps.

The priest from Morgarten married them in the early evening, a clear and bright one to celebrate the summer solstice. A trio of musicians played a hauntingly melodious tune on the alphorns that had been brought down from the upper pastures to accompany the bride and groom back from the chapel. The only flat area big enough to accommodate all the tables pulled from kitchens and a couple of barn doors set up on trestles was the courtyard between the toll tower and their chalet. Magda didn't think she'd ever seen the hamlet look so beautiful. The rosy glow of a midsummer's sunset matched the sashes on Brigitta's dress, and everyone declared the celebrations a success.

Magda was glad not to have the distraction of Sébastien's presence with so much to organise.

But she would soon wish all three of them had been present that evening.

✠ ✠ ✠

Several of the village lads had found their way up to the lookout platform at the top of the tower. They later said they'd been flicking cherry stones on the flat floorboards up there, a surface with no furniture or guests to impede their game.

The wedding party had eaten their fill of roast mutton and turnips. The fine nebbiolo wine that had been transported from Piemonte, organised well in advance by Mihal, was almost finished. The guests were sitting at the tables with full bellies, telling the stories of growing up in the villages, the tricks they would get up to as children and the alliances they had seen formed between couples in the two villages.

One of the children in the tower began squealing and screaming. At first Magda thought he was jubilant about having beaten his friends at some game. But when everyone looked up, they could see the child pointing urgently to the west. His companion jumped at the bell rope and Magda at once felt a spike of alarm. When they followed the child's pointing finger, she thought it was the knights coming late to the celebrations. But as she squinted at the horses, she realised there were more than ten armoured soldiers trotting along the path from Morgarten.

'Habsburg troops,' said Josef, spitting anger from his mouth. 'Hide what you can in the chalet, Magda. They will be ravenous as it's the end of the day. And we know their greed can twice match their hunger.'

With the help of a couple of the women from the village, Magda began clearing the table of leftover food and carried it to the kitchen.

'Maggi, I think you should take Brigitta to the sleeping alcove,' said Edgar. 'To protect yourselves from any vitriol these men might be ready to sling.'

Magda suddenly thought of Walter's mother. When had there ever been a friendly visit from the Habsburgs?

'I'll not abandon the villagers to deal with these men alone,' he continued. 'You stay with her in the house. We don't want their eyes falling on you either. You've already attracted too much attention in the neighbourhood.'

Magda wished Sébastien was there with them. She retreated with Brigitta to the house, telling her new sister-in-law to hide in the alcove behind the curtain.

'The last thing we want is to tempt them with a maiden not yet bedded on her wedding night,' said Magda.

'Bit late for that,' giggled Brigitta nervously. 'We'll close the shutters and peek through the gaps. We have kitchen knives to protect ourselves.'

The wooden shutters were closed across the two windows as the Habsburg soldiers cantered through the gap in the stone wall and into the courtyard. Each with an eye to the slits between the slats, the women watched the arrivals scattering chickens under their hooves.

'Heinrich von Hünenberg,' growled Magda under her breath. It was the first time she had seen him close up. One of his lackeys carried his banner. The soldier raised his helmet as he guided his horse towards one of the tables that still bore the remnants of the feast. Magda thought his looks were even more ugly than his reputation. He lowered his lance and speared a remaining hunk of bread that Magda had prepared with the last of the wild garlic, morsels of smoked pork baked in its midst.

'Herr Meier! Pray tell, what are you celebrating with our neighbours?' von Hünenberg asked Magda's maternal uncle from Morgarten. He angled the bread aloft on the spear towards the men behind him, still mounted on their horses.

'We are celebrating midsummer, and we invited our friends and family to celebrate,' said Josef.

'Did I ask you, old man? Speak now, Meier!'

'Josef Stauffacher tells the truth,' Urs Meier said with a shaky voice. 'We are celebrating the solstice.'

'Stauffacher, eh? Are you a relation to Commander Stauffacher?' The soldier turned to Josef. Urs Meier winced in the background, realising his error at revealing Magda's father's identity.

'A distant relative,' Josef lied. 'Second cousins, perhaps.'

The soldier stared at Magda's father long and hard, then glanced towards the chalet. Magda instinctively drew in her breath and withdrew from the gap in the shutter, even though von Hünenberg wouldn't be able to see her. Brigitta did the same, withdrawing into the dark sleeping alcove, her eyes wild.

'Hide yourself, Bridgi,' whispered Magda. 'We still don't know their intentions.' Her curiosity pulled her back to the window.

'And where has all the food and drink come from for this celebration?' asked von Hünenberg. 'I see remnants of a feast here. Have your neighbours been bringing goods that should be taxed and paid for before they leave the gates of our territory? Where is the money that will pay the duke's levy?'

Magda could see her father's ears turning red even in the dusk and hoped this wasn't going to escalate. If the Morgartners were to be fined for bringing the celebrations across the border, Magda hoped he could keep his temper and allow Urs Meier to do the talking.

'People of Morgarten: you will be required to pay a tax for your frivolity. We will come to your homes tomorrow to collect what belongs to Duke Leopold and his brother, the Austrian king. You will not be permitted to use what is rightly his to supplement festivities within the Confederation! Be home with you now, to prepare your goods for taxes.'

The horses were becoming restless, some of them sawing at their bits. Heinrich von Hünenberg's beast pawed at the ground with its hoof.

One of the three boys who'd been on the lookout platform suddenly burst from the door of the tower and slid down the wooden handrail. His eyes were wide with terror from the commotion. All of four years old, he would be looking for his mother. He was one of their village boys, Jorath, belonging to a family who lived just beyond the mill.

'Stop! Stay where you are, lad!' Magda's father called to him, his hand held out.

But the boy had only one thing on his mind, to seek the safety of his mother's skirts. He darted across the courtyard and instead of going around the perimeter of the tables, ran straight through the line of horses bunched up in a group, their riders still in their saddles.

Two of the beasts reared at the sudden movement. One of them was von Hünenberg's mount. Its legs sawed in the air and a hoof glanced off the boy's head. As his little hand fled to his bloodied temple, the boy lost balance and sprawled on the ground. The great horse balanced for a moment on his hind legs before its descending hooves thumped onto the boy's back. Over the squeals of the beast, everyone standing in the courtyard could hear the crack of the boy's spine.

After a moment of silence where all they could hear was the jangle of bridles, the clinking of spurs and the puff of a horse's breath, a high-pitched wail echoed across the courtyard. The mother of the boy ran to her son, knelt down and touched his broken body. She cradled his head and let out a mournful cry, rocking him in her lap. That he was no longer living, no one was in doubt.

Magda sucked in a breath behind her hand and she began to shake.

In the courtyard, her father stood his full height and held his hands up, pushing the air in front of the soldiers. The soldiers' beasts backed away without direction from their riders, as though Josef had magical control of them. The crowd couldn't see the expression on the soldiers' faces as they were wearing helmets, but a tragic heaviness lay in the air between the troop and the villagers.

'Be gone with you, vile Habsburg parasites!' Magda's father yelled.

'Be happy that you no longer have to raise a stupid child who would rather run in front of battle-ready soldiers than take the safe route to his mother,' said Heinrich von Hünenberg. 'Your village is better off without the boy.'

Josef began to advance towards von Hünenberg, seemingly undeterred that he was on foot and the soldier was still in his saddle.

'Why, you...'

There was a shout beyond the crowd. Josef paused.

'Jorath! Jorrie!' a voice cried, and the circle of onlookers broke open to reveal a man running towards them from the direction of the stream. It could only be the father of the slain child. He was wielding an axe. Edgar followed him, trying to prevent more mayhem.

From the doorway of the chalet Magda stared down at Jorath lying face-down, lifeless. His arm was bent at a strange angle and his legs lay twisted like the straw-stuffed limbs of a doll she'd had as a child. His mother leaned over the tiny body, sobbing into his neck. At that moment, Magda wanted Jorath's father to break through the arms that restrained him, raise his axe and smite Heinrich von Hünenberg. She wanted more than anything to see him dead.

Magda felt Brigitta come to her side, heard her shaky breath over her shoulder.

'What happened?' she asked.

'One minute the little mite was playing a game, the next he was killed by a Habsburg horse. It's terrible. Terrible. Poor little Jorrie.'

They turned to each other and hugged, tears dampening both their faces.

It was time to put an end to the constant torment of the people of Morgarten. Time to stop the unfair pillaging in the name of taxes. Time to lift the line of the border between their two communities. Time to stop the constant threat of invasion.

With a sense of doom, Magda could not even begin to imagine the extent of retribution that would come from all of this.

Chapter Twenty-One

8th July 1315, Bürglen and Luzern

WALTER

W alter had wanted to stay for Magda's brother's wedding, but felt like an interloper. Once he heard the Frenchmen wouldn't be there, he'd been more comfortable about travelling home to Bürglen as soon as the rains had abated.

There had been more meetings between various military factions within the Confederation to try and agree on their future goals. Despite the vote in Morgarten, not everyone within the Confederation was in favour of expansion either. During a visit to the barracks in Altdorf, Werner Stauffacher suggested Walter should be sent as a spy to Luzern to seek information about the intentions of Duke Leopold's troops. Discretion was essential, but Walter's knowledge of tongues and dialects meant he would have a better chance at gauging the mood of the people.

Was he willing to throw himself into that kind of danger?

Walter agreed to travel under the guise of Mihal's apprentice by barge northwards on Lake Luzern. The boat called at Brunnen, where Walter was sorely tempted to disembark and head up towards the Aegerital. As he gazed towards the pass, dominated by the Mythen Peaks to the east, Mihal nudged him on the arm. 'She got to you, eh? A lovely lass, indeed. Now if I was thirty years younger...' Mihal paused. 'I wouldn't leave it any longer to make your thoughts known to her.'

'Is it so obvious? There's someone else who's also attempting to secure her affections.'

'Never trust a Frenchman,' said Mihal with a smile. 'I'm not sure her father would approve of that match. Losing his daughter to a foreigner. And an exiled one at that. But if there is no one else making a claim, he might not have a choice. Don't wait, Walti.'

'I may need more than just a little courage.'

Mihal looked at Walter, his stare made more intense with the fullness of his bushy brow. The older man reached into one of the saddlebags hanging on the rump of his mule. 'Here, take this.'

He gave Walter a small clay pot. Walter placed it in his palm and opened the lid. A stringent aroma pinched at his nostrils.

'It's a salve, made from the oil of the camphor tree, amongst other things. Extremely precious, brought to southern Europe from China. It has been blended with butters and other oils to form this healing cream.'

Walter's eyebrows furrowed and Mihal continued. 'For Magda's hands. She has a juniper salve that I brought her last year made by my cousin in Graubunden. I told her I would source her more when it ran out. But perhaps you should be the bringer of more relief for her reed-beaten hands. This will have a far greater healing effect on the discomfort and her scars.'

Walter smiled. He thanked Mihal, knowing he was receiving late payment for errands he had carried out for the old man as a child. He tucked the little pot into a pocket on the chest of his tunic and vowed to speak his mind the next time he saw Magda. His tongue was so often silenced in her presence.

The barge sailed on towards the port of Luzern on the west branch of the lake. The impressive anvil of the Rigi, seen from almost everywhere in the Confederation, was joined in the background by the Pilatus mountain, hemming in the city to the west. Where the lake emptied into the wide funnel of the Reuss, a new lookout tower had been constructed in the middle of the river. It reminded Walter of the toll tower in Schornen.

'Holding back the waters to build that tower must have been a near impossible challenge,' he said.

'The *Wasserturm*,' said Mihal. 'The townspeople couldn't think of anything more inspiring to name it than the Water Tower, despite the immense trials in its construction. It's only accessible by boat.'

Their barge docked, and they made their way downstream on the northern bank towards the city, with Mihal's faithful mule at their side.

'If you're so interested in the tower, I should introduce you to the architect of a plan to build a bridge across the Reuss,' said Mihal, and then in a whisper: 'He's a Confederate sympathiser. His work would make a good excuse for engaging with him.'

They soon approached a group of men building what looked like giant wooden trusses. Two burly carpenters were cutting through a large beam with a double-handled crosscut saw. Walter stopped to look over the shoulder of the one who was directing the others. He had several parchments with drawings and numbers written on them.

'We're building a covered bridge across the river to connect the two banks,' said the man, noticing Walter's interest.

'So I hear from Mihal here. That's a very ambitious project, impeded I'm sure by the flow of the river.'

'The plan is to use the tower as an anchor in the centre to stabilise the bridge in the strong flow.'

'I can't imagine how many years that will take. Do you think you'll walk across it in your lifetime?'

The architect gave a cynical laugh. 'At least it will keep me employed and allow me to put bread and cheese on my table until my grave. For that I'm sure my family are grateful. They are less impressed with the amount of time these calculations take to ensure the bridge's integrity. I work on it for many more hours than I should.'

Walter imagined this man would be paid well. A bridge at this point on the river would increase the city's accessibility tenfold, with the expansion of the town on the south bank where trade routes heading in either direction could cross. Although the lakes were still being used as the principal form of transport, as new villages sprung up on the surrounding land, Walter foresaw more travel by road.

'Are you a builder? A draftsman? I'm in desperate need of someone with a sensible head,' the architect asked.

'No... I'm afraid not, but I have a fascination for bridges.'

Walter had never seen anything as magnificent as the plans the man had drawn up. The bridge would dogleg across the river via the *Wasserturm* and would be capped with a roof for its entire length. This was a profession he could see himself entering if his feet and his nose ever failed him.

'My stomach is rumbling, Walter,' said Mihal. 'Why don't you have a look around and I'll meet you back here for an ale and a *Chuechli* in a little while? Then we can make a plan of action.'

'Well, I won't keep you from your calculations,' said Walter to the architect, pressing his palm to his chest and giving a short bow. 'I've yet to see the remainder of the town, so I'll be on my way, but may call back on my return.'

'Pleasure was mine,' said the architect. 'Keep your wits about you. There are many strangers about today.'

Mihal was already walking towards the tavern under the *Rathaus*, reaching for the hitching post to tie his mule's reins. Walter continued along the St Karliquai, hugging the city wall on the north bank of the fast-flowing Reuss. He passed officials heading to their rule-making at the *Rathaus*, tradesmen and farmers coming and going to the *Kornmarkt* and pilgrims on their way to worship at the Roman basilica on the slope above town. The ringing of the bell striking the hour in its tower attracted Walter. He thought the melody would have pleased Magda. He wanted to get a closer look at the clock whose hands he'd seen glinting in the sunlight from the boat. He turned towards it through a dark passageway leading under the city wall at the Nölliturm, a small, round tower on the edge of the river.

The sunlight shining brightly at the other end of the short passage was suddenly cut off as a cloth was shoved roughly over his head and eyes. A foul-smelling hand covered his nose and mouth, pressing the filthy material against his tongue. Walter reached for his *baselard*, now a permanent feature at his hip, but a boot kicked his hand away. There was more than one assailant.

'Trying to hide your wealth under a well-worn jerkin are ye, stranger?'

The fetid breath wafting from the mouth of the robber smelled like rotting meat.

'I assure you, I am far from wealthy,' said Walter, trying to mimic the robber's guttural dialect as closely as possible.

'Peasants don't go wandering around wearing such a fine weave. Your undershirt has given you away, liar. Rich liar,' said the robber.

Despite his predicament, Walter acknowledged that Magda would be proud to have her fine work recognised. The thought that he might never get back to Schornen to tell her soon wiped the thought from his mind. He swallowed as he felt the cold blade of a knife against his neck.

Chapter Twenty-Two

8th July 1315, Luzern

WALTER

'H and over your money, lad,' said a second voice as hands
patted around his jerkin.

Walter reached for his coin pouch, more concerned that they
would find the salve that Mihal had given him not an hour before.

'Hey! Hey!' A shout echoed along the passage with the sound of
feet slapping on the paving stones.

There was a scuffle, some grunts, and Walter was thrown to the
ground, his hip crashing painfully onto the paving stones with the
hilt of his dagger between. He ripped the cloth sacking from his
head and spat the dirt and fibres from his mouth. He couldn't see
at first, his eyes taking a moment to adjust, but the receding shouts
of his assailants meant they had been chased away by whoever was
now hauling him up from the ground.

It was the architect and the two carpenters he'd seen on the
double-handled saw.

'I thought as much,' said the architect. 'When you left us to
walk up river, I saw those two shady characters following you and

reckoned there'd be trouble. You're not used to the city are you? Should be careful here.'

'I don't know how I can thank you,' said Walter.

'Did they steal anything?' asked the architect.

'Thank God, no. Please, let me buy you an ale and a meal for your trouble. And for your men...'

Walter reached into the pouch tucked inside his shirt and handed each of the workers a coin.

'I'd like to have a chat with your boss on his own, if I may,' Walter said to the carpenters.

They turned to head back to their sawing, saying it was really no trouble, that their boss had really done most of the threatening to scare away the culprits. Walter smiled at the architect. 'Come. Let's meet Mihal back at the tavern. Are you and your men from the city?'

'My family is originally from Engelberg. But we moved here when my father sought his ambition for building work with higher pay.'

'Engelberg. Still a true Confederate, then?' Walter asked in a whisper.

The architect nodded with a tight smile, looking around the street warily.

'Thomas Bossart,' he said, stopping and holding out his hand.

'Walter Tell.' Walter grabbed his hand, uttering his name without thinking.

Bossart raised his eyebrows. 'Any relation?' he asked as they continued to walk together to the tavern.

'Son.'

They approached the tavern under the Rathaus. Bossart sat opposite Mihal and Walter on a stool padded with the pelt of a goat.

'Must be tough fighting for your place in the world after the big man's reputation,' said Bossart. 'You look like you'll do a fine job, though I'm not sure how you would have fared against those men.'

'What men? What happened?' asked Mihal.

As Walter recounted the attempted robbery, Thomas Bossart's friendliness put him at ease. It confirmed Mihal's comment when they first arrived that he must be a true Confederate sympathiser. It may have been unwise of Walter to have given away his identity so readily. But instinct had told him from the start the architect was friend, not foe.

'On the other hand, a curious mind will get far in life,' said Bossart.

'That's my intention,' said Walter. 'To remain curious.'

'You'd be wasted as a warrior,' Bossart replied. Walter was about to say something to affirm this, but Bossart continued before he had a chance. 'My father was a master builder. He worked on this very structure we're sitting in. His team built those arches over there leading to the cellars. They form the foundations of the magnificent towers and turrets above.'

'Did he support your wish to become an architect?'

'Not at first. He said there was no money in it. He tried to tell me tradition dictated that builders and their designers were one and the same; a team who should put their brains and brawn together. It's true, there should be communication and comprehension between the two trades, but I saw my father build things as he went along. That might work for a village barn, but not for these tall city buildings.'

'I imagine a bridge takes a great deal of planning,' said Walter.

'Yes, it's precision work. Calculating the weights, the chords, the bracings, the struts. I'm more a mathematician than an architect. When I think about my father's ability to calculate, he could barely work out how many ales to order for his fellow workers at the end of the day.' He nodded his head towards the two carpenters across the street, who had returned to their laborious task of sawing the beam, and Walter couldn't help thinking of fathers who have different expectations for their sons. Every so often the blade of the saw came to an abrupt halt when the teeth caught in a knot.

'Are people here content to be part of the Habsburg alliances?' Walter asked with his voice lowered.

Bossart spat in the dust beside his feet. 'Are you mad? The entire region of Luzern would pay dearly to become part of the Confederation. But you should be careful who you ask these questions of. The majority of the Luzerners are not happy with the Habsburg rule, but the Austrians have infiltrated our society to the extent that you sometimes can't tell them from the locals.'

'Once I heard your accent and you mentioned Engelberg, I felt I could trust you. I know how much of a stronghold the town is to the south of the Confederation.'

'Ha, yes, dialects! Ask an Austrian spy to speak, and his tongue will always give him away.'

'You cannot exercise enough caution,' interrupted Mihal. 'Heinrich von Hünenberg and Duke Leopold now have more local support in their military and spy network. Don't rule out hearing local dialects spoken in their midst.'

'Have you heard rumours that Duke Leopold is planning to attack the Confederation?' whispered Walter.

Bossart's eyes darted about the crowds walking along the riverbank.

'Hush, lad, you must not speak of this. Let's go downstairs to the cellars. There is someone I think you should meet.'

Walter left some coins on the table, and they descended the stone steps into the cellar. In a corner was a table upon which sat a candelabra dripping wax onto the raw wood.

'This is the *Stammtisch* for the *Rathaus* officials,' Bossart said, nodding to the three men sitting around the table. 'In recent times this table has hardly been empty with men who gather to speak of the future of our canton.' He turned to the men. 'Gentlemen, there is someone who would like to meet you. The son of Wilhelm Tell, Walter.'

All three men stood and introduced themselves, saying it was a pleasure to meet the son of such a fine warrior.

'Young Tell here is fishing for news of the political climate in the city, wondering whether Duke Leopold's troops are preparing for an attack on the Confederation,' said Bossart.

One of the men cleared his throat and twirled a moustache that sat above a beard the size of a marmot. 'This city gained its independence from the Murbach Abbey over a hundred years ago. We fought hard then, and we sure as hell would like to fight hard now to regain that independence,' he said.

Another of the men took a swig of his ale, and his mug hit the table a little harder than perhaps was intended. 'A string of Habsburg dukes secured an authoritarian net around the city long ago,' he said. 'The people are quietly angry that we didn't forcefully act to join the Confederation in 1291. They were too lethargic, in my opinion.'

'There is, however,' said the man with the moustache, 'an underground group here which is forming an alliance with the surrounding villages to seek independence from Habsburg rule. It would help their mission greatly if you could discreetly take news back to Stauffacher and his generals about our desires to unify.'

Walter reflected on the plan to train the men of Morgarten and Schornen to defend themselves in the event of an attack. 'If you have men with military experience amongst you, they should be prepared to defend themselves in the event of an uprising,' said Walter.

'Of course, but I would rather see an offensive on a greater, combined scale,' said the third man. 'These Habsburgs are like a pest. If we can raise enough military support, we can at least ring-fence the whole area with troops, perhaps even win the allegiance of those communities between here and the Confederation to expand the borders of the nation.'

Walter wondered whether the number of ales they had consumed was fuelling their enthusiasm. These thoughts were rather ambitious, but it was exciting to hear such eagerness to join the Confederation. Luzern was a big city with a significant population. 'There are those within the Confederation who think political and military control might become unstable with such an expansion, but many of us are trying to assuage their concerns,' said Walter.

'I can see how the smaller communities might feel they would lose control,' said one of the men. 'But I know for a fact the villages and hamlets within our canton are not happy being ruled by an Austrian despot.'

'Hurry back home, Walter, lad. Tell your people how keen we are to join. But tell them to beware. Duke Leopold is greedy. He plans to marry soon, and will be moving his seat from the castle his family has occupied for many generations back east to Austria. It has been said he wants to try and secure the land between to ease travel between the two strongholds before he goes. Which includes the Helvetic Confederation. From what I have heard amongst the Austrian troops and traders, he could be invading within the year. He wants your land back, lad.'

CHAPTER TWENTY-THREE

July 17th 1315, Aegeri Lake, off Morgarten

SÉBASTIEN

Sébastien and his colleagues left for several days to scout the abbey in Einsiedeln. They told no one of their destination. With the promise of training the troops, people had stopped asking what they were doing in the valley.

In Einsiedeln they counted troops, horses and the various weapons available in the small garrison next to the abbey. They noted the military routines and the switch of guard duty. They studied the habits of the brethren in the cathedral, the plans of the halls, corridors and tunnels of the cloister. And they committed the lie of the hills and the trails surrounding the valley to memory.

They arrived back in Schornen dusty, hot and tired. While Yves and Grégoire sought the cool of the tower, the only thing that could take away the uncomfortable heat of the journey for Sébastien would be a good bathing.

As he walked towards the lake, picking a path on the southern edge of the receding marsh, he saw a boat floating offshore and wondered who was fishing at this time of the day. It couldn't be Edgar, as he had greeted the knights from the mill as they arrived.

The lake surface was as smooth as melted lard on a hot griddle. Long stretches of thin cumulus clouds reflected on its emerald surface, their images completely still as though set in ice. The water was far from freezing. Trout flies danced, tempting the perch who rose from time to time to kiss the surface, leaving widening rings where their lips broke the surface.

As he drew closer and the boat came into full view, a smile cracked the dust on Sébastien's face as he recognised Magda's chestnut hair shining in the sun. Rather than alert her to his presence, he sat on a rock in the trees close to the shore and watched her. The shadow of the forest brought the hint of refreshing air down the slope. He removed his shirt to let his body cool.

Magda pushed her hair back from her face. Her forehead and cheeks were flushed with over-exposure to the sun. She pulled in the fishing line, the hook still holding her bait. She must be frustrated that the perch were no longer biting; they'd be seeking the colder depths now the sun was high. She grabbed the oars and manoeuvred the boat towards the shore. Stepping out, she placed her bare feet in the stony shallows before hauling the boat half out of the water. Sébastien stayed in his hidden spot.

Magda pulled a basket from the stern and sat on a rock to gut her catch. She placed the bloody innards on the ground, perhaps to dry them out and save them for the chickens. As she gutted each perch, she placed it on a layer of leaves in the bottom of her reed basket. The innards were gathering a cloud of bright green flies, so she covered them with more foliage. Although she was in the shade, Sébastien saw a rivulet of sweat run down her temple onto her neck. He was stirred by this vision of her doing something as simple as gutting fish.

When she'd finished, he expected her to take her catch back to the hamlet. He was ready to abandon his swim and decided he'd let her leave, then catch up to her and offer to carry her basket.

Instead she looked out at the water for a moment, before standing up and untying her bodice. Sébastien stared, the alabaster skin of her arms and breasts appearing as she peeled away her clothes. The crumple and swish of her skirt masked his gasp as she wriggled out of the rest of her clothing. She walked naked into the lake and sank into the depths with a sigh. Rolling onto her back, her hands moved to keep her afloat and her chestnut tresses fanned out on the surface. Her perfect body ghosted under the surface as she concentrated on the sky.

Sébastien pulled his gaze from her beauty and looked up to see what had attracted her attention. Black specks of swallows flitted back and forth, squealing their melancholic song of summer, plucking insects from the air. He stared back at Magda, and without thinking of the consequences, bent down to untie the laces on his boots and remove them. He undid his belt and buttons on his trousers and let them fall to the ground. The buckle clinked against a rock and there was a sudden commotion in the lake.

Magda's arms splashed as she looked towards the forest, eyes wide. Her gaze fell on Sébastien standing on the shore. 'What are you doing here?!' she said. 'Can't a woman have any privacy while attending to her personal needs?'

Her eyes widened when she realised he was completely naked.

'And those of the community,' he said, touching the basket with his foot, disturbing one or two flies. 'Although I fear if you leave these little fellows here much longer you will find a rapid decline in the village population.'

The cover had slipped off the top of the basket. Sébastien reached down to put it back in place. When he looked up, Magda had turned away from him, snakes of water-darkened hair now trailing over her shoulders.

'Do not underestimate how hard I've been working! There were way too many tiddlers; I had to throw back ten times what I caught. If you will kindly step away from the shore and make your way back to the village, I will be able to leave the water.'

He waded slowly into the depths, his heart pounding. Magda turned to face him, her chin barely above the surface.

'Stop, now, Sébastien de Molay, before you get us both in trouble,' she said, although her voice was wavering with less conviction.

He was weak with desire, could not stop, and as he made his way towards her through the water, he saw the defiance go out of her eyes to be replaced by a longing that went entirely against the words she had moments ago uttered.

Their mouths met and his hands swept over her body, the water transforming their roughness to silk against her skin. He lowered his mouth to her nipple and she gasped. He was sure she felt the same flash of heat streaking to her lower belly as him. Her hips pushed towards him and her thighs parted of their own accord. He needed no explanation of the desire they both now felt.

She pulled him towards her. It seemed like such a natural thing, to consummate their passion. Despite his other obligations and the celibacy to which he had once sworn, he could not help but think God had surely intended humans to enjoy the pleasure of each other's bodies if He had created them in His own image.

At the thought of God, Sébastien hesitated. Such weakness in the face of temptation. What on earth was possessing him? 'We should not be doing this.' His voice rasped.

She shook her head, but held him tighter.

'No... yes. Sébastien, I want this more than anything else.'

And with an audacity he would not have anticipated, she reached down under the blood-warm water and guided him inside her.

'It's all right, *ma belle*, no pain?' he asked, sensing a little hesitation at first.

Her answer was in the fingers now clawing at his shoulders, drawing him to her.

'Don't stop,' she whispered, moving against him.

Having found the right depth of water to hold them both, Sébastien lifted Magda's legs and wrapped them around his waist. The angle of her hips brought him deep inside her and he tipped her chin to look at him.

They rocked together until Magda gasped with the same little cry of pleasure in the toll tower some weeks before. With his release and the slowly diminishing thumping of his heart, came the weight of guilt and the promise he had broken. The promise to his fellow Templar Knights, the promise to his life's cause and the centuries-old protection of the Holy Grail.

Even though his coupling with Magda could go no further, his heart feared what he might have started.

CHAPTER TWENTY-FOUR

17th July 1315, Schornen

MAGDA

S o this was love, thought Magda, aware that they had sealed a
sacred thing. She was surely now Sébastien's forever.

They floated in the shallows, drifting between sun and the shadow of the forest. Her head rested on Sébastien's shoulder, the solid beat of his heart against her ear. She felt so free under the heat of the sun, in the coolness of the water, with the liberation of no clothes.

The shock of his presence had lasted the blink of an eye. She had no regrets. As he had stood naked on the shore with no sign of modesty, as hard as any animal Magda had ever seen ready to mate in a field, the memory of what he'd done to her in the tower and now there in the water reverberated in her belly. She could easily have swum away. But instead she'd swum towards him, yearning for those hands on her body.

Now Sébastien kissed the top of her head and smoothed her hair away from her brow.

'They'll be missing you in the village, I imagine.'

Sébastien shifted, and Magda unwound her legs from his hips.

'Probably not me, but certainly their midday meal. Let's hope the flies haven't got to it. I'm not looking forward to lighting the fire in the chalet. It's already stifling in the kitchen. When will the storm break this heat?'

'Perhaps I can help you set a fire in the brazier in the courtyard instead. We can cook on that.'

'That would be wonderful,' she said, her heart singing. *We* can cook.

'Wash yourself well, *ma belle*. To rinse the seed away,' said Sébastien.

As he turned towards the shore, she wanted to ask how he knew of such things. He waded out of the lake and she studied the muscles in his legs contracting along his thighs with water sluicing off him. His wide shoulders topped a broad back rippling with muscle, his skin a pleasing olive hue.

She followed him out of the water, suddenly shy. She dried herself on her apron and handed it to Sébastien to do the same.

'You must forgive me, Magda. I couldn't stop myself. Your beauty knows no bounds, *ma belle*. One day, you must find it in your heart to forgive me.'

'I wanted it too,' said Magda, curious at his choice of words. 'No one is at fault. It was a beautiful thing. There will be many more pleasures. Much more happiness.'

He lifted a finger and pressed it to her lips.

A cold frisson of melancholy calmed the hot pulse still singing in her belly. Was there a doubt that she could become his wife? She wanted to stay there, make him hers again. Make him commit to her heart. But they had to get back to the village or Sébastien's head might be on the block.

They fetched the fish basket and pulled the boat through the reeds, tying it to the mooring at the end of the beach. They made their way back to the village along the narrow path above the marsh, Magda holding her boots in her hand.

'I'm so glad you sought refuge in our valley. I'm curious, though, why you're so keen to help us defend Morgarten and the pass?' she asked.

'You are good people, good citizens. We want to help; that has been our mission in the past and will carry into the future.'

'The hamlet is still reeling from little Jorath's death. I almost wish the men who you're helping to hone their skills would simply take their revenge. Get the threat of a Habsburg attack out of the way.'

'It takes time to turn a peasant into a knight, Magda.'

'Walti thinks you're keeping a secret. One that has nothing to do with helping to defend our nation.' The mention of Walter's name triggered a spark of guilt. Here she was, walking next to the man who was the cause of Walter's uncertainty.

'It's Walti now, is it? I thought he was merely an acquaintance. Your *ami* is a young man with ideas that stray.'

'He doesn't believe you can be repaid for your services. He thinks you're here for a bigger prize.'

'And not the exquisite weaver from Schornen?'

Magda punched Sébastien gently on his shoulder.

'He has a vivid imagination,' continued Sébastien. 'We will be remunerated for training the soldiers. You do not need to concern your pretty head about where our wage will come from.'

'But you must be destined for better things. With the history of what you did in the Crusades.'

Was it her imagination, or did she feel an uneasiness come over him, a hooding of his inner thoughts? The moment of silence rang a small bell of alarm in her head.

'The drought has stilled the mill wheel,' said Sébastien, changing the subject as they walked past.

'There are other things we can be doing in the meantime like threshing new grain or drying the hay. And fishing,' said Magda with a smile. 'The milling can wait. It's not our main income. I can still weave by hand.' She placed the basket in the shade of the chalet and climbed the steps. She called to him before entering. 'If you set the fire in the brazier, you can share a meal with us. The embers in the chalet have gone cold. You'll have to use your flint.'

As she prepared the fish on an iron grill, she watched Sébastien shave curls of wood from a dry log and set his flint to a fistful of them mixed with some dried grass. He stacked some twigs and placed larger pieces of wood as the fire in the brazier caught. She reflected that the method of setting a fire was no different for the French or the Confederates. How they wooed their women was altogether a different matter.

When the flames calmed, she placed the grill over the brazier. As the fish sizzled, each one covered with a twig of juniper, she wrapped a stale loaf of bread left over from the day before in a dampened linen cloth and placed it near the warmth of the fire to freshen.

When her father and Edgar returned from the forest with Grégoire and Yves dragging sacks of logs behind them, she spread the meal on the table and they all ate together. She tried to catch Sébastien's eye, but he ignored her, perhaps to avoid anyone else noticing the passion between them across the table.

Afterwards, she cleared the remnants of the meal, plates and mugs away. She took the fish bones and heads and placed them in a pot of water above the fire to make a broth over the last of the heat. She threw the gutted innards and scales to the chickens, far enough away from the house that they wouldn't bring a stench in the heat. The men went back to the forest to continue with the wood. They had intended to work in the village, but all agreed it would be cooler at elevation amongst the trees.

Sébastien said he would stay behind to sharpen the axes that had been blunted during the morning's work. Magda was secretly pleased. No one questioned his motive to do so. The sultry weather had changed everyone's ideas about which tasks were the most important and which ones required the least amount of effort. Whatever it was the others thought Sébastien had been doing all morning, he'd come back with damp clothes; the others must have assumed he'd done enough sweating for one day.

Once the others left, Magda turned to him. 'I have something for you.'

Climbing the steps to the chalet, she went inside to the alcove behind her sleeping cot and pulled out the sewing and embroidery she had done for Sébastien. It was wrapped in the original silk cloth the yarn had come in, and she carried it with reverence down the stairs and across to where he sat in the shade of the tower. The tall building was now casting a welcome shadow over the rear of the courtyard.

Sébastien stopped his sharpening and lay the axe carefully across the chopping block. He leaned the whetstone with the pouch against the block on the ground and wiped his hands down his now dry trousers. He looked up at Magda, his eyes shining with an excitement that was different from the one she'd seen when he set eyes on her body. She experienced a tiny stab of jealousy and stared down at the cloth in her hand.

'You finished it!' he said.

Her envy forgotten, Magda smiled and nodded, as though watching a small child about to open a St Niklaus gift. He lay the package across his thighs, carefully unfolded it, then pulled out the bag Magda had woven and sewn, the yarn glinting even though the sun was not shining directly on it. It was as though he had infused it with a holy light. He pressed his hand over the crimson cross of the Knights Templar she'd embroidered onto the front of the bag.

He closed his eyes, and seemed to utter a silent prayer as his fingers caressed the threads. Magda's mouth opened a little. She was witnessing something she could not fathom. When he opened his eyes, his look was glazed, as though his thoughts had flown to a distant place. Magda felt insignificant as she stood there in the courtyard, knowing her presence was forgotten.

'Tell me what the bag is for,' she asked, kneeling down in front of him and bringing his attention back to the present.

'It is not yet in our possession. But as soon as it is, this sacred bag will protect the identity and the power of a great object,' he said with an emotion Magda had never heard him use.

He was speaking in riddles. Power? What power? Are we not all privileged to be alive because of the power of God? He appeared to change in that moment, though, as if his allegiance to whatever this thing was would never include Magda. As if he was bound to some unknown passion in his soul, a calling she knew nothing about.

Their heads were still close and Magda wanted to kiss him, but he pulled away before she had the chance. Thinking of riddles, a memory of Walter Tell's complete faith in her and his mouth on hers at the *Mittenfastenfeuer* all those moons ago came to her unexpectedly, flooding her with yet another wave of... what? Guilt or regret? She and Walter could have such a life together, but her heart sang every time she looked at Sébastien.

Chapter Twenty-Five

1st August 1315, Rütli Meadow, Urnersee

WALTER

The Tells were heading to the annual outing at the Rütli Meadow on the southernmost branch of the Lake Luzern. They were going to celebrate the anniversary of the signing of the *Bundesbrief*, the birthday of the Confederation Helvetica.

Some people came over the high jutting peninsula where the Confederation bordered the outlying communities of Luzern. Some, like Wilhelm and Walter, came by water. The journey from their end of the lake was easiest by boat, the steep cliffs bordering the narrow fjord virtually impassable.

Wilhelm had contracted a deep rattling cough a few days before, and Walter wondered whether it was wise for his father to be making the journey this year. But he would never have suggested he stay at home. He was looking forward to seeing colleagues from all over the Confederation, some of whom he only ever encountered at this annual gathering.

As they sailed up the centre of the lake, his father pointed out to all those on board a rocky outcrop at the foot of the Axenberg cliffs and boasted about his sailing expertise.

'I navigated the small boat to shore during a terrible storm. Is it already eight years ago?' His audience made the appropriate noises. 'After my confrontation with Gessler in the Altdorf town square the night before...' Walter would be the one who would later be called upon to recount the apple incident. '...I was chained up by the bailiff and thrown into the boat. The Habsburg guards were under instructions to take me to Luzern the following day. But in the wild storm, the boat almost sank. I kept telling them I could help. They eventually relented and unlocked my shackles so I could guide the boat to safety. I made my escape unscathed and travelled overland to face that bastard Gessler who was already on his way back to the Luzern garrison. We met at Küssnacht. I finally put an end to him with a crossbow and the bolts I stole from the boat.'

A cheer went up from the listeners. It was a story Walter had heard every first of August since. It was not the first time most of the passengers in the boat had been reminded of it. It kept the heroic legend of Wilhelm Tell alive, but also the nightmare of the apple incident. After eight years, the legend had a jovial edge to its telling, listeners all congratulating Walter's father for his defence of the nation.

But everyone had forgotten that it was his father's rage for what they had done to Walter's mother later that night that spurred him. Wilhelm hadn't known at first, because he'd been chained up and forced to lie in the bottom of the boat all night while they waited in vain for the storm to abate. It was only when he overheard the guards talking about ransacking the Tell home the next day that he was driven to fight off almost a dozen men to escape and take his revenge on Gessler.

Ever since that day, the threat of a Habsburg invasion had been growing. It was long past the point where anyone would apportion blame to one person. Whether Walter's father had incited Duke Leopold's vitriol eight years before or not, at some stage, their nation would again need defending from his troops.

+ + +

The first thing Walter noticed as the tree-shrouded path from the jetty opened onto the freshly scythed grass of the Rütli Meadow, was the sun setting flame to Magda Stauffacher's wild curls. She was standing behind a long bench, next to her sister-in-law Brigitta, serving *Most* out of a large clay jug.

Groups of people were greeting each other, old friends and distant relatives. Soldiers wandered amongst the crowds, making sure there were no Habsburg spies present. The younger attendees gaped wide-eyed at politicians and warriors they had only heard about in legends.

As his father greeted old friends, Walter was asked several times by children to recount the apple incident. Each time, he tried to entertain them with a realistic telling of his fear, holding the tension of the story in that dreaded bolt for as long as possible before it hit the mark, a vain hope that repeating the event might finally assuage the devils that plagued his dreams.

Josef and Edgar were talking to Werner Stauffacher. As Walter approached with his father, the latter broke away and greeted the two of them heartily, embracing Wilhelm and then slapping Walter on the shoulder. Josef and Edgar shook their hands. The guarded mistrust Walter had previously seen on Magda's brother's face was replaced by something he could only describe as affection.

'It's good to see you, Walti,' he said, and the diminutive use of Walter's name felt familiar rather than mocking.

Walter looked about for the Frenchmen but couldn't see them. It was right that they shouldn't be there. They weren't part of the Confederation, despite their recent promise to help train the untrained in the fundamentals of war in Schornen and Morgarten. They were still foreigners, and Walter was sure he wasn't the only one who didn't trust them completely.

Once greetings and small talk were out of the way, Walter walked across to greet Magda. She smiled openly and put down the jug she was holding. Walter manoeuvred his way around the back of the bench to kiss her three times on the cheek in the familiar greeting of people who consider themselves no longer strangers. She hesitated for a moment and looked up into his eyes. Walter couldn't for the life of him read her expression.

'Walter of Bürglen, we have missed you in the village,' she said.

The flush that rose to her cheeks made him want to dance, but the guarded look in her eye made him wary.

'I see you have set your weaving craft aside to show off your talent as a serving girl. Could you spare me a mug, *Fräulein*?'

'Stop it!' Magda laughed but picked up a mug and poured a healthy portion of the brew anyway. She handed it to Walter.

'I see you've been far from idle with your embroidery since the last time I saw you. The blossoms on your bodice are quite exquisite, and you've used some of the dye for your yarn that we made together.'

He was trying to break the ice for what he really wanted to ask.

'Together? Walti! You know the work was all mine!'

Walter pouted dramatically, feigning hurt. Magda laughed, which made him feel better.

'While I dyed the yarn, do you not remember fletching a hundred arrows?' she said. 'For that alone, our community will ever be grateful. You've found a place in the hearts of many of our people.'

But not yours? He wanted to ask. 'And is your holy work complete? Can I see the work you did for the trouble it took to procure you the madder root?' In that moment, Walter wished he hadn't asked the question. Magda's smile fell from her face and she took a deep breath. Her thoughts must have turned not to the task she had completed, but to the knights who had asked it of her.

'You know I cannot speak of this with you. It's a secret mission.'

Walter frowned, and looked around. 'If they are to save our land, just three men on their fine horses, then why aren't they at these celebrations? My father has not yet had the pleasure of meeting them, and I'm sure Stauffacher would want to introduce them to the people and have them recognise their *charitable* contribution to the Confederation's defence.' Walter regretted his sarcasm as he saw Magda's jaw clench. He wanted to hear her say that the Frenchmen had no place at these celebrations. She pressed her lips together with an expression he was sure both her father and her brother had witnessed over the years of her fighting for her place in their family.

'I... don't know. I assumed they would be here, but perhaps they will pass by later. Have you seen my uncle Werner? Doesn't he look magnificent in his commander's uniform?'

'Indeed, but a strip or two of red cloth wouldn't go amiss on his colours. The Confederation should decide on a colour for its flag. How about the colour crimson for our land? I'd make it my lifetime mission to procure you the madder root and you could be the weaver of the nation's banners.'

Magda laughed, and the tension lifted. They chatted about Mihal, how his knees had been bothering him and his sadness at having to change his favourite mule who had grown too old to carry his wares. They talked of Brigitta and Edgar's wedding, the terrible death of the little boy Jorath, how Brigitta had been forced to leave the planting fields several times over the past weeks due to sickness and how there might soon be another mouth to feed in the Stauffacher household.

It was the perfect opportunity for Walter to say that there was plenty of room in his own house and that he would happily ask Josef for her hand. But he suddenly imagined Magda living in Bürglen, with no mill for her spinning and no loom for her weaving. Still, taking a breath, he knew there was surely no better time. 'Magda, there's something I've been wanting to ask you...'

Magda's head turned towards the forest. Walter followed her gaze to where the three Frenchmen were walking together out of the trees towards the party. Their timing could not have been more unfortunate. They were without their horses, but looked no less imposing. Although dressed as civilians, there was no denying their knightly stance and their soldierly intent. Walter looked down at his messenger's clothing, feeling only slightly comforted that he was wearing the soft undershirt that Magda herself had woven with her hands, right next to his skin.

Walter stayed by Magda's side rather than return to his father. Wilhelm was occupied anyway by the usual banter with people he had not seen for many moons. But Walter didn't get a chance to restart his intended proposal. They were always surrounded by people.

The villagers from nearby carried tables to the flat part of the meadow. Walter was asked to help open the trestles and put up the benches so the feast could be enjoyed in conjunction with the speeches. By a lucky manoeuvre he managed to seat himself next to Magda at her table, when another of the women took over her turn with the serving duties. But by an equally unlucky turn, Sébastien de Molay was the man who sat at her other shoulder. Walter caught Edgar looking at all three of them, a slight frown on his face, and Walter almost laughed out loud. He wasn't the only one feeling truly confused.

Thus commenced a double ploy to gain the attention of the most eligible spinster at the table.

Before that battle could begin, a cowbell rang out at the top of the meadow and the call for silence marked the beginning of the speeches.

Werner Stauffacher stood on a sawn log to make himself visible above the crowd, though the slope of the meadow meant that he already towered above most of those present. The only person who surpassed him in height was Wilhelm Tell.

'Welcome today to the faithful and brave forest people who have travelled from far and wide to help celebrate the anniversary of the Confederation, only two dozen years old,' he began. 'I'd like to be able to tell you that our farms and forests are secure, but there has been a growing threat.'

There were mumbles and whisperings in the crowd.

'The security and safety of our borders is once again in jeopardy,' Werner continued. 'We have three brave young men from France to thank for agreeing to show our farmers how to wield weapons. Anyone whose communities straddle our borders can take something away from their teachings. If you have a chance today, it would be good to listen to how those of you who are not salaried soldiers can help defend the Confederation.'

Walter leaned towards Magda while all heads were turned towards the commander.

'I am surprised the presence of your friends has been accepted so readily by Commander Stauffacher and his army. I would have thought military pride would prohibit any outside help.'

'You still speak of them as if they are the enemy, Walti,' she whispered back. 'When will you accept that they are here to help us? We have protected them as fugitives and they are returning the favour. They have been in conversations with my uncle and his generals as allies, not enemies.'

Magda's tone bordered on affection for the Frenchmen. Walter felt his head go hot. Had something happened between Sébastien and Magda?

'Do you remember our discussion about the three feathers the day we made the arrows and the dye in your kitchen?' he asked.

'Of course, I shall never forget. It means that in a time when every man in our village is taken in battle, I shall still be around to fletch an arrow or two. Our next adventure, Walti, will be to teach ourselves how to use the weapon from which they fly.'

Walter bit his lip.

'Remember I told you about the strongest feather, the cock? Look at how we are spinning around you like the hen feathers. I believe you are that stabilising point for us, Magda, but it would be useful for all of us to know where your arrow will eventually land.'

Walter could tell she was wrestling with something in her conscience. He wanted her to know he was still there for her. He suspected the Frenchmen weren't intending to settle long in the Aegeri Valley. Magda remained silent, but Walter wasn't expecting an answer. Not here. Not now.

His conversation hadn't gone quite to plan. By the end of the afternoon, Walter still hadn't had a chance to address his feelings further for her. And he was less than happy to be travelling back to Bürglen in the opposite direction to Magda and the Frenchman.

Chapter Twenty-Six

2nd August 1315, return to Schornen

SÉBASTIEN

'What is so special about this thing you're keeping a secret?' asked Magda. 'I've heard you and Yves and Grégoire discussing it. I don't understand everything you're saying, but I can tell from your voices it's very important to you.'

It was more than four moons since the knights first rode into Schornen, and Magda's keen ear was apparently picking up some of their language. The knights should have been practising caution when discussing their plans.

'It's an object cast from the mysterious power of God Himself,' Sébastien said, urging his horse over a washed-out section of trail.

They were returning to the Aegeri Valley, a journey that would take two days. Yves and Grégoire had ridden on ahead to Einsiedeln to prepare for what they now referred to as 'the extraction'. Magda was astride Obéron while Sébastien remained on foot, leading him by the reins. They could both have settled comfortably on the horse's back, but Edgar was ahead of them, walking, and it would not have been appropriate for them to share the mount, although

Sébastien had thought of nothing else since they disembarked at Brunnen. Sitting with Magda in front of him on Obéron's back would have been a far greater pleasure than walking in his heavy boots. But that very action would likely lead to a yearning neither of them could satisfy and it wasn't fair to Magda to be leading her on any more. The way she looked at him hopefully... she was expecting him to ask Josef for her hand. He wished he hadn't weakened that day in the lake. He should have been more responsible. Their union had been something powerful, something divine. But after this was all over, she would undoubtedly end up getting hurt. Their cause had no room for a wife.

He'd planned to break this gently to her on the way home, but Edgar was with them constantly and Sébastien didn't want the inevitable emotional scene such a declaration would lead to.

'This thing is cast from His mysterious power? That sounds more like a mighty weapon to me,' said Magda. 'Is it something to be carried in battle?'

'In a way. Our armies are ultimately controlled by the Church. Unfortunately this still means there is anguish and sometimes brutal killing. I suppose it could be considered a weapon if it got into the wrong hands.'

'Surely God wishes us to learn humility and respect for each other. I don't believe he ever intended us to raise weapons and go to war,' said Magda.

'That's another subject altogether – the digression of men – but this object has a special history. One that is completely the opposite of death and destruction.'

'You're being mysterious now, Séb. I hope you'll tell me this object's history when you're ready. Are you guarding any more secrets from God?'

'I don't keep anything from God. I just don't believe in Him the same way many others do. It is something we knights often discuss. We worship Jesus Christ and God Himself. The people of the

Holy Roman Empire answer to the Pope. And the Pope's special belief has turned my stomach in the last years. How can one person have sole access to God's thoughts and intentions? That was the privilege of Jesus, His son. And the Pope is not Jesus.' Sébastien chewed on his lip, pulling his cropped beard upwards with his teeth. Had he said too much? This philosophy was perhaps too complicated for a weaver girl to understand.

'Look at how we've been punished with the drought,' she said. 'Our people are good; they pray and work. But still he chooses to starve us. He's not always kind, and that is confusing sometimes.'

'I agree fear does not always harbour respect.'

'Take the story of Noah. Surely that's not true. Can you imagine enough water to fill our valleys to the tops of the peaks? I thought it might happen in spring, but really, it's impossible. If God was attempting to purge the evil people, why do the likes of Heinrich von Hünenberg still walk this earth? Sometimes I wonder whether these stories have been made up to promote the Church's inter-pretation of what is right and wrong without those events actually happening. Those with power will always try and fool the people. If you're a good person, you should know this deep in your heart.'

'You are very perceptive, *ma belle*. With the right teaching, you could become a wise sister,' he said with a smile.

'Hmm, a nun.' Magda narrowed her eyes. '*Monsieur*, do not forget that I – we – have already sinned in the eyes of God. He would not allow me to wear the habit, and if he could, he would probably strip you of your crusading banner at the same time.'

Deep down inside, he was still torn about the divinity of their union. He placed his hand briefly on her thigh, bouncing gently against the saddle. His hand felt the heat of her skin all the way through her skirts. She would make someone a fine and passionate wife one day. But he could not take her as his own. He was already committed to another cause.

He would have to tell her soon.

Chapter Twenty-Seven

12th August 1315, Morgarten

MAGDA

Sébastien, Yves and Grégoire were now deeply involved in teaching the young and old of both villages their fighting techniques. One sultry afternoon when Magda's work at the chalet was complete and she had no desire to weave in the heat, she and Brigitta made their way to the field between the villages where they had set up what resembled a theatre for battle.

The knights had fashioned three bodies from reeds stuffed into hemp bags no longer fit for grain. They tied the openings with willow saplings and attached them to stakes driven into the ground. Old and broken baskets topped two of the figures to resemble heads, and on the third they used an overripe gourde riddled with worm and not fit for a soup.

Using a handful of halberds that had been brought from the garrison in Altdorf, the Frenchmen showed the villagers how to use the weapons, slicing the axe blades at the bodies and turning the lance heads to pierce their torsos. If all else failed, and the shaft of the weapon should break, the Frenchmen showed them it could be used as defence against enemy swords. Magda initially saw little point in using such a narrow piece of wood as a shield, but Grégoire demonstrated by placing one foot behind the other for strength and thrusting a piece of wood in various positions across the faces of the figures, which would surely have broken their noses and cheekbones if they had been real soldiers, even wearing helmets.

Edgar was amongst the crowd of men, listening intently to the knights' instructions. Yves handed him a halberd and pointed to the figure with the gourd-head. Someone had drawn an angry face on it with a charred stick.

The crowd of men were lethargic in the heat, wiping their brows on their arms. They could barely hold their halberds upright.

'They will never be able to fight off Habsburg soldiers. Look how weak they all are,' said Magda.

'Eddi will fare better,' said Brigitta. 'Look how his muscles flex. All those years at the mill have strengthened his shoulders.'

Magda smiled to hear Brigitta speak of her brother so. They had been married barely two moons, and they were still as in love with each other as the day Edgar reached manhood some years before. Magda's gaze flicked wistfully to Sébastien. Since their return from the Rütli Meadow more than a week ago, he had made no effort to try and meet her alone, and Magda's confusion was growing.

'Isn't he handsome?' said Brigitta.

'Hmm,' said Magda and then cleared her throat when she realised Brigitta wasn't talking about Sébastien but about her brother. They turned to watch Edgar. He faced the puppets on their stakes in a warrior's stance. Yves addressed him and the other men with a raised voice. Magda hoped the valley had been scouted for Habsburg spies.

'Imagine these are your enemies. You must summon the strength from here.' Yves thumped his torso. 'Use anger to drive your determination. Think of the Habsburgs stealing your crops and herds, using your hard labour to surrender to the Duke who sits in the Habsburg Castle in Aargau feeding his fancies. Once he has conquered your land, imagine him taking your women and using them for his pleasure, dragging them back to his dungeons. When he has achieved his victory here, you will all be fodder for the rest of his filthy clan!'

The men roared and Edgar's brows furrowed as he pressed his mouth in determination. He ran at the effigy, raising his arms. The curved axe-edge of the halberd glinted in the hazy sun. He brought the blade down on the gourd and it split asunder, pieces of stringy flesh and seeds splashing to the ground. He drove the blade of the halberd into the heart of the figure, and a crack echoed through the forest as the stake holding the model soldier snapped like a twig.

There was a moment of silence.

'*Verdammt*!' shouted Edgar. 'We will eliminate the Habsburg filth from our land!'

The crowd cheered. Men gathered around him to clap him on the shoulder. Grégoire tried in vain to reconstruct their number three Habsburg soldier as the men took their place in the queue to practise their battle moves. But the gourd was unsalvageable and the hessian torso had split asunder. It had spilled its contents of seeds like the guts of a mortally wounded peasant.

Magda was impressed with the incitement, but doubtful about the numbers of men who'd turned up for training. When she turned, she noticed her sister-in-law had gone pale and was staring at the yellow mess on the ground amongst the broken pieces of gourd flesh. Brigitta held her stomach, and Magda managed to catch her before she collapsed to the ground in a faint.

She'd suspected, but now it was confirmed. A new member of the family would soon be amongst them to help defend their land. Her smile faltered, not because she would soon be sharing a noisy house with a new niece or nephew, but because by the time the little one had grown tall enough to hold a halberd, she hoped desperately that they would still *be* a Confederation.

Chapter Twenty-Eight

29th August 1315, Schornen

SÉBASTIEN

L a canicule had lasted even longer than the never-ending rains in spring. The fear of too much water back then when the knights were trapped in the flatlands outside the Confederation was now a distant memory compared to the disaster of parched fields around the Aegeri Valley in this heat-wave. The ribs of the cattle and sheep grew more prominent every day. The farmers could bring the animals to drink from the Aegerisee, but the grass had stopped growing.

This was the season farmers should have been filling their barns with hay in preparation for the winter, so the worry extended beyond when the weather would finally break. The bounty Magda brought to the table in the form of meat-rich meals was shadowed by the fact that almost every day Sébastien and his colleagues were asked to slaughter the cows that had become too weak to stand. Magda's smoking racks couldn't cope with the volume. Red flesh had started to taste bitter on all their tongues.

The stream running down to the mill from the pass had ceased to flow, despite Magda telling Sébastien in spring that this had never happened in her lifetime. The pond next to the mill became stagnant with thick weeds clogging the surface until it dried up altogether. Mosquitoes thrived and no one could escape the stink from the centre of the hamlet.

Even the flies seemed to have abandoned the cows on the pasture, which meant there were an abundance of them around the toll tower and in the Stauffacher chalet. Added to the oppressive heat, indoors was the last place anyone wanted to be.

There was coolness up in the forest where the slope faced the north. One morning, a shepherd reported seeing a suspected spy on the ridge below the Wildspitz. Sébastien, Yves and Grégoire left their horses in Schornen and climbed the ridge on foot through the forest to patrol the slope and see off any marauders.

It was a particularly sultry afternoon. The type of weather that might fray tempers. The men crept stealthily through the pines beneath the ridge. In addition to seeing off intruders, they took the opportunity to study the ridge opposite the lake for a notion that had come to Yves the week before. In the event of an attack, they would take advantage of the land itself to defend Morgarten and Schornen.

As a twig snapped under Grégoire's foot, the dry undergrowth rustled ahead of the men and they spotted movement through the ferns. With rapid hand signals to form a triangle, Sébastien advanced on a figure creeping through the forest. When the other two had encircled the intruder with two short whistles to each other, he shouted at the figure.

'*Sors de là, allez-vous en!*'

The man, for now he could see this was no beast, ran up to the ridge where Grégoire and Yves would intercept the trespasser. As he turned to join his colleagues, a flash of golden material caught his eye down the slope. Was a second trespasser hiding in the trees?

As he slid down the steep slope, weapon drawn, he discovered it was no stranger. '*Voilà ma biche!*'

'Sébastien! How long were you watching me?' Magda gasped, her eyes misted with the guilt of having been caught taking a nap.

His shout must have awoken her. She was struggling to sit up, a hand at her chest.

'I have not been *spying* on you, Magda. I have saved you from a surely savage death,' he said, although he suspected the interloper was nothing more than a hunter, wandering into Confederate territory by mistake, rather than a Habsburg spy with fatal intentions.

'Oh no! A marauder? I might have been slain. How stupid of me to have fallen asleep.' Her voice expressed fear, but there was a glint in her eye. 'When I first heard movement, I thought you might be a fox or a chamois, but a stealthy animal would not make such a noise.'

Sébastien smiled and hummed acquiescence. He looked about them. This part of the forest barely saw the sun, even in high summer. The trees offered a wisp of coolness with the occasional breath of air. It filtered through to take the weight off the stuffiness in the valley. Magda sat up and leaned her back against a tree. A basket lay at her side. Sébastien bent down and peered in. A few blackberries lay in the bottom. He took one and pressed it against the roof of his mouth. A cool sweetness burst on his tongue.

'I didn't have much luck; this is a paltry collection,' said Magda. 'They look desiccated from having spent too long on the bushes. This year's brambles will give a sparse harvest.'

'You're much too close to Habsburg territory,' said Sébastien. His boots crunched across last year's fallen larch needles as he sheathed his sword and helped her stand up. Forest debris, needles and leaves fell from her skirt. She must have been sleeping a while.

'Let's head back to the village. I'll help you down the slope.'

Their boot heels stamped the steep slope to take hold, releasing the intoxicating smell of balsam and pine. Glimpses of the lake sparkled through the trees – a deep turquoise from the algae growing in the increasingly warm waters. There was a deep tinge of something ominous reflected from the sky, and Sébastien prayed it would not be long before there was rain in the valley. It was true, none of them could stand this sultry heat much longer.

'Why were you following me?'

'I get no thanks from the fair maiden for saving her skin?'

'Of course, thank you. I'm sorry. My fright made me speak out of turn. I hadn't intended to keep my outing secret, but... we are in the middle of nowhere. Were you purposely looking for me?'

'You should exercise caution, *ma belle*. You have no idea who could be seeking the cool of the forest up here.'

'And so what were *you* doing here in the first place?' she asked with a hint of suspicion.

'Surveying the forest and chasing away a trespasser with Yves and Grégoire. Then I found you sleeping, your beautiful neck exposed and ready to meet a Habsburg dagger.'

Magda frowned and put her hand to her throat.

At that moment they heard a whistle somewhere above them in the trees, two short and one long rising and falling tone. Sébastien replied with four clipped whistles through his lips.

'Grégoire and Yves have chased away the intruder. It must have been a hunter rather than a spy. It is unlikely they have bloodied their swords. They'll come down via the ridge to avoid showering us with rocks and forest debris. We'll see them at the bottom.'

'You conveyed all that information to each other in a series of whistles and four short peeps?' she asked, her grumpiness forgotten for a moment.

'We've worked so long together, we know how to communicate the essentials. We anticipate each other's reactions.'

'Do they *know* about... us?'

Sébastien couldn't lie. But he didn't need to confirm it. Magda could see it on his face.

'The very same unspoken knowledge that passes between you and I,' he said. Did she feel sullied somehow? That was never his intention. Though the whole affair had been a mistake, he could not change what had happened between them. He never boasted about her with his colleagues. But at this point, probably nothing he could say would make her believe it.

Even in the heat, her sweat-dampened blouse open at her neck and the delicate bone at her collar was crying out for his fingers. What he wouldn't give to lie down with her on the cool moss of the forest floor.

But there was enough of his duty to the Templars and enough of her dignity to protect to fight the desire. She was compelled to deny him something she still wanted as much as she did, for he could see it through this mood she had fallen into. She would only let them both have what they desired with a promise of commitment. And he couldn't give it.

'What were you looking for?' she asked, interrupting his thoughts.

'Apart from the trespasser, we've been studying the ridge across the valley. We think we have an alternative plan of defence if we can't provide enough troops and weapons to face up to Leopold's army.'

Magda peered through the trees, the top of the ridge opposite obscured by pine branches at this level.

'What miracle did you see up there to save our village then?'

Her sarcastic tone warned Sébastien she was still not in the mood for jesting. 'A steep slope, loose rock, boulders with the capacity to roll, and an army of tree trunks ready for battle.'

Magda looked at him sceptically. 'I don't know why you keep up this farce. You know as well as I do there are not enough weapons to defend the gateway to the Confederation. There are not enough capable men to ward off a thousand Habsburg troops. Why do you keep up their expectations? If all our men die, who will harvest the fields, turn the mill, father our children? We will be nothing without them.'

'Oh Magda, you have little faith. You have truly relinquished your belief. Your men have grown proud, are enthusiastic about their new abilities to defend and possibly even attack. They feel useful. They feel patriotic. They understand the importance of keeping something that has become theirs through generations of caring for the land and the riches it provides. Belief can work wonders for an army, no matter how small.'

At the word 'belief' Sébastien now wondered whether he was doubting his own.

'Well I for one cannot *believe* God continues to punish us by keeping the rains from us. Perhaps I have never understood His seemingly random choice of who gets to survive or experience happiness or remain sickness-free throughout their lives. How can people have belief in the face of such continuing tragedies?'

Her dark mood deepened, and it seemed nothing Sébastien could say would drag her from it.

'If you did not have two sides of the fortune, Magda, you would have nothing to compare to paradise.'

She stopped, and put her hand to her forehead.

'I'm sorry, the heat is making me fractious. With so many cattle dying, it's hard to remain faithful.'

'Then we should discuss something more cheerful than battle plans and the victims of drought.'

He leaned towards her with the intention of supporting her on their descent through the trees, but her mood had sunk to the extent that she snatched her arm away from him and continued her journey down un-aided, using the trees to rest against like stepping stones.

'Is a kiss and the feel of my body the only thing you want of me? To lure me into sewing your secrets and keeping you fed? This is hardly the moment for folly.'

'I was only trying to help,' he said, realising she had misinterpreted his approach.

When they reached the shore of the lake, Sébastien was shocked to see how far the water had receded since they had swum together several weeks before. The beach had widened to a band of rounded grey pebbles scattered with the dried sticks of last year's reed stalks. The heat hit them out of the shelter of the forest and a deafening chorus of crickets robbed the senses.

He waited while Magda looked longingly at the water. 'I must get back to the village,' she said abruptly. 'I will be missed.'

'The entire village is under the soporific spell of the heatwave. No one will miss you. I can guard you if you care to bathe, Magda.'

'Like last time? Is your mind only on one thing? Where's your piety, and right after we have been speaking of the Lord himself. If you want me that badly, you can ask Papa for my hand.'

Without waiting for an answer or to see how her comment was received, Magda swung the basket onto her arm and made her way back to the village, finding a path almost directly across the swamp instead of along the shore. The marsh had dried so hard, Sébastien could have put his fists between the cracks in the mud.

In her current mood, he wasn't ready to tell her why asking for her hand was an impossibility.

CHAPTER TWENTY-NINE
6th September 1315, Schornen
MAGDA

'Suspicion must not fall on the Confederates.' A French accent brought Magda around from a deep slumber. 'So those who might still support Leopold will turn against him once and for all.'

The sound of pots and bowls being moved around her kitchen fully wakened her. Daylight shone through the edges of the shutter on the far side of the bed, telling her the day was not yet over. But she couldn't place the time. There were several people in the chalet. She lay quietly in the sleeping alcove, disorientated by the unaccustomed sleep in the afternoon.

'We shall need to redirect the scent onto those Habsburg pigs if we are to convince the people of their lack of trustworthiness.' She recognised the voice as Uncle Werner's.

'It serves two purposes. Our reward, and disinformation for the people. They are already worried about your lack of resources, troops and weapons,' said Sébastien.

Magda heard Papa's grunt of agreement.

'We have to stir them for the fight, stamp out the indifference to a possible Habsburg rule. Eliminate their lethargy,' said Edgar.

'How will we lead the abbot off the scent? We have to retrieve this object.' Now Yves was speaking.

What object?

She lay still, not wanting to let on that she was in the house, unsure what they were talking about.

'I think I know just the person,' said Edgar. 'Walter Tell. If we can drip-feed the boy enough information about the movement of Leopold's army and Confederate raids due to this damned drought, he'll ascertain a picture of the theft that will seem real to both sides. He is thorough in his work, so we must be even more thorough in our deception. You must leave him clues.'

Theft? What *deception* were they talking about? It sounded like they were dropping Walter in something he knew nothing about. Magda suddenly felt protective towards Walter. She had more respect for him than her own brother.

'The Tell boy must never find out,' said her father.

Magda had heard enough. She moved her legs over the edge of the cot and strode towards the kitchen barefoot. She threw the curtain back. She was livid that they didn't think she was old enough to keep their secrets. Of everyone now in the kitchen, she was the one who had the closest ties to Walter. Magda focused on the face of her father staring back up at her in surprise, matching the faces of the other men at the table.

'What must Walter never find out?' she asked, looking from one face to the other.

Magda instantly berated herself for her impatience. It might have been better for her to stay where she was, hidden behind the curtain in the alcove, in order to find out more about what was going on. Looking from man to man, she met only closed faces.

Sébastien turned to her, the intensity of his stare making the blood rise to her cheeks. She'd been mistaken, thinking she could walk in on this conversation. Although Walter treated her as his equal, these men did not. The last thing any of them wanted, as she stood in what was no longer her own kitchen, was her opinion on Walter Tell.

Her gaze wavered from Sébastien's face to her family sitting at the darkened end of the table. Uncle Werner's bearded face looked grave, his eyes creased as though the sun was in them. A vertical groove in the space between his brows accentuated his seriousness. He darted his brother a look.

'You'll not utter a word of what you have heard, Magda.' Her father was angry.

'Of course not, Papa,' she said with less aggression. 'I should not have interrupted you.'

If the others hadn't been in the chalet, he might have raised a broom to her hip. She'd spoken out of turn.

Magda narrowed her eyes. This was no longer about her friendship with Walter. Or trying to protect him from a miscarriage of justice. This was about something altogether far more serious. Sébastien's jaw was set, and Magda had no idea what was going through his mind. Could he have been jealous about her question, that she showed so much concern for Walter? She said nothing more. Should she be more concerned for Walter's safety or for the deception that Sébastien seemed to be hatching with her family?

☩ ☩ ☩

'You should be careful about showing your emotions when others are around,' Sébastien said.

They were sitting in the shade on the steps leading up to the tower. The setting sun was hitting the west walls of the chalet across the courtyard. The flies were enjoying the warm wood on the side of the house in the dying heat of the day. Magda watched the insects as they took off and settled, searching for some tiny sustenance, their shiny green bodies glinting in the sun.

'Your feelings are easy to interpret,' continued Sébastien. 'It's those pretty grey eyes. Like silver. I know you're feeling as though I have somehow taken advantage. You are mistaken about my love for you, Magda. It is there. It's just that I have other... responsibilities.'

'Is there someone else you've never told me about? Did you leave behind a wife, a family in France?'

'No. I've not had time for such things. My marriage is to something altogether bigger. Although you are truly irresistible, my heart is not completely yours to take.'

'You can have mine, if it would help.' She bit her lip. Offering something for nothing was not her usual trade.

'I know I have that,' he said with a sad smile. It's just... I'm constantly battling to keep space there for an obligation, the goal, if you like. It is not a person I have pledged my allegiance to. It is the Holy Spirit. And now you come along, and you're eating away at little pieces of that, and I must not sway from my mission. If I suddenly disappear, you must not pine for me, Magda. I'm so sorry, I know it's not what you want to hear, but I will never be yours.'

Magda felt a great stone in her throat. When she swallowed it away, tears still threatened to spill. And then the fire of anger roiled in her gut. That was perhaps the easiest emotion to anchor to. To protect some of her dignity. Although the intensity of it soon made her feel quite ill.

'You might have told me that before you cast your magic on my body. I'm already past the age a woman normally marries.'

'We are a paragon, you and I, Magda. Like Mary Magdalena and Christ. Lovers with no future. You even have her name.'

'They were only lovers in spirit, surely?'

He tipped his head, but did not deny it. 'As much as they wanted each other, they could never marry. His responsibilities were too great. She knew that in the end.' He paused. 'You will still make someone else a very good wife.'

Magda sighed. She didn't want to hear pity in Sébastien's voice. The mixture of emotions was not sitting well and she was overcome with a feeling of nausea, the disgust, at the advantage he had taken of her, bubbling like a bad mushroom in her gut.

CHAPTER THIRTY

19th September 1315, Schornen

WALTER

The storm broke about an hour out of Schwyz. Walter almost turned around and returned to the barracks. He could stay there until the painful pelting of hail had ceased. But it was clear after the rumbling of thunder which had started early that morning that this storm was likely to go on all afternoon and through the night. He had to deliver the latest weaponry details to Josef in Schornen in all haste. And after all, he didn't mind the soaking as it cooled the anticipatory heat of seeing Magda again.

Once on the lower slopes of the great Mythens, though, Walter felt frighteningly exposed. Lightning bolts were striking all around and thunder bellowed between the peaks. His clothes and pack were soaked through. He hoped the rains wouldn't last for more than a few days so he could eventually dry everything out. On the other hand, the land had been parched for many weeks. Walter could almost feel the earth sighing with the pleasure of sucking in some much-needed water.

The track grew slippery, with the hard ground unable to absorb the first downpour.

Walter reached the saddle of the pass in the middle of the night. To avoid waking everyone in Schornen, he bivouacked in the forest. It was still raining when he awoke from a restless sleep. Although the temperature had not dropped much, the fact that he had not moved all night in soaked clothes brought on a bout of shivering.

When he walked down to the hamlet from the pass after first light, he glimpsed the three horses of the Frenchmen tied in the shelter of the barn at the back of the courtyard. His heart dropped. He'd hoped they would be on one of their mysterious missions, somewhere far to the south.

A thin wisp of smoke rose straight up from the Stauffacher's chalet, defying the pressing weight of the rain. Either Magda or her sister-in-law would be preparing a hot drink for breakfast. He hoped they could spare an extra cup around the table.

'Walti! How wonderful to see you! It has been so long,' Magda greeted him. 'Thank you for bringing the rains. I wonder if you could lighten the intensity for us though, most of it is running straight off the land into the lake.'

'I'll do my best, if you can spare a warm broth or a tea for this cold, damp soul.'

Walter waved his hand at the sky in the gesture of a sorcerer. As though his spell had worked, the rain began to ease. A brightness infused the still-thick clouds, likely the result of the sun rising over the pass to the east. Magda stopped in the middle of the courtyard, one hand clutching the milk pail handle, the other clamped over her open mouth in surprise. She stared at Walter through the drizzle.

'I assure you that was not my doing,' he said.

Magda laughed. 'You shall nevertheless be rewarded, Walti. Come and warm yourself at the table. Papa, Eddi and Brigitta are stirring. Your company will be welcome.'

He followed her up the stairs to the kitchen, glancing once towards the toll tower where the knights must be sleeping.

Magda served a fine porridge for breakfast with a warmed compote of blackberries.

'It's the first hot meal I've enjoyed since the beginning of the heatwave,' she said. 'Thank goodness it broke yesterday. It's also the first time I have not minded lighting the fire. I hope autumn will not be thrust upon us too early. We still need the grass to grow a little to feed the skinny cattle and cut hay for the winter months.'

The sweet smell of the warmed fruit brought everyone to the table. Josef seemed genuinely pleased to see Walter. Edgar was concerned for his wife, who hurried out of the chalet to attend to her morning toilet with hardly a greeting. He followed her outside.

'With child,' said Josef, waving his spoon in her direction. A speck of milky oats landed on the end of the table. 'Can hardly hold her water for a few hours at a time. We are only at the beginning and already the babe takes up all the room in there.'

'Papa!' admonished Magda, but lay her hand affectionately on his shoulder as she carried the pot back to the stove.

Edgar came back alone.

'She'll be back shortly. She's delicate. Let's hope it means the lad is strong,' he muttered.

Another expectant father referring to his future child as a son. Walter wanted to tell him boys might be a lot less trouble, but without women the likes of Magda, their lives would be a much harder place.

'I brought a current list of weapons from the garrisons in Schwyz and Altdorf and an assurance from your brother that they should be able to mobilise within a day if necessary. I think you can rest a little safer, knowing there is a contingency plan and a warning system.'

'Except the entire number of troops we can muster will still not equal even one of Leopold's garrisons,' said Josef. 'And by the time we see them coming, it may be too late. I'd like *that* message to be taken back to Werner.'

'The knights are waking,' said Edgar, coming in from outside. 'They're planning to head up to the north-eastern ridge today to ascertain the damage from the rains. The trails will need to be kept open if we are to enable rapid access for the men from the village. Completing their training is more important than ever.'

'Perhaps you'd like to go with them, Walti? I think it would be good for you to see first-hand the resourcefulness of the men and the potential natural weapons and tools we have available to us up there. I think you'll be surprised.'

The last thing Walter wanted to do was spend a day with the Frenchmen, but he could see the sense of being able to take back their ideas and to deliver a clear plan of the physical positions of defence to his father and the commander's garrison in Altdorf. For all his passionate pacifism, they were sharing ever more strategic details with him.

'Can I go with them, Papa?' Magda asked.

Walter marvelled at her continued curiosity at what was going on in the world.

'No, for goodness sake, you will stay here. It's too hazardous up there on the slope. There is still a danger of mudslides, not to mention Habsburg infiltrators.'

'Are you upset that I would dirty my skirts, or that I might not be back in time to prepare your lunch, Papa? Why do you never let me go on adventures?'

'Aren't you a little old for that, my dear daughter?'

Josef turned to Walter. 'The more she whines, the more I think it's time I married her off,' he said and guffawed.

Magda looked painfully awkward and all Walter could do was blush. It would have been the perfect opportunity to tell Josef he would be happy to take her off his hands, but Edgar was pulling his beard at the end of the table with a look on his face that was enough to keep Walter silent.

✣ ✣ ✣

The rain eased to a light drizzle as Walter walked reluctantly with the Frenchmen up the trail to the north-eastern ridge. The penetrating heat of the sun gradually forged through the clouds, causing a steamy humidity to rise up through the trees.

The path had washed out in two places, but with the aid of branches cut from trees with their *baselards* and placed across the slippery gulley, they were able to pass. The knights would send a group of men up from the village to reinforce the path with stakes and logs when the rain had completely stopped.

'It's unlikely the Habsburgs will attack now. The rains have made the swamp impassable and they would have nothing to feed their troops, with the food stocks so low in the village. I believe we shall have a reprieve for the next month at least,' said Sébastien.

Walter bristled at the use of the word 'we'. These men would never be true Confederates. He clenched his jaw and remained silent.

As they climbed higher towards the ridge, the forest opened up to a small clearing. A great dark object lay across the shepherd's path leading to the high pasture.

'It's a stag! Judging by his antlers he was an old fellow. What a beauty!' said Grégoire in French.

'What, or, should I say, who do you think could have killed it?' asked Yves.

Walter didn't want to let on that he'd understood, but walked around the bulk of the animal's body. A handsome burnished mane flowed fluffy and blood-free down the animal's neck. He put his hand on its magnificent antlers. 'He was struck by lightning,' Walter said in wonder. 'Look how his left antler is charred, and his eye is milky. There are marks on his shoulder, the fur is singed. And look!' He lifted a chunk of flesh the size of a fist that had blown clean out of the stag's rump. It was lying an arm's length beyond the body with flies now buzzing over it.

'It must have happened last night. The maggots have not yet hatched.'

'We'll split the carcass between the four of us. He could be a tough one, but a little venison will be a pleasure tonight after the old mutton and stringy beef we've been eating,' said Grégoire.

Walter was tempted to defend Magda's cooking, knowing she would have been the one preparing their meals. Yves and Grégoire continued to survey the area for the lie of the land, the looseness of the rocks and the potential for logging, while Sébastien and Walter set about butchering the meat. Walter felt Sébastien's eyes on him as he split the animal down its belly to haul the weight of its guts out of the carcass and leave it on the mountain.

'Less to carry,' said Walter, and Sébastien nodded.

As Walter worked, Sébastien sat back on his haunches.

'If anything should happen to me, Walter, I want to know that you will look after Magda.'

Walter looked sharply at him but held his tongue, something he had done too much of over the past weeks. Sébastien's presumption that Magda was somehow already his made Walter seethe inside.

'I know you consider her a... special woman,' continued Sébastien.

Walter felt his face redden and was angry at his own inability to hide his feelings. But it finally loosened his tongue. 'How can you presume to know what I feel?' he said. 'Are you implying that I am second best? Or second choice? Have you already asked for her hand?'

'No... I... It's not so simple.'

For the first time Walter heard uncertain confusion in Sébastien's voice. Jealousy was inflaming Walter's emotions and he felt a tiny thrill of satisfaction. 'What are your plans, you and your men? I can't imagine a guardian's wage for the safeguard of some mysterious goods will satisfy you for long.'

Sébastien tipped his head. 'We may be moving on by the end of the year. I know you are aware of our history, what the Knights Templar stand for. Even though King Louis and the current Pope are seeking to have us destroyed, there are others who know God's work needs to continue in the Holy Lands. Those who do not denounce us will help us to avoid the men who think they can manipulate God's will.'

Walter was relieved that the Frenchmen might soon be leaving the valley. What could be so important that it would carry them away from somewhere they'd felt safe over the past weeks? He vowed not to let Sébastien take Magda with him.

'I will always do what's best for Magda.' Walter paused. 'But not because you have asked it of me. We are... close. You cannot take her away from her family, her world.'

He wanted to see a reaction, but Sébastien simply smiled, and Walter wondered about the extent of his feelings for her.

'Although I have the feeling that's exactly what she is craving,' said Sébastien. 'But in reality a life on the road would not be a suitable one for her. There will soon be no room for everyone in that chalet, with the first of what I'm sure will be many babies on the way for Edgar and Brigitta.'

Walter was beginning to feel uncomfortable with the conversation turning to domestic matters. They both knew Magda would make a good wife. His one fear was that should Magda be presented with two proposals, who would she choose? He hacked angrily through the last of the bones, separating limbs from the stag. He didn't need this Frenchman worming any more emotional opinions out of him. 'Let's get this meat down to the village before it becomes fly-blown and begins to rot,' he said.

They tied the two halves of the carcass to strong branches. When Yves and Grégoire returned from the ridge, the four of them carried an end each down the path, leaving the animal's entrails for the crows and foxes.

They feasted on venison that night, and Walter's belly was warm and full when he went to his bivouac in the forest, preferring to stay there rather than the tower with the Frenchmen. The night was not clear, but the rain had ceased, and he tied an oiled cloth between three trees above him to keep any sudden shower from soaking his bedroll before settling down to sleep.

In the dead of the moonless night Walter was awoken by the sound of horses' hooves. He wasn't sure of the time. In the darkness and with the sounds coming from the courtyard, it seemed the knights were saddling up their beasts, attempting to prepare their departure with as little noise as possible. They quietly led their horses away from the hamlet before mounting them. As he strained to listen, he ascertained they were heading up towards the pass, away from the Aegerital, into the Confederation. He wondered if this signalled their permanent departure, especially after what Sébastien had asked him the day before.

He fell back to sleep and by the time he awoke it was well past dawn. As he sat up and pulled the creases out of his clothes, he realised he must have dreamed about the Frenchmen leaving in the night. Their horses were still tied under the shelter, saddled up and ready to ride out. He shook his head, tidied his pack and made his way to the courtyard. As he passed the horses, one of them stamped and puffed, and Walter put his hand onto the beast's rump to reassure it of his presence as he passed. Its pelt was sticky with sweat and a thin lather laced the area around its flank. Walter frowned, and headed to the trough to splash water on his face, thinking it must have been the humid weather that caused both him and the horses to sleep so fitfully.

Later that afternoon, Walter sat at the table with the others to whet the stag pelt so Magda could begin tanning. Edgar had asked him to stay a day longer to help with the task. The teamwork was efficient. Edgar and Sébastien removed the antlers from the beast's head and cut them into sections to use later as hilts for tools or weapons. Magda served them hunks of fresh bread, herb butter and mugs of *Most*. The mood was jovial, brother and sister happily commenting on the re-growth of the pasture and the return of the water level to a regular flow so the wheel could turn at the mill.

The echo of a call against the walls of the valley and the stumble of a donkey's hoof on the rocky trail down from the pass drew their attention. A young monk waved frantically from the beast's bare back. Sébastien and Edgar stood up in alarm.

'He brings bad news. Do you think we should prepare for battle?' asked Edgar, collecting the mugs with an air of urgency.

'No, wait,' said Sébastien. 'If this was about mobilisation they would have sent a soldier. He's not a military messenger. Let's wait to hear what he has to say.'

'What is it, brother? What has happened?' Edgar asked, as the monk approached.

'It's the abbey, sir... sirs. It's been sacked.'

'Einsiedeln? Sacked? What madness do you speak?' asked Walter.

Josef came up from the mill to see what the fuss was about.

'The abbey at Einsiedeln has been sacked, Papa,' Magda said.

Josef told the monk to sit. Magda poured him a mug of *Most*.

'What happened, brother?' Josef asked, shooting a look at Sébastien that Walter could not interpret.

'It happened in the night. Several valuable items were stolen. One of the other brothers tried to stop the thieves and was injured in the confrontation. They don't think he will make it through the day.'

Sébastien drew in his breath, and looked at Yves. Magda's hand flew to her mouth. 'Oh! I have just finished sewing an order of robes for the abbot. This is a terrible thing.'

'Do they know or suspect the identity of the thieves?' Grégoire asked.

The monk shook his head. 'No, but I have to go to Altdorf after this, so Stauffacher's troops can be made aware of the theft. The small garrison in Einsiedeln is in disarray. The soldiers there are far from capable.'

Josef cleared his throat. 'It sounds to me like your tracking skills might be required, Walter. You must go to Einsiedeln. I'm sure the church will reward you if you can give them any clues as to this terrible crime.'

Walter was sure the abbot had intelligent brothers in his midst who could pick apart this theft. Above all, it was now some time since the thieves had left the abbey. He thought it a little odd that Josef was insisting on his engagement when Einsiedeln was a day's walk away.

But Walter, naturally, was willing to take up the challenge.

CHAPTER THIRTY-ONE

20th September 1315, Einsiedeln Abbey

WALTER

'Did anyone witness the murder?' Walter asked the deacon, a thin, nervous man who had been assigned by Abbot John to help him.

'No. One of the altar boys heard a loud shout, but by the time he had run from the sacristy to the chapel, the culprits had already fled with the statue and the treasure,' said the deacon.

It was only the second time Walter had seen a dead body. The first was his mother eight years before. Back then, she had appeared to Walter to be sleeping, but the villagers had soon taken him away from her until his father's return, so he hadn't witnessed the collapse of her body into post-death deterioration.

Brother Francis was altogether something else. With almost two days having passed since his death, his face had taken on a grey, ceramic hue. And although his eyes were closed, as if he was still in slumber, it was a slumber riddled with nightmares. His lightly bearded jaw still held an expression of anger, or intense pain. He looked like the Böögg on the top of the *Mittenfastenfeuer* bonfire in Morgarten.

The monk had been lifted from where he had fallen and was now lying on a table in an ante-room. As Walter gingerly turned Brother Francis' head to examine the gash on the back, he held his nose with his other hand against the stench of the body that had released its bowels. The amount of blood loss was only noticeable on close inspection. It had matted the monk's tonsured hair and had soaked almost entirely into his brown robes, turning the colour of the cloth itself.

Walter was no medicine man, but it was obvious the single wound was caused by a split in the skull. Walter had known since childhood how head wounds can gush, and he guessed this cut had caused him to bleed quickly to death. The smell of rusting metal had infiltrated his robes, only marginally less pungent than the general stink of death.

'Come, come. It is imperative that we recover the most important item that was stolen.'

Walter frowned. Surely it was more important to bring a murderer to justice? Church treasures were material objects. What could be more important than the life of a brother? Walter held his tongue. The deacon and the abbot surely had their reasons.

'The culprits murdered Brother Francis, so we must gather the clues from the theft to track down the thieves,' said the deacon.

'This is true, but a closer examination of the wound might help determine the origin of the weapon,' said Walter.

'We don't have time for that,' said Abbot John as he entered the chamber.

Walter raised his eyebrows before the abbot continued.

'Brother Francis is in heaven now. It is imperative – imperative! – that we find the stolen treasures.'

Walter felt this reaction from the abbot was most ungodly, but he followed him into the body of the cathedral.

They approached a small chapel where a wrought-iron gate had been left open. A dark brown patch stained the stone floor in front of the building. This was where Brother Francis must have fallen. Walter guessed that he had been pushed hard to the floor, and his skull had cracked against the cold stone.

'This is where she stood,' said the abbot. *She?* 'Our Lady of the Hermits. The Black Madonna.'

Abbot John crossed himself. Walter looked inside the small chapel. He saw only an empty plinth where a statue must have stood. The glint of something caught his eye by the hinge of the iron gate. Someone must have forced the gate open, for the lock had been broken with a heavy object, perhaps an axe. A tarnished *Kreuzer* lay next to a leather-bound button on the floor. Walter picked up the coin, distinctive with its eight-pronged cross and half an eagle's wing.

'Habsburg currency,' he said.

More precisely, it was one of the coins minted during Duke Leopold I's reign. It was the first major clue that the culprits of these crimes were the enemy of the Confederation.

Walter's attention turned to the button. It was coal black, with a faded ochre stripe across its centre. The colours of Austria.

'Do you have a lad who can run fast? A messenger?'

The abbot nodded. He called to an older monk praying near the altar and asked him to fetch someone from the cloister.

'Can you tell me exactly what was stolen?' Walter asked while they waited. 'I should record the objects. It's possible the thieves will have left the region in different directions, but some of them could be traced if we are hasty.'

The deacon shook his head, but distractedly listed a handful of items, a gold dish, a corolla, some pendants. The abbot stood beside them, wringing his hands. The theft was now two days old. Walter was still mulling over why they weren't nearly as upset about the loss of the young brother who had attempted to stop the culprits as about the treasures themselves.

'I'm so sorry for the loss of Brother Francis,' said Walter, hoping to elicit some words of sorrow for the human tragedy.

The deacon continued to shake his head. 'Yes, yes, of course. The loss.'

Abbot John was growing more and more distraught. His breath came in little puffs, and Walter wondered if he was going to have a bad turn. Walter's comment didn't seem to calm his anxiety.

'Herr Tell, it is most important that you find the statue of the Black Madonna,' said the abbot. 'You must concentrate on its recovery before the other items – the gold and the treasures. The Black Madonna – Our Lady of the Hermits – is worth more than you can possibly imagine.'

Walter's frown caused the abbot to sigh and lean on a pew. The deacon drew the back of his hand across his brow. A ceramic statue would have no monetary worth. Walter understood that it was revered by believers, but a new one could surely be modelled by any number of religious artisans.

'The Black Madonna has been with us for more than four hundred years,' continued the deacon. 'She is a sacred artefact. She has special... powers. Pilgrims have come from all over the continent to touch her feet and be healed. She has been protected here for centuries. It's not the first time a brother has been killed protecting her honour.'

Walter resisted rolling his eyes. What magical powers were being fabricated by the Church to control the people? Priests had already instilled the fear of God in most of the population.

'When was the last time? It sounds like she has caused quite some trouble during her existence. Four hundred years?'

'She was once housed in a chapel on Reichenau Island in the middle of Lake Constance, then moved to the hills above the lake, not far from here on the Etzel Pass. She was guarded by a hermit,

Brother Meinrad, and so became known as Our Lady of the Hermits.'

A memory came to Walter of the conversation about *La Ténébreuse* the day he first saw the knights in the tavern in Altdorf, and later Einsiedeln had been mentioned. He couldn't shake the thought that this was somehow connected. Abbot John hurried on, as though he realised his story would keep Walter from his search.

'She is not so large, maybe half your height. You must recover her for us. She cannot fall into the wrong hands.'

Walter didn't want to sound blasphemous, but a brother had lost his life. 'I knew there had been a theft,' he said carefully. 'But I didn't know until I arrived here that a man had been murdered in the process. And you're telling me a significant number of valuable objects were stolen. But you're putting more value on a statue than the life of a man or wealth that could be used for the community. This I do not understand.'

'No, you do not understand. The Black Madonna does not have a price. Her value is more than all of Leopold's coffers, all of the gold in Rome and Constantinople. If you are not committed to her recovery, then perhaps I should find someone else to do the task.'

'No, no, I will help you, Father. But I feel it my ethical duty to find out who murdered Brother Francis, and whether those who took the Black Madonna also took the abbey's treasures. I assure you, for my fee, I will try to recover what you wish as well.'

The abbot sighed. 'This mighty monastery in Einsiedeln was built for a growing brotherhood of Benedictine monks to protect the Black Madonna. They felt she should no longer be kept hidden from the pilgrims who seek to worship at her feet. It was the Lord's will Himself to ensure she could be available to help those who suffer. She has been sitting in this chapel niche for more than 300 years, until the theft just two days ago.' Abbot John swayed on the spot, grabbed his rosary and let out a passionate sob the likes of which Walter had never seen a holy person perform. He was tempted to cross himself. The atmosphere of the cathedral thickened with incense and the dull light of the evening.

One of the great wooden doors opened and another monk led in a man who was dressed in the apron of a cook or a butcher.

'Yes, what is it?' the abbot asked distractedly.

'This is the village butcher, Herr Kälin,' said the monk. 'He says he saw men running from the town around the time of the theft.'

The man, whose brown and green stains on his apron suggested that not only did he bear the juices of several carcasses, but he might have mistakenly sliced through the gallbladder of some winged creature in the process.

'They weren't simply on the run,' he said. 'They were galloping, on horseback. But let me tell you, they were no ordinary thieves' horses. Those beasts were of fine stock. I would say they were Habsburgs soldiers. They were trying to hide chain mail under their cloaks. It was soldiers, Father.'

'Had they come from the abbey?'

'Must've. They'd come through town.'

'Which direction did they head in?' Walter asked the man.

'West, towards the Sihl Valley.'

The Sihl River ran out of the lake of the same name. It was the route Walter had taken to reach Einsiedeln from the Aegerital. It would be the route he would follow to return. He wanted to take his time to track the horses along the way. He tried not to allow anger to cloud his judgement. He wanted to be sure.

'Where is your messenger boy?' Walter asked Abbot John.

They both turned as a young apprentice rushed in through the northern door. He had likely come from digging in the cloister garden as he had earth on his hands.

'Are you ready to leave?' Walter asked doubtfully.

The lad nodded, lifted his robes over his head and let them pool on the floor at his feet. He was wearing lightweight trousers and a loose tunic underneath. He must be no stranger to running messages; his robes would have hindered his run.

'You will tell Josef Stauffacher this: "Habsburg troops have stolen the artefacts from Einsiedeln Abbey, and will likely head to their castle in Aargau." After you've delivered this message you must continue to Altdorf and alert Werner Stauffacher and his troops. Give them exactly the same message along with any other notices Josef might give you in Schornen. They will know what to do.'

'Why wouldn't he go straight to Werner Stauffacher? The army must be mobilised,' said Abbot John.

'There is a group of capable mercenaries in the Aegerital who may be willing to help recover the missing treasures from the Habsburg Castle in Aargau,' said Walter. 'Go now, lad. Speed is of the essence.'

The boy bent down to retie his bootlaces in preparation for departure.

'I believe this is a provocation on the part of Duke Leopold,' Walter told the abbot. 'It could be interpreted as a declaration of war. A few religious artefacts might not be the only thing the Habsburgs intend to obtain.' He cast his hand around him, visually encompassing the rich interior of the church, his message perfectly clear.

'And why don't you deliver this message yourself?' asked Abbot John.

'I want to track these horses. If they are soldiers' horses, they will be well shod. If they've taken a different direction, then I should follow them, perhaps ascertain their route back to Aargau. It's possible they will not head directly there. They might divert to Zürich where it would be easier to hide the objects in a busy city rather than take them back to an isolated castle where they would be at risk of siege.'

The abbot nodded.

'Wise words. Then you should waste no time.'

They followed the young messenger lad out of the cathedral and watched him run along the road leading to the Sihl Valley. It was now afternoon. At the speed he was moving, he would reach Schornen by nightfall.

Walter took some refreshment from the bakery opposite the cathedral and set off along the same route, wanting to use the light before it faded. He took much more care than the boy, keeping his eye to the path for signs.

There were heavy hoof prints in the softer parts of the earth beside the trail. The angle of the marks indicated the horses had been travelling at great speed. They'd made no effort to travel off-trail and hide their route, but they probably hadn't counted on a tracker. In any case, this was the only way in and out of the west end of the valley. The path split at the valley's exit at Beaver Bridge. Walter would have a better idea of their destination once there.

He hadn't been walking long when he spotted a small shiny object on the path. He bent to pick it up. It was a square buckle from a boot. It sat in the curved dip of a hoofprint. Not only had it come to rest after the rain storm three days before, but during or after the horses had galloped past.

It was nothing like a buckle seen on a boot in the Confederation. This buckle spoke of opulence, perhaps a valuable attachment on a soldier's uniform holding armour to his chainmail. But it didn't look like a Habsburg buckle either.

But Walter *had* seen something like this before. On the French knights' boots that held their spurs.

He thought about the butcher's comments. Soldiers' horses. They could have been knights' horses. And this buckle could have flown through the air and landed in the imprint of this horse's hoof only seconds after being severed from its boot. Not more than a day or two ago.

Walter thought back to the objects he'd found at the gate to the little chapel in the abbey. Had the coin and the button been strategically placed to point the finger of suspicion in an altogether different direction? Had it been someone's intention all along to send him to investigate the crime?

The clues were adding up, and coincidence was not something he trusted in his mystery-solving. Walter was quite sure he wouldn't need to check where those hoof prints were heading at the end of the valley.

And something else came to him. *La Ténébreuse.* 'La' meant the thing needing protection was female. 'Ténébreuse' could mean something, or *someone* dark.

The Black Madonna.

A flash of anger coursed through him at the confirmation of the deception.

Why had they done this?

Chapter Thirty-Two
22nd September 1315, Schornen
MAGDA

M agda abandoned her loom as soon as she heard the bell in the toll tower. She crossed the courtyard with her hand over her brow to see who was arriving from the lake.

'Not that way, Fräulein Magda. From the pass,' the lad called from the tower.

'Then why did you ring?'

'He looks awfully agitated.'

Magda turned to see Walter jogging down the path from the pass. Even from this distance she could sense anger sliding off him like knives.

Magda bit her lip. The knights had left that morning, ambiguous about their destination. Magda assumed they were on the trail of the stolen church treasures. She now wondered whether Walter's anger was connected to them in some way. The frown on his face gave him a rugged handsomeness, but it was obvious his regular good humour was lacking.

'What has happened? Is the monastery in uproar?'

'Not as much as you would expect, considering one of the brothers has lost his life brutally at the hands of the thieves.'

Magda put her hands to her mouth. 'Oh, that's terrible! The messenger boy didn't say. A man of God, murdered! Who would have done such a thing?'

Walter pressed his lips together. 'I need to speak to your father.'

'He's at the mill. I'll fetch him right away. Go to the kitchen. You'll get cold quickly out here in the breeze. Brigitta is in there. She'll serve you some broth.'

Magda began running to the mill, but halfway down the hill had to stop, feeling quite faint. She must have come out into the cool air too quickly. She rubbed her temples and slowed to a walk. As she crossed the stream she cupped her hand and took a sip of water. She fetched her father and walked with him back to the chalet, not wanting to miss any of Walter's conversation. News of the murder would provide the village with some macabre gossip. When they arrived back at the courtyard, Walter was still pacing back and forth outside.

'Come into the chalet,' Josef told him, which made Magda think there were some things her father might not want the villagers to hear.

As the two of them walked up the steps to the kitchen, Magda grabbed a handful of kindling as an excuse to the enter the house.

'The brother who tried to save the treasures died,' Walter said as Magda tipped the kindling into the basket at the side of the stove and restoked the fire. 'But he didn't accidentally die defending the abbey and the treasures. He was pushed, his skull dashed on a stone step in the cathedral. It was murder.'

'This is tragic,' said Josef with a frown. 'But it's not the first time thievery and murder have gone hand in hand.'

A muscle ticked in Walter's cheek. 'It may not have been intentional – although I find it hard to believe that an injury so severe could be anything else – but I think you know the identity of the thieves. And I think you knew the identity of those thieves before you even sent me on the mission!'

Magda gasped. This was quite an accusation.

'Get to the cooking, girl,' yelled Josef.

Magda turned to the bench beside the stove where a handful of vegetables lay. She picked up the knife and looked at it uneasily.

'I found a clue.' Walter said as he slapped something metal down on the table. 'And it wasn't the ones that they'd intended me to find.'

Josef and Magda squinted at it in the dimness of the kitchen. Magda's heart flipped at the forthrightness of Walter's fiery look at her father.

'It's a buckle. But it's not one from a Confederate soldier's boot. Nor is it from a Habsburg soldier. It's a design only seen on the costumes of the aristocracy of, let's say, the French. Or one of their soldiers.' Walter looked pointedly at Magda. 'Or one of their damned fugitive knights.'

Magda chewed her lip.

'Before I found this last clue, a set of others had been laid to point a finger at one or more of Duke Leopold's lackeys. The messenger boy who was sent, first here and then to Altdorf, will now have spread the news through the Confederation. My findings will eventually be declared false. Someone has made me look like a fool. And I intend to find out why.'

Josef pulled out a chair. 'Sit down, Walter. Calm yourself. You have every right to be angry.'

Magda's mouth hung open, her eyebrows raised.

'Continue your duties, Maggi. And make sure nothing of what you hear now leaves this house.'

Walter slowly pulled out a chair on the other side of the table and sat down.

'What I don't understand, sir, is why you would make me look so much like a fool and exactly what role the Frenchmen have played in this farce.'

Josef cleared his throat. 'There are still many who believe they'll be safer under Duke Leopold's rule. They don't understand that their livestock would be seized and their harvests ravaged. They had to be convinced. Unanimously. We have always respected democracy.'

'But you sent the Frenchmen to rob the abbey! This is not a democracy. It is corruption! It's obvious to me the stolen treasures will pay them for training your villagers. But at what cost? The life of a monk! As much as I am a religious sceptic, and I believe the Church's treasures should be distributed to feed those in need, this is the least holy act I can think of!'

'How can they possibly have stolen the treasures from Einsiedeln if they were here during the night?' asked Magda.

Her father shot her a look that silenced her. Then he looked down at the buckle and would not meet Walter's eye. 'You know we could not pay the knights the fee they require for such military training,' he said.

'But they are fugitives!' said Walter. 'Wouldn't keeping their secret be enough? Ach, this disgusts me.'

'There is something else, Walti. Something else I have been sworn not to discuss. And I will uphold that promise. I'm sorry it was you who has been used as a scapegoat, but your honesty shines through, and we could not be sure you would be swayed to see our point of view. We will be faced with battle soon, and everyone must be on the same side.'

Walter combed his fingers through his hair. Magda had never felt so sorry for him. But pity was the last thing he would want from her now.

'*Gott verdammt*, a man died, Josef! A man of God!'

'I regret that, of course. I never expected that to happen.'

'You were party to this plan?'

His silence answered the question.

Walter continued. 'Apparently one of the pieces they stole was an important religious artefact – the Black Madonna. Couldn't they have just taken a few gold pieces and melt them down to justify their reward?'

Josef's frown deepened. 'That statue is what the pilgrims come to see from across the entire continent,' he muttered, almost to himself.

Walter stood up, dipping his head as he went through the door to the landing. 'Where are they now?'

'I don't know,' said Magda's father.

Walter looked into the darkness of the kitchen at Magda, and she lowered her gaze to the chopping board.

'I think there is more importance to what they have stolen than any of you have been told.' Walter walked down the steps to the courtyard.

'Where are you going?' asked Magda, drying her hands on a cloth and following him out of the chalet.

'Have they left anything in the tower? I want to take a look.'

Magda looked at her father standing beside her on the landing. He closed his eyes and nodded once. She took the key for the tower off the hook by the door. Since the day the children had played on the lookout platform and one of them had been killed by the Habsburg soldiers, they had kept the tower locked for the short times no one was up there. The change of watch had not yet come by to collect the key.

'Walti, I had no idea,' Magda said as they crossed the courtyard.

'I know, Magda. I'm sure you would have said something if you'd known. They kept it from you for good reason.'

'I heard conversations between the knights and my father that I didn't fully understand. I didn't realise there was a deception.'

'I could tell from your father's frown that he didn't know about the Black Madonna. Did Sébastien ever mention anything to you?'

'Not directly, but he speaks of an object that is the reason for their existence. Something so holy they have been sworn to its protection.'

She wondered how much Walter suspected had gone on between her and Sébastien. She'd have liked to let him to know there was no future for her and the Frenchman, but it would likely not improve his mood if he heard regret along with the knight's name on her tongue.

Magda unlocked the door to the tower and let Walter step through before following him in.

'They don't usually leave their things here when they depart. But since we've been locking the tower, they did leave a few bits and pieces this time. I haven't disturbed them.'

Walter was already shaking his head as he looked at a couple of leather saddlebags leaning against the wall, an oilcloth, a folded blanket, and a handful of wooden plates and pottery mugs they would normally take with them when on their longer travels.

'*Verdammt*. It's not here,' Walter whispered.

'What were you expecting to find?'

'A statue. About so big.' He held his palm above the floor at hip height.

'The Black Madonna?' Madga laughed. 'How would they have been able to move her?'

'I don't know. I don't know how they'd manage to gallop at speed away from Einsiedeln with such a bulky item between them. The smaller items would be no trouble. But I can't imagine the Black Madonna would have survived the journey on the back of a galloping horse.' Walter continued to look under the knights' things, between the folded blanket and behind the leather bags. 'So wherever they've gone now, they weren't intending to camp out,' he said almost to himself.

'I don't know where they went. I thought they had some kind of guardian work to carry out. They cannot possibly be thieves. And murderers. They were here that night.'

'Are you sure about that?'

'Well... I... don't know.'

'On that same night, I was convinced I heard horses leaving, but then when I awoke in the morning, the knights' horses were here. As I passed them to come to the courtyard, though, I found their rumps still warm. Warm enough to have worked up a sweat in the hours previously. Those horses were not sleeping during the night, and neither were our so-called allied knights.'

'I can't believe it,' said Magda.

'I have to return to Einsiedeln,' Walter said suddenly. 'Immediately.'

'Why? I'll ask Papa if I can come! There's no danger now. We know why he didn't let me come with you before. Wait here, I'll ask him.'

Magda crossed the courtyard back to the chalet, where her father sat at the table in the kitchen in deep thought, his chin resting on his hand.

'Papa, Walter wants to return to the abbey to continue his investigation. If I go with him, I can take the robes they commissioned that they will surely need.'

'You're needed here, Maggi.'

'Papa, those robes are too bulky for one person. This is an ideal opportunity.'

'And alone with Walter...'

Magda huffed. 'I'm an adult now. Quite capable of taking care of myself. Walter has proven himself a trusted friend. Brigitta will take care of the household while I'm gone.'

Walter appeared in the door, his tall body blocking the light.

'I'll be leaving at dawn tomorrow,' he said. 'I've a feeling there is more to this whole crime than I originally thought. I'd be happy to have Magda accompany me. Our journey will take us over the Morgartenberg and along the length of the nation's border into the neutral lands of the abbey. There will be less danger along that route.'

Magda's father nodded slowly. He didn't say no. She beamed at Walter, her excitement growing. To leave the valley twice in one year was adventurous – first to the Rütli Meadow and now into the depths of the Schwyzer countryside.

Walter cleared his throat. 'However much of an emotion against the Habsburgs you and your brother Werner Stauffacher were hoping to stir amongst the people, does it not make you uncomfortable that you might have been double-bluffed?'

'Tomorrow then, first light,' growled Magda's father. 'Then hurry back when you have solved your riddles. And make damned sure you protect my daughter with your life.'

Chapter Thirty-Three

23rd September 1315, the Pilgerweg to Einsiedeln

WALTER

The following morning Walter and Magda walked up the trail towards Morgartenberg. They had split the load of the four bulky robes between them. The cloth was wool, and a lot heavier than the linen Magda usually wove. Walter didn't think she'd properly considered the weight it would feel by the time they'd been on the road for some hours.

'The abbot requested these be delivered before the first chill of winter,' she said. 'Papa knows there may not be another opportunity. It has been a while since we saw Mihal and he would be the only other trustworthy choice. But we don't know when he will return. And Papa might not admit it to you, but we need the money.'

'It's a shame the Frenchmen couldn't have delivered them for you on their odious mission,' he said sarcastically.

'Oh, Walter, I'm sorry they made you feel bad.'

'Of course I feel bad! I was used!'

'At least Papa trusts you in my company.'

'Perhaps Josef is relieved to have some breathing room with you gone for a few days. Your chalet must be getting quite crowded now with Brigitta having moved in. I imagine your father is keen for you to find yourself a new home.' Walter looked at Magda sideways to see how she received this statement. She suddenly skipped ahead without saying anything, and if Walter were to guess, he thought it might be so he wouldn't see the colour that had risen to her face. She must surely realise that he would say something at some stage. Did she think she could survive as a spinster? Or did she believe a certain deceitful Frenchman would eventually declare his love for her?

Magda had become a good friend. If she were to refuse him, he didn't want to stew in the rejection for the next few days of their journey. He would ask her on their return to the Aegeri Valley. But he could at least do some fishing in the meantime. 'You seem to enjoy seeing new vistas, visiting the countryside. Do you think you'd ever consider leaving Schornen to live somewhere else in the Confederation?'

If she were to wed Sébastien, where would they settle? He should stop his jealous thoughts. She surely wouldn't be there with him now if there was the hint of a betrothal to the Frenchman. But what folly might Sébastien have told her to bewitch her as well?

'Do you mean Bürglen, Walti?' she asked.

'Well, yes, maybe. Or perhaps a bigger community, like Altdorf.'

'I wonder what it would be like to look after the household of the indomitable Wilhelm Tell.'

Walter's racing heart spiked with the shock of her statement. Did she realise what she had said? Did she assume he would ask her to be his wife without him having uttered the words? Then Magda laughed out loud, and he wondered whether her comment was in jest. Why must these things always be so complicated?

'Honestly, Walti, that thought frightens me a little.'

His heart dropped. He was about to say something when several crows, disturbed by something in a tree above them, took off in unison. Their wings sounded like the slapping of thighs, their cawing like the cynical judgemental laughing of a group of men. Knights perhaps.

'This is exciting,' said Magda, not seemingly fazed by the birds. 'You must let me know if there is anything I can do to help. It must be so satisfying to solve your riddles.'

She must not have realised that the solving of it would confirm Sébastien's guilt. For a moment he could almost hear Mihal's voice inside his head contemplating the riddle that was Magda Stauffacher and the complication of human emotions.

'We'll deliver the robes to the abbey, and then I want to re-trace the route out of Einsiedeln. I want to question the butcher again.'

✝ ✝ ✝

From the same ridge where the stag had been struck by lightning, they walked down to the vast moor spanning the meandering Beaver River. Walter scanned the flat valley for signs of the enemy. It was easy to see across the plain, but they would have to be more cautious when they entered the gorge leading up the Sihl Valley.

The onset of autumn had turned the marsh grasses rich golds and reds. Between the tussocks or where the tough grass had been cut for cattle fodder, mauve autumn crocuses carpeted the fields. This marshland was a hundred times bigger than the one on the outskirts of Magda's village. It never drained, even in summer, due to the shallow slope of the high, boggy plateau.

The abbey and the Habsburgs were often in dispute about who owned this land. Nevertheless, the Confederation had already drawn the area within its own maps.

'Have you ever seen a beaver?' Magda asked.

Walter shook his head. 'I've heard they've almost been hunted out of existence. If you want to see one, you have to get close to the tributaries that spread across the moor, and at this time of year, the waterways are mostly overgrown.'

'This is the first time I've been here, although I've looked out over the valley from the Morgartenberg. I should come down here more often. Look at these reeds! They're more flexible and softer than the woody ones we find in our marsh.'

'No time to stop and harvest today, Magda.'

Walter glanced to her hip to make sure she was still carrying the *baselard*. Today it would not be for work, but for protection. And at that very thought, a flash of movement down by the river caught his eye. Magda was stretching her neck and rolling her shoulders.

'Stop! Hush. Take your pack off and crouch a moment. I've seen something,' he said.

She did as she was told with a sigh and Walter could tell her load had weighed more heavily on her back as they'd journeyed. He shifted his own pack off his shoulders.

They waited. Whatever or whoever was moving may have seen them and would have stopped to assess the situation exactly as they had.

'Here, let me take the robes for you. I can see they're becoming heavy.'

'Maybe one. I can manage the other.'

Walter took an extra robe from Magda's pack.

'You must be able to run if necessary,' he said, and she didn't complain.

They ate some dried meat and drank from their water skins, knowing they could refill soon at the river. Walter re-packed the three robes and tied them tightly to keep them as compact as possible, all the while keeping his eye on the place he had seen movement across the plain.

After several minutes Walter saw movement again.

'Deer. A mother and two fawns,' he said with relief in his voice.

They continued down to the river to fill their skins. From Beaver Bridge they followed the Sihl River upstream through a winding rocky gully with giant pine trees rising each side. The sun was low in the sky somewhere behind them and the crystal water of the Sihl River cooled the air along their path. Walter was happy to increase their pace to keep warm.

Once they reached the top of the gully, they skirted the Sihl Lake. The spires of the abbey came into view in the distance against a sky turning mauve in the evening light. Magda's eyes widened with wonder.

'Einsiedeln,' said Walter.

'This is the place the pilgrims all talk about. This is what they travel so many miles to see. I've always wanted to visit. I almost came with Mihal once, but the time was never good for Papa. Every spring, the pilgrims come through our valley, for no other reason than to visit this holy place and place their hands on the feet of the Black Madonna.'

Walter rolled his eyes. 'What is it about her? Why are people so fascinated with an object made by man that comes from the earth? People should be praising the sun that grows the crops and the rain that keeps water flowing in the streams. It would be the reverse of a blessing if our fountains ever stopped and crops ceased to grow.'

'Apparently she has cured pilgrims of their ailments. Even if it's not true, people have to have something to believe in. If God doesn't show himself to us in the physical sense, then an image of Mary is the earthly miracle that they can touch, I suppose. The mother of Christ. The mother of God. Everyone understands the cycle of life. Not everyone completely believes the Holy Spirit, but some of them change their minds when they have something holy to touch.'

'Then we must find her. This Black Madonna. I hope she hasn't been destroyed, though I doubt they would have allowed that.'

Magda looked at Walter. 'And who might *they* be? Do you mean the knights?'

'It's possible this was all planned,' he continued. 'That I should be the one to return the Black Madonna to her rightful place.'

'You're speaking in riddles now, Walter.'

'Do you remember the special yarn you received to weave the cloth for the knights?'

'Of course!'

'How big was the pouch you created?'

'About so big.' Magda held her hands apart, to the size of a large gourde.

'Then I don't believe they were intending to steal the Black Madonna. I don't believe that's what they were truly after.'

Magda frowned, but before she could ask what he meant, he increased his pace. 'Come! It's late,' he continued. 'We'll find lodgings at the cloister. There's a small convent of sisters. You can sleep with the nuns and I'll stay with the monks in the monastery. And in the morning, I believe we shall find our designated route.'

The nuns welcomed Magda with open arms, as though she was a long-lost sister on her own personal pilgrimage. Walter briefly worried she might find a calling amongst them, but shook his head of that thought, knowing deep down it would never be so. He tried to push suspicion to the back of his mind that there might be another reason she would never be pure enough to join a community of sisters. She had somehow become so much worldlier than when he'd first met her in spring.

✠ ✠ ✠

The next morning they found each other in the cloister garden and after breaking their fast in the modest refectory, they headed to the house of worship.

The dullness of a misty dawn did not diminish the beauty of the painted arches inside the church. The frescoes told tales of angels and kings and joy and persecution, while at the altar hung a vision of the great suffering Jesus withstood on the cross. Magda looked up and stared at the figures and paintings while Walter searched for Abbot John. He found him in the sacristy.

After they had divested themselves of the four robes, the abbot fetched a box from the treasury. He held Magda's wage for the robes out to Walter without hesitation. Instead of taking the money, Walter turned to Magda and indicated that the abbot should give it to her directly.

'That's Fräulein Stauffacher's wage and no one else's,' he said, looking at Abbot John, who raised an eyebrow.

'Thank you,' said Magda, smiling at Walter but holding her palm out for the money.

He turned to the abbot.

'When were you alerted of Brother Francis' death and the theft in the chapel? Can you give me a more precise time?'

'It would have been before Matins. Deep in the night. Most of the brothers were sleeping. It was unfortunate that Brother Francis had come to the cathedral. Only he would know why. Perhaps a disturbed sleep, a need to cast an extra prayer before the chapel of the Black Madonna. Most unfortunate.'

Abbot John had calmed since Walter last saw him and was now clearly saddened by Brother Francis' passing. He crossed himself and muttered a few quiet words of prayer.

'The trail is getting warmer for me, Abbot John. I hope to solve the mystery soon.'

'Then why have you returned to the scene of the crime? Should you not be in pursuit of the culprits?' he asked.

'In good time. Peace be with you.'

Magda's eyebrows raised. Walter thanked the abbot for his time, and Magda thanked him for the work she'd been entrusted with.

As they left the cathedral, Magda counted her coins and pocketed them in her skirts.

'I know full well that there are others in this community who could have carried out the weaving and sewing of those robes. Is it wrong to feel pride that my reputation has led the church to ask for my work rather than theirs?'

'I think you can allow yourself a little pride, Magda. It's a different kind of pride than the one the bible calls a sin. A certain amount of pride keeps the quality high in our work. And I believe that is no bad thing.'

'Are you cultivating a little piety, Walti Tell?' She smiled at him, and they walked down the main thoroughfare to the butcher's shop.

CHAPTER THIRTY-FOUR

23rd September 1315, Etzel Pass

WALTER

'Exactly what time did you see the horses galloping towards the Sihl Valley?'

They were standing in the entrance to the abattoir. Magda held a hand over her nose and mouth and Walter imagined the stench of raw meat was turning her stomach. It belied her normally strong constitution and he raised his eyebrows. Herr Kälin's apron over his vast belly was still covered with the same dubiously coloured stains Walter had seen two days before. The butcher put down his cleaver and scratched his head before answering. 'Would have been before the dawn prayers in the abbey. I was up early. I know the time because not long after the horsemen passed by, the bells rang for Lauds. The moon was still high, so there was no mistaking what I saw. Are you doubting my report?'

'Not at all,' said Walter. 'I just need to be sure of the timing.'

They bid farewell to the butcher and Walter was relieved to step into the fresh evening air.

Magda stood with her hands on her hips, taking deep breaths. 'What does this all mean?' she asked as they turned towards the lake.

'You'll see. I hope.'

Instead of following the Sihl River, they veered away from it and hugged the lake shore.

'Where are you going now?' asked Magda. 'Why not back down the Sihl Valley?'

'Several hours passed between the knights leaving the abbey and the butcher seeing them galloping down the Sihl Valley. That means they spent some time here in the region before hurrying back to the Aegerital at great speed.'

'So where did they go between stealing the treasures and riding back?'

'That is precisely what I – we – are here to find out. It hasn't rained since the theft,' Walter said, his eyes not wavering from the track. 'So the horses' hoof prints should be easy to follow. I hadn't concentrated on them before because the only way out of the Sihl Valley is down the river, and I picked up their tracks from there. But they went somewhere else before heading down that gorge.'

Walter and Magda walked onto another track leading up through the Finster Forest towards the Etzel Pass. Magda lagged behind. Had Walter underestimated her strength in view of his renewed enthusiasm to solve the mystery? 'Are you feeling weary? Should we rest?' he asked.

'I don't know why I'm so tired. I slept well last night. I think maybe my legs aren't used to all this walking. I don't want to hinder your work. I'll be fine!'

'This is not a contest, Magda. My legs have been walking the countryside for many more months than yours. You don't have anything to prove to me.'

'I wanted to thank you for your actions back there in the abbey,' she said. 'Making the abbot give me my wage. Did you see the look on his face?'

They both laughed and Walter passed her his water skin before taking a drink himself, so as not to make it look like he had stopped only for her. When he started walking, he slowed his pace imperceptibly so it wouldn't look like he was favouring her tired legs.

After an hour, they approached the ridge leading up to the pass. Magda put the back of her hand to her forehead. 'Oh, I didn't know it would be so far!' Her boot rolled over a stone on the trail and she stumbled. With the pack unbalancing her, she put her arms out in front of her to protect herself as she fell.

Walter rushed to her side. 'Are you all right? Let's stop and rest here. We'll have something to eat. Restore our energy to climb to the top. Oh, your hand! It's grazed. Here. Let's sit.'

Magda sat down on a mossy boulder at the side of the path. Walter remembered Mihal's little pot in the pocket of his jerkin. He held Magda's hand and rubbed some of the salve across her knuckles where they had scraped. 'I don't know how much further we have to go, but it can't be far,' he said as his fingers gently massaged her hand.

'Oh, that burns!' said Magda and Walter looked at her in alarm. 'In a good way.' She smiled at him. 'Thank you; it does feel better.'

Walter was impatient to be on his way, but didn't want to hurry Magda. His hopes were raised as he'd seen more than one well-shod hoof print in the soft ground on each side of the trail.

He sat and chewed on a *Landjäger*, a square sausage of spiced dried meat that Herr Kälin had given them for their journey. A small stream ran down through the woodland not far from the path and Walter re-filled their water skins. By the time he returned to Magda, she was standing and ready to be on their way.

'I feel splendid now – if you'd just let me have a little of your *Landjäger*. It will give me energy to make the last distance to the summit.'

Walter handed the rest of it to her, happy to be able to share something as simple as a sausage. As they reached higher altitude, the trees began to thin, and between swathes of mist winding through the forest, they were afforded a spectacular view of Lake Zürich. Beyond the hills to the north, another ribbon of water hazed against the landscape in the distance. Lake Constance. It was too far away to detect, but Walter imagined the island of Reichenau sitting in its midst. Beyond that, the land flattened out along the great Rhein plains. It felt like they could see as far as the fabled Schwarzwald from there.

Where Walter had been in a hurry moments before, he now stood still to take in this wondrous sight.

'Come on, Walti, isn't time of the essence?' Magda mimicked Walter's voice perfectly and barged past, striding onwards. He smiled and followed. At the pass, a seldom used path led up towards a rocky cliff. Instinct told Walter he should take the trail.

'Do you know where you're going?' Magda asked.

'No, but something tells me we don't have far to go.'

She shook her head, droplets flying from her curls from the condensed vapour of her breath. She silently followed.

Around a curve, a scattering of rocks lined the path. Beyond a firepit was a steep cliff with the roots of trees growing in and out of the clefts of rock. Around it was evidence of a wooden beam and shingles that would once have been the roof of some dwelling. Apart from a pile of pine branches lying against the cliff, it was a long time since anyone had been here, and Walter suspected that the original hermitage had long been burned to the ground or dismantled. But the feeling in his gut was that he had found the right place. Not least because there was a fresh pile of green horse-dung not far from the firepit. It was no more than two days old.

'Lovely,' said Magda. 'They could have tied the horse away from the fire. I think that's rather rude. This looks like it might be someone's house. Not in a very good state of repair, mind.'

Walter didn't say anything, but suspected the pile of dung was exactly where it was meant to be found. He began searching the ground around the ruin, kicking at rocks, cutting away at the bushes with his baselard.

'Walti, look what I've found!'

Magda had lifted away some of the pine branches, exposing a crack in the cliff that was big enough to squeeze through.

'Well spotted, Magda. But be careful, it looks like the perfect lair for a bear. Let me go first.'

Walter squeezed his way through the crack in the rock. A cave opened up, but it was too dark and he couldn't see how far back it went. 'I'll have to light a fire at the entrance,' he called back to her, his voice echoing in the dark space.

'Might you need this?' Magda pulled the stub of a candle from her pack.

'Aren't you a clever girl! I have a tinder box, but a candle is more useful.'

She beamed. 'I had to get up in the middle of the night to attend to... you know. I took one of the convent's candles and forgot to put it back by the cot in my cell. A patch of luck, I'd say.'

Walter took the tinder box from his pack and from a handful of dried moss gathered on a rock, managed to light the candle from the flames.

'Let me check for bears, then I suspect I shall be needing your help,' he told Magda. 'So don't go far.'

'I want to see what's in there too. I'm not going anywhere.'

Walter entered the cave. There was no evidence of any large animal. He reached out for Magda's hand, to guide her across a pile of rubble at the entrance. They entered the main part of the cave, a space larger than Walter's chalet in Bürglen. The first thing they both saw, leaning against the back wall, was a statue of the Virgin Mary holding her baby. Both with black faces. The Black Madonna. Our Lady of the Hermits. Magda crossed herself and fell to her knees.

'You knew! Walti, you knew!'

'We must take her back to the abbey. Here, help me carry her out.'

'She's much smaller than I expected,' said Magda.

Between them they manoeuvred her out through the cave entrance and laid her carefully on the ground, face up. Walter rolled the statue carefully onto its side, revealing a hole in the back that had been somehow sawn out of the fired clay. Someone had been careful not to break the statue. Part of her torso was hollow.

'Whatever was in here was the object they were after,' he said.

Magda placed her hand into the space to feel if anything was still there. A look of wonder appeared on her face and Walter thought for a moment she was going to pull something out, like the tricks Mihal often played out of his hat when they were children. She felt around inside the body of the Black Madonna for some time, before disappointment registered on her face.

'What do you feel, Magda?'

She shrugged and pulled out her hand. 'Nothing, Walti. It's empty. Whatever was there has gone. But...' She held up her hand, fingers splayed, and turned it over and back and as though searching for something on her hand.

'Look, Walti! Look at my hand!'

He took it gently. The bruised skin from her fall was now smooth and pale.

'And my scars from the reeds! They've almost gone!'

Walter had a sudden urge to kiss her hand, and placed his lips on the middle of her palm.'

'Oh, Walti,' she said with a smile as she pulled her hand slowly away. 'You are such a romantic. What do *you* think was in there?'

'I don't know. But I hope I'm not crushing your belief when I tell you that Mihal's healing salve has quite possibly done this to your hand.'

Magda shook her head. She must have already made up her mind that Our Lady was the purveyor of miracles. Walter didn't have the heart to argue with her.

'Whatever was in there was destined to be carried in the pouch you made for the Frenchmen,' he said. He still couldn't bring himself to call them knights. They were becoming less chivalrous in his imagination by the day.

Chapter Thirty-Five

24th September 1315, Schornen

MAGDA

A t the back of the Etzel cave the Black Madonna had appeared larger than any human. But when they laid the statue in their arms between them, she seemed to shrink. It was easier for Walter to carry the Black Madonna back to Einsiedeln by himself. The path was narrow, so Walter wrapped the statue in his sleep blanket while Magda carried his pack, almost empty after having delivered the robes to the cloister earlier.

When they arrived at the abbey there was much celebration. They set the statue down in front of the chapel's iron gates and it was as though a tiny smile had curled itself onto her beautiful black lips. Magda was so happy she hadn't been destroyed. Although someone had emptied her treasure, she was whole. People would still revere and worship her.

Once prayers had been uttered, the Black Madonna was placed on the plinth in her chapel, the damage at the rear invisible. Amidst all the excitement, it was apparent to Walter and Magda that the abbot had no idea anything was missing from inside the statue.

Abbot John spoke only of arranging to have a cloak woven and sewn to honour her return and cover the hole in her back.

Magda's hand tingled as she stared at the face of Our Lady of the Hermits. She lifted her fingers to trace the sign of the cross at her forehead, chest and shoulders. She was filled with inexplicable joy.

Brother Francis was to be interred two days later to allow the monks to mourn him properly after the return of the Black Madonna. Walter was paid his reward for the recovery of the statue. He thought it odd that nothing was mentioned about the other stolen treasures. A handful of jewels, a gold chain and a platter were still missing, but nothing had been more important, apparently, than the recovery of the Black Madonna.

'Your Frenchmen will know the whereabouts of those other treasures, Magda, but after all the deception that has gone on, I doubt we'll ever know what they intend to do with them. Lodging, feeding and clothing themselves will naturally be in their plans, but I suspect there was enough gold to ensure all three of them could do that ten life-times over.'

Magda pursed her mouth, but stayed silent.

They were invited to stay at the abbey. It was too late in the day to start the journey back to the Aegerital. It would have meant travelling at night. Although it may have been safer for them to travel under the cover of darkness, the clear night threatened a heavy frost. In addition to which, the brothers wanted to share a meal with Magda and Walter to show their appreciation.

After prayers, they were invited to a table so rich and full of food, for a moment they believed the drought of the past summer had never happened at all. Walter thought the monks could teach the Confederate farmers a thing or two about how they tend their crops in the cloister garden.

After dinner, Abbot John stood up with a flourish and asked Walter and Magda if they wanted a story. Walter inclined his head and Magda clapped. 'Oh, yes please.'

Spurred by Magda's enthusiasm, Abbot John began.

'Imagine if you will, the Etzel Pass. The year, 861, the date, January 21st – the middle of winter. Our beautiful lake was frozen, the surface pale with new snowfall merging with the surrounding landscape. Hermit Meinrad was returning from Einsiedeln with his weekly ration of bread, smoked meat, cheese and dried fruit when it began to snow hard. Through the blizzard he was approached by two men. Thinking they were pilgrims seeking benediction, he prepared to give them a blessing. But as they approached, their shadowy forms radiated an evil malevolence.'

Without thinking, Magda placed her hand on Walter's leg under the table next to her. He leaned towards her. 'I can see you enjoy a little theatre,' he whispered.

Abbot John held up a finger.

'A gloved hand grabbed Meinrad's neck, lifting him from the ground. Fear pulsed at his temples. Fingers and a thumb dug into the hollow space under his jaw, clutching his windpipe. He felt something pop in his throat.

'This is quite macabre,' whispered Magda. 'But look how the abbot is acting his part. He is quite magnificent.'

Abbot John displayed surprising agility, leaping about the theatre stage of his imaginary Etzel Pass, holding a claw-like hand up to an imaginary victim's jugular. Some of the monks had begun to whisper amongst themselves. Walter suspected it was a story they had heard a hundred times before.

'"You have something we want, old man," said the other stranger with a heavy foreign accent. Meinrad caught the flash of a blade in his peripheral vision. His feet left the snowy ground once more. The hand released his throat – a momentary relief – before his neck began throbbing. "I know not what you seek," said Meinrad.'

Abbot John put on a painful-sounding rasp, a fine likeness of someone who might be choking with a pair of hands around their throat.

Magda pressed her lips together.

'This could get even nastier. Are you fine to listen to the rest of this tale?' Walter quietly asked Magda.

'Of course,' she hissed back and Walter smiled.

The story was like a legend his relatives might tell around the brazier on a warm summer night in Bürglen. The abbot was unusually animated in the telling of the tale that likely bore some truth.

'Meinrad understood these evil strangers were not looking for money or food.'

They were not looking for the Black Madonna either, thought Walter.

'Meinrad was thrown onto his back and his cloak was ripped from him. They cut the wool of his shirt from his neck to his navel, but the attacker's blade was carelessly wielded, and they sliced open his torso like the belly of a pig.'

Magda drew in her breath, but the abbot continued.

'Meinrad gasped as his inner organs were exposed to the alpine cold. His attackers tore the key to the hermitage from around his neck. Meinrad would have wanted them to consider repentance for their violence before the eyes of the Lord, but he no longer had a voice. He wasn't much longer for this world. Silence was his better option. "You will make the task easier for both of us if you tell us where it is, old man," said the thief who held the key. "We have travelled a whole continent to put an end to your Christian trickery." Meinrad attempted to croak a reply, but it hurt too much to speak. The man ground his boot onto Meinrad's broken arm, and air hissed past the hermit's injured vocal chords. But his belief in God and the importance of his secret kept him from spilling it. He focused above him on specks of snowflakes flying across the white sky like celestial angels. He might soon be joining them in the kingdom of heaven, but he was determined that no torture would reveal his secret to these men. They broke into Meinrad's refuge and ransacked the place, but they couldn't find what they were looking for. Because Our Lady was hiding in the secret cave behind the hermitage. Meinrad had ensured her safety for thirty-four years and wanted to ensure her safety for hundreds more. And, these men were not as clever as you two young believers.'

Walter smiled at Magda, who filled up with pride on his behalf.

'Meinrad had faith that the Lord would ensure the safety of Our Lady. He would be rewarded for his silence and his sacrifice in heaven. Those evil men finally put an end to poor Meinrad's suffering with the single fell of an axe.'

'Oh!' squealed Magda, with a hand to her mouth, then waved her hand for the story to continue.

'Once the villagers discovered Meinrad's body, they sent a messenger to the Benedictine brothers on the Island of Reichenau in Lake Constance. Another guardian was sent to protect Our Lady and another after him, until the Abbey of Einsiedeln was built on this spot seventy years later.'

Magda clapped her hands and her face shone. The monks cheered and touched their beer flagons together.

'And so, my dear young believers, you have become part of the history.' Abbot John's eyes twinkled as he addressed Walter. 'I never imagined the thieves of two days ago would repent and return Our Lady to the original hermitage. We shall be forever grateful for your clever deductions, and you will forever be blessed.'

Magda smiled beatifically. She was having a hard time holding her tongue about Walter's religious beliefs and for the moment avoided eye contact with him.

CHAPTER THIRTY-SIX

25th September 1315, Schornen

WALTER

The following day, Walter took advantage of the reverence Abbot John seemed to have for the two of them to secure an agreement for weapons to be forged within the walls of the cloister under the guise of farming tools for the Confederation. Walter told him he would try to arrange for iron to be delivered to them as soon as possible.

Walter and Magda bid farewell and took the path down the Sihl Valley, across the moorland and over the Morgartenberg back to Schornen. Magda was not feeling well, and put it down to eating too much food at the feast the night before. She seemed so poorly, Walter wondered if she had drunk too much of the monastery's rather powerful mead, but he couldn't recall having seen anyone pour the amber liquid into her cup. His resolve to talk to her about their own alliance was thus delayed yet again. He didn't want to ask such a romantic question while she was feeling so miserable.

As they came over the ridge and descended towards the village, they could see a number of people busy at work along the pathway between Morgarten and Schornen.

'They're erecting blockades!' said Magda. 'Why would they do that?'

The men were constructing cross-struts of wood.

'Mihal was right,' said Walter. 'It looks like rather than uniting the two communities, Schornen is beginning to cut itself off.'

'They would never do this without reason. Too many families would be split up. There must be the threat of a siege. Morgarten should still be protected. Remember Duke Leopold thinks the people there still respect his rule. We can still maintain contact through the high forest trail, but a stranger to the valley would not know where to find it.'

'It may be a precaution. But after what we've learned, it could also be to provoke an attack by the Habsburg troops. I'm beginning to see that this whole thing has been planned since those damned Frenchmen entered the valley back in spring.'

'Could they have had war on their minds even back then, when they arrived as fugitives? I cannot believe it,' said Magda with a frown.

Walter stared at her.

'Believe what you will. Do not forget that a man of God has been murdered.'

Magda chewed her lip and continued down to the hamlet. As they rounded the eastern side of the chalet, Sébastien came out of the tower and down the steps. Walter slipped the pack from his shoulders, let it drop in the courtyard and rushed headlong into the Frenchman's chest. He swung wildly with his fist, but only managed to knock Sébastien on his muscular neck. Sébastien's hand rounded to a fist as he regained his balance, bent his knees and turned his shoulders to face the fight.

'Sébastien! Walti! Stop!' Magda shouted.

Walter took another swing with his fist and found his mark on Sébastien's cheekbone. With a look of almost amused surprise, Sébastien lifted his hand to the side of his face. Finally lunging at Walter, he grabbed both his arms. Muscles bulging, Sébastien held Walter's arms behind his back. If Walter had been carrying either a crossbow or a sword, a bolt would have found its way through Sébastien's heart by now. As it was, he only had his fists. Sébastien's size and strength meant Walter was eventually overpowered. All he was left with were his words.

'Murderers! You killed Brother Francis!' Walter yelled. 'I don't want to hear any of your Christian excuses for why you've done this thing.'

'Steady yourself, Walter,' said Sébastien without rancour. 'The death of Brother Francis was never meant to be. He was in the wrong place at the wrong time.'

'That's no excuse! You of all people know life is sacred.' Walter tried twisting himself out of Sébastien's hold.

'You must listen to us, Walter. I won't let you go until you calm down.'

'Ach!' Walter knew he could never overpower Sébastien. His struggling began to weaken. The other two knights were watching from the doorway to the tower. They'd initially raised their swords, but now let them hang at their sides.

'Brother Francis was trying to prevent us from accessing the chapel,' said Sébastien. He was doing his rightful duty in protecting the Black Madonna. What was supposed to be a gentle push out of the way turned into a trip and a fall on the floor of the cathedral. There is no denying that his death is a tragedy, but I can assure you it was not intentional.'

Walter sighed. His bubbling anger wasn't helping. It was making him weak.

'Did you at least find Our Lady of the Hermits and return her to her rightful place?' asked Sébastien.

Walter finally stopped the struggle. Sébastien let go of his arms, but kept his hands ready for a further fight.

'Yes, they are still celebrating today in Einsiedeln,' said Walter. 'But it seems contrary to the life lost under the roof of the church. Brother Francis will be mourned, but his sacrifice did not take precedence.'

'The Lord knows when those will be called back to him,' said Grégoire.

'As someone who prefers to seek justice without violence, I'd be tempted to turn you over to the abbot if I was physically capable, to reveal your true identity. Especially as you are the ones the Pope seeks to burn at the stake as heretics. I'm sure this would give him untold pleasure. A valid reason to seek your heads other than the whim of his partner in crime, King Louis of France.'

'On that, then, we are agreed, Walter,' said Yves. 'All is not holy and pure for the head of the Holy Roman Empire upon his throne of deceit in the Vatican.'

Walter turned and walked away from them. He stared at the lake in the distance, across the border in Habsburg territory. He would prefer to fight this battle with words, but it would not bring Brother Francis back to life. He re-arranged his pack in silence. He had to leave as soon as possible, to take both the positive agreements and the negative threats back to the garrisons in Schwyz and Altdorf.

The knights returned to whatever tasks they'd been doing and no more was spoken about Walter's outburst. Once they were out of hearing and before Walter departed, he turned to Magda. 'I have your best interests at heart, Magda, always. I hope one day you will see we could make a great team. You know what that means. That we would be together. If it helps your decision, know that I would always have you at my side and treat you as an equal.'

Walter held her stare for some time before leaving, but not before he'd seen a softening of her face.

CHAPTER THIRTY-SEVEN

28th September 1315, Schornen

SÉBASTIEN

'I think I have a right to know what it was for. After all, it was the most difficult yarn I have ever dyed and re-spun and the most challenging of any design I have woven,' said Magda.

They were sitting at the table in the courtyard. Sébastien was rubbing pig fat into the stirrup straps he had removed from his saddle. 'I cannot show you,' he said. 'If there's to be an invasion of the Confederation with Schornen as the gateway, any treasures here are not safe. It has been hidden well, and when the time is right, we shall be taking it to safety.'

Magda held out her hand. Thinking this was a gesture of some kind, Sébastien took it and looked into her eyes.

'No! Don't take my hand. *Look* at my hand,' she said, irritation creeping into her voice.

He looked down and moved his thumb over her fingers and knuckles. The skin was surprisingly smooth, and her blemishes had cleared. He raised his eyes to hers in query. He almost pulled her palm to his lips, but checked himself. Any moments of fancy were now a thing of the past. It was torture for him, but he must not lead her on.

'Look at the skin. I put this hand inside the Black Madonna, touched the place where whatever you took out was sitting. What is this magical thing you have, Sébastien?'

Sébastien shifted on the bench and looked around the court-yard. They would be leaving soon to find a new protected place for this thing they had kept a secret for so long.

'I'll tell you the story, and then perhaps you'll understand why... we cannot be together. But you must promise not to say anything. Keep this thing as our secret in your heart.'

'I'll tell no one, Sébastien.' Magda's rosy lip trembled and her eyes pooled with tears. 'After what we did together, our union, there is surely no reason for us to be kept apart.'

She looked at him, searching his face. One tear jewelled on her lower lash and escaped down her cheek. Sébastien swallowed, his heart heavy. Magda had been touched by this thing, and she de-served to know the truth, deserved to know why a religious brother had accidentally lost his life trying to protect what held it, God rest his soul. She deserved to know why he had to continue the mission of generations of his Templar-privileged ancestors.

'A thousand years ago, the Black Madonna was sculpted and fired by a Moor brother from northern Africa who'd been living amongst the brothers in Reichenau since childhood, rescued from slavery.'

'Abbot John didn't tell us that part of the story,' said Magda.

Sébastien bit his lip, hoping he was not making the biggest mis-take of his life. 'She was created for a purpose,' he continued. 'To hide the chalice that Christ drank out of at the last supper and that he shared with his disciples. The Holy Grail was sought after by many people who believed it had great powers, powers that were of its own manufacture and not because it was cupped in the hand of Christ.'

Magda stared at him, her eyes wide. 'The chalice still exists after all this time? This is a wondrous thing!' Her tears seemed now to be forgotten, encouraging him to continue.

'It was the mission of our ancestors to ensure it was housed safely in the protection of the Christian church. It was taken away from lands ravaged with religious wars at the time, so it was hidden in the statue by the brothers on the island of Reichenau. They were to protect the Black Madonna and the Grail at all costs until the day perhaps the Messiah himself would return to claim his own vessel.'

Magda's hands covered her mouth.

'A chalice of miracles! Of course!' said Magda. 'The rest we know from the abbot in Einsiedeln. Poor Meinrad, in his little hermitage next to the cave. Such a brutal murder back then. The thieves never found the chalice. His dwelling must have butted up against that cliff and they didn't know about the cave. Meinrad gave his life, as Brother Francis did. Is that why you say we can never be together? Because this is your life's purpose? This is your obligation?'

Sébastien lowered his chin, still wrestling with this dilemma, his emotions swinging wildly from one destiny to the other. He'd been on the point of telling his colleagues he would break from the trio, settle in this little mountain community, make a peaceful farmer's life for the remainder of his days. But his original mission was reignited the moment they took possession of the Grail. What life could he possibly offer Magda as a Templar Knight?

'But surely Grégoire and Yves can continue this mission. Does it really need three of you?'

It was as though she had read his mind. This was his dilemma, that he could give up his mission for her, renounce God, settle with Magda. Although she had shed a tear, he wasn't even convinced he would be her first choice. He thought of Walter and how he and Magda were really the perfect fit for each other. Born on the same land, growing up with the same traditions, speaking the same strange guttural language. She wouldn't be the first person who had to choose trust rather than lust. That was a privilege usually awarded to the men of the community.

'All three of us have sworn an allegiance to guard the *Saint-Graal*. My grandfather told me that one of our ancestors was saved from a mortal illness by drinking from it. I have an obligation... I wouldn't be here today. We've always known of its hiding place; it has been our biggest secret for centuries. Our station in Troyes was part of the protection to the west of the Rhein. None of us will give up. That would be a failure. We have been together for more years than we haven't. The relationship and our role are things more powerful than we understand.' He picked up her hand. 'The Holy Grail cannot be allowed to find its way into the wrong hands. Whole legions would kill for this.'

'And the treasures from the abbey?' Magda wiped the tears on her face with her sleeve.

'They will not be missed. They are likely already forgotten. What use are they to the village in their current state? Now we have returned the Black Madonna to her rightful place—'

'Walter. It was Walter who returned her.'

'I meant "we" as in the allies of the Confederation. I hope you haven't forgotten that we're on the same side, Magda, even if your friend Walter is currently not of that opinion. The Black Madonna has inadvertently become a holy figure.'

Magda drew in her breath. 'Shouldn't every image of the Mother of God be deemed holy?'

'Of course. What I meant was, the statue has gathered a reputation over the years as a holy icon capable of healing sickness, delivering miracles. But it is not the Black Madonna herself that has manifested these wonders. It is what has been hiding within her for the past thousand years. She has been returned, but her powers have not. The brothers at Einsiedeln believe in the powers of the

Black Madonna. In turn it will help pilgrims maintain their own belief. Belief alone does amazing things. This—' He lifted Magda's hand. 'Does not happen to everyone.'

Chapter Thirty-Eight

11th October 1315, Schornen

MAGDA

Magda and Brigitta were working alone in the kitchen making a sauce for a doe that Yves had hunted for them a few days earlier. The animal had been hanging at the back of the barn, high enough that the foxes and wolves could not reach it and close enough to the house for the ravens to leave it alone.

Brigitta stopped her work briefly, and pressed her fists into the area either side of her spine in the small of her back. She wasn't near term, but her bump was beginning to make certain movements uncomfortable.

Magda cleared her throat. 'This is the second moon that I've missed my own bleed,' she said.

Brigitta stared at her with wide eyes.

'The French knight? Or our Walti?'

'Sébastien,' said Magda, suddenly flooded with shame.

'Then he must take you as his wife. You will likely satisfy your travelling whims if you do. Eddi reckons they won't stay beyond the year end in the Aegerital, even if there is no war.'

'He will not take me. He says he has a higher mission. Godly duties as His servant.'

'Does he know you are with child?'

Magda shook her head.

'Then you must tell him! Surely he will change his mind. You're a catch for any man with your cooking and sewing cleverness. What greater pull is there than the love of a woman? They are not priests or holy men. Why can't they take wives?'

'I don't know. Clouding judgements maybe. A promise they made as Templar Knights. A sworn allegiance between the three of them. It is not until this year that I understood what love can do to a person.'

'Ach, Magda, you've been so careless.'

'It was only once, Brigitta, and I was sure I'd washed out the seed.'

'That's not quite how it works. I thought you were wiser than that. Oh Maggi, what are you going to do?'

'I don't know! I don't know.'

'And what of the Tell lad? Josef thought that match was already made. What will he do when he finds out you are with child? Have you lain with Walter too? Perhaps you should, so you can pass off the child as his.'

'I can't deceive Walter like that. He's been so good to me. He has become such a good friend.'

'Friends don't keep secrets from each other, Magda.'

Magda suppressed a sob. 'I'll be labelled a harlot, perhaps a witch, sent from the village.'

'They won't send you from the village. But Eddi will be angry. Who knows how many little ones will be running around this chalet before too long. Both he and your father were counting on having you married off before then.'

'Please don't tell my brother. I haven't decided yet, but you must swear to this secret.'

'Have you tried swallowing a mix of mountain *Kräuter*? Perhaps a concoction of juniper and belladonna?'

'I'm not sure I want to.'

'Well, don't keep saying you don't know what to do, Magda! This will be a disaster for you! If you don't do something, it will soon be obvious to all.'

'But... the baby.'

'How can you look after a child with no husband to bring food to the table?'

She thought Brigitta would be understanding, especially with her own child on the way. She thought there would be another side to the dilemma that her sister-in-law would favour. But Brigitta was likely looking forward to the day when two women weren't running the kitchen in what was effectively her household now. Mainly Magda wished she hadn't told Brigitta because, although her solution made sense, it wasn't what she really wanted.

'Can you prepare me a recipe? One that won't kill me, too?' Magda narrowed her eyes at Brigitta, whose expression softened.

'Yes, Maggi, let's try that. I will ask my Aunt in Morgarten who has some knowledge of herbal medicine. I won't tell her who it's for. It's a shame Mihal's not around. If he comes, we should ask him.'

'Oh, I don't think I could tell him. Think how disappointed he would be in me.' Magda placed her hand over her lower belly. Could she already feel a slight tightening of the skin? She thought of the precious baby who was growing inside her. How could other women bear it, when the chances of survival to childhood and beyond to adulthood were so slim? How could they stand to lose their babies? It was such a waste of life to be rid of the child. She still wasn't sure she could do it. Because she was already completely in love with what was not yet hers.

✝ ✝ ✝

She cried all night after she'd swallowed the potion Brigitta's aunt made for her. She could only think of herself as a murderer. In the end it made her sick for two days and she could keep no food down. Any of it she did manage to keep passed through her within the hour. The potion didn't work. The tenacity of that unborn child reminded her of the strength of its father. At the end of the two days feeling they would both surely die, she decided to keep the baby, despite the dismay she would face in the village as a fallen woman. Magda wasn't yet sure how she could manage, but she had her weaving and her sewing. She'd yet to work out what she would do once the chalet was too small for the entire family, but she became determined to support them both.

The knights were away for the whole time Magda was ill. The longer she nurtured her secret, the harder it became to imagine she would ever tell Sébastien she was with child.

By the time the knights rode back into the village, a far greater storm was brewing on the horizon. The life of an unborn child was the last thing on anyone's mind.

CHAPTER THIRTY-NINE

30th October 1315, Altdorf and Arth

WALTER

Mihal wasn't hard to find, with his mule tied up outside the Bären Tavern. Walter was happy to patronise the place as it was one of the only taverns in Altdorf whose windows didn't face directly onto the market square that held so many bad memories for him.

'Walterli! Come over here and join me! Fräulein, a jug of mead for my young protégé!' shouted Mihal as Walter entered the establishment.

'*Heb Schnurre* – shut your trap, old man!' said Walter, his tone a mixture of jocular affection and admonishment.

It was time for Mihal to stop using Walter's well-known childhood nickname, not to mention this wasn't the moment to announce a stranger's presence to all and sundry. Mihal's words implicated the truth of Walter's message-errands, as everyone seemed to know around here that Mihal wasn't merely a travelling medicine man. But with enemy ears in every corner, Walter might be taken for the spy that he seemed to have become.

'Werner Stauffacher has asked to see me this afternoon at the Altdorf fort,' said Walter. 'But I'm glad to see you first. What did you learn in Zug on your last visit? Do you think Heinrich von Hünenberg is readying Leopold's troops for an attack?'

'It appears that way.'

Mihal was suddenly serious, managing to put his overindulgence in mead to one side. The business of war was never enlightening news. 'They've been moving troops gradually out of the walled fort and along the north shore of the lake towards Arth,' he continued. 'I can't imagine it's convenient to set up camp and temporary garrisons in this increasingly cold weather, so I don't think this is a chance training manoeuvre.'

'Werner will have surely sent his spies into the canton of Zug from the Confederate end of the lake,' said Walter. 'I hope he has a better idea of numbers. My worry is if they're concentrating all their efforts on a possible attack through Arth, they will be ignoring Morgarten and Schornen. Which would leave it wide open for the Habsburgs to attack there.'

'Good luck convincing Stauffacher,' said Mihal. 'He's a lot less flexible than his brother in Schornen.'

'I worry about the hamlet. The first snows have fallen on the Wildspitz and the Zugerberg,' said Walter. 'The cattle and sheep have long been brought back to their farms at lower altitude. Any shepherds up on those exposed ridges would freeze to death within a day. We cannot risk posting men up there. Damn this unpredictable weather. Freezing cloud can be a slow killer.'

'And you haven't even considered the alphorns filling with snow.' Mihal chuckled, and Walter experienced a flash of irritation.

The mead had not been completely without effect then. He calmed, silently forgiving the old man for his misplaced humour.

✝ ✝ ✝

Leaving the centre of town, Walter approached the fort on the river plain between Altdorf and Flüelen. The tall square of solid log walls built on top of sloping stone foundations dominated the landscape of the Reuss Valley.

Two towers were visible from ground level, one at the north and one at the south corner of the fort. The wooden gate was open as Walter approached the entrance in the north wall. A cart full of wood was being pulled by two sturdy mules into the fort. A group of guards waved the cart through and closed the gap to the entrance as Walter approached.

'Hoi! Walter!' a voice called from the tower above him.

Walter squinted against the sun. The voice had come from a head wearing a helmet and he had no idea who it was. When the soldier lifted the headgear, Walter recognised the face of a lad he'd known a few years previously in Bürglen. He and Friedrich used to trap rabbits together in the Schächen Valley.

'It's fine!' Friedrich yelled to the guards. 'You can let him through. Don't you recognise the offspring of our great Wilhelm Tell?'

Walter waved to his old friend and the guards moved reluctantly aside. Walter rolled his eyes. Their boredom was apparent at having to guard a gate in the centre of a nation that had not recently experienced threat. They would probably have relished driving a sword through him as a suspected enemy spy.

Inside the fort, layers of buttresses and beams criss-crossed the open interior, securing the timber walls. A warren of small huts against the western wall housed various work stations for the soldiers: blacksmiths, carpenters, food stores and a kitchen. Stables lined the east side of the fort. Walter glanced at the horses. Several fires burned in the grounds. The whole fort had been constructed round a water source that had been capped. It flowed through a metal pipe and splashed into a long stone trough in the centre.

'What's your business?' asked a guard, looking with distaste at Walter's civilian clothes.

'I'm here to see Stauffacher.'

'*Commander* Stauffacher to you, lad,' said the guard and Walter resisted another eye roll.

From what he could see, there were barely fifty horses in the fort and certainly less than a thousand men. The soldier led Walter to one of the huts. Werner Stauffacher sat at a table with a pile of parchments and a pot of wax seal at his side. There was a stool on his side of the table, but Walter chose to stand. 'There aren't as many men here as I was expecting. It has been rumoured you're moving troops from the garrison in Schwyz closer to Arth. Have any already gone from here? It would be hard to hide their mobilisation from the spies on boats travelling on Lake Luzern.'

'Have you been getting information from that nosy Graubundner, Mihal?' The commander sighed. 'Yes, he's right. What good is a garrison here in Altdorf if an attack is to come through Zug to the Confederation?'

Although it would only have taken a minimal garrison to stop an attack by water from Luzern, it was widely known that Duke Leopold didn't have a significant sailing fleet. It confirmed Walter's fear that there weren't enough troops available to cover all western points of entry into the Confederation. 'Do you really think there will be a Habsburg offensive before winter?'

'We must be prepared for that eventuality. Rumours have been rife. You only need to ask your friend Mihal to know there've been unusual movements of troops from Argau to Zug.'

'Will a Confederate troop be sent to Schornen?'

'I know you're an ambassador for their protection and not simply a messenger, Walter, but the likelihood of an attack through the Aegerital is almost non-existent. The passage up through the Lorze Gorge is treacherous, and now winter approaches, access over the Zugerberg is impossible. Heinrich von Hünenberg will concentrate his troops to attack the border at Arth.'

'But is there a contingency in case you are wrong?'

Werner Stauffacher gave him one of his trademark scowls. 'If you see a Habsburg banner in the Aegeri Valley, you're fleet enough of foot to bring us numbers within a few hours, surely. The villagers are prepared. The Frenchmen have seen to it. We cannot afford to station men there *just in case.*'

The commander raised a hand to a soldier at the entrance; the conversation was over.

As Walter left the shelter, he passed a young lad bringing the commander a bowl of stew and dumplings swimming in a lake of yellow fat. Walter wrinkled his nose. As he walked across the fort, he called to Friedrich in the watchtower. 'Can you spare a moment? Can someone cover for you?'

Friedrich turned to his colleague in the watchtower and came down the ladder. When he reached the ground, he removed his helmet and they shook hands. 'It's good to see you, Walti! Pacifism is suiting you well.'

'Hush, Freddi, that's a swearword around here,' said Walter, smiling.

'I hope you feed yourself better than the gruel we get here. You always were handy at the stove.'

Walter recalled Werner Stauffacher's unappetising-looking stew. 'What's your role here, Freddi? Are you always on guard duty?'

'Mostly, but I've been picked a few times as a messenger between the barracks here and in Schwyz. I shall probably be called upon once we've set up the camps at Arth. I can still run, Walti. Do you remember our races up to the forest in Bürglen?'

'Indeed I do. I have a favour to ask you. If you have to act on it, I promise you will be well paid.'

Friedrich's brow creased.

'Do you know the hamlet at Schornen on the other side of the pass leading to the Aegerital?'

'I haven't been there, but I know the path that leads to it from the road to Beaver Bridge. Isn't that where the commander's brother lives?'

Walter nodded. 'Directly over the border is Morgarten on the shores of the Aegerisee,' he said. 'The village is unanimously in favour of joining the Confederation. But Werner Stauffacher says he doesn't have enough men to send extra support to defend the vulnerable location.'

'He does have his hands rather full weighing up the possibility of a Habsburg attack here,' said Friedrich. 'There have been rumours. That's why we're mobilising to Arth. We leave in two days.'

'I think there's a possibility the Habsburgs will attack through the Aegeri Valley. Not just at Arth. And the commander has no contingency plan for this. I think it's because he doesn't have enough troops,' said Walter.

'Come,' said Friedrich quietly. 'I'll walk you to the gate. We are dallying and the others will become suspicious.' They made their way past the rows of horses. 'It's true, I don't think there are enough men to defend at Arth,' he whispered. 'It's no surprise he would ignore Schornen.'

'He thinks the men in the village can defend themselves and drive Leopold's troops back. He even agreed for them to be trained by mercenaries. But they would still need support in the event of an attack. It's a death wish on the village.' Walter swallowed and cleared his throat. 'I need someone who can signal the alarm if Duke Leopold attacks through Arth. And if there is to be sign of an attack at Schornen, I will bring notice of it in return to Arth and Altdorf.' Walter wasn't even sure Friedrich would agree. He would be going against orders by leaving his troop to deliver such a message.

'Werner Stauffacher is a hard leader,' said Freddi. 'But he doesn't always make good decisions. He has alienated some of the troops in this garrison and is concentrating his efforts on mobilising those in Schwyz now. Leopold and von Hünenberg haven't left Zug yet, but it could be next week or the week after. I hope the commander can organise his own troops in time.'

'Let us hope,' said Walter, almost to himself.

'It doesn't surprise me that he would let his own brother perish, Walti. Gone are the days when the passionate faith in your father's beliefs ensured the security of the Confederation. If for any reason I don't leave with the troops in two days' time and it's not me who delivers the message, I will make sure I find a fast-footed runner. You can count on me.'

Chapter Forty

5th – 9 th November 1315, Bürglen to Schornen via Arth

WALTER

'I imagine it's too late for me to give you a quick lesson on the crossbow,' said his father as Walter prepared his pack. It seemed the chalet where he'd grown up was shrinking as he aged. A little like his father, perhaps.

'You're disappearing, so I have to cook my own meals,' his father continued. 'Anyone would think you've finally decided to leave home for good.'

The last statement was mumbled with affection.

'I'd already have been gone for much longer if I'd joined the army, Father. How quickly you forget. I'm leaving you some money so you can get yourself a decent hot meal at the inn from time to time. I've made a *Brei* that will last a few days if you add more milk. The neighbour's chickens are still laying well, and there's plenty of dried venison in our store. You won't perish.'

Father and son hugged and Walter shouldered his pack to be on his way.

'Stay safe,' said his father as Walter closed the door to their little chalet.

He walked quickly towards the lake, avoiding the fort by hugging the river. He asked the crew on board the boat where the least dangerous place to disembark might be with so many brigands and spies about. Tempers were rising on the borders and a group of tradesmen had been killed on the northern shore recently.

'Too many Habsburg infiltrators with over-sensitive fingers on their bowstrings,' the sailor told him.

He left the boat at the now familiar port of Brunnen. But instead of climbing to the Aegerital, he travelled directly west to Arth. The fort wasn't as big as the one in Altdorf, but an additional camp was under construction, using the outer walls of the fort to protect the troops against the worst of the weather. Tents were being erected to house the soldiers who would soon be billeted from other towns. At least Werner Stauffacher's troops seemed more organised here.

The village of Arth was a scattering of houses along the shore of Lake Zug with a church at its centre. Werner Stauffacher had given Walter a seal so he could enter the fort, which was set back from the lake on slightly elevated land. Walter thought back to his agreement with Friedrich and wondered if or when he would arrive with his troop. He hoped the commander wouldn't get wind of Friedrich's promise, especially if his friend was forced to find someone else to run a message up to Schornen.

Walter talked his way up to the watch tower. He wanted to see for himself the lie of the land. The Habsburgs didn't have enough boats to shift that many men and horses on the lake. The town of Zug was roughly two hours' ride from here, but it was hard to see where Duke Leopold might set up camp. Riding directly from Zug would mean exhausting their horses and men right before engaging them in fierce battle. They might set up camp on the narrow band of pasture along the eastern shore of the lake. As yet, though, there was no sign of any encampment. If they were more organised than the Confederates, their deployment might only be days away.

✠ ✠ ✠

Walter climbed the road to Schornen with a heavy heart. He wasn't sure how he was going to tell the villagers that they would be unlikely to have any support from Magda's uncle in the event of a Habsburg offensive.

As Walter crossed the pass into the Aegerital, a bitter wind from the east blew a flurry of snow across his path. The fat flakes looked like cherry blossoms, but the vision was soon dashed as the icy cold found its way through the seams of his jerkin. An ominous veil of grey cloud had begun to shroud the mountains.

Schornen looked deserted. Corn snow and frost carpeted the dry pasture in the shadows between the buildings. The wind was blowing the smoke with such force from the fires, it seemed none were lit in the community. As Walter picked his way down the trail, Magda appeared from the milking shed under her chalet carrying a pail. Her head was covered with a shawl, clasped with one hand under her chin, while the other hand carried the milk, her head down.

Walter stopped briefly to watch her walk up the steps to the kitchen. A lock of chestnut hair blew across the angle of her cheekbone. Could it be she had become more beautiful in his absence? The howling wind covered the sounds of his feet on the gravel and the air chilled the sweat on his back. He hurried past the chalet towards the mill.

'Edgar, Josef! *Hoi zäme*!' called Walter as he entered the mill. Even with the tall building's door closed behind him, vapour from Walter's breath floated on the air.

'Walti! What news? Is my brother sending a troop or shall we be saved from providing the soldiers from our meagre stores?'

'I fear it is the latter, Josef. It's time to test that allegiance with your Morgarten brothers, because the one with your own blood running through his veins is doing nothing to protect you down there in Altdorf.'

Josef frowned. A curse was surely silenced on his tongue. 'The knights are due back any day from the south. They are scouting a trail. I believe they will leave before the winter sets in, even if Leopold hasn't attacked by then. There is already much snow at the Gotthard Pass and they cannot risk waiting longer for their onward journey.'

'Perhaps you should meet with the elders of Morgarten. The villagers must be ready at any given moment to defend.'

Josef nodded. 'Mihal says it looks like they're preparing to move out of Zug.'

'They haven't yet set up camp near Arth. I assume you have a permanent watch in the tower. Any sign of an encampment over there?' Walter pointed to the shores beyond Morgarten.

'No. Not yet,' said Josef.

'That gives you a few days. I think it would be wise to move your wives and daughters to the village over the other side of the pass. There are very few places for the innocent to hide here in case of battle.'

'You're right, lad. We've already been transporting food and grain over there to avoid any troops robbing our stores bare. The Schwyzer villagers have offered their homes to the young and old.' And then more quietly to himself: '*Verdammt*, Werner. What are you thinking?' He shook his head and regained his focus. 'Come, Walti, you will bed with us in the chalet tonight. We'll find room for you. The tower is too cold for sleeping and anyway it is full of weapons. The Frenchmen have found accommodation in Morgarten.'

Walter was relieved that Sébastien and his colleagues were no longer staying in the hamlet. He wondered how Magda would feel about him sleeping under the same roof as her, perhaps even in the same room. At the thought of her, she opened the door of the chalet.

'Walti! What news? Are those Austrian brigands going to leave us alone now until spring?' she asked.

The look Josef shot his daughter wiped the smile from her face and she bit her pretty lip.

'Come, Walti, Papa, we have lamb stew tonight,' she said as they stamped their feet on the veranda, shed their coats and closed the door.

The shadows under Magda's eyes belied the worry that was now confirmed for her village.

After dinner, they prepared their beds. Magda slept in the cot near the fire. Walter and Josef slept on the other side of the room, while Brigitta and Edgar stayed in the alcove. No one slept much. The wind howled around the chalet for most of the night and battered the shutters. It wasn't the weather that caused Walter his sleeplessness. He was painfully aware of Magda sleeping the length of a table away from him across the room.

But he must have slept towards morning. When he awoke, there was an eerie silence. At once he knew it had snowed. It was still dark, but when he went out, a violet light hung over the village. The wind had kept the snow from settling on the flat pastures but it had drifted up against the buildings. Edgar joined Walter on the veranda.

'It's hard to believe anyone would attack in this weather,' said Edgar.

'It won't last,' called Josef from inside. 'Winter hasn't set in just yet. It's the same every year. Always a warm spell before the solstice. I think we should meet with the Morgarten elders soon whether the knights are here or not. This weather will only speed up Duke Leopold's campaign.'

✝ ✝ ✝

By sunrise, although the sun could not be seen through the thick grey cloud, Walter left with Josef and Edgar for Morgarten. The trail through the forest was choked with drifts and the heat of their feet soon melted the ice on their boots, soaking them through. Walter barely glanced at the swamp to his left where reed heads were spitting off their white winter caps in the wind. Their journey was doubled by having to skirt each of the blockades along the trail. Clumps of snow fell from the pine branches, finding their way down the necks of their coats and filling their footprints behind them.

Keeping half an eye on the dark sentinels of the trees, the first chalets of Morgarten appeared like ghosts out of the white land-scape. Josef made his way directly to the closest farm, leaving a trail of footprints across the snow that had covered crops and pasture alike. Once there, the children were sent out to various houses in the village to gather the priest and the village elders back at the farm.

When there were enough people present, Josef addressed the gathering. 'There will likely be an attack before winter truly sets in. Walter here says Mihal has confirmed this from his discreet inquiries in Zug. But...' Josef sighed. 'My brother Werner doesn't believe Duke Leopold or Heinrich von Hünenberg will attack through the Aegerital. He knows your stance as Confederate sym-pathisers, but he cannot spare any troops. This will undoubtedly hurt us more than it will hurt Morgarten.'

'We cannot sit here hoping they will not come,' said the farmer. 'We must help you defend. You will not be alone.'

'How can you possibly win?' asked the priest. 'Your men will be outnumbered ten to one at least, even with the farmers from Morgarten. And they will face warriors. With armour and quality swords. Your men are only peasants.'

Walter clenched his jaw. They didn't need a priest to point out the obvious. 'Find a group of men who can scout the perimeter of the village both night and day, perhaps under the guise of shepherds checking roaming sheep, to report on any unusual movement or camp formation.'

Josef took up the conversation. 'Von Hünenberg won't know the state of the swamp. The waters of Lake Zug will have receded, much like Aegeri's, so they will assume the land is passable, perhaps even frozen. That is already a deceptive advantage.'

'They may have waited until now, knowing your stores are well stocked for winter,' said Walter. 'If there is anywhere you can hide even half of them, you will avoid starvation. They may think you are their allies, but that won't stop them robbing you of your food.'

'We are going to do a stock-check of weapons today and tomorrow. Your barn on the top field is halfway between our two villages,' said Josef, addressing the farmer. 'It would be good to place at least two guards there at all times.'

'We'll move the hay and straw currently there to a barn higher up towards the forest,' he replied.

'Leave enough in the barn to cover the weapons in case...' said Josef. 'If we are forced to retreat, there is a chance you will still be protected by Leopold's army. We have to hope our alliance is still a secret.'

'We'll go back to Schornen now and wait for the knights to return. As soon as they do, we'll meet the men and set out our plan of action. In the meantime, be vigilant.'

Walter, Josef and Edgar returned to Schornen on the same trail. Their toes, which had just regained feeling, were once again subjected to the chill of the snow.

As they approached the courtyard, one of the watchtower lads was jumping with agitation. 'I see smoke from several fires, Herr Stauffacher! They are setting up camp near the Eierhals, on the pasture. They're closer to Morgarten than they are to Aegeri, that's for sure!'

Josef and Edgar stared at each other, father and son with their mouths set in the same grim line. Magda stood on the veranda with her hands to her mouth and fear in her eyes. The battle raging inside Walter paled in significance now. There was little point in declaring anything to her at this stage. They all had something bigger to fight for right now.

CHAPTER FORTY-ONE

14th November 1315, Schornen

WALTER

The Frenchmen arrived back the following day. They immediately came to the chalet to hear the news. Josef and Edgar
welcomed them in. Their boots and coats brought melting snow
into the house and the little kitchen soon filled with the musty
smell of wet wool.

'The men of Morgarten and Schornen are as ready as they'll ever
be,' said Grégoire. 'You should be proud that your young men
who started the spring as farmers have ended the year as warriors.
It's time to show Duke Leopold he cannot march all over Europe
grabbing everything he wants. This nation is braver than I ever
imagined, filled with such determination to keep your independence and indeed expand the borders. I'm proud to have been a
part of this.'

Josef drew his fingers through his hair but displayed no pride on
his face. Walter never imagined he would hear any of the knights
admit such a thing. When they arrived in the valley back in spring,
their attitude conveyed only disdain for Morgarten's lack of prepa-

ration for war. Now that they'd been told they couldn't count on their own army, Grégoire's speech only vaguely assuaged the despair Josef must have been feeling. Especially when Walter remembered the Frenchmen's ulterior motive – to retrieve whatever it was they had taken from the abbey in Einsiedeln.

But Walter couldn't forget that they had at least given *something* back to the village. They could have simply marched into Einsiedeln and taken those treasures without such a complicated premise.

✚ ✚ ✚

Walter left with the Frenchmen to show them the stockpile in the farmer's barn outside Morgarten. They arranged to distribute the weapons to the men of both villages and, once they were armed, would clarify the defence strategy.

Until the men had been rounded up, Walter agreed to help spread the word to the houses in Schornen. They must prepare their families and take as much of their remaining food stocks as possible over the pass to where they would be safer. Mihal, who had returned to help, agreed to take the frail and infirm on his mule.

The first house Walter intended to call upon was the little chalet next to the tower. Persuading Magda to leave with the others might be difficult, but Walter was hoping she might have a moment to talk to him about something else. He wanted to say something now while he had the confidence. Dear God, they could all be dead by tomorrow. He didn't want to think about the consequences if the defence of the hamlet went wrong.

When Walter arrived in the courtyard, a warm glow shone welcomingly from the kitchen. The shutter had been left open to help pull the fire and dry out the earlier presence of damp bodies. Blue smoke puffing from the gaps between the roof slates told Walter it had recently been rekindled and a damp log had been put on the flames. It was rare to build up a fire indoors. Usually coals were brought from the brazier outside. But everywhere was now dripping wet with a fine drizzle and melting snow. As Walter was about to cross the courtyard, the shadow of Brigitta passed the window, and he hesitated. He would rather talk to Magda alone.

But before he could change his mind again, Brigitta caught his eye through the slats. He heard her exclaim '*Walter ist da!*'

Seconds later, Magda opened the door and came down the steps to the courtyard, shrugging her shoulders into a sheepskin coat, which Walter eyed with envy. He was unsure whether the tremble of his body was due to the cold, or nervousness for what he was about to ask.

What to start with? News of the enemy camp, to persuade her and Brigitta to retreat over the pass? Or his own emotional declaration? He didn't know which would take the most convincing. He was quite sure Magda would be right there on the front line raising a weapon to fight the Habsburg soldiers given half a chance.

Magda walked towards him. As Walter was about to lift his arms to her – he would later wonder what he had intended to do – there was a short, sharp shout from the lookout platform on the toll tower and a great rushing sound came from above. A single thump, like the falling of a heavy rock, echoed in the courtyard. After a moment of confused silence, Magda squealed and then the lad in the tower began frantically ringing the bell.

Walter turned to see Magda standing in the midst of white wisps of smoke, floating up around her, as though she had brought a log from the fire out with her from the chalet. She tried to move away, but something was holding her there.

Walter looked down to where an arrow had pinned her skirts to the ground. As they both stared at it, flames began to lick upwards, the dark amber of the dyed cloth hiding the magnitude of the fire. Brigitta screamed from the veranda and ran towards them.

'Lie down! Lie down!' Walter shouted to Magda.

Magda looked at him. She was rooted to the spot. This was surely a Habsburg arrow.

As she sank to the ground, Walter looked to the sky, afraid more arrows might follow. He took his dagger and grabbed the material of her skirt where the smoke had not yet hidden his view. He rolled her as gently as he could and ripped part of her skirt from below her waist. He threw the burning material towards the firepit in the middle of the courtyard and turned back to make sure no part of Magda's body was in danger. A red mark seared her leg from her knee to her thigh, and Walter thought how angry it looked against the paleness of the smooth skin on her other leg.

'We must move you, *Schatz*,' said Walter. 'In case more arrows are coming.'

It was the first time he had uttered an endearment, but this wasn't the time for either of them to ponder its consequence. He dragged her towards the shelter of the chalet steps. Scraping up a handful of snow, he placed it gently on the burn.

By now Josef and Edgar were running up the hill from the mill and Brigitta came out of the chalet and stood at the top of the steps.

'Brigitta, it may not be safe. Stay under the cover of the roof!' said Edgar.

Brigitta dithered on the steps, obviously wanting to help her sister-in-law. 'I'll fetch something to place on the burn,' she said, turning back into the chalet kitchen.

'I must find the archer who fired this,' Walter said urgently as Edgar arrived before his father. 'I don't know how fast your men can run or if they are already giving chase.'

'Go! Catch the culprit,' said Edgar, and Walter was surprised he hadn't taken it upon himself to put up a chase.

'You'll be safe in Brigitta and Edgar's hands.' Walter placed his hand on her cheek, and she put her own palm to the outside of his fingers, nodding in silence.

Walter leaped up and turned to leave.

'Gather more snow. Keep the skin cool,' he shouted as he ran off. 'Do you see the archer?' he shouted up to the lad as he passed the tower.

The boy pointed, and although Walter couldn't see from his position on the ground, he narrowed his eyes and followed the line of the boy's finger when he'd scrambled to the top of the border wall.

Tumbling down the other side, Walter ran as fast as he could in the direction the boy had pointed, wondering how the marksman had found his way through the scouts around Morgarten. He was spurred on by a burst of anger that the arrow could have killed Magda had she been any closer to Walter at that moment.

He skirted the swamp and raced through the forest, the tree branches now higher than his head, having shed their weight of snow. He ignored the burning sensation in his lungs, ignored the icy chill of the mud on his boots. When he came out of the forest on the other side of Morgarten, he stopped, caught his breath, and imagined he was looking for one of the rabbits of his youth. His eyes scoured the pastures, sweeping from the forest trail to the lake, carefully scanning for the slightest movement.

There! Behind the church, beyond the field where the pyre had burned for the mid-Lent festival. The archer was struggling through the slush, his quiver bouncing against his back, the bow in his hands. Walter couldn't fathom why the man would have shot a single arrow; he might now be returning with information about their barricades and weapons to his camp. Walter clenched his jaw and pursued. He began to gain ground on the archer, who spotted him and threw his bow and quiver, now hampering his escape, to the ground. Walter ran faster, his lungs burning and his boots slipping through the mud like butter, the stuff of nightmares. But he was still gaining.

Walter was within shouting distance of the archer when a sharp pain in the back of his leg pulled him up. A torn muscle. He must not let the marksman get away! He must stop him from arriving at the enemy camp. This archer who had almost killed Magda must be stopped at all costs.

Walter pulled his dagger from his hip, kissed the hilt for luck and drew his arm back. He slung the knife through the air, recalling the perfect aim he had achieved for the wolf several weeks previously.

In the dimness of the drizzle, Walter couldn't see the trajectory of the knife. But he heard the cry and he saw the figure stagger. He continued running towards the man, who was now limping. When he reached the archer, he pushed him to the ground. The dagger fell from the archer's leg, the blade tinging on a rock. Walter threw himself onto the man's chest, grabbed his jerkin with both fists and shook him. His head bounced again and again on the ground.

'Who leads you? Duke Leopold or Heinrich von Hünenberg? Who?' Walter shook the man again.

'Von Hünenberg will destroy your little village. He will eat your women and children for breakfast and spit out their bones, heathen,' said the man.

'How many men?' More shaking. 'Speak!'

'More than you can cope with. At least five hundred,' said the archer with a sneer. 'And all of them ready to put themselves between the legs of your women.'

A roar pushed its way out of Walter's chest, and he lifted the man and smashed him against the ground. The vision of his mother came to him. Again and again. Until the archer's head lolled and there was no more resistance.

Shocked, Walter stopped and stared, his heart still pounding. What had he done? The archer wouldn't be carrying his message back to the Habsburgs, that was now certain. His head had smashed against a rock. Shame chilled Walter's head, knowing it was anger that had fuelled his actions. He picked up his dagger and left the marksman on the field. His comrades would find him. He collected the bow and the quiver and jogged back past Morgarten to the tower in Schornen.

Edgar called to him from the top. 'Not something I thought I'd ever see. Walter Tell carrying a bow and arrow,' he said with a laugh.

It wasn't until Walter heard Edgar's mocking but affectionate laughter, that he realised that he'd not only just killed his first enemy soldier, but he'd killed a fellow human being, the thing he'd said wouldn't solve their nation's issues. The very thing he said he would never do.

Chapter Forty-Two

14th November 1315, Schornen

WALTER

Magda had been carried into the warmth of the chalet. Walter barely had enough energy to run up the stairs. She was lying on the cot near the fire and smiled as he came through the door. Brigitta was placing strips of linen soaked in water across the burn. When Walter came in, she looked up at him with a nervous smile.

'How is it? Can I take a look?' asked Walter.

Magda lifted her skirt. A grimace clouded her face when she moved her leg.

Sitting on the edge of the cot, Walter reached into his jerkin for Mihal's pot of salve.

'Oh God, Walti, an arm's length here or a moment sooner, and that arrow might have found your head!'

'Or yours, Maggi. If you hadn't stepped back at that moment... Are you all right? I'm afraid your skirt is a little shorter than this morning. Tell me this is not one of your special tricks to make me notice your fine legs.'

She laughed and Walter was pleased her fear had momentarily diminished. He dabbed a little salve on the burned skin. Magda sucked in her breath.

'Did you catch him?' she asked.

Walter nodded and bit his lip. His loss of control, the anger. What had he done? Magda put her hand on his arm.

'He would have killed one, or both of us, Walter. Someone was going to perish in all this. Ouch!'

'I'm so sorry.' Walter returned his attention to the burn. 'We must make sure no infection gets into this raw skin. I fear there may be scarring.'

'When the knights talked of their colleagues burning at the stake in France, I kept thinking it must be the most painful way to die,' she said. 'Dying of cold or drowning just doesn't conjure the same fear as that. Thank you, Walti. Thank you for coming back.'

'As soon as you feel a little better, you and Brigitta must retreat over the pass to protect yourselves. Do you think you will be able to walk?'

Magda began to cover up her legs with the remainder of her skirt. 'Yes,' she said, not meeting Walter's eye.

Walter pressed his lips together. He was about to say more, when the sound of running feet and an urgent, familiar voice was heard outside in the courtyard. 'Walter! Walti!'

Friedrich. This could only mean more bad news. Although the enemy hadn't yet followed up their single flaming arrow with an offensive, it was surely imminent. Walter kissed the pads of his first two fingers and pressed them onto Magda's lips before hurrying out of the door.

Friedrich was in the courtyard bent over, hands on his knees, catching his breath. 'No point... going back to Arth,' he said. 'Stauffacher... assembling a troop... but they may not make it in time.'

This was positive news, but Walter wondered why there was a change of heart. Friedrich reached into his pocket, pulled out a note and held it out to Walter.

'"BEWARE MORGARTEN",' Walter read out loud.

Friedrich had begun to recover from his run. 'The note arrived wrapped round the shaft of an arrow. Someone warned us.' He took another deep breath. 'Why would they warn us in advance of an attack? There is no surprise in that.'

'Foolish pride, perhaps,' said Walter. 'They've done the same here, but sent a burning arrow without a message. Perhaps they're goading a community who they think has no possible way to defend themselves.'

'I don't see there is any advantage to this message at all, but I came anyway,' said Friedrich as Walter pressed a *Taler* into his palm. He would respect the promise of payment even with the threat of war on the doorstep.

'They won't know how we've been training these past months,' said Walter. 'We all know how inflated Duke Leopold can get. Some of his decisions have never made sense. Whatever it means, an attack is imminent here as well.' He ran up the steps to the tower and scrambled up the ladders. Friedrich followed behind.

When they reached the lookout platform, the lad on watch was leaning over the rail. His eyes squinted in the direction of the lake, as though half an arm's length would help him study the landscape better.

'I see them now, setting up camp. There are a dozen fires, maybe more. Shall I ring the bell again, Master Tell?

'No. Not yet.'

Walter chewed his lip. If the warning bell rang, the enemy would hear it too and rally faster. The distribution of weapons to the men in Morgarten wasn't yet complete. By keeping the bell silent, they might buy themselves a little more time before the main attack.

'How are your eyes?' he asked the lad. 'Are you able to see if they start to approach from Eierhals? You must sound the alarm as soon as you see troops mobilising, as soon as the horses come.'

'Yes, Herr Tell.' The lad paused. 'Is Fräulein Magda going to be all right?'

'I hope she'll recover. She's a strong woman.' Walter tried to put Magda from his mind. He stared at the peninsula between Morgarten and Aegeri, gauging the size of the camp.

'I'm not sure of numbers, but there could be soldiers gathered on the fields out of our view,' said the lad.

'I don't believe they'll attack after dark,' said Walter. 'Finding a route through the swamp is perilous at night. They probably know we've set blockades on the trail. Keep a watch for any movement at all, especially through the forest above the main village. The Frenchmen should be returning soon. If you see horses that are not theirs, then ring that bell as hard as you can.'

Walter looked towards the mill on the other side of the stream. The building lay silent, the waterwheel stopped since there was no grain left to grind or wool left to spin. The flow was diverted into the stream that flowed under the border wall through the swamp to the lake.

On a flat rock next to the mill Edgar and Josef were handing out the last of the halberds to the Schornen men. Edgar kept the last weapon for himself and the two of them made their way back towards the tower. Walter and Friedrich slid down the ladders and hurried down the steps to meet them in the courtyard.

'How is my sister?' asked Edgar.

'I've treated the burn on her leg. She should be fine, though perhaps a little too scantily clad in this weather until she can weave herself a new skirt,' said Walter.

Edgar could have taken Walter's jest as inappropriate, but he was suppressing a smile.

'Who is this?' asked Josef, looking at Friedrich, who had stopped at the fountain to take a drink and was now limping towards the group.

'Freddi comes with a message from the Arth garrison. They fired an arrow there as well, but this one had the words "Beware Morgarten" on a piece of parchment wrapped around the shaft. The camp is expanding near Aegeri. Battle is imminent,' said Walter.

'Why would they do such a thing? Have they been drinking too much mead?' asked Edgar.

'Possibly,' Josef answered. 'But I don't think they have any idea about what's been going on here over the past weeks.'

They all turned to the sound of horses trotting nimbly down the trail from the pass to the tower. The Frenchmen were returning. It was time to exercise their plan.

'Leopold's soldiers are fools, thinking they can taunt us so.' Josef spat and rubbed it with his boot into the dirt at his feet. '*Messieurs!*' he called to the knights as they pulled up their horses. 'Let us gather the men. It's time to rally our troops.'

✝ ✝ ✝

They gathered on the pasture between Morgarten and the first buildings of the Schornen community. Josef stood next to the Morgarten farmer who had cached the weapons. The men from both villages spread out in front of them. Walter tried to keep despair from seeping into his thoughts.

'We may be outnumbered when they come, but each and every one of you has taken not only a piece of the French knights' knowledge, but also their courage,' said Josef. 'You've given your energy and shown your patriotism to fight for what you know is right. We're grateful that the brothers of Morgarten join us in our defence of this gateway into the Confederation. All that is left now is hope that we can succeed.'

The Morgarten farmer took over. 'We have the advantage of surprise on our side. Without many weapons, we are using what nature has provided. No amount of armour can stop your ammunition – the trees and the mountains will be our allies. Those who have been assigned to their positions on the ridge above Morgarten will head up there before first light. The archers amongst you will be ready next to the marshland and those of you with halberds will be led by the knights to stop any enemy soldiers who manage to get through.'

'Von Hünenberg's men will be expecting the marsh to be frozen,' said Josef. 'That will work in our favour. Your efforts will help us fight for our homes, our livelihoods, and we will defend them with all our strength. Let this finally unite our families as part of the Confederation!'

As if a curse had been cast, the wind sighed through the pines, carrying the threat of more snow as the light began to dim at the end of the day. Wrapped in coats and animal pelts, the men dispersed, heading to their stations. Walter was still sure the Habsburgs would not attack after dark. But the Confederate allies needed to be in position in case. It would be a long night.

Walter made his way to his post on the southwest ridge of the village. On the way he passed Brigitta's father Berndt and a youth huddled together on the lower slope. The older man sat with a crossbow on his knee, the younger one with a bow on the ground at his side. He was shivering, but Walter knew it wouldn't be from the cold. He pulled a small flask from his jerkin and handed it to the old man. 'A little kirsch might help you both.'

Berndt nodded his thanks. The lad took nervous sips from the flask until the older man took the flask gently from him. 'A mouthful is enough for courage, lad. Any more than that and it dims the wits and thins the blood.' He turned to Walter. 'Thank you, Walter. God speed.'

Walter climbed to the rocky outcrop with a sweeping view of the valley and the Figlenfluh Ridge above Morgarten. It was almost dark now. The glow of more than two dozen fires dotted the Habsburg camp, but there was no movement. Walter hoped that Freddi could reach Werner Stauffacher in all speed and beg him to spare a troop of soldiers for Schornen. Time was running out. They might not arrive in time, if at all. But until the bell rang from the tower, Walter felt useless.

With the darkness came the cold. Walter had been given an extra pelt, but his lack of movement caused the cold to penetrate and his body shuddered from time to time. Sounds were magnified in the blindness of the narrow valley head. A crack echoed from the other side of the village. Walter sensed the Schornen men tense with expectation. But the faint crump of snow falling to the ground revealed that a branch had snapped under the weight of it.

The moon appeared only once in the night. Its cloud-diffused light on Walter's eyelids made him realise he'd been in a state of half slumber. Once it had set in the pre-dawn darkness, above the high-pitched honk of a coot somewhere in the swamp, Walter thought he could hear human movement: the unfolding of tent skins, the donning of armour, the saddling of horses and the dull ring of weapons being prepared. Metal against metal.

Heinrich von Hünenberg was waking his troops and preparing them for battle.

CHAPTER FORTY-THREE

15th November 1315, Schornen

MAGDA

T he four most important people in Magda's life were involved in this battle. She wasn't going to simply hide and
wait for news of their fate.

Edgar and her father had wanted her to go with Brigitta and
the other women. They'd taken as many of the livestock as
possible to the village over the other side of the pass. Mihal
had arrived to help transport the old and infirm with his faithful mule. In the mayhem of animals, children and the elderly
struggling up the slope towards the top of the pass, Magda
had taken the opportunity to sneak back to the village. She'd
watched Walter running from building to building. She didn't
set a fire for fear of him discovering her there and forcing her to
leave. If only she had more experience with weapons, she would
disguise herself as one of the men. She could think of nothing
more satisfying than driving a pike through their enemy.

She was shivering when she woke in a darkness tinged with the deep blue of pre-dawn. She dressed in double layers and ate some stale bread, wiping it around the previous day's lard in the pan.

At first light she climbed the hill to the south of the village where Walter would be. There was no path; she picked her way over the rock-strewn field above the gorge where the trail led down from the pass. She held her skirts, now at different lengths on each side, away from her bandaged leg.

The steep cliff on the southern end of the lake was inaccessible from the lake. The Habsburg troops would have to pass to the north, through the swamp, and couldn't reach this area. She was high enough above the marshland to witness the battle from any direction. She would simply need to keep an eye out for stray arrows.

She imagined the enemy arriving in their hordes, searching the outbuildings for food stores. Most of the village's grain and preserved foods had been moved several days ago over the pass to dry barns on the Schwyzer farms. The rest of the textiles were hidden in the mill. They didn't have time to move them out of the village to anywhere safer. At least for this, they were prepared to foil the Habsburgs.

Walter was somewhere further along the rocky outcrop where she now stood. He was to be the signaller. Although it was still dark, she knew vaguely where he was and at the very least would be able to find him when he blew the alphorn.

They had abandoned the idea of a lantern. The weather was still unpredictable and a light may not be visible in the gloom. It would be impossible to see in the event of a sudden blizzard.

Magda remembered the knights studying the opposite ridge from here all those months ago when they first arrived. It was a perfect lookout for the exact moment that the enemy would pass the narrowest part of the valley before the mill and the saddle of the pass. The rock wall leading from the toll tower to somewhere below her looked insignificant from this height. She prayed the enemy wouldn't get through, but doubts were beginning to flicker in her mind. Those campfires looked far more numerous than she had imagined. She continued to scramble up the slope to the ridge, limping slightly as her delicate skin chafed against the bandage.

As the sky lightened, Magda made out Walter's silhouette on the same rocky outcrop she had stood on with Sébastien in the spring. An alphorn lay on the ground at his feet. Standing tall, Walter was like a commander, ready to take charge of an entire army. He turned at the sound of her swishing skirt and a footfall against gravel.

'Magda! You should be on the other side of the pass,' he called down to her in a forced whisper. 'What are you doing here?'

'I can't stay back there not knowing what is going on, Walti,' she said as she joined him, catching her breath. 'And if they decide to wait another day until darkness to attack, I can help keep you awake. If necessary I can be a messenger.'

'You will do no such thing. If any messages need taking to our front line, I'll be doing the delivering. Here, let's sit a little lower so we are not seen from their camp when dawn breaks. When the battle commences, these rocks can protect you from any stray missiles.'

'How did they gather in so many numbers without the people of Morgarten noticing?' asked Magda.

'The Habsburgs are not known for their stealth, so I'm wondering the same thing. Perhaps von Hünenberg has begun to learn from his mistakes.'

'What are the arranged signals?' asked Magda.

'After the initial bell from the tower, I will sound one blow when they reach the end of the lake, and shall repeat a shorter two-tone blow when they arrive at the critical point below the ridge.

'Look! They are moving!' said Magda.

As though the lad in the tower had heard her, the bell began to ring, echoing a frantic warning across the valley. Von Hünenberg would be in no doubt that they were aware he was advancing. There was no avoiding confrontation now.

The enemy troops were too far away to be seen individually, but Magda and Walter made out a mass of men on foot, behind some mounted soldiers. The combined breath of their beasts rose in a vapour cloud as they began to move.

The troop advanced as a solid unit, a giant dark arrowhead moving across frosty pastures. They looked frighteningly magnificent, even from a distance. Magda swallowed. They must number several hundred at least. The mounted soldiers kept their angular line, the horses at the head of the cavalry prancing as they were reined in to match the walking pace of the troops on foot. The jingle of bridles and the clink of armour drifted to them across the swamp. The mounted soldiers held their spears and halberds upright, their shafts wavering like reeds in a Föhn wind.

She wondered how many troops were currently advancing on Arth. The difference there was that Commander Stauffacher's army was waiting for Duke Leopold's soldiers. How could a handful of lowly peasants deal with Heinrich von Hünenberg's troops now moving towards Morgarten?

As the enemy came level with the end of the lake, the formation condensed as the troops were forced onto the narrow trail between the swamp and the forest. The horses could only walk three abreast, leaving themselves in a position of vulnerability from the side. Walter took a deep breath and blew the alphorn as steadily and as long as he could. It was hardly melodious, the tone as his lungs emptied honking the out-of-tune crack of a beginner. Magda thought he could use a few lessons, but marvelled at how much air he could hold.

As the enemy drew nearer, Magda thought she could feel the hooves through the ground. She now clearly heard the screech of armour hinges and blowing horses rattling their bridles. A weak rising sun shone briefly through the cloud and glinted off the helmet of the man at the head of the formation. Heinrich von Hünenberg. He looked imposing and confident. Hope sluiced out of her like snowmelt from the mill pond.

They were well beyond Morgarten now and had veered off the blockaded path through the forest where the horses could only pass in single file. But as they reached the pastures where they had earlier that year slaughtered Schornen's sheep, they quickly reformed the battalion and continued their steady movement forward towards the upper marshland, and the walled border of the Confederation.

At the base of the wall on the east side, the remaining village men who weren't up on the Figlenfluh waited, crouching in the shelter of the rocks. Farmers and herdsmen held on tightly to their crude weapons, swords, halberds and a variety of bows and crossbows. They were all waiting for Walter's sign.

As the Habsburg troops began to cross the reed marsh, the soft ground caused some of the beasts to stumble, and the battalion appeared to falter. A number of commands, incomprehensible from a distance, were delivered in the strange dialect of the Austrians, but they didn't stop the advance.

'Shouldn't you be giving the second signal now, Walti?' asked Magda.

He shook his head. 'The intention is not to block their way. That will not stop them. They would retreat and find a way around the obstacles later. The intention is to inflict damage. To make sure the troops are compromised so as few as possible return to their garrisons. By the time they limp back to their castle in Habsburg, it is hoped they will have little intention of ever attacking again.'

Magda could hardly believe he was saying this. Walter the pacifist.

The enemy horses now appeared unsure, some advancing faster than others as their hooves met varying solidness of ground under them. The men on foot began to bunch up behind the cavalry. Magda looked at Walter, but still he waited. The knuckles of his hand clutching the neck of the alphorn were as white as the snow at their feet.

A company of men at the back of the battalion stopped and knelt down in the muck of the swamp. As they raised their weapons, Magda saw they were archers. A pot of burning pitch was passed along the ranks. They dipped their arrows and bolts and placed them in their bows and crossbows. As the first set of arrows flew straight and true over the border wall to Schornen, the squeal of a horse echoed across the valley.

The foot soldiers carrying swords behind the horses were now directly below the Figlenfluh Ridge opposite them.

Walter stood on top of a rock, lifted the alphorn and took a few deep breaths.

He blew again and again, repeating the two-tone tune they'd all agreed beforehand. This time he kept his tune. It took a while for the sound to reach the opposite ridge, but when it did, the logs and boulders finally began to roll.

Chapter Forty-Four

15th November 1315, Morgarten

MAGDA

As the thundering mass rolled down towards the enemy troops, burning arrows continued to rain onto the hamlet over the border wall as the archers were unaware of their fate. The enemy battalion soon stopped as one, seemingly confused by the thundering din above them. Magda imagined them looking up with horror at the approaching doom.

The projectiles piled onto the battalion, crushing everything in their way. The valley was a chaotic jumble of hewn logs, boulders, uprooted trees, horses and troops. Earth and dust rose in a blinding cloud at the bottom of the slope like smoke. The continual rumbling under Magda's feet was like the earth tremors Omama had described to her in her youth.

Magda could no longer make out anything through the dust cloud, but in the hamlet she saw that the barn next to the chalet was now a roaring pyre, along with several other buildings around the mill. She looked on in despair. Flames licked close to the roof of the chalet. How could she save their home from here? She gathered her skirts as though to run back down the hill.

'Please, Magda, stay here now,' begged Walter. 'It's not safe to go back.'

As the cloud of dust and debris cleared above the battlefield, the men of Morgarten and Schornen scrambled over the border wall where they had been hiding and ran towards the Habsburg troops. Sébastien led them with Grégoire at his side, their mighty swords drawn and ready. Yves was up on the Figlenfluh Ridge with the other men and would be making his way back down to the valley, following the trace of their natural missiles. Magda wondered what the knights had done with their horses. They must have decided not to ride into the swamp. Seeing the Habsburg horses in difficulty, they must have abandoned their mounts.

The battle cries of the knights and the villagers were now audible over the dying thunder of the barrage. Magda's gaze was drawn back to the mayhem. 'Oh my Lord, look how they are trapped. Those poor horses!'

The few Habsburg soldiers who were still upright finally reached the outskirts of Schornen. In some places the reeds came almost up to the heads of the foot soldiers. The men of Morgarten swung and slashed and stabbed their halberds and swords into the midst. Their open mouths were silent for a moment. And then their furious battle cries reached Magda's ears.

A line of men returned the enemy crossbow fire from behind the border wall. They may not have had the aid of pitch, but their bolts reached their mark over the tops of their own men running into the melee.

But the enemy troops kept coming, blind to the destruction behind them and the danger ahead. Enemy soldiers stumbled over the top of their fallen comrades, pressing their bodies under the mud. They drowned their own troops in the marsh and then gained purchase on their bodies to continue the onslaught. They ran over the floundering horses, whose nostrils and eyes had filled with filth and whose legs were tangled in the unforgiving blades of the reeds. They ran over the tops of the logs and boulders that had filled the gully and created a difficult path for the troops to scale.

The Morgarten men roared into the midst of bodies, brandishing their home-forged weapons, the echo of their voices turning the defenders from a hundred-fold to a thousand in the echoes between the hills.

And suddenly Magda saw Sébastien fall. She recognised the blond curls of Grégoire seeping out from the sides of his helmet as he bent to help his fellow knight.

'No! No! No!' she cried.

Walter followed her gaze, and put his hand on her shoulder. She looked at him, and he pressed his lips into a line. There were no words.

Magda put her hands to her mouth, torn. She wanted to run down there, but knew she'd be putting herself in grave danger. As though reading her mind, Walter shook his head.

'He must still be alive, or Grégoire would not be protecting him so,' he said.

From the ground, Grégoire was protecting Sébastien's body and fighting the oncoming troops above him.

Over the sound of the battle in the swamp, the bell in the toll tower began ringing again. Magda turned to look east towards the pass. Confederate troops! A thousand of them! Men poured over the pass, running down the trail, their armour seeming not to hinder them.

'They took the message on the arrow seriously,' said Walter. 'Thank God for Friedrich!'

The Confederates ran through the hamlet and over the wall, flowing towards the Habsburg horde who had found a way through the first defence, smiting them and continuing to destroy those who were still stuck in the swamp. The bloody battle continued with a rising madness Magda would never have expected.

☩ ☩ ☩

Magda's attention wavered between Sébastien and the horse nearby that she had first seen floundering in the swamp. It made a series of guttural grunts with each effort to rise out of the quagmire. It proved to be impossible as she watched a useless rear hock flailing from its haunch. The animal would never gain purchase upon the softness of the marshland. Its rider had long ago been dragged to the depths under the weight of his armour. She couldn't take her eyes off the death throes of the beast and was worried its body would crush those of the two knights close by.

Her ears rang from the clanging of halberd against sword, and rock against armour. And the horrifying sight of men who could not contain their lust for battle even after the battle was so obviously won. As the battle began to peter out, the Confederates claiming a sure victory, she admitted she'd never seen such carnage. Bodies and severed limbs and heads lay everywhere, haphazardly scattered in the marshland like a field of marrows and gourds.

'I never imagined such senseless destruction of life,' she murmured, tears running down her cheeks. She desperately hoped that Sébastien had survived. 'Would this have taken place if we all hadn't been deceived? I'm so sorry. I didn't know the significance of the abbey's theft at the time. I made a promise to Papa to keep you in the lie, Walti, my love...'

Victory cries from the Confederate soldiers began to filter through the sounds of dying men and horses. As the words died on Magda's lips, it was only then she realised Walter hadn't said anything, that he was no longer at her side. She turned to stare at his body crumpled next to her on the ground.

CHAPTER FORTY-FIVE

15th November 1315, Morgarten

MAGDA

A stray Habsburg arrow had pierced Walter's jerkin, severing Magda's recently embroidered handiwork on his chest. The bright green thread she had used to sew the leafy design was now soaked with his lifeblood, transforming the colour to the putrid dark brown of the autumn swamp.

The expression on his face was one of shock; he couldn't speak. Magda feared even if she could muster the strength to remove the shaft, the arrowhead might stay in his body. She knew nothing about wounds a weapon could inflict. She had to get him back down to the village where she might find some help.

'Walti, can you move? *Mein Gott*, you're bleeding so much!'

Magda placed her hand on his forehead. She avoided looking at the shaft sticking out from below his shoulder. She took off her coat and laid it on the ground, instantly shivering, either from exposure to the cold or fear of losing Walter. Her hands hovered over him, then moved him limb by limb and gently pushed him onto her coat.

'I have to drag you, Walti, there's no other way.'

He winced and groaned and tried to help shuffle himself onto her coat. She wasn't sure she could muster the strength to move him, but as God was her witness, she would try.

Her coat slid over the frosty ground with Walter lying on it, the sheepskin he'd brought with him the night before now covering his body. Magda could only pull down the slope in bursts. Her heart hammered, knowing that every bump over the rocks or tussocks of brown grass could be causing him agony. She was torn between getting him as quickly as possible to the hamlet and causing him as little discomfort as possible.

Pulling and tugging, her wrists and hands aching with the cold, she managed to drag him to the edge of the village. Once on the flatter ground, progress slowed. Every few pulls, she checked the wound at his chest. The shaft of the arrow still pointed towards the sky, the cock and two hens mocking her as their feathers caught the wind. So far there was no great welling of blood; it seemed the arrow had not touched his lungs or his heart. But if his wound was not attended to, he would either die of poisoning or he would lose too much blood to matter.

Men were still stumbling out of the swamp, some of them with horrendous wounds; some of them simply in shock. Magda didn't know whether there would be enough men left standing to help any of their people. Those who weren't injured were still coming down from the ridge on the other side, mentally exhausted from the bloodbath they had helped create in the swamp.

Magda's arms burned with the effort of pulling Walter. Her hands were cold and losing their feeling. Her fingers kept slipping from the cloth of her coat, soaked in melting frost and snow and Walter's blood. Slowly they made their way towards the mill. The closer they came, the heavier the weight of Walter as they reached flat ground, and Magda began to stagger, trying to suppress the sob in her throat.

A small crowd was gathered on the dry beaten earth of the forecourt of the mill. Magda saw the familiar flash of Grégoire and Yves' chainmail.

And then her heart dropped. Sébastien lay on the ground between them, a deep crimson gash in his thigh exposed through a tear in his leggings. His skin lay open like giant lips, globules of yellow fat spilling onto his inner thigh. The white smoothness of his leg bone shone like the centre of a lily, making Magda's stomach turn. Grégoire looked up as she approached. His eyes, red-rimmed through the dirt on his face, were bright with unshed tears.

Yves' face collapsed in a grimace as Magda indicated Walter on her coat. She could pull him no further. On the last tug across the ground, he uttered a cry of pain before losing consciousness.

Yves examined the shaft sticking out of Walter's chest. 'It has not reached his heart, but his breathing is laboured. I fear it may have pierced a lung. Oh God, Sébastien too! This is terrible, terrible!'

Magda stifled a great sob. She could not believe that the two men she loved most had both been injured in battle.

CHAPTER FORTY-SIX

15th November 1315, Schornen

SÉBASTIEN

Fire raged in his leg. The pain was like nothing he'd ever experienced. From the thigh up to his hip and into his back he experienced a burning, dragging ache. Along with his roiling stomach, both legs began to tremble uncontrollably. He saw starbursts in front of his eyes whether they were open or closed. He stayed as still as possible to relieve the waves of pain searing through his body.

Sébastien looked at his friend Grégoire. A greyness tinged the skin under his ice-blue eyes. The seriousness of his injury was confirmed in the strained lines of his friend's face.

He turned to Magda, crouched on the other side of him. Beyond her skirts, Walter lay on the ground, the shaft of an arrow sticking upright out of his chest below his shoulder. Sébastien squinted. Walter's chest still rose and fell with his breath. Would he live?

'What are you doing here, Magda?' yelled Josef, striding over from the base of the ridge. 'I might have known you would not go with the others, but thank God you're safe!'

'And then I would not have been able to help! Let us not waste our talk on something that did not happen. I'm so glad *you* are alive, Papa. Now we need to save these men!' Magda's voice broke.

As her father looked at both Walter and Sébastien, they all saw hopelessness in his eyes.

'What can I do, Grégoire?' asked Magda. 'What does Sébastien need? How can we help Walter? I wish Mihal was here.'

'Sébastien is losing blood fast.' Said Grégoire. '*Mon Dieu*, Magda, it does not look good. And if we don't take that arrow from Walter's chest he will die from poisons in his body. And yet if we do take it, he may bleed to death.'

Magda tugged the shawl from around her shoulders and folded it many times to make a pad. She knelt beside Sébastien and placed her palm on his chest. He held her gaze, not wanting to blink for fear of losing the look in her eye; of love, of pity, of a faint hope that he would survive.

'Press this to Sébastien's wound,' she said to Yves. 'The bleeding must be stanched while we think. We have to think!'

'Magda,' Walter groaned

'He has come around!' she shouted.

As Walter opened his mouth to speak, Sébastien saw a fleck of blood on his tongue. Magda must have noticed it too. If he was bleeding inside, this wasn't a good sign. He lifted his head.

'No, no, no! Walti, don't move. Lie still.'

Walter tried to grab Magda's hand, tried to speak, but could do neither.

'I can't lose *both* of you.'

Sébastien heard the whisper from her throat, strained with an exasperated helplessness. He kept his gaze on them both. Walter closed his eyes, the grimace on his face showing his pain. Magda touched his cheek. When she turned back to Sébastien, her eyes were flicking from him to Walter. He was losing a lot of blood, too much, but could see for himself the position of the shaft in Walter's chest.

'Grég!' Sébastien rasped.

His dear friend approached, then leaned down to hear him better. Sébastien took a sudden inward breath and panted while pain cast its singing net over his torso. 'She cannot know how badly I suffer,' he told Yves in his own tongue. 'Walter must be saved.' He grabbed Grégoire's jerkin to pull his face even closer to his own so he could whisper in his ear.

'Fetch the *Saant Graal*,' he told him.

'It's that bad?' Grégoire asked as he pulled away.

Sébastien nodded, his eyes narrowing as another chill shook his body.

'If by God's grace I end up living, I will surely lose this leg. I cannot...'

Grégoire stood up abruptly, turned away and ran towards the toll tower.

'Where's Grégoire going? What is he doing?' shouted Magda.

'Be calm, Magda,' said Yves. 'It will be all right. We must take the arrow from Walter's shoulder.'

She looked at Walter, then turned to Sébastien. He smiled weakly.

'Your skin is as white as a heron's feather, Sébastien! We must bind your leg, stop the flow. It needs a suture.'

'My artery is cut. There is no one here skilled enough to sew the vessels that deliver my life blood. I am not in pain, Magda. Just very tired. You must see to Walter. You and Yves must take the arrow from his shoulder. Grég will bring something to help.'

'But Grégoire has gone! What are you saying? I can sew,' she said, though Sébastien saw her swallow.

Yves touched her on the shoulder.

'The arrow must come out, Magda,' he said. 'Josef! Can you fetch a bottle of kirsch from your kitchen?'

'This is no time to drink yourself into oblivion to forget what you have seen, young man,' said Magda's father in confusion.

Sébastien smiled.

'No, it is for the wound,' said Yves. 'It is something we learned in the Crusades. Alcohol can help stop rot setting in around a wound. Please, fetch the kirsch.'

Walter raised his hand again, made a guttural sound in his throat, pointed to his jerkin. Magda looked inside his pocket and pulled out a small flask. She opened the cap and sniffed. Her head recoiled and the unpleasantness of the contents was made obvious by the twist of her mouth. 'Papa, wait! There is some kirsch here.' She drew a deep breath. 'Hold him, Yves. Gently.'

She opened Walter's jerkin and pulled back his undershirt. Sébastien winced at seeing the wound. Yves held Walter down. Josef held the flask. Magda placed her palm on Walter's chest and pulled the shaft of the arrow with her other fist. Walter screamed. Magda let go, tears filling her eyes.

Sébastien prayed for her to have courage. She must know that this thing should be done without thinking too hard. She set her mouth, stood as though to gather her strength and pulled the shaft again. This time the arrow resisted for only a moment, then pulled free. The tip steamed with blood, flesh and the heat of Walter's body. The wound looked red and raw, but the arrow was free. Sébastien let out a long breath.

Josef passed the flask to Magda.

'Do I just pour it on?' she asked Yves.

He nodded and she poured the remaining clear liquid directly on the wound. Walter shouted out. The movement caused a welling of crimson blood. Magda pressed the cloth of his undershirt over the wound. Then closed his jerkin to attempt to keep him warm. Her hand felt something hard and round in another of Walter's pockets.

'The salve!' she shouted, and Sébastien looked on curiously.

She pulled out the ceramic pot. Fumbling, she managed to open the lid and exposing the wound again, applied a salve around its edges, wiping the continually welling blood with a piece of Walter's torn shirt. The tatter of cloth was soon soaked through.

'Tear my shawl in half! If you can find a length that is still clean!'

Yves went to Sébastien, removed the pad and did as he was asked, finding part of the material that was not soaked in blood. Magda pressed the cloth against Walter's wound.

'I don't know what more to do! Do we let the poison bleed out, or try to stop it?'

Yves shrugged in ignorance.

'The *eau de vie* should help to stave off infection.'

Magda looked up to the sky, as though uttering a silent prayer. Sébastien smiled; that his Magda could still summon God in moments of peril. A flash of movement in the forest caught their eye. As Grégoire emerged from behind the toll tower holding the specially sewn pouch, Edgar appeared from the trail leading to Morgarten.

'Eddi,' whispered Magda. 'Thank God he's safe.'

Magda looked back down at Walter, whose eyes had closed. 'Walti! Stay with us!'

She had eyes only for Walter now. It was as it should be.

'Perhaps it is best he stays unconscious,' said Yves. 'To ease the pain. A man can die from that alone.'

'I think we are losing him anyway,' said Magda with a sob.

'Yves, don't scare the girl,' Sébastien admonished, his voice now strained with his own suffering. 'There is a way... Grég is coming.'

It was the last thing he could say before his eyes fluttered closed.

'Eddi, can you fetch blankets from the chalet? The men will be suffering from the cold.' Sébastien heard Magda's voice as though through a thick fog.

He opened his eyes a fraction to see Magda patting the sheepskin over Walter's torso. But his thinly clad legs remained exposed to

the elements. Edgar turned towards the chalet without complaint. Grégoire arrived with the cloth bag Magda had woven
and sewn for Sébastien, the crimson cross shining brightly
against the pale linen background. Sébastien took a breath, and
suddenly felt no pain.

Inside this pouch was the thing that had become a dangerous secret, for which the one life lost at the beginning of this
whole affair was nothing compared to the carnage they had all
witnessed that afternoon.

Grégoire placed the bag on the ground and took out the
sacred chalice; Sébastien thought how ordinary it looked. Not
like the shiny communion cup in the chapel in Morgarten and
not like the carved gold goblets on the altar in Einsiedeln. This
one was tarnished, a little grubby. But it held such power.

'Bring water directly from the spring, Grég,' said Yves. 'It
must flow directly into the cup from the source, and you must
bring back as much as you can.'

They watched Grégoire approach the stone trough in the
centre of the hamlet where the spring water harnessed at the
village's source flowed directly from a pipe. He filled the cup
to the brim and walked carefully back to the group of people
gathered round the two bodies on the ground.

Josef stood with Walter's bloody arrow in his hand, a tiny
piece of flesh still sticking to the blade. He looked at it and
threw it to the ground behind him where a rose of colour
spread in the snow.

'Séb! Séb, *reveil-toi*,' said Yves, gently shaking Sébastien by
his shoulder.

Sébastien opened his eyes wider. He didn't have long now.
His eyelids wavered, his gaze losing focus.

'*Pas moi*. Walter,' he croaked. 'Walter first. He must be saved.
I... it is my time, and there is not enough for both of us. I have
lost too much blood. *C'est trop tard*.'

Yves took a sudden breath, an inward sob. He closed his eyes and briefly lowered his chin. Then he sighed and looked straight at Magda. She curled her free hand into a fist and bit down on her knuckle.

'Walter must drink. He must finish the water in the cup. Every drop,' whispered Sébastien.

Magda looked down at Walter. He was unconscious but moaning a little.

'It will spill. You'll have to sit him up,' she said.

Together Yves and Grégoire lifted Walter, supporting him under his arms. He shouted out and his jerkin fell open. The rag fell away from his wound. Everyone gasped to see a fresh welling of blood.

'Walti, you must drink the water,' she begged.

He opened his mouth as a few drops moistened his lips. Magda poured a little water into his mouth and waited for him to swallow, to make sure he wouldn't choke. She leaned in towards his face.

'Walti, you must wake up. Enough to drink the water. Can you hear me?'

He didn't move. Magda was staring at his mouth. His pink lips trembled a little, the tip of his tongue lying against his lower teeth. She moved closer and keeping the cup straight, she kissed him fully on the mouth. A single tear ran from the corner of Sébastien's eye.

'Please, Walti,' she whispered into his mouth.

He opened his eyes as Magda pulled away, with a look so intense, Sébastien saw her blush.

'Here. Drink.'

Pressing his lips around the rim of the cup, he drank. His swallows became stronger and stronger until he had finished the cup. And for the first time that day, he smiled.

'Whatever magic has just happened here, I believe you will live, Walti. Thank God,' she said.

Edgar arrived from the chalet, and covered Walter with another soft sheepskin. Magda touched his cheek, and Sébastien's chest constricted.

'Quick, Edgar, you must refill the chalice! Hurry!' shouted Magda.

She turned to Sébastien and knelt beside him.

'The pain... It is not so bad, *ma belle*,' he said.

She looked down at his legs as they continued to tremble.

'How does your body still have the strength to do this?' she said and laid her hand on his cold thigh.

'Walter will make it,' he told her.

Magda looked over to where Walter lay on the ground. He took a deep breath and released it slowly, as though the pain over his upper torso was floating away.

'You have sacrificed yourself for his survival.'

'Magda, you know we could never be together. I have already told you my faith lies elsewhere.'

She leaned in, so no one else could hear.

'But I am carrying your child.'

Sébastien sucked in a breath. He furrowed his brow. Joy flooded his weakly beating heart, the pulse of it fading in his throat. And immediately following, he felt the cold sorrow of despair. A child! Would it have made a difference? It was too late now. He felt the burn of tears at the back of his throat.

'You will make... exemplary parents.' Sébastien groaned as a wave of pain hit again. 'I'm honoured for Walter... to be the father of my child.'

'What if he won't have me?'

'He will. His love for you is great.'

'Would you have drunk from the cup first if I'd told you sooner?'

Sébastien closed his eyes tight. He knew he was beyond healing. 'He will have you. He will raise the child as his own. The child will have a... special message for the future of this nation... for the future of humanity...'

And with the effort of those last words, Sébastien simply closed his eyes, sighed his last breath and sank into the welcome darkness of eternal sleep.

Chapter Forty-Seven

30th November 1315, Morgarten

WALTER

I t was the first Sunday of Advent. Snow flurries whirled around the courtyard between the toll tower and the Stauffacher chalet. Although Walter had been offered a bed in the Morgarten Inn, the tower seemed to be the only place in the newly united villages where any kind of order had been restored. It wasn't until morning when he woke without a fire in the building that Walter partly regretted his decision. He hadn't been offered a bed in the chalet, but this was probably because Josef detected a new emotional tension between his daughter and Walter. The barn had burned to the ground in the battle, but the stone tower stood with its roof intact.

Bodies were still being pulled from the swamp closer to the lake. They were carried and placed on a slope beyond Morgarten away from both villages, to avoid water sources becoming tainted with disease and to stop the stench of death rising from the marsh, despite the cold. It was decided the Habsburg bodies would be burned. The elders considered erecting a memorial, perhaps to avoid future generations farming on earth poisoned by enemy soldiers, but mainly to remember the strength of their own defence and honour their own dead. It would be discussed the following spring.

Morgarten was now unofficially part of the Confederation Helvetica, and a new treaty was being drawn up. As Walter was still recovering and couldn't yet travel far, his writing skills were employed to draft the initial documents. He used birch parchment scrounged from the Morgarten church. When he was well enough to travel in a few more days, he would take these documents to Schwyz and Altdorf for military approval. They would be re-written officially by a scribe engaged at the Capuchin Monastery above Altdorf.

The Holy Roman Empire had finally agreed to relinquish part of its rule over the nation. The Confederation Helvetica not only had independence in the middle of Habsburg territory, but it had also begun to gain a foothold in the neighbouring cantons who were desperate to escape Duke Leopold's rule. The Confederation would soon grow, increasing its land area, absorbing a more diverse population. It would secure the axis of one of the most important trade routes in Europe across the Gotthard Pass.

Of the entire troop of Morgarten men and Confederate soldiers, losses after the battle amounted, unbelievably, to only around a dozen. Those who survived, though, had more blood on their hands and consciences than was healthy, and Walter hoped he would never have to see such a conflict again in his lifetime. Although he hadn't seen the last madness of it, Magda was a witness to the battle in its entirety and recounted the horror to him later. Even those admitting defeat amongst the Habsburg troops with the intention of retreating back to the castle in Aargau were brutally slain before they could leave the Aegerital. A battle-fuelled madness had infected many an ordinary man that day. And one thing Walter couldn't ignore was that any determination to remain pacifist had been negated by his input into the military strategy and the slaying of a Habsburg marksman.

Sébastien was buried behind the chapel in Schornen at the base of the trail leading over the pass to the heart of the Confederation. Walter would be forever in his debt for allowing him to drink first from the Holy Grail. His pain had subsided almost immediately after emptying the cup and his wound was healing well. The muscle that had torn in his shoulder was binding, and if his lung had been compromised, there was now no sign of it.

But their individual beliefs had turned on their head. Now it was Walter who was willing to accept a miracle, and Magda who was keen to learn the ingredients to Mihal's healing salve. Nevertheless, her curiosity was not without a degree of wonder.

'When I saw blood rise in your throat, I thought you were done for, Walti. It's truly a miracle. The Grail is not something of this earth, but then neither is God. It makes you think, doesn't it?'

They were standing beside Sébastien's grave, looking back towards the community of Schornen. The brown reeds of the swamp were broken and crushed where the battle had taken place.

'I no longer wish to speculate,' said Walter. 'I've been known to question the existence of the Holy Spirit, but it's hard not to believe in His power now. Whatever happened that day, it allowed me to wake from the throes of a deathly wound to look upon your face.' He turned to look at Magda and she smiled sadly, glancing down at the mound of fresh earth under which lay Sébastien's body. Then she reached for Walter's hand, and gazed up into his face with a different, hopeful look.

'Walti, there is something you must know before you spill what I know is on your mind.'

He tilted his head, encouraging her to continue.

'He sacrificed himself for us.'

'I don't understand. He died at the hands of a Habsburg sword, but I'm sure he was a worthy soldier, fighting to the end. He was doing what knights do.'

'Yes, but he might have survived if he'd drunk from the chalice.'

Walter pressed his lips together, but didn't say anything.

'He never forgave himself for what happened following the sacking of the abbey,' Magda continued. 'That they kept their secrets from us. That they were indirectly responsible for the death of Brother Francis. That they used you as a pawn in the deceit to make the people of the Confederation believe that what happened in Einsiedeln was the thieving work of the Habsburgs.'

Walter frowned. 'I know that. I've recovered from the... humiliation.'

'He had an obligation to a higher calling. The thing the knights committed themselves to all those years ago is beyond the ruling of King Philip and now Louis of France or the Pope in Rome.'

'So he should have saved himself for his mission. Stayed alive to continue the holy work he and his colleagues were meant to undertake.'

'There is something else that complicates everything.' She paused. 'I'm carrying his child.'

Walter swallowed. This was no surprise. There had been signs. But it still caused a strange feeling of confusing, almost detached pain, to hear her say the words. 'Then I understand even less why he would allow me to live. Surely a man's greatest achievement in this world is to raise his sons and daughters.'

A sad smile flickered at Magda's mouth. She seemed suddenly unsure of herself.

'The thing is, he could never take me as his wife. His life's mission could never have included a family. But I think he had someone in mind to take that role.'

'Magda, I...'

'Oh, Walti. You are such a *good* person. You are godlier than anyone I know. It fills me with such joy that you treat me as an equal. If Séb were still alive, don't you see? He would still have gone to his calling. He would not have stayed with me, even though I carry his child. In saving you, and knowing how you feel about me, he hoped... I'm so sorry.' Magda placed one hand over her heart and the other on Walter's arm. Her eyes shone with tears. 'I gained your friendship, your trust and yet I have betrayed you.'

'There was no betrayal, Magda. I am a victim of my own pro-crastination. I should have declared my love for you long ago.'

Walter bit his lip. It was the first time he had used the word 'love'.

✝ ✝ ✝

They crowded round the table in the Stauffacher chalet kitchen. Walter, Josef, Edgar, Grégoire and Yves. Magda and Brigitta flitted back and forth from the stove, delivering warm food and mugs of mead. It was the last evening the two remaining knights would be in the hamlet. They were to leave the following day.

'The Confederation has strengthened its reputation as a warrior nation, so there will hopefully be less thievery along the trade route to the Gotthard. Our work in the valley is done,' said Grégoire.

'And we have to find another safe home for the Grail,' added Yves.

'Can I see it one more time?' Magda asked. 'Before it leaves us.'

Yves reached into the leather bag tied across his shoulder. They had never revealed its hiding place in the forest above the village before the battle, but now its power had been unveiled, letting it out of their sight was a risk they could no longer take.

He placed it in the middle of the table between two guttering candles. Behind Magda a soft glow came from the coals on the fire. But it seemed to Walter that the chalice glimmered on its own, in the middle of the table, despite its age-old tarnish. The dim light that had previously been cast from the paltry light brightened a little in the faces of those around the table.

'Can I?' Magda nodded at the cup.

Yves nodded and she picked it up with reverence, turning the bowl in her hands to examine the intricately carved patterns in the brass, emphasised by black tarnish fixed deep into their lines. Walter was overwhelmed with a sudden feeling of gratefulness. Magda handed the cup to him.

'One more time. You should hold it one more time.'

Walter took it from her and looked in the bowl. The brass inside was golden, as though someone had spent hours with a soft cloth polishing it to a sheen. He wanted to believe. He wanted to believe it was here that a miracle had taken place with a simple filling of water from the village spring. He recalled the pain in his shoulder when the Habsburg arrow had hit. He recalled the delirium and the searing heat of the wound. And he recalled drinking the sweetest tasting water, as though it were an elixir of life. The pain simply flowed away and he fell into the deep sleep of healing. He remembered Magda's soft hands on his chest, her fingers against his forehead, the lilt of her voice as she begged him to live.

'Whatever this thing is,' said Walter, 'Whether it be a thing of God or a thing of magic...'

'It requires belief, Walter. A belief in the Holy Spirit,' said Yves.

'And what is the difference? Between that and magic? We have never been shown God, and magic is an unseen deception that may simply be the ordinary idea of man. Some things happen by chance. The minuscule chance of a man on his death bed whose own body fights the wounds that ail him.'

'Or God's healing in imparting the knowledge of the herbs in Mihal's salve,' said Magda with reserve in her voice.

Grégoire went to speak, but Walter raised his finger to silence him. 'There is another explanation. Perhaps this Grail has been

forged from a blend of metals with a lucky combination of prop-
erties to heal infection in the body. You will call it a miracle, and
for years to come the stories will be embellished, just as the stories
of the son of God have been embellished. I believe Jesus was an
ordinary man, just like you or me. If indeed he drank from this
cup at the last supper, perhaps its "magic" protected him when
the barbs of Judas' nails cut into his body on the cross, so later he
could stand up and walk away. God imparted that knowledge too,
the forging of the Grail. But as I sit here today, healthy, with all my
faculties, I am happy to accept the miracle.'

Grégoire turned to Magda, tears on his face. 'God rest
Sébastien's soul,' he said.

Magda chewed her lip, but her eyes remained dry and she turned
to smile at Walter. And at that moment Walter knew beyond doubt
he would offer her his hand in marriage. The love in her eyes was
directed at him. And he could tell by her look that she wanted him
to ask it. But it wasn't his place to ask in front of the men who were
like Sébastien's brothers. To prove his point, Yves spoke to Magda.

'The very thing that might have saved his life is also the thing
that would have determined his future without you, Magda. He
was devoted to protecting this Grail. A group of us has always
been assigned to protect the routes to where it has been hidden for
centuries and its consequent safeguarding. It is what our ancestors
once carried before what others might call our army to protect
the worshippers of Christ in the Holy Lands. We knew when we
arrived in the Confederation what we were looking for. The fact
that Philip of France had declared us heretics meant that we had
to change its hiding place before it was jeopardised. This was what
Sébastien had devoted his whole life to.'

Grégoire cleared his throat. 'We're leaving tomorrow. Sébastien
knew this, and nothing other than his death would have prevented
him coming with us. He made a promise. It's in our code of
honour, a promise etched in our souls. The task has fallen to us,

and it pains me that Yves and I must carry on alone. We will likely be on the road for the remainder of our lives, always seeking a safe place for it.'

'Do you really believe that Christ himself drank from the cup?' asked Walter.

'The stories recited to you in church tell the truth. I know your scepticism. It is up to you to interpret these holy scriptures as you wish. Perhaps now you will have a different view of the church.'

'Joseph of Arimathea was the first to covet the Grail,' said Yves. 'Although it wasn't until much later that the descendants of Christ's disciples were obliged to develop their knightly expertise to continue its protection.'

'Joseph! Like you, Papa. Who was he?' Magda asked Yves.

'He was the first after Jesus to drink from it. He was the one who took Jesus down from the cross and carried his body away. God would have given him strength to do this through drinking from the Grail. Sébastien believed he was himself a descendant of Joseph through the generations.'

Walter thought of Séb's dark skin, his swarthy looks. How he looked more like a native of the southern lands who had occasionally been seen travelling through Bürglen and Altdorf on the trade routes than a man of the north.

'Then why didn't Joseph share the water with Christ himself, to bring him back to life?' Magda voiced Walter's own thoughts.

'The reason for Christ's death is a lot more complicated than that, Magda. He had to die; it could not be any other way. He had to prove to the people that he was mortal. It was to make the people believe in his earthly existence. To try and convince them to share his benevolence and kindness.'

Walter thought of what Magda had described at the scene of the battle. Men who were thirsty to take the lives of the enemy, an enemy who was essentially ruled by the Holy Roman Empire through the puppetry of Duke Leopold. Somewhere along the way, a conflicting set of values had been created by man in the name of God.

For Walter, it was time to get back to immerse himself in the simple values of human compassion and community.

CHAPTER FORTY-EIGHT

9th December 1315, Brunnen

MAGDA

It was the third time Magda had been out of the valley within the year. She was so excited, and imagined she could easily get used to travelling – satisfying the dreams she'd had since she was a child. She never tired of listening to Mihal's stories of far-off lands. She still had a yearning to discover the world beyond the little alpine valley, despite finding herself in a yet-to-be-revealed family situation. She refused to believe a baby would tie her to the village, as she'd seen so many other women simply resign themselves to a life of endless pregnancies of which only a third of their offspring reached adulthood.

Memories of her baby's father, the handsome knight, tumbled less frequently through her mind. They had all mourned his loss after the remaining knights had departed. But then she had been mourning Sébastien's loss from the moment he had told her he could never be hers. That half of her heart that had kept beating for him was now blossoming with the prospect of allowing the other half to fill the space completely.

Much depended on how Walter would react when Magda saw him in Brunnen. There was always a danger that his eye would be drawn to a maiden with less burden.

They were on their way to Brunnen to witness the signing of a new charter. Magda's father had already departed to confer with her uncle Werner in Schwyz. He would be joining them there later, so Magda was chaperoned by Edgar. Brigitta stayed at home. She said she felt too cumbersome in her pregnant state and insisted the affairs of the nation should be left to the men. To be fair, she had grown quite large, and Magda wondered with a little worry whether she was carrying twins. Brigitta hadn't wanted Magda to go to Brunnen either. She didn't approve of her interest in political matters.

Magda's own pregnancy wasn't far behind Brigitta's. She'd only recently begun to show – but was managing to hide it beneath her thick winter skirts and cloaks. It was only when she took off her clothes in the rare privacy of the chalet and placed her hand on the rounding swell of her lower belly that she allowed herself to think about what was growing there. Despite having helped Edgar deliver dozens of calves and lambs in her lifetime, she still marvelled at the miracle of life growing inside her. But something would have to change imminently. It would soon be obvious to everybody, especially those living in the confines of their little chalet.

At least she was no longer feeling tired and faint. Apart from Walter, Brigitta was the only person who knew her secret. If her calculations were correct she would be birthing in spring with the lambs.

Magda was dreading her father's reaction. By the next moon, many more people would know she was carrying a child. Then it would no longer be a secret. But whether the two people who were still alive would reveal the secret of the baby's paternity remained to be seen. Her dilemma would be solved for better or for worse in Brunnen.

She felt fit, having walked several times a week between the hamlet and Morgarten since the battle, re-establishing contact with relatives they hadn't felt safe visiting before for fear of Habsburg brigands who might be hiding along the forest trails. Now that Morgarten was part of the Confederation, enemy raiders had all but disappeared.

A new, smaller watchtower had been built in haste at the western entrance to the village of Morgarten, which gave a clear view to the end of the valley and the pastures surrounding the crescent-shaped Aegeri lake. Enemy trackers and spies returning to the scene of the battle in the weeks afterwards in the hope of scavenging useful trinkets, tools and weapons were threatened and fought off by the villagers if they even attempted to trespass into Confederate territory. They had soon slunk back to Zug and Aargau with their tails between their legs like shamed dogs. Those farmers whose tempers were still heated from the battle ensured that the enemy stayed away. Before long, marauders ceased their provocation altogether.

Magda's father and the farmers in Morgarten were already talking of digging trenches through the swamp to drain the water and turn the land between into pasture. The defence skills of the villagers were no longer in question. The land could be put to better use.

✥ ✥ ✥

Brunnen was in the heart of the Confederation, so the danger of meeting bandits along their route was even less likely than in the Aegerital. Their troupe took on a festive atmosphere as it expanded. Mihal joined them, journeying from the northern shore of Lake Zürich. He had met with relatives from Graubunden and received news that his family were safe and healthy. He wouldn't be able to get back home until the snows melted in spring.

There had been a light snowfall the day before they set out, but not enough to spill over the tops of their boots. In her pack Magda carried goat cheeses and pots of redcurrant jelly to contribute to the feast that would follow. They donned their thickest socks and mittens with their warmest pelts and hats for the journey. Along the way they sang songs and told jokes to keep themselves warm and maintain their high mood.

When they arrived in Brunnen, the temperature had risen to accompany the jovial mood and the sun shone brightly on the courtyard in front of the *Rathaus* where people had begun to gather. Dignitaries had come from Schwyz and Unterwalden to join the people in the beautiful town at the centre of Uri, where the Alps climbed directly out of the lake to dizzying heights. Their peaks glistened with snow in the sun. Boats and barges were tied up to the jetty on the lake. Gulls and terns soared playfully on the wind, looking for spare morsels from the tables being set with food and drink that would be shared following the speeches and the signing of the charter. The charter that Walter had helped to draft.

Magda's heart lifted when she saw him. He asked her to sit with him and his father at a table near the lake, and her hope blossomed. She looked towards her own father and he smiled with a twinkle in his eye. He would approve of her betrothal. *If only Walti would ask!*

Magda couldn't wait much longer, and might be the one to have to do the asking. A part of her wondered what was causing his hesitation. Perhaps he'd decided he didn't want her, didn't want to raise someone else's child. Her worry that another lass had caught his eye over the past weeks seemed unfounded, as he was alone apart from his father. Magda only had to remember the way he looked at her to be sure she hadn't misinterpreted his feelings. That, at least, still shone from his eyes.

Wilhelm Tell asked Walter to recount the events of the Battle of Morgarten. Those around the table hung on his every word.

His father exclaimed at the ingenuity of the villagers' defence, the thunderous rolling of the boulders and tree trunks down the hills, the destruction of the enemy troops. He would be gaining vicarious pleasure from hearing of the Habsburg army's demise, retribution for the terrible things they had done to Walter's mother all those years ago.

Walter spoke of the arrow that wounded him, and Wilhelm placed his hand on his son's shoulder, then squeezed it tenderly, a gesture that told everyone he was glad he hadn't lost the only remaining member of his family.

'It seems my notoriety might always be founded on the end of someone else's arrow,' Walter said without rancour. He left out the telling of the miracle of the Grail, making it sound as though his injury had not been serious. They'd been sworn to secrecy about the chalice by Yves and Grégoire.

'And what of those knights who helped train your peasants to defend those filthy Habsburgs? When I met them at the Rütli Meadow in the summer, I hadn't realised the extent of their devotion to train our people. Are they here? I'd like to thank them personally.'

'They've moved on, Father. They are travelling south now, continuing the journey they started all those months ago. Don't worry, we gave them a good send-off.'

A brief moment of sadness flooded Magda as she remembered the humble gathering at Sébastien's grave.

'I met two Frenchmen travelling through Altdorf heading south a few weeks back,' said a farmer sitting opposite Wilhelm. 'But it couldn't have been the knights. For a start, there were only two of them, and they were dressed in pauper's clothes, and it looked like the beasts they were riding were cart-horses.'

Magda remembered the morning Yves and Grégoire left. Their fine horses had not been stabled since they arrived back in the Aegerital. The barn had burned down in the battle. The animals had grown thick winter pelts as protection from the mountain cold. Rather than brushing them clean, mud from the swamp was left on their hocks and rumps following the battle to disguise their breeding. But Magda imagined the knights still had their weapons at the ready to defend the treasure they were carrying.

Sébastien's fine black beast had been led to Magda by Yves, who placed his reins in her hands. She had put her cheek against his soft muzzle, and took comfort in his fruity warm breath blowing in her face. There was no cart in the village to bring them all to Brunnen, so Magda had left Obéron with a farmer in Morgarten. She would collect him on her return. He would be a welcomed addition to the household. His days of riding into holy battle were over, but until Magda's future had been decided, he could be used as a valuable part of the farming community, to pull a plough and deliver wood. As she'd led Obéron into the farmer's barn, he nickered a friendly greeting to the cows and donkey stabled there for the winter. She had looked into his sad black eyes, quite sure he was aware his master had gone. She promised to come back and fetch him soon. He had become part of Magda's destiny. He even had a strong Germanic name, though when she talked to him, she voiced the soft accented version Sébastien had used.

She hoped he would eventually keep the blisters from Walter's feet.

'I hear your riddle-solving skills were useful to the cause, Walti,' said Wilhelm, bringing Magda's thoughts back to events leading up to the battle.

She felt Walter's turmoil. There were only a few of them who would ever know that truth. He'd kept the whole story even from his own father. Walter's smile didn't reach his eyes. Before he could answer, there was a commotion from the steps of the *Rathaus*.

'People of the Helvetic Confederation! It is done!' shouted Werner Stauffacher as he emerged through the heavy wooden doors, holding a document aloft. 'I have here in my hand the *Bund von Brunnen*.'

A group of men crowded onto the forecourt of the *Rathaus*, and Werner Stauffacher waited for them to quieten.

'The leaders of Uri, Schwyz and Unterwalden have signed this pact. We now have a sworn confederacy!'

As the commander talked of allegiance and strength and growth, a warm feeling of pride flowed over the gathering. Some of them, though, had still not forgotten the horror of the battle.

'What does this mean?' Magda asked Walter in a whisper.

'The leaders of these Confederate cantons have promised mutual military assistance,' he said. 'Although there was victory at Morgarten, there were still factions of the army that weren't involved in the campaign. This has ensured your uncle's command of the entire Confederate military.'

'It makes the alliance solid, supporting the charter sworn in Rütli fourteen years ago,' Wilhelm added. 'We are now truly a nation.'

'And we can expand our borders, take in more villages and towns,' said Walter.

'There is talk that Stauffacher will ask for your diplomatic skills between the Confederation and Luzern,' said Wilhelm.

'From my visit to the city earlier this year, I wager they'll be the next canton to seek to join the Confederation. It would be exciting to have such a city with an important trade centre at the heart of our nation.'

'The signing of this pact is the first step towards Duke Leopold being forced to conclude a truce,' added another man across the table.

'Perhaps you should seek a seat in parliament when we have enough men to form an official government.'

Walter smiled with pride, but didn't say anything. He looked at Magda a little shyly. 'That depends,' he said quietly. 'I would not want to force my partner to go somewhere she doesn't want to.'

'Oh Walti, take me to Luzern!' blurted Magda without thinking. 'I'd love to go to the big city. Perhaps I can take my craft there – find a buyer for my wares!'

'I'm not sure your father would approve,' he said, standing up.

'What do you mean, "approve"? Where are you going?'

'If I am to take you with me, I need to seek his permission to wed you, Magda.'

Magda could not stop the widest of smiles across her face, and those around the table began cheering and applauding. Magda believed she saw a twinkle in old Wilhelm Tell's eye.

'Then I shall be the first to welcome you to our family, Fräulein Stauffacher,' he said. 'I'm honoured that these two great family names will be united. The perfect alliance.'

Magda looked over to where her father was now standing, listening intently to Walter. Moments later he touched his shoulder and shook his hand. Magda felt a warm glow inside. They would be married.

She placed her hand on her belly. It was not a moment too soon.

✠ ✠ ✠

Magda and Walter stood side by side on the shore of the *Vierwaldstättersee*, looking west over the water towards Luzern. The celebrations for the signing of the charter were still going on in the background and would likely continue well into the night. Walter took her hand, held it to his lips, and a frisson ran through her.

'Are you sure about this, Walti? Can my love possibly make up for the way I betrayed you?'

'It was not a betrayal, Maggi. Love can make people do things that don't always make sense. You weren't yet mine when Sébastien took advantage of you.'

'It's a strange thing to love two people so much, Walti, but a love that is based on respect and friendship is the strongest kind of love. That love will always win.'

'Did Sébastien know? Did he know you're carrying his child?' he asked.

'Not until it was too late.'

Walter looked up to the sky, avoiding Magda's eyes. 'I made a promise to Sébastien to always look after you,' he said. 'Maybe he knew.'

'You don't mind, that our firstborn will not be your own?'

'We could not have been more different, the Frenchman and I. But somehow, through all the deceit and competition for your attention, I believe there was a quiet respect between us in the end.'

Magda reached up to touch Walter's cheek. 'What do we tell my father, the others? I am already beginning to show.'

'I'm sure he will forgive us for the timing of events,' he said.' We'll make him or her *our* child. And then we'll give him or her lots of siblings, fill our new nation with a bright young future.'

He kissed her then, and there was still room deep down in her belly for the fire to ignite. She knew this passion would grow to something more powerful than what she had with Sébastien. She would make sure of it.

They drew apart and returned to the festivities under the watchful eye of Walter's father. As they approached the tables, Wilhelm Tell stood up and his booming voice rang out over the gathering. 'Raise your cups, good people! We celebrate more than just an alliance and the future of our great nation today. We celebrate the betrothal of my son Walter Tell to Magda Stauffacher of Schornen!'

The crowd, ever more jubilant for something to celebrate, began to cheer and yodel, and Magda vowed to be the best partner a man ever had.

AUTHOR'S NOTE

The Battle of Morgarten, fought on 15th November, 1315, effectively stopped Switzerland – the Helvetic Confederation – from falling into the hands of the Habsburgs, who would later become the rulers of the Austro-Hungarian empire.

The dates of major events, and the names of the rulers, leaders and military commanders are historically correct in the narrative, while the family members, the identity of the knights and the minor characters are completely fictitious. There is no record of what became of Walter Tell following 'the apple incident' or even whether he reached adulthood.

The setting and place names are also accurate, although the exact positioning of some of the borders may not be geographically correct to the degree. The toll tower still stands in the village of Schornen with a museum depicting the events of the battle at its base. In 2013, the Aegerital celebrated 700 years since the Battle of Morgarten with a festival involving the citizens of the valley and the Swiss military. It was at these celebrations that the seeds of the idea for *The Secrets of Morgarten* germinated.

There is no proof that anyone helped the farmers and the people of Morgarten and Schornen to fight the Habsburg troops prior to the battle. Some legends say a group of Italian mercenaries were engaged to teach the art of war. But the timing of the disbanding of the Knights Templar coincided with this period, and I have borrowed those myths for the purpose of the novel.

GLOSSARY

- Bärlauch: Wild garlic

- Baselard: A long dagger

- Battle of Morgarten: A defensive mission that took place on 15th November 1315, defending the Confederation Helvetica, ensuring the independence of what is today Switzerland

- Berg: Mountain

- Böögg: An effigy or puppet made out of paper and flammable materials and placed on a bonfire

- Brei: A porridge or a soup made with grains, sweet or savoury

- Bundesbrief/Ewige Bund: A document of allegiance signed by leaders of the three forest cantons Uri, Schwyz and Unterwald in 1291. The eternal charter.

- Canicule, la: Heatwave (French)

- Confederation Helvetica: The official name of Switzerland, CH is still used today as the international country abbreviation

- Commandery of Avelleur: A modest templar fortress outside Troyes in France

- Chuechli: A small single serving tart with a pastry base, savoury or sweet

- Einsiedeln: A large cathedral and cloister in central Switzerland that was in 'neutral' Habsburg territory in 1315

- 'En guete': Swiss German (in high German 'Guten Appetit') – 'Good appetite'

- Ferkel: Piglet

- Finken: House slippers

- Föhn: A strong southerly wind that can rise suddenly in the north–south facing valleys in the Alps

- Goret: Piglet (French)

- Gotthard PassEven today, remains one of the most significant trading and traffic routes in Europe

- 'Gott sei Dank': 'Thank God' but used in the way we might say 'Thank the Lord'

- 'Gott verdammt': Blasphemy 'God damn it'

- 'Gruezi': Swiss greeting (in high German 'Gruss Gott') and 'Gruezi Mittenand' when greeting a group

- Habsburgs: The rulers of Austria from 1282 and of the Austro-Hungarian Empire from 1526 to 1918

- Halberd: A weapon with a curved blade, a small axe on the opposing edge and a spike on the tip

- 'Heb Schnurre!': 'Shut your snout,' as though to a dog (vulgar)

- Heinrich von Hünenberg: A commander in Duke Leopold I's army

- Kachelofen: A closed fireplace covered in ceramic tiles which retain heat

- Kornmarkt: Grain market, corn exchange

- Kreuzer: An ancient unit of currency in Southern Germany and Austria

- Landjäger: A long four-sided sausage of dried meat

- Leopold I, Duke of Austria: Brother of Prince Frederick of the Habsburgs

- Mittenfastenfeuer: An annual celebration half way through Lent in the Aegeri Valley

- Most: A cloudy cider, turning alcoholic when left to ferment

- Pact of Brunnen: Document confirming recognition of the Confederation Helvetica in 1291

- Pilgerweg: Pilgrims way or path

- Rathaus: Town hall

- Schatz: Treasure, used as a term of endearment similar to darling

- Schulze: Town mayor, sheriff

- See (pronounced 'say'): Lake

- Spaetzli or Spätzli: A mixture of flour, egg and water, rolled into small uneven shapes and cooked in a pan

- Stammtisch: A table in a bar or restaurant reserved for regular local customers

- Tal: Valley

- Taler: A coin in ancient Swiss currency

- Ténébreuse, La: The Dark One. Used in this fictional instance by the knights to hide the identity of the Black Madonna, the central sacred statue in the Einsiedeln Cathedral

- Walter Tell: Documented in the legend as Wilhelm's young son who had the apple shot off his head

- Werner Stauffacher: General of the Confederate army as documented in legends written about the Battle of Morgarten

- Wilhelm Tell: The mythical hero of ancient Switzerland who defended the Confederation with expert use of his crossbow

ACKNOWLEDGEMENTS

When I began studying for my Masters in Crime Writing at the University of East Anglia, I'd intended writing this historical mystery for my dissertation, but it soon became apparent that the amount of research involved meant I would not be able to hand in a complete work by the deadline. Instead I turned to the more familiar world of psychological suspense. My third novel, *The Beaten Track*, was the result.

But after receiving my diploma, Henry Sutton, director of the Masters programme at UEA, encouraged me to re-visit that first idea, and during the years since I graduated, I continued to work on *The Secrets of Morgarten*.

Sharing work amongst our close-knit Masters cohort was one of the greatest resources during that time at UEA. Many of us still help each other to this day to critique and refine our work. Thanks are owed to the entire cohort for their original feedback on the project and to Bill Ryan for his early tutoring. Thanks particularly to Antony Dunford and Natasha Hutcheson for their more recent close reading of the work in its final stages.

I am grateful also for the resources available at the Morgarten Museum, the Bundesbriefmuseum (Museum of the Swiss Charters Confederation) in Schwyz and the Landesmuseum (National Museum) in Zürich.

Thanks to Scott Pack for his editing prowess, Johanna Robinson for her astute proof-reading and Jane Dixon for her beautiful cover design.

And last but not least, thanks to my husband, Chris, who has supported me throughout my writing career, contributed his ideas, and helped to solve plot holes on our hikes around the Aegerital, the spectacular setting for the novel in central Switzerland where we are so lucky to live.

ABOUT THE AUTHOR

Louise Mangos writes novels, short stories and flash fiction, which have won prizes, been placed on shortlists, and have been narrated on BBC radio. Her short fiction appears in more than twenty print anthologies. She holds an MA in crime writing from the University of East Anglia in the UK.

You can connect with Louise on Facebook —/LouiseMangosBooks, or Twitter @LouiseMangos, and Instagram as @louisemangos, or visit her website https://louisemangos.com/ where there are links to some of her short fiction. If you'd like to receive information about new releases and be in with a chance of winning the occasional giveaway, subscribe to her newsletter on her homepage.

Louise lives at the foot of the Swiss Alps, a few miles from the scene of the Battle of Morgarten, with her Kiwi husband and two sons. When she's not writing, she enjoys an active life in the mountains.

Dear Reader,

Thank you so much for reading *The Secrets of Morgarten*. I hope you enjoyed the story.

I'm lucky enough to live in the beautiful Aegeri Valley in central Switzerland where the Battle of Morgarten took place more than 700 years ago. It has been the perfect place to research and write this, my first novel-length work of historical fiction. I fell in love with my main characters as much as they did with each other. As I can't seem to let them go, there are plans afoot for Walter and Magda to continue a little medieval sleuthing, so watch this space!

The most important people in an author's career are you, the readers, whether you are a blogger, a reviewer, or someone who simply enjoys a good yarn. A fellow author once told me that reviews are like coins – a few *Taler* if you like – in a busker's hat. I'd like to use that analogy and encourage you to leave your review on the platform of your choice. Each of those coins contributes towards an author's bread and butter.

If you enjoyed my writing, you might like to try one of my psychological suspense novels, details of which are on the following pages.

I hope to bring you many more tales for your enjoyment in the future.

Cheers (zum Wohl)

Louise

Strangers on a Bridge

How far would you go to protect your family? While Alice Reed is on her morning jog in the peaceful Swiss Alps, she unexpectedly saves a stranger on a notorious suicide bridge. But could her Samaritan deed turn out to be the first of many mistakes?

Adamant they have an instant connection, Manfred's charm gradually darkens and his obsession with Alice grows stronger.

In a country far from home, where the police don't believe her, the locals don't trust her and even her husband questions the truth about Manfred, Alice has nowhere to turn.

And she begins to think she should never have saved him that day on the bridge...

FINALIST in the EXETER NOVEL PRIZE
LONG LISTED for the BATH NOVEL AWARD

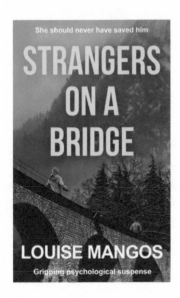

The Art of Deception

She must prove her innocence to save her son... but time is running out.

Art school dropout Lucie is on a backpacking trip across Europe when she arrives in the idyllic Swiss Alps. A holiday romance with ski instructor Mathieu takes a crucial turn when Lucie discovers she is pregnant. Spiralling into a relationship of coercion and dark domestic abuse, Lucie is powerless to escape her marriage without losing her son.

Seven years on, Lucie is serving a sentence in a Swiss prison for a murder she insists she did not commit. Surrounded by an eclectic group of inmates, Lucie must summon all her strength and intuition to uncover long-kept secrets and fight for her freedom to be reunited with her son before he is abducted by her husband's family.

The clock is ticking . . . but who can she trust?

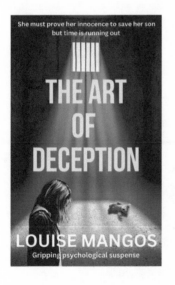

The Beaten Track

After her stalker takes his life and she's jilted by a holiday lover, Sandrine comes home from her round-the-world backpacking trip perturbed, penniless and pregnant. She meets handsome Scott, who offers her love, security and all she and her new baby could ever wish for. But their dream is about to turn into a nightmare...

Made in United States
Troutdale, OR
04/08/2024